PRAISE FOR ATTRIBUTION

2022 International Book Awards
Finalist in Best New Fiction

"Desperate for meaning and to fill the hole left by her younger brother's death, an art historian searches for a lost painting—and finds herself. Gorgeously written and as rapturous as a Van Gogh, Moore's book is a winner."
—CAROLINE LEAVITT, *New York Times* best-selling author of *Pictures of You* and *With or Without You*

"*Attribution* is an intriguing art-historical fantasia. I loved reading it!"
—EDWARD J. SULLIVAN, Professor of the History of Art, New York University

"Moore is no novice in the art world, but it is her ability to weave words into breathless imagery that sets *Attribution* apart from other novels. Combining literary fiction with suspense—and adding a touch of romance—to the mix will keep readers interested until the very last page and clamoring for more."
—BARBARA CONREY, *USA Today* best-selling author of *Nowhere Near Goodbye*

"This novel has mystery, a puzzle, romance, and adventure. The craft is strong, the characters fully human, and I never would have guessed the outcome."
—JUDY BERNSTEIN, author of *They Poured Fire on Us* and *Disturbed in their Nests*

"Linda Moore's *Attribution* is a different kind of thriller: a career and a reputation are in danger. One is of a young art history student, the other a famous . . . painter. Moore keeps you in suspense about both while painting a portrait of each rich in detail of both lives as they were lived in Spain in the 17th century and today. A fascinating, fun read, with a romantic story at its core."

—PAUL CHITLIK, screenwriter and story editor of *Bern with an E, The Twilight Zone,* and *The Wedding Dress;* WGA Award and GLAAD Award nominee, and Genesis Award Winner

"Written with a deft hand of someone who knows the art world, someone who has been immersed in it for many years, makes this novel unique and informative. The great writing craft keeps the story moving forward and difficult to put down. The three-dimensional characters are real enough to stay with you long after you close the book. Moore is new to the literary scene, but she's proven she's here to stay."

—DAVID PUTNAM, author of the Bruno Johnson crime series

"Everyone loves a whodunnit, and that's exactly what this is: a mystery of attribution. Cate, in graduate school, gets to live every connoisseur's dream: not only finding a masterpiece, but proving it. From New York to Madrid, this is a page-turner about the thrill of discovery and the pitfalls of rocking the boat!

—ARIEL PLOTEK, PhD, Curator of Fine Art, The Georgia O'Keefe Museum

ATTRIBUTION

Attribution

A Novel

Linda Moore

SHE WRITES PRESS

Published 2022
Printed in the United States of America
Print ISBN: 978-1-64742-253-0
E-ISBN: 978-1-64742-254-7
Library of Congress Control Number: 2022907466

For information, address:
She Writes Press
1569 Solano Ave #546
Berkeley, CA 94707

Interior design by Stacey Aaronson and Tabitha Lahr

She Writes Press is a division of SparkPoint Studio, LLC.

For

Alexander, Teddy, Reece, Parker, and Beckett

CHAPTER 1

$\mathcal{S}$ pider webs covered the storeroom door with taut and wispy fragments, evidence that this basement room hadn't been opened in years, maybe decades. Cate ran her fingers over the door's painted surface, cracked like an alligator's back, and with a flick, paint chips fell away, drifting down like so many abandoned aspirations. She placed her palm, fingers outstretched to cover the exposed area of yellowed paint, a surface that so resembled the faux finish on Matty's coffin the touch of it turned her cold.

Memories of Matty found their way into her thoughts, but she swept them aside as she pushed back from the door and tried the locked handle again. Without success. Twenty minutes had passed since she'd phoned security to come open the door, and her patience, in short supply on a normal day, ticked away with the clock.

This was no normal day. Today she would finish the art inventory of New York City University and dismiss the under-graduate team, now on their obligatory coffee break. She'd supervised their assignment to locate every artwork either in the remodeled vault with its climate controls or on the walls of Hamilton Hall. This storeroom was an odd room not listed nor pointed out by the registrar, but she'd noticed the door when exiting the art vault to make a phone call. Nothing should be kept outside the vault in this dank cellar, especially not art.

Anyone sensible would stop now, turn in the forms with every item checked, and tell Professor Jones the scut work he'd assigned to avoid another dissertation meeting with her was complete. Escape their cha-cha dance of her moving two steps forward with ideas and him stepping her three quick steps backward with a list of reasons her proposals fell short. The whole inventory project stole time from dissertation research. Jones might not know this room existed, but it would be just her luck if the self-important art history star had laid a trap to send her back to the basement because she'd not been thorough. A setup, a gotcha moment he would relish.

A jangle of metal echoed in the cavernous cellar. A security guard attached to the sound appeared from around the corner brandishing an immense key ring like a weapon. He scowled. "Guards don't come down here without a call from the Department Chair."

She smiled, a weak attempt to reset his unexpected attitude, and squinted to read his name badge. "Julio. Cate, from the art department. Do you have a key for this door?" She straightened the bottom of her turtleneck and pulled it to cover her worn jeans.

Julio shrugged and throttled back his attitude. "Professors' rules, not mine."

She took the clipboard from her messenger bag, brushed strands of hair from her face, and put on her glasses. "A printout with Professor Jones's note to locate every piece of art, no exceptions."

Julio didn't look at the note. He scrunched his mouth and looked straight at her with a smirk. "Jones got you doing the dirty work, eh? When the emperor calls us to come to his office, we all got excuses, everybody busy somewhere else."

"He's the boss."

Julio snickered, bent down, and struggled to try a key. "Too much rust. Haven't been used in years." He mumbled curse words in Spanish, some real whoppers, different from what she'd heard two summers ago in Madrid, or during her high school stay in Mexico City. He stood, stretched his back, and groaned. The buttons on his uniform shirt strained against his stomach, just like Dad who suffered from watching sports instead of playing them.

She pulled the water bottle from her bag and held it out toward him. "My dad's got a bad back too. Painful?"

He stared, perhaps reassessing an impression she was a spoiled art type from the Upper East Side, and then accepted the bottle. Between twists of his back, side to side, he took long drinks of water and then searched the ring for a different key. "This might be it." He bent over with a wince and tried the lock. The bolt released and the door creaked open.

"Well done." She lifted her hand to high five him.

He left his arms at his side. "You never seen me."

She lowered her hand and gave a quick nod.

"Call us to lock up," he shouted over his shoulder as he jingled down the passageway.

With a slight push, the door opened wider to a room about twelve feet square. The scent of trapped air and other smells she didn't care to think about caught her by surprise. A God-like shaft of light from a window near the ceiling shone on dust particles in the darkness and lit a lacework of—no surprise—more spiderwebs. She shuddered and studied the lacey threads for the artful sculptors, but only dust wafted in the air over file boxes stacked within a foot of the ceiling.

Those web spinners were hiding somewhere. She gazed upward, saw nothing but rusted pipes, and turned to wedge herself between columns of file boxes crammed together. She nudged one box marked "Published Dissertations 1970–1990" back into the stack and considered the weight and volume, literal and emotional, of the students' work it contained. The pressure to secure Jones's approval on a thesis topic buzzed in her ears like a swarm of hornets and renewed the urgency to complete the inventory so she could return to her research.

Another file box marked "Correspondence" protruded from the stack, and when she bumped into it, the box tumbled and folders of handwritten notes and letters toppled onto the floor. She scraped the folders into a pile. The top one had a handwritten label that read "Letters from L." One brittle envelope with no addressee contained a short note, a paragraph about brushstrokes and religious themes in artworks, oddly signed "Mother."

Her own mother barely appreciated the Baroque art Cate studied, except for the Madonna. Mom, just forty-six, kneeled more often now below Mary's saccharine face in the nave of Holy Family Church and prayed for strength and comfort that might come from another mother who'd buried a son.

Art crates, lids detached, a sure sign they were empty, were stacked at the rear of the storeroom. She maneuvered forward to make certain but saw something else—a corner of carved wood near the wall. She rocked an empty but still heavy crate, inch by inch, to move it out of the way, earning a splinter in her thumb. She'd deal with it later in better light.

A wooden chest, maybe walnut, had fat-cheeked cherubs holding a ribbon between grapevines carved into the lid. The figures surrounded a royal crest she didn't recognize. Sixteenth century, or maybe earlier, similar to the ones she'd seen in a museum catalog. The lid fell, her fingers escaping a crushing blow. She lifted more cautiously, propping the top securely against the back wall. Rumpled packing paper filled the inside. With two fingers, she gingerly removed a paper or two, then scooped bunches with her arms, praying no creature would jump out.

This chest, an object of some value, was out of place in this cellar. Incongruous and forgotten. Wild ideas surged in her imagination about why it might be here. Art history wasn't a romance novel. But people found important things all the time. Packing paper in an empty chest didn't make sense. This chest most certainly had a story.

She knelt on the filthy floor for a closer look. That a rat, by the odor of the inside, might jump out any second, forced her to fortify her resolve, plunge her arm in, and move her fingers quickly from left to right systematically along the bottom like reading Braille. Something was there, on the bottom, a frayed edge of fabric, not a rag, nor a weaving, something stiffer and rolled.

This might be *something*. Papers went flying, tossed everywhere. Until . . . there it was.

A painting. Unmistakable: a rolled painted canvas.

She stopped breathing and then gasped, breathless from the manic unpacking and the surprise that this room held an artwork after all. A canvas of some heft had been rolled a number of times, paint side out to prevent cracking, as was the practice of the last century. Rich pigments glistened in the cellphone light. She tried to lift the roll, but the painting wouldn't budge. Humidity and time had fixed it to the bottom.

With hands trembling from the fear of damaging a work that might be important or might be trash, and knowing to proceed with protocols as if it was the former, she nudged the canvas by rocking it in tiny motions. The painting loosened, moved, and to her relief, detached from the bottom. She lifted the artwork with two hands underneath like a newborn infant being brought from its mother's womb and set the canvas onto a cradle of file boxes.

The dimensions were larger than she'd guessed, maybe three feet high and twice as long. With her cellphone light, she examined the paint on the outside of the canvas and found significant craquelure showing age and potential risk due to its dry condition. Even one turn to unroll the stiff canvas might flake the pigment or tear the linen. She suppressed the urge to flatten the roll to view the whole image and instead stood back, focused on taking a deep breath, summoning patience to respect the art.

She turned the roll over and focused the light to view the edge. Could it be lapis lazuli pigment, expensive and important, only used on works that mattered, shimmering even in the dim light? Evidence the pigment had been hand-ground was revealed in the granular texture, dating it to hundreds of years of age. That ultramarine color had been applied with brushstrokes, the few that were visible worked together with exactness and then expressive freedom. She stood back for perspective to view strokes that defined realistic folds of velvet, perhaps draperies or an elegant skirt, painted in red lake carmine, another priceless color hiding under aged varnish.

She examined the backside of the linen covered with irregular slubs only found in handwoven fabric. The ground from red clay used to prepare the front side of the canvas had bled through the back.

Her heart rate increased with each bit of information tested against her knowledge of the practices of certain artists she'd studied. The style, those costly pigments, the precise brushstrokes combined with spontaneous dabs, like those royal paintings she'd studied at the Prado ... could it be?

A European masterwork in the cellar of an American university, not the attic of an English country house chockablock with such things or the rectory of a regional church rolled up in armoires that held liturgical vestments, places such things were expected to be discovered, was at the least, highly improbable.

She focused the light again at the canvas edge, doubting what her eyes, with certainty, had seen. The cracks in the canvas declared it old in a way that could not be forged. Her imagination leapt ahead with the possibilities, resisted the counterarguments, and overflowed with an intuitive conviction that this was something. Something she could not see the whole of and should not speculate.

And yet the possibility could not be denied . . . could it be a . . . she couldn't say the name. Even a solitary whisper in this cavern might let the unthinkable into the universe. An attribution so audacious, she could only shout it in silence.

CHAPTER 2

*C*ate wrapped the canvas in paper, her hands shaking at the touch of this unlikely, too soon to know, maybe master-piece. Possibilities deserved space to blossom until they were ruled out. Whatever the work proved to be, it deserved cautious respect. Rolled in the packing papers, the canvas appeared an unremarkable parcel, nothing more, and its ordinariness would enable her to carry it upstairs out of the basement. In that way, she and this parcel were similar; she could leave the basement where Jones had exiled her, move upstairs unnoticed, and when the right time arrived, reveal this extraordinary find.

No, no. That was beyond aspirational, getting way ahead of the required research and yes, her commitment to scholarship to see the whole of it, to identify with precision and references what it likely was, before racing ahead.

First stop would be the third floor Conservation Center's humidity chamber, where the stiffness could be removed and the canvas unrolled without risking damage. The hallway to the elevator was empty in both directions. Her gut told her to keep the canvas secret. It just did. The curious undergrads would ask questions, speculate, and gossip about the mysterious find. Better to see the whole thing, build a case for Jones to consider the artwork something of substance, worthy of serious study, or if research revealed the work was a pastiche, she could return it without embarrassing herself. Again. But if that red clay ground used to prepare the canvas, the handmade linen, that glimpse of ultramarine and carmine red and their granular texture led where she suspected, Jones could not dismiss the artwork.

Those factors offered clues mostly to the age of the work and the wealth of its patron, but composition and subject would provide material evidence. Chemical tests of pigments and linen fragments could identify precise dates and a list of possible artists within those dates, but style and image, that first intuitive look, seeing what the composition might disclose, could support or reject this wild hypothesis that kept running through her head.

It was noon and Mary Murphy, the Center's director, would be at lunch. Mary's Irishness, that loquaciousness, added a lilt to the dour winter and joyless academic ambiance. Mary could have answered many questions, especially about the conservation process and the operation of the humidifier, but if Mary saw the painting and shared the find with colleagues, the pretentious art cabal would opine and squeeze out a junior scholar like herself. Mary—the lovely, likable Mary—was incapable of discretion.

"Director's in London, at a conference," the clerk mumbled between chomps on her chewing gum, her attention focused on the phone receiver. The young woman, attractive, probably a student, put the call on hold and added, "Until after the holidays."

"Too bad." Cate pretended to view a brochure on the counter to hide her relief. "I need the humidifier."

"Only Mary knows how to use that thing. Register the work and put it in the storage lockers. She'll call you when she returns." The phone rang; the gal ignored the caller on hold and answered the next call.

Cate pantomimed signing and the clerk set a clipboard on the counter while she argued about an invoice with the caller. The clipboard form required details Cate didn't have, but she registered the painting as: "Unknown, European." The girl took the log back and smiled, she actually did, for the first time. Cate returned a nervous grin and proceeded through the turnstile.

The humidity chamber's instructions were written in a bad translation of German. She pieced together meanings and merged those sketchy instructions with the course demonstration she'd had at orientation. The treatment depended on the materials, the medium that bound the pigments to the linen, as well as the type of canvas, none of which were known to her. If she got it wrong, paint would flake or separate from the surface. Her minimal training had never been put into practice.

She stood, hands trembling, fearful she could harm the work, and lifted the top. The rolled canvas fit inside the chamber, a tent sort of contraption, with little room to spare. She set the dials and crossed her fingers she wouldn't find paint fragments when she opened it. She could do this, perhaps not as well as Mary, but well enough. She closed the cover.

A cast-off couch in the corner provided a perch to monitor the painting through the humidifier's transparent top. She'd have hours to observe progress and make certain no one came in to question or disturb the process, the machine didn't blow up or the building catch fire, space aliens abduct it, or whatever ever else popped into her relentless imagining that lately calibrated toward the negative.

She pushed these possible calamities aside, sunk into the couch, and her mind drifted toward home, toward sad Ypsilanti and the calamity of her life, her brother's drowning. When Matty died two years ago, she'd abandoned her doctoral program at the University of Michigan, took a terminal master's degree, and found a curatorial assistant job at the Detroit Institute of the Arts. She struggled to help her grieving family, end the deafening silence of her brother's absence, and conquer the guilt. The secret she'd hidden from them, those amphetamines she'd left on the bathroom counter, the why of Matty's death that even the coroner didn't discover, ate at every bit of her soul, her spirit consumed by what she could not, would not say. But she knew, she'd known, seen the signs when he'd returned from reckless parties. The five years between them meant she should have been a good big sister, but she'd said nothing to him or their parents about the perilous path Matty tread with the other high school seniors. He was their parents' darling boy, the one that could do no wrong, made them laugh, drew pride at every soccer match and honors that would propel this family to the heights Dad dreamed of while he worked the assembly line.

What would be the point of the truth? In their minds, he'd live forever as unrealized perfection. Matthew had drowned and whether by his own hubris or a horrible accident, she'd loved him too.

Mom and Dad had nothing left for her, didn't see that her life might have value, could be enough for them. She'd fled to New York, still in shock she'd been accepted to the doctoral program after she'd withdrawn from Michigan, but clear-eyed that at twenty-three she must embark on a solitary journey, unmoored from those rocks she'd once clung to, anchors now submerged in the tide of grief.

When she'd arrived in September, the Palladian entrance to Hamilton Hall had left her speechless with exhilaration about her future prospects. She launched herself forward to breathe oxygen onto the embers of her own dreams. And now, the idea that her accomplishments might be enough to fill the hole in their hearts slipped away each time Professor Jones rejected her work, rejected her. That revitalizing breath, spent, leaving her breathless, not an awestruck kind of breathless like when she stood before a marvel of a painting, more like gasping for air to survive.

But there'd be no quitting. How many times was that drilled into her head by her teachers, her coaches, and her parents?

This next proposal, her fourth, needed to earn Jones's support or this fragile framework of a future would collapse—again. She'd anticipate Jones's questions and nail this attempt. This proposed study of two little-known, almost unknown, women artists from the Baroque period should impress Jones with its originality and meet his demands for unique research. Few references to these Portuguese women, one a cloistered nun and the other, an unmarried woman assisting her father in his studio, existed. She'd scoured everything available in New York and online.

Jones never wrote or spoke about women artists. The Spanish Golden Age was his specialty area, a playing field he dominated—and he knew it, like an athlete in constant self-congratulatory mode. Female painters were lost from history except for Artemisia Gentileschi and maybe one or two others. There had to be more, but the notion more women existed to be uncovered did not gain his support, and support from Jones mattered.

Four hours had passed in what seemed minutes while she'd explored topics she loved, soothed by the hum of air flowing through the chamber. She rose, stretched her legs, took a few steps, and peeked her head around the corner to see what the clerk was doing. The desk was empty and the computer turned off. Maybe the clerk had forgotten she was in there and had left for a class. Cate studied the humidifier and decided to open it before the clerk returned. She closed her eyes, unable to pray since Matty died, to summon positive karma, as she lifted the top.

No paint flakes! She nudged the canvas that was a bit damp, maybe too damp. The roll moved about a foot and stopped, revealing a bit more of the image she'd spotted in the storeroom. The remaining layers of canvas clung together, still stiff. The painting would require days in the chamber to relax enough to roll out.

Days meant a lot of moisture and the paint could detach from the canvas as the linen fibers swelled. She turned off the machine and lifted the canvas to a large table. The canvas unrolled a little more, then a little more, and she positioned weights to hold each section down. But two thirds of it remained too stiff to unroll.

She could stay and sleep on the couch but looking at the stained cushions, maybe not. People had left for the holidays, but someone still could come into the room. She covered the canvas with clean muslin and scribbled a sign: "Do Not Touch." Hopefully the moist air now filling the lab would continue to relax the canvas.

She picked up her coat and computer bag to head home. Voices came from the reception area where the clerk chatted with someone. The two girls, probably students, were comparing different bars and the guys who took up residence at each. Her repertoire in such things ranged from limited to nonexistent, and she'd ceased longing for that carefree life or anything that diverted her from her career. She swept around the corner, past the desk and, with aplomb, sent words flying over her shoulder, "Have fun tonight."

The apartment she'd sublet offered refuge from the frenetic city and recovery from what had been lost in each day's struggle. The fridge contained leftover Chinese, an unpleasant dinner option but preferable to another withdrawal from her dwindling bank account. She nibbled at the tangled noodles and read course material. After a few tasteless bites, she moved the reading sans noodles to her bed, hoping the ponderous pages would bring sleep instead of a head filled with wild possibilities.

THE ALARM SHOWED FOUR O'CLOCK in glowing numerals. Images of what the unrolled painting might look like had kept her awake. Sleep was hopeless and she abandoned her bed for a kitchen chair. Old coffee warmed in the microwave energized her to review her dissertation draft. Yesterday's caffeine and yesterday's ideas, the proposal had been edited twenty times. She shook her head and chuckled more from fatigue than amusement. She could not force herself to read it again and printed it out.

Computer tabs marked the biographies of artists who might have painted the artwork resting in the Conservation Center. The list was short and she studied them all: the cities where they'd worked, where they'd lived, who they'd known, and, of course, images and dates of their works. She deleted possibilities that didn't fit, pausing to reflect and then trusting her eye to distinguish pigments and brushstrokes from what she'd observed on twelve inches of the painting, her painting.

Sun poured through the studio window. She stretched and watched clouds of warm smoke break the freezing air's grip on the sky. It was almost six and she needed to get dressed. She put on her art-people-wear-black turtleneck, a simple skirt, and black tights to protect her legs against the cold. The Center opened at seven and she wanted to be there before anyone else arrived, even though the clerk would likely be late for work after her evening antics.

The temperature hit her hard even as a veteran of Michigan winters where locals mocked complaints about the cold. A taxi would be nice, but a walk to the subway was cheaper and would clear her head. Money from her graduate grant would be deposited at the beginning of the semester in January, another penny-counting twenty days or so.

She pulled a subway token from her pocket, grabbed the train, got off at Washington Square, and sprinted from the exit to Hamilton Hall before her nose froze. She climbed the stairs to the entrance as the university clock tower sounded the chimes for seven.

No surprise—the clerk wasn't at her desk. Cate pushed the turnstile into the lab and tossed the winter gear now making her sweat onto the couch. The muslin cover appeared untouched. She put on her cotton gloves, took a deep breath, lowered her tense shoulders, and cautiously pulled back the fabric. She lifted the rolled part of the canvas, lighter and more pliable, like a patient ready for examination.

The ancillary light together with the surgical overhead lamp illuminated the table where the patient waited. She reminded herself to slow her racing heart, to breathe, and to move with purpose and precision. With a gentle nudge, the canvas rolled a bit and then a bit more until the entire thing waited backside toward her. She lifted the painting with two fingers of each gloved hand, stretching her arms out like a crucifixion to hold the painting's full width stable, and then turned the artwork to spread it onto the table. With the front side now fully visible, she held her breath to contain tears welling up in an emotion like seeing a newborn's face for the first time.

Extraordinary.

Stunning.

She grabbed her cheeks and then the edge of the table to steady herself and to quell the feelings overtaking her. Painted poetry glowed and throbbed with passion in the sterile atmosphere of the lab. The artistry, the composition, and brilliant craft made this painting an exceptional example of the Baroque period. What kicked the work into the higher levels of achievement was an unavoidable connection to the central figure's expressive face. Those poignant eyes, staring back at her, fully human and complex with feeling.

The size of the work required four steps back from the table to view the whole image with perspective. A step stool lifted her short stature another twelve inches to view it all. A woman with blond tresses wore robes of carmine velvet, the fabric she'd spotted in the storeroom. There was no signature, typical of the time. The figure stood next to crowned royalty, perhaps King Felipe IV with his upturned moustache, and pointed to a group of women humbling themselves before an angel. The composition seemed to be an allegory, perhaps from mythology like something Titian or Rubens might paint, or like Velázquez's *Las Hilanderas*, also called *The Spinners* based on the Arachne fable.

The quality remarkable, even phenomenal—there were no words. Exceeded the usual "School of"... or "Artist Unknown," often attached to works found in church rectories and palace storerooms. This painting sang, rising to a crescendo, an aria, a Gloria! *La Gloria*, that's what she'd call it, for now, until thorough research would uncover its real name.

Questions remained. The reasons such a work was abandoned, forgotten, or hidden were a mystery. That a canvas like this had been left off the inventory made the whole of it imponderable. The registrar of the university's art collection might have some old documentation, but then the work would have been carried forward in the inventory. It was doubtful that the canvas was a gift to the university. If the chest had been donated, surely someone would have looked inside. Perhaps Jones, who'd been at NYCU forever, might know something of its origins, but if he did, he would have already embraced or dismissed the work. Either way the painting would have been listed. Jones didn't know about it, she felt certain.

Clean cotton squares removed bits of moist dirt that had loosened during the humidification. With the surface cleaned, she dried and rolled *La Gloria*, first in acid-free paper and then archival board. The work needed to be kept out of sight until she had a plan. But she couldn't hide it and also study it. If she showed it to Jones, he might be convinced to permit her to work on it, openly.

She'd do it. She'd take it to their meeting today. He had to see what she saw.

CHAPTER 3

*T*he dissertation review with Jones was scheduled for ten o'clock. She took a chair in an empty conference room that smelled of chalk dust and the stuff janitors use to mop the floors and began to review her presentation about the Portuguese women. Images of a positive response from an enthusiastic Jones did not materialize. The proposal was clear in her mind, but the tension about the impending meeting stole her focus. If . . . no, *when*, things went well with her proposal, she'd show him the painting. The unmistakable mastery, evidence of hand-ground pigments, and craquelure were all no-brainers as to its age. If he agreed, then she could get grant money for chemical and dating tests to learn more. She made her way to the department reception.

Noemi, Jones's assistant, was alone in the department office. "You're five minutes early. He hasn't arrived. Weather, traffic." She shrugged. "You can wait in his office."

"Snow is really coming down. I don't suppose he'd ever take the subway."

Noemi smiled and winked. She hailed from Nebraska and was a kindred soul, bringing a softness to a sea of cold New Yorkers.

Cate went into Jones's office and sat in the Harvard alumni chair, resting her head against the *Veritas* motto embossed in gold on the top rail. She balanced the rolled canvas against the chair's arm and stared up at books stacked to the ceiling. She studied the book titles on the shelves, tempted to pull down Professor Herant Jones's *Art History of the Spanish Golden Age,* his seminal work. The names of art illuminati appeared on book spines wedged next to his. She squinted and imagined her name, Catherine Adamson, first in an autoworker's family to attend college, on a book. That a book by her would ever sit on the shelf next to a definitive expert like Jones, with three exhaustive artist biographies, an extraordinary breadth when most professors write one important book and spend the rest of their careers defending it, remained a distant dream. The acolytes trained by Jones and positioned throughout the academic and museum world secured his position with unquestioned reverence.

The mullioned windows that touched the ten-foot ceiling rattled from the storm's winds. Another tempest stirred inside and despair leveled her as she stood and stretched her own spine to its tallest height. *No quitting.* She repeated the words as a mantra, drilled into her by her parents. Self-pity was not allowed in her hometown of Ypsilanti, including questions of why Matty, why my family, why me? She could not return to the sadness with Dad's embargo on laughter. She was young and wanted to be alive, embrace life, and if she could move on, maybe they'd come too.

Noemi appeared in the doorway. "You okay in here? He'll arrive soon."

Cate nodded and sat down, crossing and uncrossing her legs to find a comfortable position. She adjusted her shoes onto the rungs under the chair, like she was five.

Hard to believe it was four months ago that she'd attended the welcome cocktail, uneasy and awkward at an event that was not part of her Michigan world. Jones greeted the male students who'd gathered around him, addressing Stephen and Leonard by their first names. He'd offered his hand to her and pretended not to know who she was. Only ten had been accepted to the prestigious program, nine men and one woman. He had to know her name.

She'd managed to respond, "Catherine Adamson."

Stephen and Leonard introduced themselves, as did four other men.

"We've never admitted anyone from your university," Jones had announced with a smirk to the guys huddling around him. Stephen elbowed Leonard.

She looked away, biting her lip. *Stand up for Southern Michigan State.* "Janson taught a class there one summer," she said, "while he was at Washington University." Stephen and Leonard raised their eyebrows, no doubt surprised by this information.

Jones sniffed. "Janson was in New York when he wrote the *History of Art.* He taught in Michigan? Really?"

"He liked fly fishing," she said. The subtext of Jones's innuendos, complete with the nuanced inflections, prevented her from saying more.

"I suppose there are worse reasons to go into the woods." Jones waited for the other students to chuckle and then returned to the subject of her admission. "Professor Meyer spoke highly of you; his letter certainly got my attention. Said you wanted to study female artists. He called in a favor. And well, here you are."

Her face turned hot at the "favor" comment, but before she could say anything, Jones shifted topics and disarmed her. "Did you find Janson's *History* lacking because he omitted female artists?"

She stared at him without answering. She'd practiced this disciplined drill of silence against Dad, a champion baiter.

Jones's eyes turned dark and he continued, "Janson didn't write about them because there *were* no women artists who met the standard of his magnum opus."

She had positioned her mouth in neutral, not a smile, not a frown. The ice cubes in the vodka tonic rattled when she'd lifted the near empty glass to her lips. "Would anyone like another drink?" They all declined. She excused herself and headed to the bar, wondering what she had done or not done to deserve this non-welcome.

GLAD TO BE PAST THOSE beginning days, she sighed and unhooked her feet from the chair rung. At least she knew what she was dealing with, and she'd come to like hanging out with Stephen and Leonard, who were as terrified of Jones as she was. But their dissertation topics had been approved.

She checked her watch and the office door banged open. Jones entered and tossed a stack of term papers onto his desk with a thud. He looked at her and said, "Oh."

Good morning to you too. She sat up straighter, if that was possible, and moved the canvas to keep it from falling to the floor.

He hung his tweed jacket on the door's hook, tightened his tie, and, with his back to her, said, "And you're here because . . . ?"

This kind of charm could not be taught.

"Monthly dissertation meeting."

He lifted the pile of telephone messages and read them without looking up. "I see. What progress do you have to report?" He raised his eyes for a moment, adjusted his tortoiseshell glasses, and returned to read messages, not even pretending to care about the answer.

She folded her hands and searched for the right response, the erudite and scholarly sentences she'd composed in her head. She knew the key points by heart but reached in her messenger bag for the proposal anyway, only to leave the bound folder closed on her lap. She had this.

Elucidate stylistic advances, compositional changes, and icono-graphic innovations by women in the early Baroque. Geez, a pompous sentence she would have never uttered a few months ago, prefer-ring clarity in lieu of verbosity.

Jones lifted his head, made eye contact, and said, "Silence. Wandering in the weeds? There is a deadline, you are aware?"

She blurted, "Golden Age of Spain. Analyze little known artworks and connect them to the early Baroque in Seville and Lisbon in the 1600s."

He scoffed. "Specifics, please. We spoke about this at our last meeting. Sevillian artists have been thoroughly studied. Scholars are expected to advance, the word is *advance,* Ms. Adamson, knowledge in their area of study."

Worse than usual, if that was possible.

"Artists from the Portuguese Baroque." She opened the folder and pulled out the two-page proposal, a précis, each word carefully chosen. She leaned across the desk and held the paper out for him.

He didn't reach to take it. Instead, he leaned back in his chair and twirled a pencil between his fingers.

She set the pages on the edge of the desk, pushing them a few inches toward him with her fingertips.

He moved his glasses higher on his nose with the pencil's eraser and straightened some papers on his desk. He turned back toward her and picked up the proposal. Without turning to page two, he said, "It's thin." He flipped to page two and shrugged. "A bibliography perhaps?"

She sank back. Topics that "advance knowledge" by definition do not have extensive bibliographies. She mentioned the meager references and mumbled in a voice so meek she couldn't hear herself. "Works by women of the era, artists overlooked by history, published writings on their works are limited and the bibliography sparse. I plan . . . hope to travel to Spain to research church and library sources that identify women . . . to compose a robust and original bibliography."

He leaned forward as if to deliver the coup de grace. "Female artists of the Golden Age? If they existed, they are mediocre or worse. Such a dissertation topic is certain to die in the bowels of the university library."

She lifted herself a couple of inches to enable her lungs to find air to speak more forcefully. "I pursued a little researched topic, per your advice."

He smirked. "And that is progress. However, the topic needs to provide insights regarding significant artists or works of the era. Bring me something I haven't heard before, but something that matters."

Jones intertwined his fingers, squeezed them until they turned white.

Show him the painting.

The paper crackled when she lifted the rolled canvas an inch or two from the arm of the chair. "What about unknown works, something hidden away, from a private palace, something maybe belonging to nobility, somebody like the Duchess of Alba?"

He threw his head back, howled with laughter. "Is the Duchess a friend of yours? Have you spoken to the curator and seen the collection they have catalogued and studied for *four hundred years*? Maybe you're coveting a research grant to Spain to drink sangria?"

She glared at him, lips pursed to keep the word "asshole" from escaping.

The painting. Her only remaining shot. That *La Gloria* represented a significant work amounted to a preliminary hypothesis with scant evidence. She ran fingers up and down the wrapping's edge. *Risk it. Show it to him.*

She pulled at her black turtleneck and smoothed the fabric of her skirt. "What about an attribution? Of an unstudied work?"

"Attribution?" He rolled his eyes and shook his head. "Let me give you some advice."

She took a deep breath and forced herself to find sincere helpfulness in his words.

"People find canvases in yard sales and oh my, they've hit the jackpot." He leaned forward and whispered a shout like a Detroit preacher. "Masterpieces do not reside in attics."

Actually, they do. Examples came to mind, examples where indeed they had lived in attics—and garages. A Rembrandt drawing found in Schenectady of all places. "What about . . ."

Jones talked over her, ranting and looking away as if pacing during a lecture. "If an art historian attributes a work to a master, he risks being sued when new information changes the authorship and destroys the value. If, on the other hand, a scholar says the work is not authentic, a pastiche, an imitation, the owner argues the case, even though collectors know nothing. Attribution is about money."

"Identifying works for scholarship, to deepen the understanding of the artist's oeuvre. . . isn't that the art historian's job?" She wanted to suck back those words.

But instead of fury, he shifted his gaze outside as if distracted by the wind's sound or the call of some distant muse. "Values in the art market create these searches for the golden find. I have a few years at this. Trust me." He lifted his eyebrows and placed a stare squarely on her face to announce the lecture had ended.

She placed her fingers on her left temple to quiet the pounding. If someone of Jones's stature declared the work was by some unknown, amateur artist, no scholar would consider the painting again. She too—she'd be dismissed. Without a dissertation, there'd be no doctorate, not even a footnote in art history.

The suffocating air of this inner sanctum where quiet competed with the wind bleating against the window added to the throbbing of her head. Her fingers released the canvas onto the arm of the chair.

Jones flipped the pencil into a holder and moved on. "What about the inventory? Did you complete *that* assignment?"

"Paperwork has been submitted to the art registrar." She hesitated. "Yes. Everything accounted for." Her voice tapered off with the non-lie, Mom's word for leaving out facts instead of altering them. The *Veritas* seal on the Harvard chair burned into her back.

Tell him. Tell him about the locked room, the dust, the cobwebs, file boxes filled with old papers. A carved chest with a painting stuck inside. Cracked surface. Lapis lazuli, carmine red pigments. And, and, and . . .

She caught her breath as if she had actually said the words. She placed her hand on *La Gloria,* steadied it against the chair, causing the paper to make a rustling sound.

Jones pointed to the package. "What have you there?"

Leaves swirled from trees outside Hamilton Hall and drifted by the office's dirty windows.

"Ms. Adamson, kindly give me your attention." He enunciated each word slowly with drama. "Did you want to show me something?"

His mood, his attitude, all wrong. All of it. Jones didn't deserve to decide *La Gloria's* fate. His arrogance, masked as erudition, would kill any chance the work could sing.

She'd birthed the painting into the light from the dark place where it had languished. The work found her for a reason, and claimed her as its protector, its guardian.

She lifted the paper roll. "Something that needs framing."

"Oh, she's a collector." He flipped the air with dismissive fingers and smirked. He rose, his back to her, to return a volume to the bookshelf. "Our time has ended. Since you have no topic, I suggest you complete an integrated critique of existing publications about Spain's Golden Age. That at least would be a service to scholars and perhaps a suitable dissertation idea will emerge."

Seriously? A self-congratulatory bibliography to promote his own work. Anger mixed with humiliation flushed her cheeks. Her lip trembled and she took a deep breath to control her quivering voice. "I'll look into it."

Get out. Get away before words that can't be erased, erupt.

She picked up her messenger bag, grabbed the painting, and mumbled something about the next meeting.

In the hallway she stumbled forward, still dizzy, trying to put her arm through her coat sleeve while balancing the rolled painting. Grade sheets and course notices fluttered on bulletin boards as she raced toward the exit.

A line of students shivering in the cold waited to place their backpacks and belongings on the security check conveyer. Both guards moved fast, inspecting parcels and purses to get the freezing mob into the building, without anyone to check people leaving the building. Her head was now in full migraine status.

One guard, a friendly guy she'd chatted with that morning, waved her out without the usual exit inspection. She weaved in and out, past the entering students, and exited the main entrance.

Brisk air hit her face and froze her tears like a slap of reality. She descended the staircase, trying to catch her breath against the cold and find her balance against the staccato thrumming of the headache. She steadied herself on the handrail only to remove her bare hand just as quickly from the icy metal. The faux Italianate lamppost made a leaning pole for the rolled canvas and freed both her hands to find her gloves. She pulled wisps of hair back into a plastic clip and wrapped a woolen scarf two extra turns around her neck.

The messenger bag slipped from her arm and knocked into the canvas. The roll teetered from the lamppost and slid onto the sidewalk like it had melted. She grabbed the roll to keep it from tumbling down the stairs into the snow and brushed drops of water from the paper covering it.

Oh shit. The painting.

She'd taken it! Removed it without paperwork, without permission.

Return it. Now.

The line of students had grown and snaked down the stairs. She walked toward the back of the line and stopped. If she went through security, the guards would require paperwork to register the art, information she did not have. She turned her head around as though an answer was somewhere nearby. Snowflakes started up again. Protecting the canvas from the bad weather came first.

Buses and taxis whirling in the traffic circle forced her to wait on the sidewalk for the light. She turned to look back at Hamilton Hall's frontispiece. Its Palladian architecture represented the rejection of the Baroque, the style of *La Gloria*. No small irony.

The traffic light turned green as the snow became rain coming down in big drops. She secured the rolled painting under her open coat, pulling the sides closed against the coming storm.

CHAPTER 4

*T*he storm continued to pound against her apartment windows all afternoon and into the night. She'd given up on sleep . . . again. Wild visions cascaded through her mind of losing the painting, having it stolen, getting caught, serving prison time, or worse, bringing shame to her family. Medical science should develop an imagination suppressant, a concoction to quash tumultuous thoughts.

The kitchen pantry, basically cabinets in her bedroom, contained a partial bag of coffee. She tossed out the half-empty Chinese cartons and prepared the brew. Coffee in a chipped mug warmed her hands and her soul too as she stared out the window into the cold searching for daylight on the horizon.

Her restless night had left her with a singular conclusion: return the painting. NYCU buildings opened in fifteen minutes. She dressed quickly in the same clothes as yesterday, packed the painting in an old art tube to protect it from rain or snow, and walked down the stairs to the street, putting forward each footfall with resolve. This escapade, this crazy journey that made her into an art thief, ended now.

It wasn't Jones's fault. No, this mistake was all on her, beginning with taking the artwork from the cellar, putting it in the humidifier, and then rushing out of Hamilton Hall because he'd rattled her. Her future prospects had to be with him, not without him. This art history journey meant everything, and hard as she'd tried, she was failing.

The sky threatened with clouds full of snow, but possibly rain if the temperature warmed. A walk in the brisk air suited her better than the subway's morning crush that was more crowded, if that was possible, when the weather was bad. She and the canvas made their way against the wind toward the university.

Building security might check the canvas, but probably would accept some explanation, especially because she was bringing it *into* the building, or maybe they'd have some benign forms to register it. A painting from a donor, an alum, a practice work or some such. That was the best she'd come up with among the dozens of choices cycling around in her head. She pulled her coat tight and clutched the painting tube with her mittens.

The tube had held a poster, now hung on her apartment wall, an image by Artemisia Gentileschi, a favorite, not only because Artemisia was female, one of the few documented in the seventeenth century, but also because Artemisia's talent rested in her representation of the female figure. A woman was not an object to be admired or worshiped, but a real person charged with emotion, anger, even violence, highlighted with light and color. Artemisia and the artist who painted *La Gloria* shared much more than the trivial connection of the art tube. The central female figure in *La Gloria* had those same human, naturalistic, emotional faces as the faces in Artemisia's works.

Artemisia lost her mom as a young girl and was raped by her painting tutor. Her father insisted she marry him, only to have the rapist refuse to do so. She survived the rapist's trial where her own testimony was tested by torture with thumbscrews. In the last four centuries, Artemisia's talent and her legacy triumphed over the tribulations of her life.

Cate waited at the stoplight where a Salvation Army bell ringer endured the cold for coins in his bucket. In two days, the university's holiday break would begin and life would get more complicated. She had booked a holiday flight to Spain using half an airline ticket left over from last summer when she'd purchased an emergency flight home for Dad's heart scare. The ticket would allow her to spend five days in Madrid before Christmas. Jones had given her a letter that would grant access to the Prado's research libraries. Perhaps the Prado's archives held a few nuggets about the female Portuguese artists that could convince Jones the topic had promise.

She'd booked a few days at a student hostel and needed her shrinking funds for food and subways in Madrid. After Madrid she'd fly home Christmas morning and face the third holiday with Matty's chair empty at the dining table.

She turned the corner toward the university entrance and quickened her steps. The walkway leading to the plaza in front of Hamilton Hall was crowded with more students than usual. Perhaps waiting for a final exam in a big undergraduate course. She started up the steps, but security guards waved at her and other students, pushing them into the plaza.

"What's going on?" she asked a young guy in ripped jeans.

"Can't get in the building."

"What about the side entrance?"

He shrugged.

She walked around to the side of the building and recognized Julio standing guard, shivering.

"Sorry, can't let you in." He was dressed only in his uniform shirt and shook as the wind blew against him.

"Looks like you forgot your coat."

Julio pulled on the long sleeves of his undershirt, the kind blue-collar guys wore in winter under their uniforms, and said, "Had to get out fast when the alarm went off."

"Alarm?"

"Yup, fire alarm, but there's no fire. We were sent to block the doors." He looked around, leaned toward her, and whispered, "Between you and me . . . a bomb threat. Some kid not ready to take an exam made a phone call. Happens every year. Got to search the whole damn building."

She nodded. Unable to come up with any other response, she asked, "How long would you guess?" She balanced the canvas under her arm.

"Don't know how long. Dogs got to check all six floors. Pain in the . . ."

An especially frosty gust burned her cheeks, and Julio shuddered. "Could you go inside for your jacket and maybe detour to, I mean, it would take only a minute, to put this in that storeroom, the one where you opened the door?" She lifted the tube.

"Can't."

He said the words with a finality that disallowed pressing him. He shivered again.

"Would you like my cap? Might keep you warmer." Every Michigander knew that a hat along with thick socks was the key to warmth in frigid weather.

Julio moved his head in a nod or a shake. She wasn't sure. She handed him the knit cap and he quickly pulled it down over his ears and held it there as though it might take flight. "I can't let you in. Really can't. I'd get fired. Or . . ." He paused. ". . . we'll get blown up. Which won't matter if I get fired, if you get my meaning."

It was her turn to shudder-nod her head. "I'm going over to the NYCU Student Union to have a coffee. Maybe you can call me when they open the building." She jotted down her number on a scrap and put the paper in his shirt pocket.

"Thanks for the . . ." He raised his eyebrows toward the hat.

Juggling the tube while keeping her hatless hair from blowing into her eyes, she made her way through the throngs to the student union building. She pushed against the glass door and a blast of hot air blew on her face. The union was packed with students who scrambled for seats, even occupying the fancy ones in the salons used by touring parents and their applicant kids. Students' legs and backpacks became a gauntlet for those trying to get to the cafeteria for coffee and breakfast. Some chose the floor over the posh couches in the foyer and spread their books and exam notes in front of them, preparing for a long siege until Hamilton Hall reopened.

Clanging trays and plates combined with the cafeteria's buzz of conversation distracted her from the derailed mission to return the painting. The smell of grease and mildew, combined with wet wool, made her nauseous. Three gals had a free seat at their table, and she asked with a lean of her head if they minded her sitting there. Without a break in their chatter, one made a hand gesture seeming to say the fourth chair was free.

She steadied the tube securely between her legs, where it wouldn't get jostled by students weaving between tables. The taciturn girl looked like she was about to make a comment about the phallic profile, but before she could, Cate shifted the tube from between her legs to the side.

A silent fog from a clash of indoor heat against the outdoor cold condensed on the windows. The girls chirped about their exams, and she remembered when she had friends like that, happy to be together for hours, talking about nothing and soothing each other's troubles.

Noemi might know when they could get back in the building, or perhaps she was wandering around somewhere nearby. She found Noemi's number in her contacts.

"Hi—was just going to call you. Got a text not to come to work. Heading back to subway now."

"What's going on in Hamilton?"

"Somebody stole stuff. The police are there now."

Shit. Stole stuff. She struggled to breathe.

"You there?"

She managed a whisper. "Yes."

"Jones emailed me to get a copy of the inventory you did or a file from your computer—we can't get to our computers and the police want it."

"Art? The cops are looking for stolen art." Cate blurted the words. If she hadn't been sitting, she would have dropped to the floor.

"Don't know. Cops are checking. Computers, files, artwork, everything."

Cate held the phone away from her face so Noemi could not hear her panicked breaths.

Noemi continued, "Do you have it—the inventory?"

La Gloria was not on that inventory. How could the work be missed if it wasn't listed? Just because the university had no record of the painting didn't mean someone, someone like Jones, wasn't looking for it.

Cate cleared her throat. "I can email the file to you or Jones."

"Jones is gone."

"What?" A shrill sound came from her throat. She plugged her finger in one ear to cut out the cafeteria noise.

"Holidays. His classes are over, flew to Europe I think, won't be back 'til January."

Of course, no full professor hung around when there were no classes. She shook her head. No way to return the painting with Hamilton Hall full of police. No chance of discussing the canvas with Jones—try to make it right, have him advocate for her in case the owner of the painting had missed it and called the cops. Not that he'd advocate for her regardless.

"Do you need to get something to him? I can probably reach him."

"No. No. It's okay," she lied.

"Going into the subway, I'll lose you. Send me that inventory and hey, Merry Christmas. Watch out for the mistletoe."

"You too." Mistletoe? She wished.

The cafeteria emptied as word of Hamilton's prolonged closure spread. She wrapped her scarf around her head, buttoned her coat, and secured the tube under her arm. Students gathered near a security guard with gold around his captain's cap.

"Your exams have been moved. Check the course website for details."

She sat down on the low wall near Hamilton Hall. Things would only get worse if she tried to return the artwork now. Her scarf slipped to her neck and her hair blew in all directions, chaos instead of the calm resolve that had begun the day.

CHAPTER 5

The subway stairs brought a cold blast and rain poured from the sky, requiring a mad dash to her building's door to find refuge from a world turned wrong side up.

She brushed the hair from her eyes, the mahogany strands now dark and dripping, stomped the muck off her boots, and fumbled with the mailbox key while holding the painting. The floor was damp and filthy from everything New York streets had to offer. Junk flyers and catalogues advertising everything from tires to wrinkle cream, neither of which she needed, were wrapped around one first class envelope in her mailbox. The letter had an NYCU logo on the return address.

She climbed the stairs to the studio, a sublet from a guy who kept the rent-controlled space while he lived somewhere in the sunshine. Subletting was probably illegal, but also cheap. Real estate fraud and art theft were two things she had not envisioned for her life. It was true New York changed people, made them into something else. But these were not the ways she'd expected.

She opened the apartment door, flung her coat to the floor, and quickly slid the canvas from the tube onto the table, relieved to find it was dry. She stared at the brown paper roll and the roll stared back, waiting for what came next. So here she was, here they were, she and the painting, locked out, cops searching, and she struggling to undo what she'd done—stolen a painting.

Stolen. Mom would not associate the word with her daughter. "What the heck?" she'd say, selecting a modified expletive with the limited options her Midwest persona allowed. Worst on that scale was "Gol dang it!" Stealing a painting would get that or maybe a first, an "F" without the rest of the word.

She needed a minute to sit and breathe. She picked up the university logo envelope. Probably another reminder of the tuition due date.

The letter was from the Dean of Humanities, Graduate Division:

> *The Chairman of your dissertation committee has notified this office that progress toward a doctoral dissertation topic, a requirement for satisfying next semester's prerequisites, has not been completed. Your Committee Chair must advise this office that sufficient progress has been made and sign the enclosed form before January 15. Failure to do so may result in academic consequences, up to and including being placed on probationary status, suspending your funding, or being asked to leave the university.*

The paper in her hand shook with the rest of her. She set the letter on the table and steadied herself on the back of a chair. Still shaking, wondering if this notification had been submitted before she appeared for their last meeting and the bastard had rejected her proposal before he'd heard it.

Of course he had. No doubt he'd deceived her. Jones didn't believe any woman, not descending from generations of art collectors or the legacy of an Ivy League pedigree, belonged in his art history program. What a fool she'd been; the quality of her work didn't matter.

She sucked back tears and frustration, unwilling to give him any satisfaction from this crushing blow. Don't get mad. Get even. A mantra from Dad.

Options were limited: push back, ask for time, insufficient notice, change advisors, change departments to woman's studies or history. Any of these would result in more cost and more time, detours from what was unavoidable—the need to convince Jones of a viable topic—before mid-January. And Jones wasn't even in town until after the holidays. Shit.

The struggle through Ypsilanti's bad schools where only ten percent went to college had motivated her, given her local star status. No one in her family had studied beyond high school and she knew no one with a doctorate. This battle wasn't only for her. Like her high school advisor had said, she was clearing the path for others. Once that would have included her little brother.

She ran her fingers along the edge of the paper covering the canvas. Taking the canvas from the university was stupid and wrong, at least in the short term. But there was no undoing the past, rewinding and editing what had happened, and she needed to stop wishing it away. Make the best of the hand dealt.

She didn't know what "making the best of it" meant, how she could translate that into a plan. She wanted to give the painting an identity, place it in the pantheon of history. That's what this art history thing was about: piecing puzzles of the past together. If she was right, the value of the NYCU's humble collection would increase and yes, Jones could get the credit, feed his ego. She'd play to his weakness. She sighed and dug deep for Midwestern grit.

She spread a clean bed sheet over the table and put on her cotton gloves. She loosened the tape and the brown paper fell away from the canvas. She nudged the uncovered painting by unrolling it inch by inch with her fingers.

The image silenced her anxiety, pushed away the wreckage she'd created, and focused her attention on the beauty, the poetry of the art. Like a lover gazing upon the face of her partner in first morning light, she studied the central figure, a young woman, who opened her hand toward a gathering of the faithful, bowing to angels who flew above her and a royal image, a king with his crown, silent and strong. The woman standing on the earth was not the Virgin nor a saint, nor an object of beauty, but a naturalistic figure, human in all respects. The figure gazed outward, connecting her eyes with the onlookers, inviting them into the scene. Simple pigment on linen executed with expressive brushstrokes came alive, a magic that, for her, was transformative and could never be deconstructed into its material parts.

Artistic brilliance glowed from the kitchen table and awaited meticulous, thoughtful, and most important, uninterrupted study. She pulled a reference book from the plastic crates where she stored treasured volumes from her undergraduate courses. Images of Baroque paintings, famous works from superstars, masters like Rembrandt, Rubens, and Caravaggio, yes Caravaggio, flew by until she stopped on the Velázquez chapter. She looked from the page to *La Gloria* and back again to images that with some exceptions differed from the painterly composition of this work. The luminosity of the colors, the ideas drawn from nature, these were people that existed and *La Gloria's* central figure shared that with many of Velázquez's works. However, this painting's expressive brush strokes had more in common with the later works.

Works painted by Velázquez's studio assistants showed similarities. Why wouldn't they? The work might be by Juan de Pareja, the slave who worked as his assistant and became an important painter, or by Martinez del Mazo, his son-in-law, but their works lacked the richness and the exuberance of *La Gloria's* color palette.

She looked up from the book to the painting. The painting might be an exercise assigned to a different studio assistant, a practice piece for a master painter—or a nineteenth-century commercial copy for Americans on their Grand European Tour, wealthy travelers who returned to cities like Cleveland and Chicago with treasures. But a copy of what? There were no compositions like *La Gloria*. Yet the figure's face was distinctive, and likely the woman had been employed as a model.

She took the bottle of distilled water she used to fill the iron and put a drop onto a Q-tip swab. The conservative intervention of dapping water might remove grime from the central figure's face and reveal subtleties of shading. There was little risk of damage if she tested a small spot on the edge. The swab absorbed the black soot and she tossed it for another. Pigments glowed rich in red and azure with texture and shading adding depth. She leaned back, adjusted the light. Spontaneous and unlabored brushstrokes scurried across the linen to form images. Under painting of pentimenti, the artist's rethinking the composition, appeared ghost-like, faint and better viewed with an x-ray.

Drawings, studies, or sketches to prepare the canvas before painting were different than overpainting what was already put down. Overpainting happened more often when the artist skipped drawing, as was Velázquez's artistic practice. She put a magnifying loupe to her eye and lowered her head to a section of thinly painted canvas, with the linen's texture visible.

There they were.

Lines, seemingly random, a twist to the body or a hand's position, that perhaps represented an idea the artist rejected. Her heart raced as more led back to her initial impression.

She pulled out Jones's tome on Velázquez. The section on technique stated, "He did not use preliminary drawings or studies, instead sketched directly into the gesso. When he changed his ideas to create the final composition, residual lines of the original sketches remained in the gesso. These can be seen in some cases with the eye alone, but are easily revealed with x-rays."

X-rays would eliminate other painters whose techniques did not match the ones used on this canvas. Chemical examination of the pigments and the particular weave of fibers in the canvas fabric could add more evidence. These tests confirmed age and location, verified whether the work was painted in Seville or Madrid, or maybe even Italy. Laboratory tests at a top research facility cost money. Money was something she did not have.

Academics sought grants for such things. The Velázquez Foundation would expect Jones, a board member there, to sign off on an application. That wasn't going to happen. The National Endowment for the Arts and NYCU grants took time.

She was not an expert, not yet. But she had intuition and an eye that had studied many of these works. She'd need more than hunches, much more. Needed them soon, by the beginning of January, latest.

Experts' preliminary comments might convince Jones to support a grant, or at least sign off on a topic of study. Experts like Cuevas, unfortunately Jones's archenemy, were in Madrid. Cuevas's books and his other writings were never on Jones's course syllabus unless the writings were assigned as a critique of bad scholarship and comparison to Jones's own ideas. Cuevas was better than Jones, but to Cuevas NYCU students were tainted as Jones's allies. Scholarship became a sham, an excuse to pummel each other.

Hours passed as she worked over a two-inch circle around the central figure's eye, using all Q-tips. The cleaned space brought out exquisite flesh tones and small dots of light from under the shadows.

The figure pleaded with her eyes, an entreaty from four hundred years ago. Women painted in this time often had their eyes positioned downward in prayer and humility, upward toward heaven in supplication, or in profile looking to the side. Natural eyes looking directly at the viewer did appear in the early 1500s, like in the *Mona Lisa*, but were still rare in the 1600s. Velázquez pioneered changes toward a more natural gaze outward.

Something else.

She stood back to study the newly cleaned face. Something beyond the brilliant composition: That model, strangely familiar, appeared somewhere, perhaps in another work.

She jumped up and searched through a stack of old exhibition catalogs and pulled one from the Metropolitan's Velázquez retrospective that she'd bought at a used bookstore. Color plates of the paintings included in the exhibition skipped between her fingers until that face . . .

"Yes!"

Plate number twenty-nine.

The figure's face was the same as the model for the weaver in *The Spinners*. That model posed for Velázquez, and the same woman posed for *La Gloria's* central figure. Those eyes, that emotional face. Unmistakable.

Models didn't travel far in the seventeenth century. The canvas had been painted in the same decade and not far from, if not *in*, Velázquez's studio in the Royal Palace. An undeniable link.

Wow. Twirls. Yes.

She fist pumped into the air. She danced around the kitchen chair, like Mom did when the tax refund arrived.

Breathless, she collapsed into the chair and grinned.

The phone flashed, a message from Mom.

"Darling, how are you doing? When are you arriving? And what do you want for Christmas? You'll probably say money, but what about a new coffee maker with those pod things? Have you seen those?" Mom was incapable of a brief message.

She'd planned to head to Michigan after Madrid, but the Dean's letter, the painting, and well ... everything. Mom's words added to the exhaustion that stole the joy of her discovery and now overwhelmed her. She needed sleep, to restore clear thinking and find some way to solve the problems that pressed on her.

She rolled and wrapped the canvas to protect it from a disaster like a broken water pipe, not uncommon in this decrepit building. A multimillion-dollar painting, perhaps tens of millions, rolled up in this cold apartment with the flimsy door chain. One of those heroin addicts she stepped over on the stairs could break in, grab the masterpiece, and pawn it for a hundred bucks to get a hit.

She couldn't leave the work in this apartment, nor take it when she went to Spain for a few days of research. Maybe she'd skip Spain and go straight home for Christmas. But Michigan wasn't safer. And she needed that time for research in Madrid. It was zero hour to make a bold move or her whole life plan would derail.

Maybe she could take *La Gloria* to Spain, see what she might learn, and get it in front of some experts or their assistants. Was it possible to carry a painting across the borders and back? Most customs people couldn't tell a poster from a Vermeer, if they even asked to inspect the luggage of a lowly student.

The best labs for Spanish works were, of course, in Spain, with experts in Madrid and Seville where the Golden Age had flourished. Get away from the tight New York art community where everyone talked to Jones. Guillermo, her Prado course professor, had agreed to help with her research, but she couldn't show him *La Gloria* until she had more supportive documentation.

She couldn't think, not now with everything she needed to do. But her brain kept churning. An appointment at Seville's Art Conservation Institute was a good first stop where she could try to get the painting's canvas dated there before the Madrid gossip started buzzing. With support, she could risk putting *La Gloria* in front of Guillermo, who might agree to show it to Velázquez experts like Cuevas.

She sat back down and slumped. There was no money for three weeks in Spain, much less for the lab tests. The familiar names in her contact list scrolled through her mind in a well-practiced exercise known to all impoverished researchers looking for sponsors.

Mom and Dad were out of the question. They struggled to pay bills with their limited funds. The debt of burying Matty hung over them, a monthly reminder of the sadness, in a windowed envelope. She could not ask them.

Her credit card approached its limit too. Maybe she'd ask for a bigger credit line. Every asset she owned—jewelry, clothes, the silver tray Gran gave her for graduation, a family heirloom—could be sold for cash. Selling stuff took time and there wasn't any, not if she was going to pull this off over the holidays.

Harry. The wealthy collector who pursued her when she interned at the Met, had funded an exhibition for which she'd been a curatorial volunteer. They had met at a donor cocktail party. Inviting him for drinks at the Algonquin and then fighting him off was an unpleasant prospect.

The retirement account from the three years she worked as a resident assistant at Southern Michigan was still intact. Basic retirement plan deduction on her pay stub felt like robbery, but a minimum was required of employees with a year of service. Even with employer matches, it didn't amount to much. If she withdrew from it, her friends in the business school had advised her, there would be penalties and taxes. Like she had a tax problem.

She sighed, exhausted from the universe blocking her every plan. She pulled out the sofa bed, slid the painting into the tube, and placed it on the bed. Her flannel nightgown comforted and warmed her as she slid into bed and reclined with a hand on the tube's edge, keeping the painting close.

Screw financial advice. She'd cash in the retirement fund and see what else she could scrounge. Nothing about Operation Velázquez had been intelligent. Why change now?

She and her new love were going to Spain.

CHAPTER 6

*T*he piano riff ringtone jarred her upright from deep sleep. She tried to focus her eyes on the time on the phone. Mom. Cate fumbled to push the button to answer and avoid a lengthy message. In the gymnastics to untangle the sheets, she fell off and sat up on the cold floor with her back balanced against the sofa bed.

"There you are, honey. Dad and I been worrying. Did ya go down that subway and never come out? Like a groundhog in a bad winter." Mom sputtered a promising laugh.

She rolled her eyes and tried to stand. "No, Mom, fell in a hole in my bed from exhaustion." Mom's jovial mood reminded her of the before-holidays, before the sadness.

"More cold than usual. Pipes cracked. Putting up Christmas for you."

Christmas would bring out old photos to add to the ones in the shrine that was Matty's bedroom. The sound of Mom's words brought a longing Cate buried with the innocent joy that once defined home, that safe place now evaporated.

"You there, Catie? Sweetie? Are you crying?"

Mom could see to her soul. Cate was bound so tight to her, wanting to break free and yet connected always. No lying to Mom either. It was like lying to herself.

She tried anyway. "A head cold Mom. Sniffles. It's been freezing here."

"You're Michigan. Ya know—ten below zero here and we're having a cookout. Your Dad shoveling snow in shirt sleeves."

Michiganders made fun of people in other states who closed down school at the first snow. No snow days for them, ever. She sucked in the tears and embraced those images until worries returned. "With Dad's heart condition, he shouldn't be shoveling snow. What's he up to?"

"Watching the golf on TV."

"Dad doesn't even play golf. Why does he care?"

"He gets to sit in the recliner, with Hound Dog by his side. Those hushed-toned announcers like a naptime lullaby."

The dog barked in the background and she pictured Hound Dog jumping up and Dad pushing him off the chair.

"Ah hell-oh. Is that you?"

"Hey Dad. Who's on top of the leader board? You should learn to golf."

"Nah. Got to join a club, pretty boys in pastel shirts, all tucked in. Got to stay here, give your mother somebody to cook for and talk to. God that woman can talk."

Mom hollered in the background, "I heard that Al."

Dad had the character of men of a certain era, bitter critic, negative about most things. Yet under it all, there was a protective love, even if you had to scrape away layers of curmudgeon to reveal it, suffocating but real.

Dad ignored Mom and asked about school.

"I'm tired. Hours in the library, research, studying paintings, you know, work."

Dad interrupted, "No kinda work that is. Looking at paintings, sitting in libraries." He stopped and then went for the usual advice. "Get a real job, make something people need."

Best not to react to Dad's taunts, but now, her patience short, she jumped in. "Like building cars? Maybe it's not lifting heavy things or assembling a truck, but people need art, food for the soul—that's my work." She wasn't about to give up her passion for art, awakened when she was ten on a school outing to the Detroit Institute of Arts. Those Murillo figures in *The Flight from Egypt* grabbed her heart as a real family, a baby Jesus that resembled her little brother and what she now knew to call naturalism in the Spanish Baroque. She'd stared at it until the teacher found her and fetched her back to the tour.

"Those cars paid for your college, Sis."

It had been awhile since he'd called her "Sis." She was nobody's Sis anymore. "Let's don't argue Dad."

"Tell those professor types, treat you nice or I'll come on over there."

No. No more disasters like her college graduation when Dad walked onto the stage after the ceremony, asked why his straight-A daughter didn't get to make a speech. Dean Collins brushed him off with a "Congratulations on your daughter's success" and a handshake.

She'd hidden a certain pride that Dad had asked Dean Collins the question. Why had Jonathan Priestly, a student riding the wave of his family's donations and alumni network, gotten top honors over a scholarship student like her with the same grades? The answer was in the question. In recent memory, no female student had made the valedictory speech.

For all his lack of sophistication, Dad saw through people and didn't hesitate to call them out. In his heart, he wanted to protect her. She knew that. And she also knew that his gruff manners could not be polished as she had struggled to polish her own. His belief every woman needed a man to defend her would never change.

"They're not being unkind, just doing their jobs. It's how it works in graduate school."

School had been a protected world where achievement was a meritocracy . . . what papers, exams, and other work earned. But winning awards and getting reference letters woke her up to a universe of biases favoring men that echoed the resentment she'd felt over Dad's support of Matty's future and silence about hers. Now she was his only child, a female child, and he was forced to choose either to abandon his aspirations for his family or believe in her future, in her, a woman.

Graduate school would be different, she'd thought. Midwest work ethic would matter. It didn't. Different lines, but lines still, were drawn around gender and class. She had no desire to change powerful men's grip on the prizes or rich kids' legacies. Friends, colleagues, even Harry, helped her with the social codes she'd never learn at home. She'd learned and would learn more about how to navigate this world that was not hers and find a small slice of success.

"Put Mom on."

"She's checking the pot roast. Takes all day to cook it."

The smells, the sounds of an unwatched television, Hound Dog barking, the political arguments, formed a mental collage. Fog would cling outside those frosty windows and create moisture on the inside where she had sat drawing images on the glass after peeling carrots and potatoes, creating dreamy visions of leaving to somewhere warm. Matty's young voice imitating sirens with his fire truck sounded with these memories. Her heart longed to return but that place had cracked like frozen pipes, damaged and unrepairable even with a thaw.

Mom fumbled the phone, mumbling about needing to wipe her hands on her apron. "When do you arrive?"

"Mom, I'm so, so sorry." She took a deep breath.

"You're not coming?"

The thud of Mom's heart breaking was too much.

She held the phone away and allowed a sob to escape. *Stay strong, hold on.* The rolled canvas sat on the bed, about to wake up.

"I have a huge deadline. If I don't get my thesis topic approved by January 15, I might not be able to continue my program."

"Well, that's a biggie. Can't you work here? I'll make Dad turn off the TV."

Cate pulled at the threads on the little rug by the sofa bed. "I need the library and . . . other resources." All true. Not really a lie.

"I will miss you so. I never sleep as well as when you're under this roof. To see your face and know you're fine. That's what I want for Christmas."

The image of Mom's protective embrace forced her to grab another tissue. "I'll make time in February." *Maybe it could happen.*

Mom paused. "Well then, get to work. We're not quitters. Never have been."

"I won't let you down." The words hung in the air, cold and empty.

Mom's voice cracked when she repeated the phrase "best daughter in the universe," as she had done since Cate left for Y camp. "I love you honey."

Cate whispered "love you too" while she bit her lip and pushed the off button again and again, three times as though the connection could not be severed.

Regrets flooded her thoughts. Mom's standards didn't permit lies or non-lies. Bruce Nauman's "partial truth," had been essential to survive high school, especially when she came home past curfew, and now to survive a stolen painting and navigate a tenuous future.

She'd be in Spain on Christmas morning, missing them more than they would know. She hadn't bought any Christmas gifts, and pangs of being selfish and ungrateful added to her guilt. She dialed a florist in Ypsilanti and placed an order for the cheapest arrangement they had.

Outside the apartment window, the winter sky spread grey over the buildings with yellow light fading on the horizon. She tiptoed in her nightgown on the cold floor over to the light switch and picked up the coffee pot to pour yesterday's coffee into her mug. The microwave warmed it to good enough. A jar of peanut butter sat alone on the refrigerator shelf next to a bottle of water. She counted the slices of bread from a loaf on the counter and added up enough meals for the two days until she left. She wiped her hands and sat down at the keyboard for a long slog through the airplane booking process.

The original ticket had been booked on a low-cost airline and the change fees were more than the whole ticket cost. The computer pinged, something popped up on the screen. Air Canada, Kennedy to Madrid via Toronto worked even though the flight began in the wrong direction. She hit the "book" button, fast, before the price disappeared or the computer crashed. She'd leave a day earlier but no matter. Less peanut butter needed.

Air Canada would fly over Michigan as the plane circled to land in Toronto. Airplane food would be an improvement over peanut butter. Yet the meal she'd want would be on the ground below her in that warm Ypsilanti house.

CHAPTER 7

*T*he last twenty hours had been a blur of airplane seats, sized for leprechauns, a mad dash from the immense Barajas airport to the train to the Nuevos Ministerios stop, and then the subway to the Atocha train station, all with the art tube under her arm, and then a collapse onto the bench seat of the cheap train to Seville, the center of sixteenth- and seventeenth-century Spanish art and trade. Her urgent mission was to get the painting to Seville's Art Institute before it closed for the holidays. Madrid could wait because its large libraries and museums like the Prado stayed open, albeit with limited staff, between Christmas and New Year's.

Guillermo expected her in Madrid before Christmas, and she had no idea if he would remain in Madrid or stay at the Prado for the holidays. She shook her head at the details she'd had no time to organize, and all she could do now was hope luck had not left town for the holidays too.

Train wheels screeched as they gripped the rails on the curves with a fingernails-on-a-blackboard noise. The frayed fabric on the armrest of the old RENFE car, a relic, testified to decades of neglect. Perhaps one of Franco's generals occupied this seat or an artist like Sorolla placed his arm on the worn velvet.

She nodded off until the engine heaved into a nondescript station of a town she'd never heard of, where smells of diesel oil and coal hung like wet laundry. She stretched her head through the window's top half hoping for cleaner air. The view offered nothing remarkable, only the sameness of the thirty-two stops this regional train would make before arriving to Seville. The fast AVE train took passengers from Madrid to Seville in four hours. And knowing there was a faster but unaffordable train, especially for last-minute tickets, only added more frustration.

She double-checked the luggage rack above her head for the tube with the canvas. Three weeks—well, two and a half with travel time—for this stealth trip was not nearly enough to validate a wild-ass theory about a masterpiece, but she had to try.

The conductor opened the sliding door to the cabin and barked, "*Billete*." He shifted from one foot to the other as she rifled through her purse for the e-ticket.

The conductor, his spine bent from years of leaning over passengers, took the paper with the bar code. His jacket cuff had frayed, soiled edges. He handed the paper back and asked for an old school ticket, but she didn't have one. He scowled.

After a standoff, grin against grimace, the conductor reached in his pocket for an orange chit, wrote something on it, and tucked it into a metal bracket above her seat. He took a real ticket from the Spaniard who sat across from her. She pulled in her knees, putting some space between her legs and the Spaniard's.

The conductor moved on. The sound of ticket punches echoed throughout the car until the noise diminished and then disappeared.

The train passed a ruined castle on a Castilian plateau, but mostly the plains rolled by as repetitive as the clang of the wheels. Her head sagged against the seat back and she jerked upright to keep one eye on the tube. The police were probably still searching Hamilton Hall, but not likely for this undocumented painting, unless somehow Jones was in the mix. She sighed, doubting herself, this path she'd chosen, and fearing the outcome.

She'd sought out Cynthia Monahan, the only woman faculty member in the art history department. Cate had confided to her the struggles with Jones and the sexist vibes from the male students.

"I suggested a couple of little-known female artists from the early Baroque, but Jones declared my proposal dead on arrival. What do you think?"

Cynthia had laughed and shook her head at the question, but said nothing.

Cate persisted. "Perhaps . . . you or another faculty member have more interest in studying forgotten women artists and maybe believe female students have potential."

The professor removed her cherry-colored glasses and sighed. "Revising history is a tough slog, that's why I prefer the study of contemporary artists. While women are better represented in art scholarship now, little has changed regarding interest in women artists. It's worth pursuing your ideas for that very reason."

Cate nodded.

"As to the chauvinist idiots, the dinosaurs that still roam these halls, there's little hope. It's your, our, reality. You can file a complaint, but it will likely make things worse, not better. I had to toughen up and so do you."

Tough. Tougher. She'd do this. Show Jones, Cynthia, everyone.

The fellow across from her juggled his papers against the rocking train. He caught her looking up at the tube and smiled. She didn't want to call attention to it and looked out the window.

The train's brakes shuddered and lurched at a crossing to avoid another train. Her knees slid into the Spaniard's whose mustache made him look older than he probably was. The painting tube flew off the rack and would have hit his head except for a quick catch on his part. He laughed.

"It's yours?"

She managed half of a smile. "You're a good goalkeeper." She stood to put the tube back, but more rocking made it difficult to secure.

He helped her into her seat, stood, and reached over her, pushing the tube behind her bag. "That should keep it from rolling."

Maybe he was being nice, but most Spanish guys couldn't be trusted. She'd learned that in the Madrid course. Guillermo took the female students under his wing and offered a Spanish twist on options for how to say "no," including the look away and say nothing strategy she used now.

The Spaniard pulled out the shelf-table between them and placed a bottle of Rioja on it. "Would you like a glass of vino?" He didn't wait for an answer to his perfect UK-accented English question and set out two cups.

"That conductor." She shook her head. "My world has a few people just like him."

"And what world is that?" he asked.

A truthful answer required an elaborate tale, information that would lead to questions she preferred not to answer.

He offered his hand. "I'm Antonio."

"Catherine. Cate." She held out her hand.

He lowered his head and instead of shaking her hand, he brushed a polite kiss on it.

She pulled away and looked out the window.

He sat up and straightened the mustache that had prickled her hand.

Kissing a hand was odd from a young person. Perhaps he was a gentleman, or a genteel provincial person.

He lifted his glass. "The tube. Are you an architect? I need an architect."

"No, not an architect."

The train's jostling sloshed the wine in her almost-full glass onto the table and his papers. Antonio took a monogramed handkerchief worn at the edges from his pocket and dabbed at the spill. "Best to drink up." Grey eyes that looked blue when he turned into the light had a wise but distant countenance. He had an attractive face in a ruddy kind of way.

He slid his papers back into his briefcase. "My neighbor's wine. We trade marmalade from our orange trees with him." He smiled.

"I like the wine, but I'm no connoisseur." She paused. "This train is so slow. Are you getting off in Seville?"

"Two stops after Seville, a little town with bad train service, Olivares. I was born there." He held up the bottle in a gesture to refill her glass.

She steadied the glass underneath the bottle. "Beautiful convent in Olivares, paintings by Zurbarán, Roelas, and others. Didn't Roelas die there?"

"You are interested in art history? Most tourists don't bother to visit Olivares. Better paintings in Seville and Madrid."

"I've never been to Olivares, and yes, a graduate student in art history." She resisted sharing too much of her story. "Orange marmalade with oranges not from Valencia but from Olivares."

"Yes. Our orange groves were planted in the days of Count-Duke of Olivares."

"The duke who ran the government of Phillip IV in the 1600s? That duke? Is the current duke your neighbor?"

"No, not my neighbor." Antonio looked uneasy. "Why not visit while you're here?"

"My days are booked in Seville, every minute for research."

"Research about what?"

She held out the plastic cup. "Is there more wine?" She sipped quietly and rested her weary head.

Antonio slept with his head bumping against the window. His long lashes almost reached the sunken places under his eyes, unusual in someone around thirty. Worries did that to a person.

She took a small notebook and a pen from her bag and wrote "The Plan" at the top of a blank page. After she checked into the hotel, she'd go to the Archives of the Indias and the Columbus Library. Maybe there were some histories, diaries, journals, or documents from ships or public authorities that would shed light on the artist's travels. Monday's appointment at the Art Institute was the only hard date booked. If the Institute said the painting was nothing, she'd return it to the chest at NYCU and end this crazy adventure. A plan evolves; it must be flexible. She put the pen and notebook back in her bag.

She wanted to call Noemi about the police investigation and what was stolen, if anything. It was the middle of the night, too late or too early, which ever, to call and it was Saturday. Nothing to be done until Monday.

A short, plump lady sitting in the next seat rummaged through a nest of brown paper in a plastic basket and pulled out a *bocadillo* that smelled amazing. A splurge in the overpriced restaurant car was out of the question. The woman smiled, showing at least two missing teeth, reached for another sandwich, and offered it to her.

"*Sí chica.* Food on the train, very bad and *muy caro.*" The woman rubbed her fingers together as if there were coins between them.

Yes to that. And the sandwich. Cate pulled back the paper and smelled the garlic and olive oil from the omelet in the sandwich. She thanked the woman, who reached across the little space and patted Cate's knee. She gulped the wine left in her glass and eyed the bottle wedged against Antonio's sleeping torso and the window. She attempted to nudge the wine free. Antonio stirred and opened his eyes.

"Would you like more?" Fully awake, he pulled the cork out and filled her glass.

"Are you hungry? We could split this sandwich."

"*Mala suerte.* I wanted to invite you to the dining car. Guess I missed my chance."

Unexplained disappointment floated over her, sensing she was missing something more than the food.

"Come anyway. Keep me company." Antonio got up, tucked his papers into his briefcase. "Finish your sandwich and I'll buy you dessert and coffee."

Her eyes met his. She paused, rewrapped the sandwich, and grabbed her purse. The tube with the painting caught her eye. Antonio would ask more questions if she brought it, but she could not leave it. She nearly bumped sandwich lady, trying to get around her and her bundles to exit the cabin. The lady looked up at her, squeezed her arm, winked, and whispered. "He's very handsome."

The restaurant car had a faded elegance of well-used linens and scratched silverware. The maître d'hôtel looked like the ticket guy, a throwback from another era with a rumpled collar and a tie that had been tied too many times. Nearly empty, a dying clientele and exorbitant prices made this rolling eatery a failed business proposition. The tottering fellow showed them to a table and handed out menus.

Antonio's face turned white as he reviewed the choices. "I haven't eaten here for quite a while."

Without saying it, the prices were a shock. The basic three-course plate of the day was seventy euros. Coffee cost five euros, rare even in NYC, but unheard of in Spain.

"What would you like?" Antonio squeaked, then cleared his throat. As though talking to himself, he said, "Don't worry about the prices."

Her host was as broke as she was. "Just coffee."

He ordered a gazpacho, the least expensive item at ten euros. The waiter delivered an ample basket of bread and butter to the table and laid out an excess of cutlery in front of Antonio, who was only having soup. She was relieved not to have to choose which implement for which course. She'd learned in college to wait and copy others who grew up with such things.

He motioned his head toward the parcel. "You never told me what is in the tube."

She moved the tube to the window side and hoped to make it through dinner without another question she didn't want to answer. "Enough of me. Tell me about you."

He chuckled. "I'm an attorney." He patted the briefcase he'd placed on the seat next to him. Apparently, he was not about to leave it in the cabin either. "Real estate, wills and trusts, contracts. Land rights. Complicated old laws in conflict with new codes."

"No courtroom dramas like Paul Newman in *The Verdict*?"

"Loved that film. Newman. Down, drunk, and broke and pulls it out against the rich lawyers." He lifted his shoulders with the exuberance of a ten-year-old about to watch his favorite team.

"Is that you? Down but not out?"

He didn't answer.

She played with the napkin on her lap, dapped her lips. "Sorry. I didn't mean to pry."

He shook his head. "Don't worry. I'm facing some big battles against the rich lawyers. I've no resources like those firms."

"Can't you charge the client?"

"I am the client, me and my family."

His spoon clinked against the china, intruding on the silence between them. She pondered her own legal problems, but the word family took her to that place like a distant echo. To Matty, there under everything always, and her part in it, her failures, that might have saved him.

Antonio changed the subject back to her. "What are your plans in Seville?"

"Work. Meet with art conservators and search for more documentation." She didn't want to say more.

"Not going to a flamenco show with a paella supper?"

She smirked. "No time for silliness."

"When you think you don't need silliness is when you need it the most." He had a nice laugh, half-chuckle with a quick shrug of his left shoulder, a talent to lighten the moment.

"True for you too?" she asked with a smile.

"Touché." Funny and honest too.

The conductor's voice came over the loudspeaker, "Sevilla. Ten minutes."

The waiter brushed breadcrumbs into a tiny silver dustpan and then produced the bill.

Antonio took a deep breath. "Waiter, this is incorrect. We had the soup and a coffee for twenty euros."

"Si and the *cubierto*, caballero, ten euros each for the seating." At the word *cubierto*, a cover charge, the waiter motioned to the breadbasket and the water bottle.

Antonio placed a credit card on the plate.

The waiter leaned down and whispered, "We require payment in cash."

Antonio rolled his eyes and searched his wallet.

She moved closer to the window, causing the tube to tumble under the table. She leaned under the tablecloth and lingered, noticing the worn state of the crumbling paint on the table's legs and avoiding the awkward moment. She lifted her head and Antonio's face flashed red. He held twenty euros between his fingers. "Could I borrow fifteen euros from you?"

Her wallet contained one twenty euro note left over from Madrid last summer. Taxi money before she got to a bank to convert the few dollars she had. She handed him the twenty without a word.

Antonio didn't seem like a deadbeat, but she learned this lesson about trusting too much with so-called boyfriends in college. She gathered up her things and stood to leave as he finished paying the waiter.

Antonio came down the hallway, his tie flopping as he raced to catch up.

"I'm embarrassed. So, so sorry."

She shrugged and lied, "It's twenty euros. Really nothing." But it was.

The train bounced on a curve and threw her into him. He grabbed her and held onto her a bit too long. "Would you be my guest for a proper meal with better food?"

"Sorry, I have a tight schedule over the university holidays."

"Hardworking student. Perhaps a coffee to give you a break from academic jail and return your twenty euros."

She hesitated. But then there were his eyes, now very blue and intense in the light from the windows. This struggling lawyer could be a mood boost, a free meal, and she might even get the twenty euros back. "You can reach me at the Alfonso XIII Hotel."

"Wow. The most expensive hotel in Seville? I misjudged you."

She bit her lip. Misjudging all around.

CHAPTER 8

*H*er red suitcase bumped, instead of rolled, along the stairs like a child's toy. She'd left the train with a brief "nice to meet you" to Antonio, who'd carried her suitcase to the platform, and then she rushed to find a taxi. Spaniards traveling on weekend jaunts queued up smoking Gitanos, those black tobacco cigarettes. That smell combined with diesel fumes from trucks and buses took her to crowded summers in Madrid. Sunlight poured in the station's exit door and was a sea change from New York's winter storms. A teenager in a parked car blasted music from the radio, a familiar tune. "Be Happy." If her arms hadn't been swamped with a bag lady level of encumbrances including the tube, she would have raised her arms to rejoice she'd made it this far.

"*¿Dondé,* Señorita?" the taxi driver asked.

"Hotel Alfonso XIII."

"Oy—the best hotel in Seville."

If he expected a big tip, he'd be disappointed. One credit card had enough left to cover the taxi ride and perhaps a meal or two, but not much more. Harry's hotel reward points would save her from sleeping in the train station. Harry had offered the points to her last summer when she went to Madrid, but she'd had student lodging as part of the program. When she decided to travel to Seville, she learned the points could be used at the Alfonso XIII and reached out to ask Harry if his offer still stood. He was a kind old gentleman . . . well, not always a gentleman. The hotel was so expensive those points were only good for three nights. To stay in Seville longer, she needed a cheap place to stay, a really cheap place.

The Alfonso XIII clung, not unsuccessfully, to the elegance of Spain's past where time had stopped in the 1920s. Hemingway, Fitzgerald, and the romantic writers of that era smoked their cigars in grand public rooms. Blue and gold glazed tiles on the floor, up the walls of the grand staircase reflected sunlight from the central patio where patrons drank sherry with afternoon tea.

The bellman led her to the elevator and then down two long hallways. He unlocked the door with a large key, not a plastic card, to a deluxe room, an upgrade, with high ceilings and large French doors. A Juliet balcony provided an expansive view of university buildings across the street where students chatted and laughed as they waited for the local trolleys. The students' exuberance made her long for undergraduate days, loads of friends united in the battle to earn a degree and faculty generals that led the charge. Graduate school replaced that camaraderie with a solo slog where students competed for star status to earn a prized academic position.

The shower ran over her body like baptismal water and rehydrated her drooping limbs. She had lost track of the travel hours or even what day it was since she'd left New York. Soft towel tufts removed the water from her wet body. Citrus-smelling lotion nourished the skin she could reach until the complimentary bottle was empty. She purred.

The king-size bed with a silk cover called to her and she answered. Thirty minutes, no more, a quick nap and over to the library before it closed. She stretched out, her head heavy from jet lag, from fleeing, from the complications of her life, sunk deep into the fragrant pillows.

A KNOCK. ANOTHER KNOCK. She stood, disoriented, to navigate the room in the darkness toward the door. Rose blossoms appeared through the peephole, until a bellman peeked his head out.

Flowers? No one knew she was here but . . . Harry, of course. She opened the door, accepted the flowers, and thanked the bellman without a tip. A note was stuck in between the roses.

She focused her sleepy eyes on the writing. "In Seville on Tuesday. Will you honor me by joining me for dinner? I will call for you at 8:30 p.m." She squinted, horrified that Harry was coming to Seville, and turned on the light to be sure she read the signature right. Not Harry, but Antonio de Olivares.

De Olivares. That *de* in front of Olivares had meaning in noble titles. Was he related to the duke? Maybe everyone in the town from nobility to laborers had that name since they came from the same place. She'd ask him at dinner.

A feeling that had not emerged in a while, so long she almost didn't recognize it, swelled inside her. An anticipation about what came next brought renewed enthusiasm about this trip. She checked the time. Only two hours before the library closed. Spain had its own work rules and often posted opening and closing hours that could not be trusted, especially during holidays.

She fluffed her hair, grabbed the tube, and stopped. Walking the streets with the painting was a bad idea. It wouldn't fit under the bed's frame as the side panels went to the floor. The only spot to hide it was the back corner of the closet behind the hanging laundry bags. An art tube wasn't a likely target in a hotel that would have lots of jewelry anyone could slip into a pocket. Steal this already stolen painting—she shook her head and closed the closet door, grabbed her messenger bag to head out.

The Columbus Library, along with the Archives of the Indias, was not "thoroughly sourced." Jones proclaimed all

Spanish libraries had been overrun with art history scholars. This library was more for historians than art types. Jones wouldn't know people at this library like he would in the libraries of Madrid and Barcelona.

The Columbus Library's heavy door squeaked when she opened it. Columbus's son had bequeathed his father's library to the Cathedral of Seville where father and son were now buried. Hernando Colón endeavored to own one of every book published. Many volumes in this library had not been opened for hundreds of years, some since they arrived from the cast-off collections of relatives of deceased noblemen. Important letters and private papers had been found, tucked in a book or an atlas, unread for centuries.

A seventy-something gentleman answered the buzzer on the secure inner door to the library stacks. "*Buenas tardes*, Señorita Adamson."

"How did you know my . . ." She paused to scope out the lonely library. The chairs and tables sat empty and so neatly in their places, it appeared no one had visited in a good while.

He held Jones's credential reference, the one for the Prado that she'd modified and sent by email. Their footfalls on the marble floors echoed against the thirty-foot ceilings as they marched past glass-fronted bookcases. He stopped at an imposing desk lit with tiny lamps, essential reading lights because the ceiling chandeliers hung so high, no light reached the desk.

"Señor Piero?" She said the name she'd found on their website tentatively because she did not expect Señor Piero greeted visitors at the door.

"I am. You're here to study Velázquez, or maybe his father-in-law Pacheco?"

This took her by surprise. Those artists' names were not in the credential letter, and she had never mentioned either one to Jones. "I'm not certain of my research topic . . . yet. Still exploring."

"You're an art historian and not a historian. In Seville, American art historians have one interest: the Master, Velázquez." He stopped and looked around. "Our library is limited for art studies. We do have a first-edition copy of Pacheco's *Arte de Pintura* from 1649. It's in bad shape but you can see it if you use these cotton gloves."

"Thank you. I have a reprint of Pacheco's book. What topics do Spanish history scholars pursue when they visit you?"

"A history professor from Salamanca came for information about slaves in Seville."

"Slaves?" She removed her computer from her messenger bag and opened a blank page to take notes.

"Seville was the shipping port to the Americas until a new port was built in Cadiz. That shipping included slaves."

She typed "Slaves," more to show interest in Piero's response than for her research. "May I see those records? I want primary sources that describe the culture of Seville during the 1600s."

Odd to think of Seville as a slave port when it was known as the center for new ideas from a new world. Educated artists and writers in Seville met in salons including Pacheco's, wrote poetry and plays, and discussed the interface of art and religion. Artists, including Velázquez, had slaves as assistants, she knew that. But hundreds of slaves being loaded onto the caravels that lined Seville's harbor didn't fit with their progressive center image.

"The volumes will be brought to you."

"Gracias. Since it's late, may I leave the books in the carrel and continue tomorrow?"

"No. Books are returned each night before you leave."

He was a kindly man and his job was to safeguard the collection. She got that, but it also meant she'd lose a half-hour each day to re-request the books before she could begin work.

Piero set the volumes down on the carrel and dust flew into the air. One massive book covered the entire desktop. She slid her chair backward to make room to open it to the title page. The volume contained passenger logs for ships going from Naples to Barcelona in 1651. A bookmark lodged in the binding marked a place and she flipped to that page, wondering why it was marked.

Calligraphy swirled and bounced outside the lines like an abstract painting defying the boundaries of a canvas. She strained to read the letters. Perhaps something about Velázquez. No "V" appeared in the puzzle of letters. The musty smell of the logbook made her turn her head for fresher air. She sneezed.

She started to close the book when Piero stepped closer and put out his hand to keep her from closing it.

"Difficult to read, *sì*? Look here." Piero pointed and drew his finger across a line that read Diego Rodríguez de Silva y Velázquez.

Velázquez's father's name was Rodríguez and his mother's surname was Velázquez. How he came to use Velázquez alone, she didn't know. The log listed Velázquez's occupation as painter and his address as Madrid. By age thirty the Master painted for King Phillip IV in the Madrid Court and had a huge reputation, enough apparently for the king to fund a trip to Naples for Velázquez to purchase paintings. Great artists like Ribera were in Naples, a part of the Spanish realm at that time.

Piero stood, pointing. He fumbled a bit and said, "Look here. The list of the Master's cargo." Piero took the tome from her hands and stood close enough that it was apparent he had not changed his shirt or cleaned his suit for weeks, maybe longer.

He pointed at a page reference at the end of the column and turned toward the back of the log. Cargo inventories. Piero's finger stopped, trembled a bit, on a line that read Velázquez with the words "Slave, male 23, called Juan de Pareja."

"Some historians think the slave didn't travel with Velázquez on this trip." Piero took pleasure in overturning the conventional wisdom, a good quality for sure.

"What else did researchers get wrong?"

He didn't hesitate. "There's more." He turned to the passenger listing and found another name. "Look, look there." The log read: Slave, female, age 25. F. T.

"He had a female slave too?"

His finger landed on the F. T.

"F. T.—maybe F. T. was a mistress? Velázquez was a loyal husband to his wife, Pacheco's daughter."

"Who knows what a man does, when he is alone?" Piero winked.

What an odd fellow. Coy, dangling ideas but not forthcoming.

A bell sounded, a chime like church communion was about to be served.

"Closing. Books must go back to the stacks. On Saturday, 7 p.m. Next Saturday we close until the New Year."

Piero lifted the books and left the desk empty except for the dust. She typed out the words "1651 trip to Barcelona from Naples, Velázquez's slave F. T.? Who is F. T.?"

She paused at the front desk and Piero handed her an identification card that would allow her to return.

"Next visit, I will have more volumes about that trip."

She thanked him, an ally, friend, perhaps. Piero didn't know it yet, but he'd joined her journey.

CHAPTER 9

*S*unshine poured through the crack in the draperies and brought a new day—a big day. In spite of bone-deep fatigue, she leapt up. Today she'd bring *La Gloria* to the Institute for its debut and share the painting with someone else, an art expert. She hopped over the cold floor tiles to check that the painting was still in the closet just as she had done after she'd toured several Seville museums on Sunday and then numerous times during the night.

A gentle knock at the door brought her to peer through the peephole.

A butler with a tray of coffee, bread, and orange marmalade appeared behind a single rose so that the blossom was the same size as the man's head. The waiter entered, averting his eyes like a horse with blinders. He fussed, placing a cloth on the table by the window and pulling back the draperies.

She picked up the folio with the bill. The waiter handed her a pen, but the check had no amount.

"*Incluido.*" The waiter smiled and straightened his jacket while she signed.

Brilliant. Thanks for the points, Harry. A no-charge breakfast with plentiful coffee added to the positive outlook for a day of progress on *La Gloria's* true identity. She ate and dressed and skipped down the steps of the hotel to embrace a history-loaded city.

The maze of the old town twisted her in circles until she asked at every corner for the Instituto de Artes Plásticas. Finally, an etched brass plate marked the building. The former convent had been appropriated when the nuns died off, leaving the place empty, now with cloistered prayers replaced by sterile labs for art conservation.

On the dot of nine, the sound of high heels on the terrazzo floor announced the arrival of an attractive woman in a lab coat with her name monogrammed on the upper left pocket. Black hair bounced on her shoulders and she pulled her coat closed over the front of her well-cut trousers.

"Good morning. I'm Doctora Isabel Maraval."

She extended a soft hand with a flawless manicure that marked the scientist as one who did not do heavy lifting or mess with solvents. No professional in Spain did physical work, the kind of work Dad respected. This create-make-work for more jobs made the Prado a better workplace than the Met, according to curator friends, where moving crates and schlepping installations forced staff at all levels to sacrifice fingernails.

A large office with fine furniture and a conference table confirmed the prestige of Isabel's position. The Institute showed off its resources and displayed the nation's dedication to the arts. Pacheco, Velázquez's first art teacher and then father-in-law, fought for artists to be considered professionals, not craftsmen, because their work's purpose was to inspire the faithful to yearn for holy paradise. Artists were God's ad men.

"*Mucho gusto.*" Cate lifted the plastic tube and placed it in Doctor Maraval's hands like a temple offering.

Isabel smiled broadly and gestured toward the tube. "It's a pleasure to work with Professor Jones's student. Please give him our regards."

Shit. Of course, she knew him. A surge of red hot went to her cheeks, a combination of embarrassment for her oversight in not expecting every art person in Spain to know him and anger that even remote art outposts circled back to Jones, all feeding his huge ego.

The Institute likely didn't know the painting was missing. The risk she was taking to show the work needed to pay off with scientific facts before anyone in New York missed it. She calmed her shaky voice with the details of her plan and a couple of deep breaths. "Yes, of course I'll tell him. Thank you for seeing me on short notice."

"Call me Isabel. During the holidays, workload goes down and space opens in our schedules. Outside labs have less incoming for chemical analyses and reduce their substantial backlogs." She motioned to follow her into the lab. "Let's have a look."

A steel-topped table, the kind used for an autopsy, dominated the laboratory space, and lab assistants prepared its surface with fresh archival paper. Isabel put on cotton gloves and slid the canvas from the tube. She unrolled the canvas onto the table, little by little, and a gasp from the lab assistants arose when the complete work was revealed.

They saw it too. Cate tried and failed to suppress a grin, the ear-to-ear kind. *La Gloria* lived decades, perhaps centuries, inside a mildew-infested chest, and her pride of bringing the painting into the world could not be hidden.

Isabel showed no reaction. She donned a pair of Eschenbach Maxdetail glasses, impressive gear for any lab, and began to examine the canvas. Mary Murphy had requisitioned these lenses, but university budget czars killed the request and students continued to use uncomfortable, basic ones.

Isabel lowered her face twelve inches from the canvas and touched two spots with a tiny brush. She lifted a corner of the canvas and brushed her gloved hand along the backside of the linen and then raised the top and then the bottom until she had viewed the entire backside. She removed the glasses and motioned toward the office.

Isabel set the magnifying glasses on the desk. "Would you like a coffee?"

"Thank you. Black please." As much as she craved coffee, she wanted Isabel's expert opinion more.

Isabel picked up the phone and asked for two coffees. Then she turned to stare at her across the desk. "The canvas is definitely old. Probably seventeenth or eighteenth century. Chemical tests on canvas fibers will establish the dates within a decade or two. We'll test the pigments and compare the brush strokes to those of other artists. Tell me what you know about the provenance."

The chest, its age, the state of the storage was not going to help the Institute's analysis, because the objects were not related. Better to say nothing about the chest, the inventory, and the rest because it would only raise questions. Keep the analysis focused on the science. "Not much is known about the provenance. It was found in a storage area with no frame or labels."

"Would you like to proceed with an evaluation?" Without waiting for an answer, Isabel pulled a form from a drawer and placed it on the desk.

Cate nodded like a bobblehead doll and then managed to speak like a client. "Will you be able to identify a location, perhaps assess the linen and pigments and connect them to artists from the time period?"

Isabel checked boxes on the form without looking up and slid it across the desk toward her. The form read Chemical Pigment Analysis, Fiber Analysis and Evaluation, and Foreign Material Extraction and Testing.

Cate tried again. "Perhaps I'm not translating correctly. Foreign Material Extraction? Did you see any foreign material?"

"I did. Small hairs, probably from a brush. We can't say

definitively before we examine them under a microscope. I recommend that, as fragments might match something we or another center removed from works we've studied."

Cate signed, pleased that she'd come to Seville.

"I'll need your authorization papers."

"Authorization papers?"

"Yes, the university's permission to sign on their behalf. We need the owner's permission before we can touch the canvas."

"Ah ah, my credentials are at the hotel. Can I fax them over?" She pulled her jacket closed to hide the perspiration on her camisole. How many lies would she need to tell before she could return the painting and make it right?

Isabel paused before replying. "That is fine. We'll need a university purchase order for the $2000 deposit before work can begin."

Two thousand! And that was the deposit. The rest—an unspecified black hole of money. Two thousand was more than January's rent in her illegal sublet and maybe her card did not have that much credit left. Her head was going to explode.

"What will the total be?" She took another breath and used Noemi's line. "The university is on a strict budget, grants are drying up for new projects." Cate looked around the elegant office. "The US government doesn't support the arts like Spain."

Isabel laughed. "We have an economic crisis in Spain. Forty percent unemployment for people under thirty. I got this position because someone died."

Cate checked a laugh before it escaped—nothing laughable about that. She sat upright in the chair, set her coffee cup down, and presented her most professional self. "Getting the university to do anything over the holidays could be a challenge."

"We can wait until after the holidays. The total cost can't be determined until we have completed the work and calculated the work hours. Likely many times the deposit."

Not possible. Everything was gone from her retirement account; this painting was her future.

"Can you accept an American Express card?" She saw Isabel's reaction and added, "To expedite things." An international transaction over the holidays might take days before she'd get the call about credit limits.

Isabel shuffled papers on her desk and leaned forward. "The Institute does not accept credit cards. We only do bank transfers between institutions."

The hurdles kept coming and these impediments weighed her down without a partner, an accomplice to help or a pal to share the disaster she'd created.

Isabel punched the top of a ballpoint in and out and stared at her. "I know university accounting can take time to issue a check. Over on the exhibition side, we have a gift shop and perhaps they can do a credit card transaction for us."

"That would be so much ah . . . faster. I can get reimbursed when I return." *If only it were true.* Cate managed a weak smile. She signed the paper authorizing the work and handed the clipboard with her credit card back to the assistant.

"The analysis will take about a month."

"No, no. Not a month. I need to return with the painting in two weeks before classes start in January." *Was that a mistake? To share that much with her.*

Isabel shook her head. "The whole lab is closed between Christmas and New Year's, and then there is the Fiesta de Tres Reyes. We only have this week."

"My dissertation committee meets in January. I'd hoped your analysis could be part of it." *A non-lie, sort of, or maybe wishful thinking.* "What about a preliminary review?"

"No guarantees. Something this valuable requires precise, careful work."

The pressure mounted and she formed a checklist of compelling reasons for expedited treatment. "I appreciate it. If there is anything I can do, let me know."

What did Isabel say? Something this valuable, "this valuable." Whose art did this expert believe was laid out on the laboratory table?

CHAPTER 10

*A*ntonio waited in the hotel lobby, seated on a carved chair suitable for a bishop. He was taller than most Spanish men and looked regal sitting in front of the Mudéjar tile walls. The grand chandelier sparkled and blocked her view of him as she descended the stairs, until she turned on the final landing. This dinner was to be a distraction to take her mind off her problems, have a good meal, and hopefully recover her twenty euros.

But in this moment, like something out of a movie, the evening promised more. He rose to greet her at the bottom step and kissed both her cheeks, lingering on the second one. Definitely more.

A bellman standing near the elevator stared and then averted his eyes.

"A surprise for you," Antonio said.

She was about to say she didn't like surprises, but at seeing his little-boy excitement, she held back and let herself be guided by the elbow past the doorman, outfitted in a ruffled collar and carrying a spear-like standard reminiscent of Velázquez's *Surrender of Breda*. The streetlamps threw golden circles onto the cobblestone walk. The sound of horses' hoofs clip-clopped as they made their rounds leading tourists past historic landmarks.

Antonio stopped in front of a carriage hitched to horses with gold-trimmed bridles. He bowed and held out his hand for her to climb up to the leather banquette.

She placed one foot on the wobbly step. Her foot slipped, sending her backward. She grabbed his arm, laughing. *Not funny, nervous and awkward.*

When she was safely seated, he climbed next to her. The horses jerked and sent her sliding closer to him. She adjusted herself with some space between them, held firm to a strap on the side.

"Like that train ride to Seville," he said.

"This is better." She waved her arm at the ancient city before them, the yellow buildings glowing in the light of antique streetlamps. "The view and the night air, it's wonderful, and calls for a slow pace." The horses clopped along, navigating the narrow streets where cars weren't allowed, past the Alcázar used still by the king and queen when they visited Seville. Parents sat in plazas beneath tree umbrellas and watched their children kick soccer balls in the dim light. She didn't see them, instead she saw Matty doing the same when he was that age. She'd lingered too often on those reminiscences and now longed to enjoy something, to jettison that heartbreak and to feel this, this moment, here with Antonio, still undefined except the anticipation something good might happen.

A stoplight turned red and they waited on the corner where a newsstand with lottery tickets posted on every empty space did a brisk business with Spaniards lining up to take their chance. Tempting, seriously tempting, buy a chance to fix her life, then she heard Dad's advice—lotteries take a fool's money.

Antonio was distant, his excitement about the surprise turned to something else, nervousness, worries, or boredom. They had little in common, except they were both broke. She'd met him on a train and he owed her a dinner. "Where are we going?"

"A favorite. In Barrio Santa Cruz, the old city."

"Sounds perfect after the couple of days I've had."

"Has Seville been unkind to you?"

"Bureaucratic hurdles. Presenting credentials. I'm sure it will all work out. What about you?" She forced a smile, wishing she hadn't mentioned any details.

Antonio didn't answer, like his thoughts were elsewhere.

The Columbus Library was closed on Tuesdays. She'd skipped lunch, wasted another day wandering around Seville.

She wrote a permission letter in legalese on the university stationery authorizing the Institute to inspect the painting, adding forgery to her crime sheet. She shook her head at the shame, the legal consequences, if Isabel was not convinced by a paragraph with a scribbled signature of a make-believe dean. After she'd faxed it over, Isabel hadn't called, and the credit card charge had been processed. The why of this good fortune eluded her but no reason to risk total collapse by asking questions.

The carriage stopped in front of a stone arch with a plaque that read "Restaurante San Marcos." She exited with more grace than she'd entered. Antonio paid the driver, without incident. Perhaps she'd been wrong about his finances.

The portal led to stairs going down into a cellar. They walked through a narrow passageway to a room that bounced candlelight off limestone walls. Classic Moorish arches held up the ceiling and created alcoves with intimate tables covered in white cloths. They squeezed into seats at a table so tiny their shoulders touched.

Campari and soda, she told the waiter. Campari was something she'd had only once but the medicinal elixir fit her mood. Antonio ordered Scotch and they settled into their stranger status, empty words, attempts to ignite a common interest.

"I love the old arches. What do you know about the history?"

"Mudéjar era, twelfth to fifteenth century." He raised his glass to her, and she saw him through the red of the Campari.

He studied the menu. "Do you feel adventurous? The special Andalusian plate?"

He didn't wait for an answer. His take-charge manner with polite but rhetorical questions surprised her, in a good way. Antonio consulted the waiter and chose other items with unfamiliar names. The waiter nodded in approval, "*Muy bien. Perfecto. Bien*, Don Antonio."

Antonio lifted his glass. "To a beautiful dinner companion."

She smiled and sipped. "The waiter knows you."

"I've come here for a long time and my father before me. He loved the history that fills this place. After the conquest, Jews hid from forced Catholic conversions in this cellar."

"This was a secret hiding place?"

"Yes. From the street you wouldn't know it was here."

"Are there lots of hidden places in this quarter?"

"Seville is an old city with secrets uncovered when new construction happens. By the way, did you find what you needed in the library?"

She straightened her black skirt and crossed her ankles. She didn't want to share about her search. "The library was closed today." The conversation died and she tried again. "Thank you for the roses. Brightened my week. How is your legal work going?"

"Many challenges. I inherited a home in Olivares, too big for a bachelor, nearly a ruin. Like all old houses, the upkeep is . . ." He shook his head and made a whoosh sound alluding to unimaginable expenses. "Now we face legal questions about the ownership."

He finished his drink and scanned the room with that same distance he had on the train. He avoided looking at her, holding his cards close, keeping his own secrets. This could be a long night with both of them avoiding everything important.

The waiter arrived with a plate of unfamiliar food, nothing from any tapas menu she'd seen, and she regretted not speaking up when asked to order.

The waiter announced, "Cod fish rolled in a *buñuelo*."

Antonio broke the silence and showed his delight at the tapas. "Burdens trouble you too. Many thoughts going through such an intelligent head."

He was sweet, in a Spanish kind of way. She sipped the *tempranillo* wine the waiter chose, soothing the struggle to edit out what she could share with this stranger.

The arugula garnish looked mean, and she pushed the leaves to the plate's edge. "Let's don't spoil our dinner with troubles."

"Let's trade. You take my problems. I'll take yours. A new head worrying about something different might produce an innovative solution. Why not?" He laughed.

The list of "why not" was long and serious, including talking to a lawyer about theft, forgery, and more. Her need to get a doctorate, lift up her parents, in this moment seemed unworthy excuses of her character deficiency. Stealing to feed your family or save a life was a worthy defense. At times, it felt she was saving a life, her own. She'd probably never see him again but still.

"Ah Antonio." She shook her head for a moment and chose the least secret of her problems. "Ok. Most urgent. Before tomorrow, I need to find another place to stay, somewhere cheap."

He leaned back in his chair, laughed, howled, and then leaned forward, taking out that monogramed handkerchief to wipe his eyes.

"How is that funny? Sleeping in the park is not funny."

"Sorry. So sorry." He squeezed her hand. "The solution to your worry is right here." He pointed at himself. "My apartment in Seville. You're welcome to stay there."

She choked on her water and sputtered. "Really?" She paused and said, "Wait. It's your apartment . . . I don't want you to misunderstand our . . ."

He didn't wait for her to finish. "I have no motives. I won't be in Seville. I'm going to Olivares and then Madrid. After that, with family for Christmas."

A smile stretched her weary face. "Thank you." She resisted jumping up and kissing him.

"Not the Alfonso XIII. Just a tiny apartment."

"Doesn't matter." She lifted her wine glass toward him, feeling her worries drifting up the columns and beyond the arches.

The next plate arrived with the aroma of cognac. A familiar fragrance, one that took her back to a late-night celebration with the faculty when she'd completed the Prado summer course.

He breathed in. "*Carrillada en Pedro Ximenez*, my favorite."

"The smell is amazing." She lifted a forkful and swooned at the richness of the flavors of the pork cheeks. "*Excellente*. It's your turn."

"Turn?"

"To tell your worries. I owe you a sympathetic ear."

"Let's not ruin this fine meal." He motioned for the waiter to fill his glass.

"Come on, that was the deal. I'm waiting." She tapped her fork on the plate. An echo, too loud, bounced against the vaulted ceiling.

He launched into a story with such speed it forced her to concentrate and made her realize how her Spanish fluency, developed since high school from a home stay in Mexico and a summer in Madrid, still needed improvement.

"The developers are trying to take my family lands. The deeds that prove we are the owners either have gone missing or never existed. These ancient properties are rarely questioned because the owners have been on them for centuries. Modern legal titles just don't exist. There's a royal grant, now missing, that gave the land to my ancestor."

She switched to English. "A royal grant should be in the National Library. I'm a researcher and royal decrees are well documented, although sometimes not always in the correct location or filed in the right year. Which king?"

"Felipe IV."

"Phillip IV. Olivares? Antonio de Olivares? The Count-Duke?"

"He's my ancestor, although I'm not from the main family line."

She couldn't control her mouth gaping. "Really? The Conde-Duque de Olivares."

"The Duke's official relatives exist in Spain, England, other countries, many generations since the 1600s have held the title."

"Is one of them challenging you?" That sounded like prying, a step too far.

He turned away and then looked back at her with a calm face. "I don't want to think about it now. How are the langoustines? Isn't the sauce amazing?"

"Shall I add the royal land grant to the list I'm researching?"

"Is your project during the reign of Felipe IV? What artist are you researching?"

Perhaps she could share the artist's name. Just the artist's name. No mentioning the painting. "Velázquez."

There it was, out into the universe.

"Why didn't you say something? He painted a portrait of my ancestor, the Count-Duke of Olivares. We have another portrait Velázquez painted. A small one."

"Wow. I'd love to see it some time." Maybe Olivares was worth a trip.

"Yes and soon, because I need to sell it and maybe another painting for the taxes on the estate and legal fees for an expert title search. Family pieces, so few left, so difficult."

"Estate? A palace?"

He squirmed. "Not what you think. Crumbling and cold. Chopping wood for fireplaces, no central heat. But on the good side, no need for a gym membership."

She laughed and tried to come up with an image of him chopping wood in his lawyer's suit and tie. Antonio, a guy who owns an estate, does manual work, practices law, has noble relatives and burdens of his own. His face seemed older and more tired in the candlelight than the one that greeted her in the hotel lobby.

She lifted her hand and placed hers over his, and then withdrew it to raise her glass. "To conquering worries." She got it, got him, and longed, as perhaps he did, for someone to listen, to understand and to care.

The waiter brought flan swimming in a rich sauce that smelled of oranges, vanilla, and cinnamon.

Antonio picked up his spoon. "Flan solves everything. Join me."

She laughed. "And Grand Marnier."

"No French liqueur. We drove Napoleon out of Spain. This sauce, *puro* Seville oranges. Grand Marnier was made from them too, but the French would never admit it."

They enjoyed the flan in silence until the waiter cleared the plates and brought the bill. Antonio put a credit card on the little tray with the check.

He had invited her, of course, he would pay. She finished all the wine in her glass and reassessed the good man who sat across from her.

A grey-haired man in a cut-away jacket, perhaps the maître d', walked up. "Don Antonio, we can't accept this." He held up the credit card.

Oh God. Not again? She could not afford this one. Her face burned. He could do dishes while she walked back to the hotel to never, ever see him again.

Antonio turned white, then stood. The man rejecting his card embraced him, patting his back several times.

"Cate this is Geronimo, the owner."

"Señorita." He kissed her hand. "Don Antonio never pays here. What his grandfather did for my grandfather. We never forget."

She looked down at the floor, embarrassed, but relieved that she'd held back her anger, for once.

"I want to pay for this excellent meal. My American friend thought the food exceptional."

She nodded. "Best I have had in a long time." It wasn't difficult to beat peanut butter.

"Take your card back my Lord, it's my honor to have such a fine person visit my restaurant." Don Geronimo rushed away to some other patron.

She smiled. "Generous man. You're pretty good at getting free meals."

He coughed into his napkin and lifted his head. "I almost forgot." He handed her a twenty euro note.

She mumbled thanks, embarrassed at her nudge to remind him. Twenty euros could buy her groceries for the next couple of days.

"What did your grandfather do for Don Geronimo's family?"

"He hid them during the Civil War at our estate. Franco's troops were executing those who sided with the Republican forces. Long story."

"I'd like to hear it someday. You never answered me. Is there still a duke?"

"A number of disputes about what happened to the title when the first Count-Duke died, leaving a bastard son." Antonio took back his distance and paused. "The family split even though Don Gaspar, the Duke in the painting, acknowledged his paternity. That son died without heirs, but the family did not know there was another bastard son from whom we are descended. When the Duke died, a different branch of the family took over the title."

He folded his napkin and stood. "A beautiful night. Shall we walk back to the hotel?"

She restrained her joy at the word hotel. She'd leave the evening with something better than a fine meal—a place to sleep tomorrow. She took his arm for him to guide her over the cobblestones until they reached the hotel.

"Here's my address. I'll phone the bar downstairs to give you the key." He handed her a thick business card and kissed her on both cheeks. Her heart sank that he didn't give her an actual kiss. But no, this was good, better, less complicated.

In the room, she kicked her shoes off and set his card on the desk. "Well done, Antonio. Antonio de Olivares, Familia de Conde-Duque de Olivares." She put the card closer to her eyes and read from it again.

Antonio—Count-Duke, maybe a duke, a count-duke, a pretender from a different line. What mattered was something else, something different, almost connected, but not, not ready to believe he cared. Not yet.

CHAPTER 11

$\mathcal{B}$reeze from the Juliet balcony in the hotel room separated the sheer curtains to reveal centuries-old buildings in the moonlight. There was no one to talk to, not Mom, not Noemi, certainly not Leonard or any of her classmates, no one. Calling her college roommate to say she'd gone to dinner with a duke would result in questions, for which she had no answers.

Not cute. Handsome, Antonio was *guapo*. That smile that almost made a dimple but not quite, his face had a boyish charm that morphed into a rugged unshaven face late in the day. Something else, though, made him different from others, something inside. He didn't talk about whether Real Madrid would win the championship or if he would make partner in a law firm. He had a mission that drove him—his family, a responsibility from the centuries that landed uninvited on his doorstep. His background differed from hers yet they both were burdened with the worries about family, the future, and their responsibilities for both.

She pulled her computer from the bedside table to her lap. She searched his name and Wikipedia pages appeared, including his relative Don Gaspar de Guzman, Count-Duke of Olivares. King Philip IV, who was only sixteen when he was crowned, named Antonio's relative a grandee. Olivares was reluctant to give up any titles, so he called himself Count-Duke. Why not? Was his wife the Countess-Duchess? *Good morning Countess-Duchess.*

Spain struggled during the so-called Golden Age. The royal treasury spent the colonies' gold, couldn't protect their extensive empire but fought wars trying, bills mounted, and it ended badly. Antonio's relative, the Count-Duke, was exiled from court, a sad ending for a great man.

The day had consumed her with mixed emotions and she had nothing left. She set the computer on the nightstand and turned out the light. Tomorrow she'd move to Antonio's apartment. The apartment could be a disaster. If it was full of cockroaches that would be a no, she couldn't live with cockroaches. What if it had no Internet, heating, or elevator? The answers didn't matter. The apartment was free and the rest, well, she'd deal, just deal with it.

She punched the pillow one way and turned to the other side. Sleep wasn't happening, not with the moonlight through the window. Her phone pinged, a text reminder from the building manager that because of the New Year's bank holiday, the rent was due before the end of December. She checked her bank account. If she paid the credit card bill, she couldn't pay the rent. She should have sublet the place over the holidays, Airbnb. A lost opportunity.

She'd pay the $2,000 credit card for the Institute deposit and think about the rent later. No crying over spilled cream, one of Mom's modified clichés. Maybe Westside Property Management might agree to a partial rent payment, or she'd just pay less and hope it would take time for them to realize the payment was short. Lost in the mail, deposited to the wrong account, the list of possible excuses (or partial truths) ran through her head. NY tenants got months, sometimes years, before eviction occurred. That could ruin her credit, future employment, especially at public institutions. This was not how she imagined her life.

She ran her hands through her hair and squeezed her temples between them like Munch's figure in *The Scream*. Funny to be worried about eviction, which wasn't a crime, not like criminal, prison kind of crime, nothing close to stealing a painting. No one would hire an art curator with a record as an art thief. And forgery, yeah, that too.

A few deep breaths could not stop the looming migraine. She could not undo what was done and needed to focus on the one thing that would make this crazy trip and insane spending worth it: proving the painting was by Velázquez. On Thursday, the preliminary pigment testing and fiber evaluation results would be available from Isabel. Tomorrow was Wednesday and time was evaporating. She'd check out of the hotel, move to Antonio's, and hit the ground running, scouring Seville for references to the painting.

THE MORNING WIND BLEW AGAINST her wet hair that smelled like apricots from the hotel shampoo. She stumbled up the irregular staircase of Antonio's building with her rolling suitcase. No elevator. The stairwell had cobwebs in the corners but no spiders in sight. His tiny apartment was cleaner than the stairs leading to it. One cupboard was empty and the only other one had salt, sugar, two cups and two plates.

A familiar jar of NesCafé had some crusted grains inside, putrid stuff, but any caffeine in a storm. She boiled water and searched for a spoon. The first drawer was filled with papers, the one on top stamped "Past Due" in red. Seville Electric Company for three hundred euros, due six months ago. Poor Antonio. She'd worried about Internet service—the power turned off would be much worse.

She sipped a bit of the NesCafé and spit it into the sink. Nasty. Even in poverty she had standards. She'd find somewhere with proper coffee and a free Internet connection.

A plastic armoire served as a closet. She unzipped it and

hung her good suit next to a tweed jacket and Antonio's brown dress slacks. She reached for a hanger and bumped against Antonio's jacket that smelled like his cologne. She drew in the smell and remembered last night.

She pushed it away. No time for a relationship. She lifted the hanger with her suit and hung it outside the armoire on a hook behind the door.

She reached in the suitcase and pulled out a pair of black leggings and a sweater, also black, and checked her watch. Almost mid-morning, the day was disappearing. She'd get her coffee, head to the library, pour over the ship logs, and persuade Piero to find more primary sources for her project.

THE LIBRARY DOOR WAS UNLOCKED and she walked in to find Piero at his desk. He rose to greet her. She kissed him on both cheeks, like a friend.

"Good morning, Señorita Adams. Your carrel is waiting for you." Piero fidgeted with his hands and his face twitched, a kind of nervous tic she hadn't noticed on Saturday. He was old and no doubt had many health problems, but he'd kept working like so many Spaniards.

"Could you bring me the ship logs from my last visit?"

He nodded and disappeared. The cavernous space was empty, every seat available except one. A young man glanced up and then returned to his computer screen.

She walked to her desk and brushed the dust away. A wind blew from somewhere in the drafty building. Tall stacks covered the walls to the ceiling connected by narrow metal walkways and staircases rattled when anyone used them. The volumes waited in silence for someone to mine the information. The possible finds gave her goose bumps. A decade in this place might produce dozens of research topics, original ideas that *advance* knowledge as Jones would say, information that would revise history or reveal unknown information.

Piero approached, his hands empty. "The ship's log is missing. I'm sorry."

"Missing? Did you look in the shelving bins from Saturday?"

"Yes. Then I searched the stacks."

The library predated the Dewey decimal system. Over time, resources became archived in erratic ways, systems of filing changed, misfiling happened, titles misread. Some libraries didn't even have a complete list of what they owned. Last year, a visitor to the National Library in Madrid uncovered a Rembrandt sketch tucked in an atlas. Uncatalogued treasures waited to be discovered in places like Spain and Italy.

"Perhaps someone else is using it."

A ridiculous comment in this room of empty tables.

Piero whispered, "Very strange." He looked over his shoulder and shifted from one foot to the other, pacing a few steps in between.

A chair scraped against the floor, drawing back from a table not visible from where they stood.

Piero looked from side-to-side and leaned closer. "This week . . ." His voice trembled and he struggled to recover. "I'm the only one here. Only one key. I put that ship's manifest on a shelf, awaiting your return."

Footsteps sounded on the hard floor and a fellow with a messenger bag disappeared between the bookshelves. The library door creaked opened and clanked closed.

She shook off a chill and focused on Piero, a frail man. "Don't worry. Perhaps the cleaning crew or maybe . . ." she hesitated, "you forgot? Got distracted?"

Wrinkles covered the old man's face and he stammered a bit. "I do misplace things, believe me, but this time, I was sure."

His head moved up and down, like nervous shaking. "It's back to those days. The days of the caudillo . . ." He looked over his shoulder and leaned, looking for something or someone in the rows of bookshelves.

"Franco, the dictator?"

More headshaking. "A hard time, a complicated world."

The notes she'd taken on Sunday were incomplete. She'd recorded "F. T." in her notes and wrote the referenced volume title from a card Piero had given her, but left off the date and page number. A mistake she'd not make again.

"Can you keep looking? I need the complete reference. Perhaps there is another record of Velázquez's slaves."

"Yes. Yes. Come with me." Piero took her behind his desk to a room that contained globes with misshapen continents, sea monsters, Neptune and other gods.

Piero opened a large volume to a page with a map of Seville dated 1620. "Look."

The page displayed a street map. The binding of the book was worn and some of the streets were illegible. "It's the tax collector's book, all of the houses, including the home of Maestro Pacheco, his daughter and his son-in-law, Maestro Velázquez."

"Is there more material about his Italian trip?" The street name was partially gone but read "Padre Luis——"

Piero didn't answer her but read aloud, "Padre Luis Maria Llop. Street name. Number 1. There the Master was born. Over here is Calle Limones, Pacheco's studio."

She typed the street names into her phone.

"Everything is not in books. To walk the streets where the giants walked. Perhaps something speaks to you."

A noise, a falling book perhaps, dropped from behind a door she'd assumed led to a closet. Piero avoided her eyes and continued to point out Sevillano landmarks from the 1600s. He couldn't have missed that sound.

She took a step toward the door where the noise came from and pointed in its direction.

Piero looked and then looked away. "*Ratones*. Rats. The library can't get rid of them." His voice quivered.

She nodded with an uneasy shudder. Piero was lying.

The noise was something. The library's labyrinth of puzzles couldn't be solved in the time she had. "Piero, will you keep searching? So I can record that reference or find another."

"What exactly you are looking for?"

She didn't want to mention the painting. "I am looking for references to artworks. Perhaps they traveled as cargo, shipped from Italy with Velázquez."

"Ah—the catalogue raisonné. You find it at the Museo de Artes Plásticas's library."

"Keep looking for the log. I appreciate your help."

VELÁZQUEZ'S BIRTHPLACE WAS ON THE way to the Museo. The house, a simple facade with a stone lintel, had been converted to an architect's office. Velázquez would have liked creative people working there. These buildings would have been stripped of their contents centuries ago and would yield nothing for her research.

Calle de Limones wasn't on any contemporary map, and so she took a seat in a pleasant plaza with a WiFi café. Sunshine warmed the chair where she sunk down, rubbed her eyes, and tried to figure out how to get some productive work done until the Institute had the lab results.

A waiter arrived, asked for her order, and bustled off. The *café con leche*, with its warm milk, took the chill from her hands and her soul. Brainstorming with smart art historians, sorting out a direction of where to search and for what, collegial discussions to kick around ideas would be a huge help. This secret project demanded she have those conversations with herself, and she tried to believe that would make her stronger. She could do this.

Concentrating on reading what she'd written became too difficult. Children on Christmas holiday played tag in front of tables in the plaza. Their carefree shouts were nothing like the world of academic rigor, intense wringing of hands. Even Christmas would become just another workday for her. A teen about sixteen, younger than Matty was when he died, kicked a soccer ball that knocked into her. She stood and passed the ball with a solid strike to the sweaty boy. Her heart paused at a distant memory and that amphetamine bottle, that damn bottle.

Inside the little café, the espresso machine coughed and huffed steamed milk as she waited to pay. The waiter had his back to her and washed coffee cups while he managed the machine in a marvel of multitasking.

He turned around and placed a white saucer with a paper scrap in front of her without her asking for the bill. The body language of the café needed no words.

She tossed two euros on the plate and looked around for the restroom. The café was empty except for a man at the counter drinking coffee. His face appeared in the bar mirror when she walked to the WC, and that face was familiar. She knew only a handful of people in Seville and it was unlikely they might know each other.

She locked the bathroom door and when she was washing her hands, looking in the mirror, it hit her. He was the man in the library, the one with the messenger bag, but why in this neighborhood, this café off the track, far from the cathedral and the library?

She unlocked the bathroom door and saw the guy disappear out the back door. She followed him and stepped outside.

He stood near the trash cans, smoking a cigarette.

"You were at the library?"

He crushed the cigarette into the pavement with his foot and bolted. He called back, "Be careful, Señorita. Be careful."

"Careful? Careful about what?"

She went back into the café and left through the front door. Combined with the lost books in the library, this day was turning into a web of oddities.

No one followed her the few blocks to the Museo de Artes Plasticas's library. The automatic glass doors separated when someone stepped on the mat, a convenience for patrons with loads of books. The reception area had high worktables with computers for searching the archives or ordering a book to be delivered to the desk, a real contrast to Piero's operation. Thousands of entries for Velázquez popped up. The catalogue raisonné, the annotated compendium of all known works by an artist, which would include works lost to fires, wars, and careless heirs, if they had been recorded anywhere, would be faster than individual references.

She waited on a plastic bench with arty metal legs and watched the buzz of students, future experts perhaps, coming and going. A clerk called the numbers on her ticket and plunked three enormous tomes onto the counter.

She staggered under the weight of the volumes before she found an empty seat. The first catalogue had torn pages, pencil markings, and a broken spine. The worn condition of Velázquez's catalogue supported Jones's "thoroughly researched" statement. The catalogue listed citations to letters, royal edicts, or invoices, documents written in Velázquez's time. Perhaps she'd have that eureka moment of a misinterpretation or a bad translation, or a hallelujah of something unnoticed by researchers.

Reading the three volumes was slow going. She recorded dates and locations of works painted based on where Velázquez lived at the time. Errors repeated from scholar to scholar, all trusting the established gods of their fields. Velázquez's birthdate had been recorded incorrectly and many scholars repeated the error. Art history was not a romance, nor a thriller. Not at all. The work was drudgery, plowing through pages and pages of details, looking for that needle, that shiny reward to justify the butt-numbing sitting.

She lifted her heavy head to study the people at her table and returned to the books. Three missing paintings were described in words without images. Could her painting *La Gloria* be one of the three lost works? *La Gloria* had been trimmed, cut to fit a frame or a space, and the exact dimensions and the complete image could not be known, although enough was left that one could envision the remainder. She sketched what the missing bits might look like and returned to the chapters of works after the second Italian trip. None of the missing works matched or even came close to *La Gloria*. She lifted the volumes and placed them on the return cart.

A night chill spread over Seville. She stopped to buy something for dinner, something cheap. Warmth came from the glow of the taverna's windows reflected onto the damp streets. Inside patrons, families, or old friends, still visible through the foggy windows, lifted their glasses, laughed, and chatted. Streetlamps lit the way back to the empty apartment.

She'd splurged on a cheap wine, a Rioja for three euros, at the bodega near the fishmonger. She'd planned to open it tomorrow to celebrate the Institute's report, but a glass or two tonight might help her sleep. A Spanish bachelor pad would have to have a corkscrew, unless Antonio drank his wine in the bars with life-long friends.

CHAPTER 12

*T*he clock tower, part of an old palace a few streets away, chimed nine times, but the Institute's door remained locked. Her watch confirmed the old clock got it right. This whole trip, maybe her future, depended on what Isabel would tell her about *La Gloria*, and any delay translated into anguish a normal person would not understand. A stiff wind froze her face. The backside of the building where the employees entered provided refuge from the wind swirling leaves and trash around her. Checking the front entrance, again and again, from the corner of the building had no effect on opening the Institute. Today she wanted—needed—answers: answers to questions about the painting and how it might become a key to open doors for her.

She turned back toward the employee entrance.

Him. Again.

Señor Library-Café-Alley trash cans. He exchanged a glance with her and disappeared into the employee entrance. *What the heck. He worked here?*

The fire of anger along with the bitter cold burned her cheeks as she marched to the Institute's main entrance. Isabel needed to explain why her employee was stalking her. Yes, she had questions about more than *La Gloria*.

A twenty-something, dressed de rigueur in black with fashionista rings on four fingers of one hand and a tiny diamond in her left nostril, fiddled with some keys, taking her time to open the entrance door.

"Dr. Isabel Maraval. Nine o'clock," Cate said. She could not suppress the sarcastic emphasis on the time and then quickly adjusted this misdirected anger and added, "*Hace frio.*"

The girl rolled her eyes, maybe guessing Cate's insistent tone resulted from the 9:15 late opening and not the cold. The annoyances had grown beyond those two.

Maraval appeared in the lobby. "Come in, Ms. Adamson." Isabel had abandoned their first name status with a cold and unwelcoming voice.

"Dr. Maraval." She nodded and brushed past the art scientist who held the secure door. Best to hold back on assumptions. Isabel might not be aware of this employee's behavior and she didn't want to alienate the deputy director whose help she needed.

Dr. Maraval closed the door and sat at her desk.

Cate opened the conversation with gravitas to match Isabel's tone. "I am anxious to hear your report on the painting, but I need to ask you something urgent."

"And I also have questions for you," Isabel answered.

She ignored Isabel's comment, skipping past what those questions might be, although a flicker about forged documents crossed her thoughts. "There's a young man working here, he came in the employee entrance. I saw him."

"Is there a problem?"

"He's been following me, stalking. I'd say that's a problem. Who is he and why am I seeing him everywhere?"

"We have 130 employees working here. Do you know his name?"

"How would I know his name?" Employees working nearby stopped and turned their heads at the tone of her voice. "I saw him at the Columbus archives, later he was in a café miles from the library. I asked him why he'd followed me, and he ran. He's here, this morning, working here. Who is he?"

The woman across the desk from her folded her hands and rested them on top of her white lab coat, like Buddha. She leaned forward. "What *is* going on, Ms. Adamson? Tell me, who are you?"

"Doctoral candidate at NYCU. You know that."

"That part is true." Isabel waited. "We verified that."

Cate exhaled, trying to silence the crushing boom of her heartbeat, sensing what was coming next.

"That authorization letter is a fake. There's no Dean Grant at NYCU. Did you think we would not check? It's what we do—authenticate canvases, paper, signatures . . . and people."

That letter had been a reckless move, a desperate effort to save the journey, a failure to think things through . . . through to what? A better fake letter? She needed to respond, explain her rush to leave New York, university bureaucracy, the holidays, or something, anything. Excuses ran through her brain, rejected by her as fast as she could think of them.

Change the subject, the best defense is a . . . ignore her. "You accepted my payment. In the United States that constitutes a contract. I expect you to fulfill the services I paid for."

"Yes we charged the card, the first sign something was not right. No legitimate researcher pays with her own funds." The art conservator leaned back in her chair, smug, and straightened her lab coat, brushed away some lint.

Cate's head shook even though she willed it to nod in agreement. Visions of a jail cell, the inevitable outcome for the thief she was. But Isabel had not mentioned the painting's ownership, which was a bigger crime.

"My intuition tells me you're not a fraud," Dr. Maraval said as she got up from behind the desk and sat down next to her. "I'm sorry Enrique upset you. He's a part-time intern, mostly works in the shipping room. I asked him to follow you. His report confirmed nothing unusual. Searching the library, doing research on Seville and its artists, what I would expect from someone attempting to attribute an artwork."

There was more to this. Isabel could not be trusted. "That you sent him after me makes me wonder who you are. Why would you suspect anything but what you found?"

"You must admit the credentials, the forged letter, the payment—we were obliged to investigate."

"I'm still confused about Enrique. What was 'Be careful?' A warning? A threat? What was that about?"

"He said that?" Maraval shifted her position, sitting back in the chair, an angry flush visible on her cheeks. "I have no idea. I'll need to ask him." She paused and went on the attack. "Why did you lie?"

Memories of her mother's interrogation after some high school prank flashed in her head. Exhaustion, fear, and an urgency to get information about the painting sent her to her roots, her Midwest openness, the truth will set you free and all that Mom drilled into her. Her dishonorable tale erupted, uncontrolled it spilled onto the desk, filled the room: Jones, dissertation topics, no women artists or mentors, the inventory, the chest, the accidental theft, her bank account. All of it. She had to take a breath, disappear the tears and at once, became both relieved and regretful.

Maraval's demeanor, including her silence, told her she'd trusted the wrong person. Cate had put herself at risk, and Enrique too.

Isabel removed her glasses, reached over to touch Cate's wrist, and said, "I believe you."

Isabel handed her a tissue and said, "Would you like coffee?"

Before Cate could answer a simple question in her muddle of guilt and fear, Isabel left the office and returned with Ms. Fashionista carrying two demitasse cups on a small tray.

Dr. Maraval finished her coffee in a single gulp. "I'm sympathetic. My own story has a parallel to yours. Am I not the first woman in leadership of any Spanish conservation lab? Certainly you didn't meet women managers at the Prado."

Cate nodded like a robot without feeling a sister-connection with Isabel. Isabel was too calculating, the genuine-meter did not register.

"Is anyone aware of this artwork?"

"Jones had left for the holidays." She shifted in her chair, reviewing in her mind that last meeting in Jones's office, the day she and the painting left the university. "You're the only one to see this painting. Why do you ask?"

Maraval sighed with a smug look that seemed like satisfaction, or maybe relief. "Okay." Isabel continued, "The director doesn't need to know about this project, but I will not put my job on the line, not for you, not even for this painting. We must follow protocol."

Cate froze on the words, "even for this painting." "What did you find out?"

Isabel looked like she wanted to take her words back. "The work is interesting." She stood and moved to the wall where she scribbled an extended timeline on a white board. "Look at these dates, based on carbon testing of the materials." Isabel pointed to the numbers written there: 1620–60.

Oh wow. Velázquez's productive years. Exactly what she hoped.

Cate tried but couldn't stop the grin growing on her face. She cleared her throat, trying to keep her excitement from erupting and regain her professionalism, seriously diminished with the emotional collapse, but held back any comments.

Dr. Maraval pointed to another column on the board. "The linen fibers, bits of wood in the creases left by the stretcher bars, and the tested pigments indicate those dates."

Cate stayed silent. No reason to influence the discussion with her assumptions.

"But there are problems."

Her grin fell away. Cate croaked out, "Problems."

"The brushstrokes are different than the ones observed in computer analyses from possible artists from the Golden Age of Spain."

"Could they be from conservation work done years later? Infills of paint?" Cate asked. Velázquez's work was not known to have had much conservation work, especially paintings kept for centuries in the royal apartments. But it was doubtful *La Gloria* was one of those.

"The strokes are too extensive and large to be conservation work, unlike detailed repairs modern conservators make."

This information undermined the hopeful date range facts. One element or detail that didn't fit or modern pigments that couldn't be explained would kill the attribution. The unthinkable had to be asked. "Is the painting a copy of another work? Another artist's hand behind the brushes?"

"Perhaps. The European academies had students sit in museums and make copies. Thousands of them exist. This painting is likely one of those."

"But what about the canvas fibers, the wood fragments, and the pigments that are seventeenth century?"

"Students and good forgers often use discarded canvases bought in flea markets. The canvases are old, but the pigments are not."

"But you just said the pigments on this work are old. You saw the skill, the artistry. You called it *valuable*."

"I was speaking about forgers in general." Dr. Maraval, unflappable, refuted each argument Cate offered in support of the canvas while Cate's head went elsewhere. Maybe it was Isabel's job to reject the hypothesis, if there was one.

"Even students and forgers have their moments."

Disappointment overtook her, a crushing blow after all she'd risked. Her head swirled with skeptical nagging about the inconsistencies. Maybe she inherited Mom's talent for ferreting out a lie. But she was in no position to challenge an expert like Isabel with intuition alone.

The conservator continued. "Some might go beyond the preliminary tests to infrared reflectography and other tests to see what lies beneath such as underdrawing, compositional revisions, canvas preparation compared to known works. Tests cost money. Even if you had a grant, which you don't, I wouldn't waste the money for the same conclusions."

Cate shuddered at the snarky remarks. This could not end here. There were others to consult, different experts. Guillermo at the Prado would know others, connoisseurs whose eyes on the work could rule out the notion that it was a copy.

Cate pushed back and formulated a new plan. "I'll take the work to the Prado. Colleagues there might do me a favor and put it in front of experts."

Maraval's hands began to shake and she gripped the arms of her chair as though she wanted to brace herself against the prospect of others seeing the work.

"The Prado has no time for a pastiche. You, you . . . don't . . . want to embarrass yourself."

Her nervousness affirmed Cate's instincts and strengthened her resolve. She studied Isabel's face and made a decision. "Thank you for your efforts. I'll take the painting back to New York and write a grant proposal to support additional research."

Maraval leaned forward, pursed her lips, and barked out her response. "I can't give you the painting."

"What? I don't understand." Cate's face turned hot and now her hands shook.

"You confessed to stealing it, presented forged documents, and represented it as something it is not. We need to contact

Interpol and, depending on the results, we either seize the work to keep it out of the marketplace or initiate a process that could result in the destruction of the work."

Cate gasped and tried to quell the explosion inside her head. *WTF? Destroy the painting? It couldn't happen.* "How can you take someone else's property?"

"Like counterfeit money, forgeries are destroyed. Protects collectors and institutions." Isabel pulled a form from her desk drawer and placed it with a pen in front of Cate. "If you sign here, we will proceed with the Interpol search."

Cate read the form with the intensity of a detective. Her eyes lingered on the word "dispose." She stopped. Something wasn't right.

"This line on the form for the artist's name . . . someone wrote 'Velázquez.' I never wrote that." Cate was certain about this point.

"You did; it was your preliminary assessment." Isabel folded her hands and then unfolded them.

Cate lifted the form to study it in the light. The name Velázquez had been inscribed on a piece of white tape pasted over the words "Spanish seventeenth c." Cate had been deliberately vague, wanting an unbiased opinion. "Someone altered this form, someone in the Institute."

Maraval said nothing.

Cate decided to take on this liar. "There is a problem with your conclusions, Dr. Maraval." She fixed her eyes on Isabel's and searched for a reaction. "If this is an academic copy, a student trying to study a master or even a forgery, what is it a copy of? Which painting has been copied to be sold as the original?"

Isabel Maraval pushed her chair back against the far wall. She buttoned the top of her lab coat. "Regardless, it is Spanish, art that is our patrimony, work without proper permits to leave the country. I will not release the painting to you."

Another leap that was never discussed—where it had been painted had not been determined.

Maraval moved toward the door and opened it for Cate to leave.

Cate stood and faced her. "The painting belongs to NYCU." She caught her own voice, something just short of shrill. "I'll consult with the university . . . and their lawyers."

Maraval was unmoved, no doubt recognizing a bluff from a lowly student. "I'm late for a conference at the *ayuntamiento*. Goodbye Miss Adamson."

Cate walked to the Institute's lobby. She was the guardian and champion of *La Gloria* and the artwork needed her now more than ever.

Ms. Fashionista sat at the reception, texting on her cell phone.

"Is there a conference today at the *ayuntamiento*?"

The girl put her phone down and punched at the keyboard. She read without looking up. "Conservation technology in the twenty-first century. From 10:00 until 5:00."

Isabel wouldn't return to the office today. Cate had less than twenty-four hours to get the painting back before tomorrow, before Isabel could move on her plan, whatever it was.

CHAPTER 13

The heels of her boots sounded her anger on Seville's cobble-stones with sharp, quick beats along with the music of a city alive with activity. The Institute disappeared as she rounded the corner, but Isabel's arguments, filled with contradictions, along with many nonverbal signals of a liar, lingered. The seizure and possible destruction of the work represented a drastic conclusion, far-fetched and outrageous, and would crush her mission. Isabel held all the cards.

She didn't sign the form to release the painting for more research, not that she could authorize anything. The form proved Isabel wasn't beyond forgery herself. Going to the authorities about Isabel might land her and not Isabel in more trouble. This journey was one hot mess.

A little café by the plaza provided refuge from the cold. While she waited for that steamy cup to warm her hands, she studied the plaza through the window. Two elderly women dressed in mourning sat and chatted with each other under a tree. Another old woman leaned on a cane and spoke to a some-what younger woman next to her. The younger woman did the talking and the older woman said little, nodding from time to time. Oh, to have a friend, a friend who would listen, just nod and not judge. A small boy twirled a brown leaf between his fin-gers and held out his treasure to the old woman. She enveloped the leaf and all the rest of him into an embrace that closed out the rest of the world and made the boy's cheeks glow.

A hug like that should be cherished, a masterpiece. Masterpiece hugs waited for her in Michigan. In two days it would be Christmas Eve. Mom had asked what she wanted for Christmas and had suggested a coffee maker or extra money. Her list had one gift: the painting back in her hands, to return it to the university and undo everything. Start over, leave the door locked and let the painting sleep for another century or more.

She sipped her coffee. That isn't what she wanted. She loved *La Gloria*. Someday she'd write a book about what gives an object value and why money is a poor measure for the importance of a thing. The painting was skillfully rendered, inspired even, regardless of the name-dropping value of some famous artist. *La Gloria* was a stunning artwork, and no attribution could change that whether a student, a forger, a master, or all the possibilities in between had created the work.

Coffee spilled out of the cup onto the saucer. She pulled a few paper napkins from the metal holder and mopped up the saucer and the bottom of the cup. A hand touched her shoulder.

A man's voice whispered in her ear, "Don't be afraid. Just want to talk."

Enrique! She pushed his hand off her shoulder. "Still stalking me?"

"Give me two minutes." He drew a chair out from the table near the bar and motioned for her to sit.

She shrugged and moved from the bar to the table. The waiter approached and her stalker ordered a small espresso. "Enrique—Henry." He offered his hand. "Student doing research and earning shit money for shit work at the Institute under a shit boss. I have no power—is power the right word?"

She didn't say anything. Goodbye to that naïve, trusting Midwest girl. Time to bring the New York A game.

He talked faster, as though clocking his two minutes. "Yesterday Isabel told me to follow you because she believes your painting was stolen. Or that's what she said. Isabel can be a witch when she has an idea put in her head. Do you understand my English?"

She emptied her cup and searched her purse for enough euros to cover the coffee and leave.

Enrique put his hand on her wallet and closed it. "I'll pay. I want to help you."

She shook her head. "You expect me to believe that? You're a spy for Isabel."

"Meet me at 7 p.m. behind that café where you saw me, by the trash cans."

She shook her head. "No way."

"Do you want the painting back?"

Could he do that? She gazed at him, searching for his motive, a reason to believe him. God, how badly she wanted to believe him, but was this another Isabel trick? Isabel had left for her conference, right after their meeting, but the woman could be commanding Enrique via phone or email. She had no other options except the guy sitting across from her. "And how will you do that?"

"Not easy for me, but there's a possibility. An idea how we can take it."

"What's your idea?"

"Things are not right at the Institute. Isabel is a liar. Yvonne, Goth girl at the reception, forgot her phone one night and returned. Isabel was there, talking at . . . to New York about your painting. And . . . well I don't understand. If it's stolen, procedures say call Interpol, not New York. Isabel did not call Interpol."

New York. Would Isabel have called Jones? He'd left for the holiday break and Isabel probably didn't reach him.

"I'm no thief. You know that, right?" *That was foolish, answering a question not asked or defending herself before she needed to.*

Enrique leaned back and nodded. "My colleagues say no one comes into the Instituto with a stolen work. A collector, someone clueless, not an art professional might bring a suspicious artwork. Art thieves or art dealers know about the international registry of stolen works and the seizure. That's why Isabel's idea for me to follow you was strange."

"Why does she want to keep the painting?" *La Gloria* was hers and not Isabel's. Actually, it was neither.

"I don't know. The Instituto marked three or four paintings to destroy since I came. That's many. What did she tell you?"

She took a deep breath and proceeded against her reservations. "Isabel said the work was painted over an old canvas, a copy of a famous work. She claimed the work could be misrepresented and sold as a Velázquez. She needed to keep it and call Interpol." Cate took a deep breath and said the words. "And maybe destroy it, if it was a fake."

He choked on his coffee, sputtering and coughing. "Are you serious? Does she think you're stupid?"

Well yeah. Stupid fit. She should have probed Isabel's assumptions and her draconian conclusions. The Institute's professionals are careful scientists who didn't name or exclude an artist until they'd built the case. Isabel's behavior did not fit with that approach.

"Your brain is spinning. Confused. There are differences from this work to Velázquez's works, brushstrokes that could be a result of his age, or partial painting by an assistant, or rushing to complete a commission. The report said these minor differences often occur, especially if Velázquez painted it over a few years."

"You read the report?"

"One of the technicians showed sections to me. Isabel has a different plan that we don't see."

Enrique's face revealed something she hadn't seen—an awareness, like a light switched on his fear. He turned his head and she did too, searching their surroundings, catching his fear like a contagion. The café was empty except for the bartender washing cups. Enrique leaned closer. "We need to be careful."

She paused at hearing those words again. "But of what?" She studied Enrique. "And even more strange, why are you risking your career to tell me these things?"

"My internship ends after this week, and it's been the worst experience. Isabel would not give me a recommendation. Nothing for me. Want to . . . how you say . . . take her down."

"How will you get the painting out?"

"I work alone tonight packing things. Isabel is gone, until after Christmas."

"If the painting disappears on your shift, won't you get blamed?"

"I will say you picked up the work, you had paperwork, so I released it. Intern mistake. She can't call the police if she's hiding something." He shifted to Spanish and repeated the same thing.

A simple plan might work. It had to work.

"I shouldn't have trusted Isabel." She cringed thinking of what Isabel might do with the information. Her romp through Spain needed to become a sprint, to get where she was going, without even understanding where that was, before Isabel beat her to it.

"We're the same. Idealistic and too trusting. The art world has many layers."

Yes to that. The mirror behind the bar reflected her face between the Cinzano and Illy advertisements. Enrique rubbed his chin, leaned forward, and picked up his bag. "Meet me at the café, the corner of Herrera and Olivos—7 tonight."

"Wait. Can you get the report too?"

"Files are locked up. Perhaps there's a copy in the lab. I'll try." Enrique kissed both her cheeks and left.

The kisses surprised her; in a few minutes Enrique moved from foe to ally. Or was he? The answer would come tonight.

The waiter arrived and put down the bill for her coffee and Enrique's. Not again. Un-friggin'-believable. She put precious euros on the plate.

The air temperature had dropped. She walked toward the library and her phone rang. Mom. If she answered, she was in for a long talk. If she didn't answer, Mom would call the police, the embassy, and anyone who'd listen.

"How's Spain honey? How are you doing with your research?"

She blew off the question about research. "How's the weather?" That was a mistake.

Mom went on about the amount of ice on the roads and whether the power lines might be weighed down. She moved on to a soliloquy about Christmas cards they had received and the info in those letters other moms wrote from the kitchen table covering their kids' every activity since last year's letter.

A question diverted her from the conversation: What would *her* mom write in the annual letter? Probably an exaggeration about her daughter's achievements, ahead of them actually happening and now less likely to happen. But she didn't need to worry because Mom hadn't written a letter for their family since the year they lost Matty.

Mom went on about the neighbors, the Christmas menu, Dad's good days and mostly bad days, and a hello from Dad. Cate looked at her watch. "Mom, Mom. Stop. I'd love to talk more, but I've got to get somewhere before it closes." Okay, that was a lie. "I will call you on Christmas. Love you." She didn't wait for Mom to protest, but repeated "love you."

SHE'D ARRIVED FOR THE Enrique rendezvous twenty minutes before seven and chose an outside table, in the cold without the pressure to order something. The winter moon hid behind clouds bringing snow perhaps, and an impenetrable darkness that made it difficult to navigate between tables and chairs. A young man, not Enrique, appeared from behind a tree, startling her as he headed toward a girl who greeted him with a passionate kiss. She stared at them with envy, their closeness forcing her to look away and fiddle with the sugar packets on the table.

Nothing was going as she'd hoped. In fact, things couldn't be worse, a disaster of a day except for a few productive hours researching Velázquez's brushstroke techniques.

Enrique better show. She agonized over the what-ifs: What if he didn't come, what if someone else came, what if she didn't get the painting back? Before she could add more worries, Enrique appeared. Early. No footsteps, no possibility to see him crossing the park, he just appeared and stood next to her. Poof, there in a long coat, the type men in New York wear over their suits in winter, and a hat like Bogart might have worn pulled down, blocking half his face.

She stood and he kissed her on both cheeks, again. Her new best friend. "Where's the . . . ?"

"Shhhh. Walk with me." He steered her by her elbow, keeping one arm against his body, and walked her away from the plaza, down a cobblestone street.

Three blocks later, down an alley and to a boulevard with heavy traffic, he stopped and lifted his arm to hail a taxi.

"I'm not getting in any taxi until you explain." She pulled her elbow from his hand.

"Calm down." He opened his long coat and showed her a brown paper roll. "Cameras everywhere on street corners. Up there, look." He lifted his chin toward a video camera mounted on the traffic lights. "Ever since terrorists bombed the train, we have these." He put his arm around her shoulder drawing her close like they were a couple. "I signed your name to the painting receipt. When Isabel returns and discovers the painting missing, you need to be gone. *Fuera de* Seville." He lifted his arm off her shoulder to continue to summon a taxi.

A yellow taxi pulled up to the curb.

"Do not go to wherever you stay. They can be looking for you."

"They? The police?" She hadn't considered Isabel worked with others, others besides the staff like Enrique.

"Not sure. But go away."

"My things, my computer, the research, I need them." Ten minutes . . . only ten minutes, enough unless someone followed Enrique.

"Send a friend to get them. Best not to contact me." He opened the door and nudged her into the back seat.

Before she could respond, he leaned over the seat toward her and pulled back his coat. The painting slipped across the seat and onto her lap. Then he put his hands on her cheeks and kissed her mouth.

She grinned, relieved that Enrique made this happen and enjoying that unexpected, false kiss. She ran her hands up and down the paper covering *La Gloria*, resisting the desire to verify this was the right painting.

The driver hollered something about the light turning green. Enrique cut him off. "Love comes before traffic." The *taxista* laughed. Enrique disappeared into the dark night.

She raised her palm to wave goodbye at the darkness and wondered if she should have thanked him. Car horns blew and brought her back to the urgency to leave Seville.

The *taxista* turned the corner. "Where to, Señorita?

She didn't have an answer. To where? She had to risk it. "I need to get something at my apartment. And then . . ."

To the train? A train to where? Madrid? She could sleep on that slow train and decide what came next. "The train station."

The taxi darted between lanes, doing battle with traffic.

She struggled to sit upright and hold onto the rolled painting until the taxi pulled up to Antonio's building and stopped with a jerk.

She looked behind them to ensure no one had followed. The street was empty and she exited the taxi with the canvas. "I'll be back. Need to get my suitcase. Maybe ten minutes."

"Señorita, pay the fare."

He might not wait if she paid him first. "After I return, when you take me to the train."

"Then leave the package on the seat until you come back." He put his hand on the roll and pulled.

Not happening. Would not leave this painting again. The cabbie stood between her and the building door.

"Stop that, you'll damage it. I need to get cash from the apartment. I'll be in Apt 3-B."

He shook his head.

She lifted her arm and took off her Swatch. "Take my watch for security. I'll be right back." No taxis passed by on this tiny street and she couldn't walk far with her suitcase, her computer bag, and the painting tube.

He took the Swatch.

She double-timed her steps up the stairs until she stopped to breathe on the landing below the apartment. The door was slightly ajar, a light came from inside. *What the heck? Was Enrique right?* She had turned out the lights, not wanting to add to Antonio's unpaid utility bills, and locked the door. She was certain.

Each breath came faster. She leaned against the wall and looked for a place to hide the painting. Not a good idea. She'd found courage when Dad insisted she shoot at a deer, thankfully missing, but fear froze her now. The old building key could take out an intruder's eye and then, then . . . what? If there was more than one of them, she was screwed.

She listened for voices, sounds, and heard nothing. She tip-toed the last few steps and nudged the door open wider. A man stood at the window with his back to her, turned around. "Hello."

She gasped.

$\mathcal{A}$ntonio turned her direction and sipped the last of the Rioja bottle. "Did I frighten you?"

"Yes." *More like scared shitless.* She took the canvas and placed it next to the empty tube and her suitcase.

"You're shaking." Antonio took her hands between his own and planted a kiss on them. He put his arm around her and held her like he would comfort a child. The fast breathing continued, and not from the closeness to him.

"What are you doing here?" Her question made her cringe. Jeeze, he was standing in his own apartment.

He drew back. "Sorry. I sat across the street in the bar waiting for you to come home, but you didn't arrive. So I came up, turned on the lights, and left the door ajar. On purpose."

"I saw the light. The open door . . . I was terrified."

He laughed and said, "Thieves don't leave doors open with the lights on." Then after a pause, "They tend to enter and exit in the dark." He took a sip of his . . . ah, her wine.

It wasn't funny. His explanation did nothing to slow the pounding of her heart. Possibilities of Antonio and Isabel working together crossed her mind, although it was unlikely they would even know each other. "You're in Seville?"

Antonio poured another glass, finishing the bottle. "Plans changed. I hope you don't mind I took some wine. Here, join me." He poured half of his glass into an empty one and gave it to her.

She set the glass on the counter so that he wouldn't notice her shaking hand.

"A taxi is waiting for me."

"You're leaving? Weren't you staying through Christmas?"

She stammered out the only answer she had. "I might have to go to Madrid." That didn't sound like someone about to get into a taxi and actually go to Madrid.

"I can drive you wherever you need to go. Let me go pay the *taxista*." Antonio got up and reached for his wallet.

She walked to the window and pulled the blinds apart. "Too late. He's gone . . . with my watch." She rubbed her empty wrist. Darn.

"He stole your watch?"

"Nada, it's nothing. I had to come up here to get money and I didn't want him to leave. Forget it. What brings you here?" She pretended to care.

"I came to Seville to file papers with the provincial courts before they close for the holidays. They wouldn't take the filing in Madrid because of regional jurisdiction. I wondered . . . well, hoped you hadn't eaten dinner."

What time was it? When did the last train leave for Madrid? "Lots of pressure to finish my research, make some notes and so on." And get out of Seville. "Thank you. I'll pass on dinner."

"What are your plans for Christmas?"

There wasn't a plan for the next hour much less Christmas. "Working, staying in Madrid." Ok that was a full-on lie, but she could make it true.

"Libraries close for Christmas. No one works during Christmas." He paused. "I'm going to Olivares. Come with me. The whole family gathers there for Christmas and someone new, an American, will make it interesting."

"Thanks, but I need the Internet for my research." She could not trust him. Too much of a coincidence that he had appeared now.

"Come on. We have Internet in Olivares. Full disclosure, it can be shaky. The young cousins will visit and slow it down with their games."

Spending the holidays with Antonio solved the "where to go" question and she wanted to trust him, have someone on her team. The money problem nagged at her and she had nowhere to go. Trusting Enrique had worked, but it was a gamble.

Antonio smiled, and a charming half dimple appeared. "Okay final offer: our library. The Olivares Library. You could spend hours looking at some of the resources we have. Volumes not touched for centuries. Scholars are always asking to use it, but we say no."

She had not heard this before. The library might be a gold mine or a bust with all the good volumes gone. The bigger reality could not be denied: She had no one but him and she had to trust him. Okay, not trust—trust, but watchful, cautious, and smart.

She faked a smile. "You had me at *library*."

"Wonderful." He reached out with a hug. She stood like a totem and then stepped back.

He put his arms down and took his wine glass to the sink, erasing the awkward moment. "It's settled then. The place is large enough to get lost and hide from my crazy relatives."

Her cold reaction was about her fear, not about him. But his distance showed he had taken offense. She liked him and if he was one of the good guys, she really liked him. "I appreciate the invitation. We can leave after I pack my things."

"How about if we leave in the morning?" He paused and surveyed the room. "Perhaps I can impose on you. Stay the night here?"

Her smile evaporated. Any protests about him not needing the apartment would be ungrateful. "Ah, it's your apartment." Maybe he would protect her from whatever, unless he *was* the whatever.

"If you're uncomfortable, I can stay at a friend's."

She turned to put the wine bottle upside down in the trash and moved on. "I don't have much to offer you. There's bread and serrano ham."

"Sure you don't want to go to dinner?"

"I'm more tired than hungry."

"Ok." He patted the couch and said, "I will sleep here."

She should volunteer to give him the bed and take the couch for herself. She looked around. The couch was five feet from the bed. It didn't really matter.

He got a blanket from the open shelves in this tiny studio and spread it on the couch.

MORNING LIGHT FELL ON HER face and woke her. Antonio stood by the window, his duffle yawned open on the couch ready to swallow the last items to be packed. He picked up his razor from the kitchen sink where he'd shaved and put it in the bag. He wore a crisp shirt with his jeans.

"Good morning." She stretched and rubbed her eyes, hoping he hadn't noticed her staring at him.

"Good morning, *Guapa*. Want some coffee?"

She had not moved all night. Emotionally spent, she'd fought but finally accepted a deep sleep. But now, worries assembled like prison guards watching her through the bars. Her naïve expectations had been upended by Isabel who misled her. Enrique was trustworthy in the end but had been part of Isabel's strange tactics. Piero and the ship logs, another strange happening. In five days, she had a directory of sketchy characters and questions without answers, a complex web made by an invisible spider, a mysterious opponent.

"I'll get coffee downstairs. It'll give you a chance to shower and dress. Do you take it with milk?"

She hadn't answered him the first time. "Yes to the coffee and no to the milk. And thanks, thanks for getting it."

She dressed quickly, brushed her teeth, skipped the shower, and tossed the sweats that served as pajamas into her suitcase.

Her computer sat on the kitchen table where she'd left it. She tucked her "life" into its case and packed up things from the bathroom, checked that nothing was left behind in this place where she would not return. The little black dress hanging on the hook remained. She held up the LBD and folded the top over to minimize wrinkles, hoping it wouldn't violate provincial customs to wear black to Christmas dinner. Widows wore black in Spain for a defined period of time. Art people wore black for a lifetime.

She lifted the painting and peeked under the rolled paper to make certain it was *La Gloria.* That carmine red winked back. Somehow all was right in the universe with Gloria inside the tube. She sighed, relieved she'd be gone from Seville, but suspicions and distrust would travel with her.

Antonio pushed the partially open door with his shoulder and walked in with two cups. He set his coffee down and picked up the tube. "Do you need to bring this? We'll be back in three days."

She took it from his hands and wondered why he zeroed in on the tube. "Curatorial ethics. I need to keep it in my custody." She added, "If I don't return to Seville, I will have everything with me."

"Ok, your choice. My car is small but we will make room." He held the door for her to go down the stairs and locked it behind them.

His once top model Fiat now with worn leather seats, battered and old, sped through early morning Seville into the Andalusian hills. The road stretched out ahead of them well into the distance. Frosty dew covered the stalks that remained after the harvest.

Traversing the landscape together in the cramped car, in silence, her shoulders and hands inches from his, nurtured an intimacy that relaxed her fears about him. That dimple on his right cheek made it difficult to see him as sinister. His Roman nose exaggerated a certain strength, a nose like the count-duke in the portraits. Almost but not quite the duke's nose. Thank goodness, because those were some ugly noses and puffy lips too. Velázquez got away with painting reality as he saw it. Others might have lost their jobs if not their heads. "Too truthful," Pope Innocent X said of Velázquez's portrait of him.

"If I had money, I'd spend it to know your thoughts," Antonio said.

"Artwork. How works can be viewed so differently, the eye of the beholder changes a work."

"Deep thoughts for a holiday trip."

"Not really. Art has been my passion since I was a little girl. What are you thinking?"

"How to explain you to my family. If I introduce a woman, especially at Christmas, it's something serious. They'll never believe the truth."

"What is the truth?"

"Hmmm. What's your answer?"

"We met on a train. You invited me to stay in your apartment where we slept together." She laughed and so did he with spontaneous ease.

"That's the truth, but you see my problem. We need a consistent story."

"Okay counselor. How about a non-lie?"

"What's a non-lie?"

"My mom never tolerated lying. She'd say whatever you've done, the punishment would be worse for lying." She stopped to calm the wobble in her voice. "I excelled at the non-lie, the partial truth, truth with a lot left out."

"Interesting. What's our non-lie?"

"I'm a curator doing research on the Golden Age of Seville and this painting." She tapped the tube. "I am only here for two weeks and you kindly offered to let me use the Olivares Library."

He nodded. "Continue."

"The only available days were the Christmas holidays and so here we are."

"Excellent. All true."

"A tip from an experienced non-liar: If they ask a question, ask them one in return or change the subject. If you try to answer, you might lie."

"Got it. Just like criminal law. An inconsistent story of false testimony means a guilty suspect." He slowed the car and pointed. "Look. At the top of that ridge."

Ancient walls glowed amber in the sunlight warming the hills. The structure, a classic from the Middle Ages like the castle at Segovia, fit her image of an iconic castle.

"A castle."

"Ha. Yes, that's our home. Additions built to look older than they are. My relatives liked the idea of promoting their nobility, such as it is. The castle is a non-lie. Did I get that right?"

"Yup. Obscuring the truth."

He turned off the national highway onto a rural road and slowed to avoid sheep crossing to a grassy hillside.

The castle or palace, she didn't know the difference, appeared and disappeared as they went up and then down the hills, but the house didn't seem any closer. "How far is your property?"

"We are here. This is our property, our bad road."

"Not acres, but miles?"

"Ten minutes to the house. These roads were fine for horses and carriages. Paving them, miles of them, is big money. We have a Range Rover, an old one, better for these roads. Would you like a tour around the property? Do you ride?"

"Sure." At least the remoteness made a pleasant hideout, from what she still didn't know.

Antonio crossed a bridge over a small stream, perhaps once a moat, and drove through an arch to enter a courtyard. "Ready to meet the relatives?" He turned and looked at her, as though anticipating a sign or something.

"With pleasure." She smiled, an unspoken but needed peace offering for her earlier mistrust and affirming in her own head that he was one of the good guys.

He turned off the engine. "One thing troubles me about our story."

"What's that?"

"I wish we had something to non-lie about."

CHAPTER 15

*T*he relatives had not yet arrived. The sun warmed the air, unusual for December, and this pleasant time outdoors was too good to waste. Antonio found riding boots for her behind the stable door and a pair of breeches with rusted fittings. "Hope these work. You might shake them out."

The pants fit only by cinching in the waist, but they were better than jeans rubbing on the saddle and chafing her legs. A ride on a friendly mare across the gentle hills far from the art world silenced the unrelenting thrum of stress. She patted the horse's head and ran her hands through the mane. The mare was a mount she could handle with her limited equestrian skills developed and practiced on ponies boarded at grandpa's farm.

Antonio rode with confidence over this terrain so familiar to him. He sat upright in the saddle and galloped without speaking until he slowed to take in the view above the house. The setting, the horses, and the vast landscape so much unchanged, could have been four hundred years ago with the Count-Duke Olivares riding with them.

They dismounted a mile from the house and walked the horses, with puffs of the breeze cooling their faces. All horses like returning to their stalls and some rush to do so, but she held hers back and Antonio did as well in an unspoken and tentative effort to benefit from time alone. They stopped at the last hill overlooking the estate.

"You ride well for not doing it very often. We'll go again if the weather holds."

"I'd like that. Look how the sun shines and makes the roof sparkle. I can understand why you fight to keep this legacy."

"I was noticing how your hair shines out here in the light, almost an auburn color."

She blushed. "It's brown but I'll take Titian red if that's what you see. Color changes depending on who's looking."

He tucked a strand of hair back behind her ear to keep it from blowing in her face. "Like many things in life. I behold a young beauty struggling to figure out her life. Am I right?"

"The struggling part is true. I look at those old buildings and see hundreds of years of history glowing in the light, but others might see a wreck to be leveled."

"Also true. I'm thirsty and so are the horses. Shall we go back?"

A young boy took the horses from them when they reached the barn. He was the nephew of the caretakers, home from university in Seville. She and Matty had groomed horses on the dairy farm. She'd saved the money grandpa paid them for school, Matty ... well, she didn't know what he did with his earnings, but she could guess.

The shower renewed her energy and her reason for coming. She pulled on her jeans, added a fresh shirt and the beige sweater she'd bought with a Christmas gift card from her godmother. The cashmere, the only cashmere she owned, smelled new and the quality made her feel like she'd summered in the Hamptons or something, something like Christmas with Spanish nobles.

This bedroom had not been dusted in a while, nothing a clean cloth and a few minutes couldn't solve. The canopy bed and vistas from the window seat made up for the neglected housekeeping. This place showed a sad, faded elegance of once sophisticated refinement.

She started toward the bedroom door and stopped to check under the bed where the tube remained undisturbed. Events of the last few days flipped her practice to trust first until given cause to do otherwise. Isabel had tricked her and she could not let it happen again. She picked up the tube and her computer bag, balancing them both one on each side, and walked down the three flights to the main level. She was here to study, that was their story and that was true.

Antonio waited in the foyer standing on the Guzman coat of arms inlaid in the marble. "Chain of custody. Here?" Antonio pointed to the canvas and screwed up his lips.

Her cheeks got hot. "I need it with me to compare to other works." His questioning of her work practice was annoying.

"Do I get to see this artwork, my competition, that takes your attention away from me?"

Her cheeks continued to burn, not as much from his flirtatious comment but the prospect of him or anyone seeing the painting. She'd hoped to be left alone to study. "Where is this library you hide from everyone?" She lifted her hand waiting for direction and rethinking why she had brought the painting out. Hiding the painting and assuring it was safe were incompatible with her stated purpose. *La Gloria* would need to come into the light; it was inevitable.

Before they walked two steps, an older man, distinguished in a tweed coat with elbow patches and an aristocratic demeanor, opened the front door.

"Tio Luis!" Antonio bent to embrace his uncle who was shorter than he once was due to an unfortunate bend in his back. Antonio held him away, gazed into his face and hugged him again, rubbing his deformed back. Their joy at seeing each other was contagious and Antonio's love for his family melted her distrust.

Tio Luis took his hat off and bowed. "Don Gaspar, mi conde-duque. Thank you for receiving us in your home."

Gaspar? She raised her eyebrows toward Antonio.

Before Antonio answered, a woman with at least three pearl strands around her neck and a diamond brooch on a tattered Chanel jacket came through the door chatting with Maria, the housekeeper.

"Tia Teresa." Antonio kissed both her cheeks.

"And who is this?" The woman held her hand out.

Cate took Aunt Teresa's hand and jumped to the practiced story. "Catherine Adamson. Cate. I'm an art historian doing research in Seville. Your nephew offered the resources of the Olivares Library." *Too much. Teresa hadn't even asked.*

"Of course." Teresa winked at Antonio.

She looked at Antonio, who rolled his eyes and then studied the floor in silence.

"*Encantado.*" Tio Luis kissed her hand, just as Antonio had done on the train. "Where did you find this beauty, Gaspar?"

Antonio smiled but ignored the question. "You must be tired, Tio. Do you want to go to your room to rest? We'll talk at lunch."

Her eyes followed them up the stairs and she whispered to Antonio, "Sorry. Not my best effort." She squeezed his hand, a gesture so natural it surprised her.

Antonio carried the tube and led the way to the library.

They passed a large sitting room and walked through the dining room where Maria was removing linen covers from chairs. The covers released a cloud of dust that remained suspended in the sunlit air. Juan, Maria's husband, opened the shutters and light streamed through the windows. Paintings hung salon-style from the ceiling to the chair rail three feet above the well-worn parquet floors.

Antonio went down a small passageway and pushed open a twelve-foot carved door.

The open door revealed not just any library, but an extraordinary space like the Morgan or the Strahov in Prague, with a treasury archived under a Rubens-esque ceiling, thirty feet high. Carved plaster vines decorated each corner and acanthus capitals finished the columns that held the bookcases. Volumes, ten thousand perhaps, covered the walls of two floors connected by a metal staircase and a catwalk around the second level.

"Beautiful. Stunning and so different from the simplicity of the house."

"This wing was built around 1600 and the renovations were the pride of the third duke. All yours to search." He swept his arm in an expansive arc.

Antonio's library did not disappoint. Books, atlases, and documents that could be career-defining for librarians like Piero, scholars like Jones, and students like her had to be on these shelves. "It's amazing. Gracias, Don Antonio—or is it Gaspar?"

"My relatives prefer Gaspar because that name connects to the lineage of the Count-Duke of Olivares. Historians write that the line died out, except for distant cousins, the Haros. My family knows there was another son, a bastard also, who continued the line. A family tree, somewhere in this archive, shows the details. I'm named for the son Gaspar de Guzman y Velasco."

"So your title comes from the duke's son?"

"That legitimized bastard son died a year after the famous duke, and that son had one child with his wife Juana de Velasco who died as an infant. But Juana learned her husband Gaspar had another child, a bastard, who she took into her house when her own baby died. Powerful nobles, the Haros, convinced the king they were the legitimate family and eventually the official title was swept into the Duke of Alba's line."

"How did you end up with the estate?"

"Juana de Velasco held on to this property and the books in this library, passed them on to the other bastard son she'd hidden from the world, and after four-hundred years, the estate came to me."

Cate moved her head up and down and her body in a circle, taking it all in. "This could be one of the great European libraries."

Antonio shrugged. He lifted a white sheet from the library table and another from a large globe near the spiral staircase. "I'm not sure what is here. There's no catalog."

"Sounds like a treasure hunt."

"And a lot of pressure to produce treasure." He dumped the covers in a heap near chairs around an inlaid wood table. He wiped off the table with one of the covers. "Let's see this painting that follows you everywhere."

"I'd rather work alone." She hesitated. "It's hard enough to discover the facts and objectively consider them, without everyone's conflicting ideas getting into the mix."

"I know little about art. I won't offer any conflicting opinions because I have no opinion."

She would need to show it to someone, trust somebody besides Isabel. *Arghh. And that went well.* Her growing admiration and attraction to Antonio scared her. She so didn't want to be wrong about him, like she had been about Isabel.

"Attorney-client privilege. If I break my promise and tell the world about your painting, you can take it up with the Board of Legal Ethics."

She laughed, pulled *La Gloria* out of the tube, and removed the acid free paper. She smoothed the canvas to make certain no particles were on the surface and nudged it to unroll across the table, moving with caution to avoid chipping any pigments. She paused at the final layer of paper that protected the surface and raised her eyes to search Antonio's face, filled with suspense at this dramatic reveal.

Antonio helped to remove the paper.

She laid her hand on his and stopped him.

He sighed. "Are you teasing me?"

She shrugged and removed the paper from the surface, suspending time, and watched his face for a reaction.

He lifted his eyebrows and nodded. "A worthy opponent."

"Opponent? What?"

"For your time. For you." He stood silent, rubbing his hand on his chin and leaning closer. "It's as good as anything from the sixteenth century. The color and tone, the subject. Impressive."

"It's likely seventeenth century."

"Well I confessed I didn't know much about art. That figure looking out at us is here in the room. Naturalism. Like those paintings he did in the Prado."

"He who?"

"Velázquez. The style is the same."

He said the name, that thing that she didn't want to say, as though it was obvious. He mentioned the qualities he admired, but she stopped listening at "Velázquez." She hugged him and then quickly drew back. "You do know art. You see that it's special."

"A Velázquez, right?"

"That is the complicated question since I found it."

"Found it? At the university?"

"Well, sort of." She lowered herself onto a leather chair, catching her new sweater on a bent grommet. She'd wanted to avoid this conversation.

He sat in a chair across from her. "Tell me about finding this work, include the 'sort of' parts."

He sounded lawyerly. She held her forehead. Allies would be pivotal to move forward and find success. She could not continue this journey alone.

She recounted the events, choosing the pertinent details and words with care to avoid mistakes she'd made with Isabel. In spite of her intended caution, once again everything spilled out and didn't stop until just before the Isabel chapter. She preferred Antonio did not view her as an art thief at all ... one theft was better than two, and whatever she told him made him a knowing accomplice.

She paused for two or three deep sighs to recover from her sprint of words, sinking into the chair.

Antonio focused, engrossed in the words. He listened, more like an attorney than a friend. He stood with gravitas and rang a buzzer installed in the floor by the desk. Maria appeared at the big door and he asked her to bring tea.

He pulled up a small side chair next to her. "That's quite a story, a thriller." He spoke, hesitating for a way to deliver his message. "You are aware you could be in trouble. The story . . . Jones's behavior, while outrageous, will not excuse that you took the university's property."

She sputtered at first and then blurted, "I took it to Jones who has, ah, is . . . arrogant and unsupportive. He would send it back to the cellar, deny the work deserves a clear attribution, right away without even studying it, because he didn't find the painting, wouldn't get the credit. No, I didn't show it to him nor ask permission to study it." The rationalizations, the excuses rang unworthy, and she regretted them as soon as she said them. "You agree, don't you? This painting deserves to be in the world."

The library clock ticked in the silence. Finally, he nodded. "Maybe you should have given your professor a chance?"

She studied his face and relented. "I know. I know. I've reviewed what happened over and over in my head." She lowered her voice. "One good thing, the painting was not listed on the inventory, the university doesn't have a record of it. No one will be looking for it."

He lifted his head to look at her, raised his eyebrows. "That won't matter. The university had possession of the artwork, and in Spain and the US possession matters."

She returned to the strategy that had kept her from her worst fears. "I intend to return the painting with some evidence about its history, share what experts found, create compelling facts Jones has to consider. If the painting turns out to be nothing, a studio work or a later effort by an unimportant artist, the painting goes back to the university."

"I'd counsel return the painting now. Seeking proof could take months. Tell Jones everything and make it clear your goal was to study the artwork, to find a dissertation topic, and not to sell it."

He paused, rubbed his chin, a thing he did when things were difficult, and then continued. "Selfishly, I would rather you stayed in Spain. I cannot advise you to do that. Return to New York before they find you." Antonio's voice trailed off.

Maria nudged the door open with her hip and brought a tray she set on a nearby desk. Tio Luis followed behind her.

"What's this?" Luis asked. He stood over the library table with *La Gloria* exposed to the world.

Luis added to the growing list of people. *So much for keeping the painting secret.*

"Would you like a cup of tea?" Antonio nodded to Maria to bring another cup.

Cate appreciated Antonio's attempt to distract Luis and started putting the paper back over the canvas.

"No, no I want to look." Luis stood next to Antonio to get the angle of the light just right. "Incredible. Just incredible," Luis raved.

"Let's leave Cate to work, Tio."

"Amazing."

"What, Tio?" Antonio said, and he moved to Luis's side by the library table.

She waited for Luis to answer, still holding the paper to cover the painting. What nonscholars might think could matter, but usually did not.

"I was searching the family photos last fall. The albums, they are here somewhere." He muttered and surveyed the room, then walked to the Victorian style couch, pulled off the white sheet to reveal green leather-covered albums stacked on the cushions.

"I can't be sure. The photo was old and fuzzy. I remember thinking I'd never seen that painting, not in this house anyway."

"You saw this painting in a photo?" She exchanged a glance with Antonio.

"No. I mean, yes." He seemed confused. "Much was sold when the duke your great-great grandfather needed money to pay debts. The photo is here somewhere." Luis flipped through the albums and became lost.

"If you're right, the connection would be significant, adding information to solve this painting's provenance." She wanted him to be right, but Luis was probably mistaken. Yet, this painting was different, not religious, nor a portrait. Maybe it made an impression on him.

Luis set one album down and grabbed another like a hungry man looking for a meal, oblivious to Antonio or to her or anything.

"Back to that other matter, what to do next . . ." Antonio whispered to her.

She leaned her head toward Luis to discourage Antonio from saying more. Luis didn't need to know about how Gloria got here.

Antonio nodded and whispered, "We can talk about your situation later. But we must do it soon." He continued in a louder voice, "One of our ancestors was an early fan of photography. In the 1840s he visited Paris and quietly brought Daguerre's technology to Spain."

Antonio stood and picked up the tube. "Do you want to put the painting back?" He looked into the tube. "There's something in here." Antonio pulled papers from the tube and handed them to her.

Enrique had scribbled a note that he couldn't get the official report, but he'd found a draft in the trash. She quickly hid the note in her pocket and flipped through five handwritten pages with whole sentences crossed out. She read a few lines and looked up. "I need a dictionary for these technical Spanish words. And these revisions, crossed out sentences and changes don't make it easy to read."

"Did the director go over it with you?"

"That's another story . . . for later."

"We have a dictionary." He pointed to a stand.

She turned to the last page and leaned toward him with the section labeled Conclusions and read:

The above observations and the results of scientific tests confirm the following:

—Wood fragments: +/- 300–400 years
—Red clay ground typical of those years
—Paint layer—firmly hardened, result of the drying of the paint binder
—Natural craquelure—depth indicating an age of +/- 350 years
—Use of hand-ground pigments including lapiz lazuli into ultramarine and carmine red from the insect Carteria lacca brought to Spain in the 1600s.

She stumbled on the next words and held the page closer to her eyes. Antonio took over and read aloud over her shoulder:

Canvas fiber content is composed of flax and linen grown in the areas around Madrid in the 1600s. The hand-ground blue, red, and yellow pigments tested are consistent with materials used in the first part of the seventeenth century. Certain pigments date from the nineteenth century. The ratio of these to the remainder of the canvas is small enough to be the likely result of repairs and other conservation methods applied in the later nineteenth century.

"The last sentence is crossed out." Without waiting for a response from her, Antonio continued:

The red clay ground material, the pigments, visible pentimenti and the broad brushstrokes are consistent with only one known artist working at the time and location of the dated materials, Diego Velázquez de Silva or his studio.

He paused and looked up at her, waiting for a reaction.

She reread the line underneath the strikeout again and then again with a trembling voice. The paper shook when she repeated Velázquez and she held her hand to her chest, to control the heart that raced with this affirmation.

"It's what you were hoping, what we saw?"

"Yes. Yes definitely. It's stunning."

Antonio brushed her hair from her face and smiled. He read the final paragraph:

Recommendation: X-ray analysis of underpainting, comparison research of brushstrokes and compositional and iconographic analysis with well-documented works by Diego Velázquez. Comparisons with works by the artist's contemporaries are needed for a conclusive attribution. Comparison with known missing works by Velázquez may result in identification of the provenance of this work.

Antonio squeezed her. "This what you needed to convince Professor Jones?"

She whispered, "Half of it, yes. None of these tests eliminates Velázquez as the author of the work. That's not enough for definitive attribution, but yes, the start I'd hoped for."

He nodded in approval, perhaps thinking she was in less trouble now.

"Why do you think these lines are crossed out?"

"Perhaps it's a simple edit to write the sentence better. But maybe supervisors disagreed on the final conclusion? We can't know until we see the final report."

They'd never see a final report. Isabel had eliminated those sentences, she felt certain. She leaned closer to Antonio and read again the words that *La Gloria* had passed the first preliminary tests.

Antonio returned his teacup to the tray and reached for a crystal decanter filled with an amber liquid labeled Fundador. He dusted a crystal sniffer and gave it to her while he filled it and then filled one for himself. "It's a lot to take in," he said.

She touched her glass to his, declared "salud," and sipped the celebratory brandy.

Antonio finished his in two gulps.

"The painting appears to be important, and this report influences what we do." His tone had a solemnity that detracted from the celebration, reminded her she was still a thief. "I advise you to protect yourself legally. You must." He stared at her, waiting. "That is, if you want me to advise you."

"Yes, please. I've created a mess." She fiddled with the brandy glass and set it down. "I can't pay you anything."

He put his arm around her and gave her half a hug. "I don't expect anything. I just want you to be safe. I don't care about your career. I care about you." He kissed her forehead.

She held back tears and felt that aloneness dissipating. She'd known Antonio such a short time, but he had become a real friend, maybe more than a friend. She'd tell him about Isabel, Enrique getting back her property, well the university property. She would tell him when the circumstances were right.

Tio Luis wobbled up from the floor. "*Sí*, Señor. Look at this."

Luis made his way to the desk from the far side of the library and handed them a faded black-and-white image on a metal plate, a daguerreotype. "Your great-great-great uncles. Here's Gaspar, your namesake . . . well, one of the Gaspars."

"Which one?" Antonio asked.

"Forget those old men." Luis pulled Antonio's sleeve and held the photo closer to his face so he could hold it in front of the light. "Look here."

"Cate, come and look at this." He placed the metal plate next to the canvas.

The black-and-white image was clouded with grime and obscured in low light. Five men stood near a fireplace dressed in white tie. She lifted the plate and tipped it to the light.

Behind the men was a painting with a woman, a royal figure, and others praying to angels. She lowered the plate and compared it to the canvas and lifted it to the light again to believe what she saw. The painting in the photo was *La Gloria*.

CHAPTER 16

$\mathcal{A}$ ntonio guided her to the couch and insisted she drink the water Maria had brought. "Please rest here until the dizziness is gone."

Luis paced, asking repeatedly if she was all right, and she kept nodding to diffuse his guilt about showing her the photo.

"I never expected this." She tried sitting up, but the light-headedness returned. "Do you recognize the fireplace mantle? The wallpaper?"

Antonio offered her more water.

Tio Luis studied the photo. "Not this house, possibly in Olivares."

"Somewhere nearby? If we can identify the building, possibly there are more records." She put her elbow on the pillow that Antonio propped under her head and sat upright.

Antonio placed another pillow behind her back to help her sit. "Maybe the Ducal Palace in Olivares town. Anything important in Olivares happened either in the Palace or in this house."

Tio nodded. "There was a fire. Some things burned in the Duke of Alba's collections, arson they say, and most scholars think everything burned. But before that happened Juana de Velasco sent things to the Ducal Palace, and once this library was completed, all of the books, papers, and documents were hidden here."

She sat up and surveyed the walls. "I so appreciate being able to search this library. You are a scholar Luis."

"Not scholar. Just family."

As if on cue another relative visible through the smudged window arrived at the grand entrance. The Olivares family united with the holiday reunion, unlike her own family, which had gotten smaller with Matty gone, and now, she too was gone.

She blocked those thoughts to launch herself from the couch, ready to use every moment. The search for a reference to a commission or an inventory was top priority.

"Maybe we'll find titles to the property too," Antonio said.

She squeezed his arm. "We're on the same path, searching. You for land titles and me to discover the journey of this painting from the artist's brush to Olivares or nearby, and then, the biggest leap . . . to the United States?"

"And now back to Olivares," Antonio said.

"How should we divide this up?" She'd never had a "we" before. Her spirit lightened, her weary body energized, possibilities surged.

Antonio stopped her. "I know you're impatient, but don't climb this shaky staircase. I'll pull volumes from the second level and the high shelves." He climbed a fixed ladder behind the desk to reach estate records behind glass doors.

Household transactions, everything from construction expansion, renovations, and repairs, detailed histories of monies spent and collected on the dukedom's properties, were recorded in detail. Parties and dinners where guests would have traveled days to attend filled the pages along with what was served, who was present, and even where guests sat at the dining table. Centuries of records of sheep, horses, and cattle the dukes owned. Any painting hanging in this house or the Ducal Palace in Olivares had an entry somewhere, in some year. A singular *La Gloria* entry became the hidden treasure in centuries of record-keeping haystacks.

The daguerreotype technique began approximately in 1840; the painting had to have been in Olivares before that. She scribbled a timeline on a yellow pad. If the duke commissioned Velázquez to paint the work, then it was during the duke's lifetime that ended in 1645. If Velázquez gave the painting to the duke in gratitude for his patronage and bringing him to court, then there wouldn't be a financial record.

Based on the loose brushstrokes and the composition, the painting connected better with later works, after his Italian trips, after Olivares died. Perhaps Velázquez wanted to support Olivares's bastard son's wife, Juana, and his other child that survived. The painter had a mistress too and there were rumors of a son.

Luis told stories about family artworks. One of the great-greats sold works to pay gambling debts, and another relative had many trysts.

She scribbled notes, but these anecdotes, often changed in the retelling, fell short of what was needed. Antonio relayed books from the ladder to the floor. They turned pages in a silent rhythm. Footsteps creaked against the inlaid parquet when one of them got up to replace one volume and pick up another.

Juan arrived with more logs, the wooden kind, and stoked the fire. The heat rose, filling the upper portion of the room with warmth, leaving the lower area still cold.

Antonio and Luis worked faster than she, but hopefully they were being thorough. She placed a small bookmark inside the front cover of the volumes she'd searched, a mark that she didn't need to revisit them unlike the ones Antonio and Luis were flying through, which she might need to review.

Luis hummed Christmas carols, Antonio sweated with the physical exercise up and down the ladder, and she turned pages, greeting each one with a silent wish. Maria interrupted to announce lunch was served. The men left volumes opened to the last page reviewed.

She paused in front of Gloria. Even under centuries of grime, the muted colors waited to beam their original brilliance. Gloria's eyes appeared unafraid, pleading in anticipation. *Better to leave her out of the tube, in the light of day, to breathe the air, and let her view the world as she was meant to.* This painting had come home.

Maria's niece Sandra had come to help for the holidays and laid the table with family silver and stemware. The crystal goblets bounced a rainbow of light coming through the windows. An epergne with silver arms, Rococo around 1750, English probably, balanced plates holding fruit and nuts. Something she'd never have recognized except for the internship at Sotheby's. Frayed corners on monogrammed napkins and old stains set into the tablecloth reminders of the elegance that once was.

Antonio sat beside her in the middle of the long table with the *tios* on the other side. Antonio ranked highest in this household and took the middle seat, not at the head. They sipped soup from porcelain bowls with lids to keep the liquid warm.

"A moment of quiet before relatives arrive from Madrid. The house will fill with laughter and noise, the grandchildren—well, quiet times are about to vanish," said Tia Teresa. She pushed herself into the back of her chair, sitting straight upright, hands folded across her lap with an air of satisfaction.

"How many grandchildren do you have?" Cate asked.

"We have six, but poor Gaspar's father and mother, God rest their souls, have none." Teresa rolled her eyes at Antonio. "We are waiting for Gaspar Antonio to make them smile in heaven."

"Quiet, Mujer," Tio Luis said. He leaned over and whispered something in her ear and then winked at Antonio across the table.

"Is there a shop nearby? I have no Christmas gifts for the

children," Cate said. Not that she had money to buy gifts, even for Antonio.

"We don't exchange gifts until *Dia de Los Reyes Magos*— Three Kings Day in January. No Santa Claus in Spain, at least not in this house. Tia, describe *Nochebuena*," Antonio said.

"All the family goes to Mass in the little chapel. The workers too, the ones who farm the estate will bring some of the animals, a cow, some lambs for the Nativity Scene where the children will dress like Mary and Joseph. Then a Christmas banquet in the Great Hall. One hundred people in their finest clothes, smoking we say, but in English, black tie."

One hundred. She had never been at a private dinner that large, and black tie too. "I won't be able to attend."

"Nonsense. Your research can wait," Teresa said.

"It's not that." She looked at Antonio. "I haven't brought the right clothes."

Tia Teresa smiled. "This house has trunks full of elegant clothes. They might be . . . what do Americans say, vintage. Balenciaga gowns from the 1930s that were for Gaspar Antonio's great grandmother. You are tiny, like her."

Sandra cleared the soup bowls and offered a platter of fruit. Like a skillful surgeon, Luis peeled an orange with his knife, ate it elegantly with his fork, and folded his napkin, pulling it through the silver napkin ring.

Teresa did the same and waited. In the absence of a footman like they'd had in a prior era, Tio Luis stood and pulled out her chair so that she could rise.

Teresa smiled. "Come Catherine. Let's go to the attic."

The tios walked toward the stairs, leaving them alone in the dining room. Antonio took her arm and walked a few steps to a window overlooking the decaying garden. They sat on the seat of the deep casement window, and he pulled her next to him to kiss her forehead.

She looked up at his eyes. "What was that for?"

"The tios like you. Trust me, they don't like many."

"Many? How many have you brought home for Christmas?" *That was silly.* Of course, good-looking Antonio had the attention of others. Add a title, even a controversial one, and Antonio became a chick magnet, hard to translate that into Spanish.

"None." He shook his head and rolled his eyes. "Go with Auntie. Christmas is the only time we forget our troubles, all the challenges of maintaining what once was."

The sound of truth made her sigh. "We all yearn for what we've lost."

He turned toward her and leaned in, close to her lips. Plates and silverware clattered. She pulled away and jumped up.

Sandra worked at clearing the table and had interrupted their first kiss.

Antonio snickered and led her to the stairs.

Teresa motioned from the landing to follow her up the flights of marble stairs. The steps got narrower as they passed four levels, and the glistening marble turned to simple wood. Teresa held tight to the stair rail as she lifted her frail body onto each step. They arrived at a humble door and Teresa took a five-inch key from her sweater pocket to unlock it.

Spiderwebs covered old rafters and reminded her of the locked storage where this unusual journey had begun. Treasures hidden in locked storage spaces can complicate life.

Tia lifted the lid of one trunk, pulled out mothball-smelling dresses, and moved on to a different trunk filled with more clothes. Round boxes with logos of Paris millinery shops and shelves of little worn shoes were spread under the rafters.

Teresa lifted a black lace gown with elaborate beadwork. "Imagine. This is what they wore to dinner every night. So elegant." She touched the detailed stitching. The gown sparkled even in the dim attic light. "No one did beadwork like Balenciaga."Teresa took another dress from a rack she'd uncovered by removing a muslin sheet. "*Fantástico.* The azure color goes with your eyes."

"I couldn't wear something so precious. It's small, really tiny. Look at the waist." Cate held the dress up to her figure. A silvery one, covered in bugle beads and rhinestones hung like a 1920s flapper dress and maybe had a chance to fit over her twenty-first-century hips.

Teresa bubbled with excitement. "Try it on."

It fit. Barely. The mirror reflected a woman she didn't recognize. The V-neck cut deep and revealed more cleavage than appropriate for midnight Mass.

"You belong in that dress," Tia said.

Cate looked in the mirror and nodded, unsure but pleased she could attend the dinner. At the same time, she felt out of her element in a way no dress could solve. She'd experienced a few black-tie dinners with Sotheby clients, given a seat to complete a table when a guest failed to show up. But she'd never lost the need to be consciously observant: which fork to use, where to set it down, which way to pass something, which wine went with which course, and more. Dozens of pitfalls, a minefield that would explode to mark her as a fraud, an imposter in a world where she did not belong.

At Sotheby's a grey-haired event planner had told her that rules of etiquette were created to make guests feel comfortable. *Yeah right.* However, the rules could be learned and she would learn them.

She spotted the reflection of something in the back of the room and turned to investigate. "What are these?" Gold leaf frames were stacked behind the mirror. A white sheet covered a portion of the stack.

"More of our history. All over this house."

Cate pulled out a frame, eighteenth-century, gold acanthus leaves, deeply carved and expensive. Cardboard separated and protected ten, maybe eleven more frames of similar importance. A bead from the dress caught on a carved corner and she returned the stack back against the wall, vowing to return.

"Jewelry that goes with this dress is here somewhere," Teresa muttered. "Antonio would not sell those things, not his mother's jewelry."

"Did this dress belong to his mother?"

Tia rummaged around, mumbling things about the jewelry. "This dress belonged to his great grandmother. She was a beauty, just like you."

Cate didn't think of herself as a beauty. She was smart, a scholar, but her physical appearance was unexceptional. *Presentable*, she'd call herself. "Not unattractive" her aunt had said in a typical Midwest understatement.

"Here, take this." Teresa wrapped a mottled silver fox stole around her shoulders and stood back. "You're a vision."

The image in the mirror was something from a Hollywood newsreel, complete with the black-and-white reflection in the mirror in the dark attic.

"You'll need the fur for the chill in the chapel."

"Thank you." Cate stepped out of the dress and changed back into her jeans and cashmere sweater that was ordinary now. She stopped at her room, placed her new-used garments on the bed and hurried to the library.

Antonio and Luis were drinking cognac from a crystal decanter and joking about a distant relative.

"What's this?" she said a bit too loud. "Workers slacking on the job." She glanced at the painting on the library table. She'd spent a whole hour without thinking about it.

Antonio lifted a cognac snifter in her direction. "It's Christmas, boss. We're collecting holiday bonuses."

Luis got up, poured cognac into a brandy snifter, and handed it to her. "Here's yours, *Jefa*."

She tried to smile and took a sip.

"A toast to what we found."

Antonio gestured to an open volume on the table and lifted the glass in his hand.

She raced to read a reference to a Velázquez purchase. A volume dated 1910 was open to a page listing accounts, revenue, and expenses. Under revenue, there was an entry that read "$20,000 paid by a Lady Claybourne-Brown. Painting 200 cm by 150 cm. Velázquez, ca. 1650s."

"Is that your painting?"

She shook her head. "This entry doesn't match *La Gloria's* measurements. The painting in the inventory is much bigger. But great to know Velázquez's paintings were in the Olivares collection and this is the type of entry we're searching for."

Antonio set his empty glass down. "We'll keep looking. They must have been desperate to sell that work for so little. We know they had more, at least one—that little portrait in the gallery."

Antonio pouted his lip like a little kid trying to soften the disappointment that they hadn't found the needle. He turned toward the volumes on the couch. "Let's keep looking. We have a few more hours before we dress for dinner."

CHAPTER 17

*S*he woke to a dark room and jumped up to check the time. Her little nap had gone too long. It was 6 p.m. Mass in the chapel began at 7 p.m. For a moment, she longed for those pills she'd taken during finals, given to her by the student health doctor. But she swore them off forever after Matty's death. She checked the sunken half-circles under her eyes and searched her suitcase for a foundation cover-up. She tried to fix her hair around the headpiece, but her hair looked odd.

She hadn't worn heels since high school prom, and these vintage shoes weren't a good fit. Antonio's grandmother had tiny feet, tiny everything, as she straightened the dress around her hips. Good thing she hadn't eaten a large breakfast, or much lunch.

Antonio was not at the bottom of the stairs where she expected to find him. When Spaniards say seven, they mean seven-thirty or eight or somewhere in between, and perhaps everyone was still getting ready. However, Mass was always on time. He'd be busy with such a large event, but she didn't expect to be forgotten. The house seemed quite empty.

Antonio came around the corner dressed in a black tuxedo with a white tie, his mustache trimmed and his hair neatly combed. "Oh my." He stopped like he was surprised.

"I couldn't find you. Is everything okay?"

"Not okay. *Magnífica.*" He kissed her cheek and took her hand to twirl her around. "You ... *Dios.* For a minute, you looked like . . . look stunning." He fidgeted and straightened his tie and cummerbund.

"You're looking handsome—like a hot latino actor."

He laughed and offered his arm and they walked—he walked and she wobbled —on the cobblestones. The fur in surprisingly good condition did protect against the night chill.

Antonio led her past the Nativity Scene where village children stood in for the Holy Family. Their little faces glowed with anticipation in the candlelight along the pathway.

The family pew in the front of the tiny chapel had spaces reserved for them, not marked but understood, and the guests filling the chapel seemed to follow them up the aisle with their eyes. The candlelight didn't hide the crumbling walls and mildew smell permeated the air. The congregation chanted in well-practiced responses and songs that rang out Christmas joy so familiar to her. She gazed at Antonio who stared ahead at the altar. A special affection for this new friend landed on one word, gratitude, gratitude that he'd provided her shelter in Seville, rescued her to Olivares, from a gloomy Christmas and a desperate search for *La Gloria's* past. Hopeful energy boosted her singing and the sense that she belonged somewhere, at least for this day, this night.

They filed out, crossed the gardens, and entered the ballroom that looked like a dream, something from a queen's palace. A table set with one hundred matching place settings ran the length of the room. The table glistened with silver and crystal on the embroidered linens from the Olivares' dynasty, the estate's best finery. A fifteen-foot Christmas tree filled the ballroom where three fireplaces burned and crackled. She turned her head around and around to take it all in. "Spellbinding. What a grand tradition."

Antonio's face betrayed a melancholy look that at first she interpreted as the look of a preoccupied host, but all was going well at this well-practiced event. His worries puzzled her, but this was not the time to ask. She found her place card next to his, the place of honor. Whispers about the two of them spread around the glowing ballroom and maybe that was worrying him—their non-lie faltering. She snickered when she overheard someone speculate she was an American heiress. If they only knew she was the princess of Ypsilanti.

Village girls served roasted suckling pig stuffed with chestnuts on silver trays. She patted her mouth with the monogramed napkin and sipped crisp albariño and politely added small bites to her plate. She'd wanted to take more but didn't dare test her dress.

Yet, in a minute, she would have traded this dream elegance for a plain turkey dinner on the Adamsons' table, covered in a paper poinsettia tablecloth from the Dollar Store. She could imagine Antonio, the guy without money on the train, eating mom's cornmeal muffins in Ypsilanti, but Mom and Dad, well she could not imagine them at this formal dinner in Olivares.

Luis sat on her other side and entertained her with tales about family members and guests seated around the table. Enough stories to create a telenovela. And like a miniseries, she couldn't keep the characters and their storylines straight, but that was okay. Being a passive listener meant she wasn't asked questions about her relationship to Antonio, questions to which she had no answers. Not yet. Not after only a week together.

Antonio left to smoke cigars in a nearby men only salon; his departure signaled dinner was over.

She peeked through the smoke and decks of cards and chips waited on tables. Antonio didn't seem like a gambler, especially without money to risk. What a contrast to her. She also had nothing, but she'd gambled her career, her freedom, the respect of her family, everything on *La Gloria*. Her recklessness saddened and shamed her, but she would find a way to fix it. She would.

Women retired to a sitting room, the stained wallpaper and worn fabrics hidden in the shadowy light. A ballroom chair next to a tiny table in the back of the room provided a perch to sip sherry, a fine Spanish variety, and watch from the sidelines. She preferred this place of anonymous comfort, not knowing the protocols. The women discussed why Sorolla had painted naked orphans and whether a biography of the poet Quevedo had reflected his friendship with the Count-Duke of Olivares. She'd never been at a social event in a nonacademic setting where people chatted about these things, were so informed and well read, even in a rural place like Olivares.

An hour into the women's salon, feeling the effects of the sherry, and dodging questions about Antonio, she excused herself, blaming travel fatigue. She left and wandered corridors in the house's far wing. They were empty and silent except for the noise from the courtyard out front. Family members who lived nearby in Olivares and villagers drove away shouting holiday greetings in happy, drunken voices. Tires made grinding noises on the gravel drive until the cars disappeared under the archway and onto the roads, leaving a parade of car lights in the darkness over the hills.

She hadn't said goodnight to Antonio, didn't know the rules for entering the male domain and chose to avoid an embarrassing faux pas.

A long gallery, filled with portraits, connected the salon to the ballroom. She glanced around, unable to resist viewing the paintings. She stopped in front of one canvas that could be something interesting maybe it was the portrait Antonio mentioned that was attributed to Velázquez. Tomorrow she'd return when the light was better and maybe find something to solve his financial problems.

She jumped. Antonio touched her shoulder and stood behind her.

"Come with me." He took her hand.

She stumbled and steadied herself on feet that were scream-ing for redemption.

Antonio offered an arm to lean on and they stopped in front of a woman's portrait at the far end. The subject of the full standing portrait was her, looked so much like that image in the attic mirror, or better said, the sequined dress, fur, and even the difficult shoes were all there.

"Teresa yearns for those days, the way she dressed you. Meet my great grandmother." Antonio's eyes danced from her to the portrait. He squeezed the hand that clung to his arm.

"You are Tia's recreation of her." He glowed with pride. "The sparkle in your eyes, magic in the candlelight. You, that dress . . . you are so beautiful. The similarity shocked me when I saw you."

"But I am . . . not her." She looked down at her dress and compared her outfit to the painting. Something was missing. A silver headband with two leaves of diamonds held back the side of his great grandmother's bob. "The tiara. It's stunning."

Antonio swallowed and lowered his voice. "Tia was searching for the jewelry case this afternoon and asked me where it was. I told her that the tiara was missing, one of your non-lies. Maybe a whole lie."

She looked up at him.

He looked away. "I sold the tiara in Madrid. I had to." His head dropped and stayed there.

She laid her head on his shoulder. "I'm sorry. You and your family have it forever in this painting. Art freezes the past." She paused and wished she had a portrait of Matty.

He wiped the tear from her cheek. "No crying on Christmas. What's wrong?"

"Thinking of my brother, Matty, Matthew. He died . . . drowned . . . three Christmases without him."

"Very sad." He pulled her close in an affectionate hug. "Tell me about him."

"I will someday." She pulled back and looked up at him.

He caressed her hand, held it against his face, and leaned down. He lingered there, waiting. So close, she shared the air he breathed. A force pulled their lips together as though they'd found a home.

THE EVENING HAD BEEN . . . what word? Magical? Marvelous? Magnificent? Images swirled in her head, preventing the sleep that should come after champagne, aperitifs, wine, finishing with Pedro Domenq. She stared at the inside of the bed canopy and checked the clock to see how much time had passed. The magic was not in an evening in a castle, nor the clothes Teresa had found, but in him. Antonio. Antonio. Attorney, attractive, almost nobleman, a friend of what . . . a week. A Midwest girl, with her professional aspirations, wasn't supposed to be swept away with such things. She was a woman, flesh and real, not just a brain full of facts, alive with awakened emotions she had forgotten or denied.

She sat up and rubbed her palm where Antonio had rested his head, however briefly, to bid good night after he'd lifted her onto the bed and kissed her eyes. The scent of him lingered there and she placed her face to breathe in his fragrant smell.

His family, old and young, adored him too, and their heritage, gleaming like the candles that lit the room, bound them together. She sat up, abruptly reminded of home. It was not Christmas morning in Michigan, too early to call. She would though, tomorrow afternoon.

The painting. Ugh, it was still in the library. She'd intended to roll the painting into the tube and bring it back to the bedroom after her nap, especially with all the strangers in the house. But she'd overslept and there was no time. She threw on a T-shirt, a pair of jeans, and sneakers, better than those vintage heels, and crept down the stairs. The door to the library creaked when she pushed it open.

It was there, just where she'd left it. The family party never got to this part of the house. She relaxed on the couch, gazed at the work, and ran her fingers through her hair.

A floor lamp with funky fringe on the shade lit the area by the couch. Three inventory volumes dated 1550, 1551, and 1552 were stacked next to her on the couch and she began to thumb through them. The dates struck her in a new way. The Institute reported on the unique brushstrokes, different but close to Velázquez's later works. The composition's iconography signaled memories of King Felipe IV and his prime minister the Count-Duke of Olivares, the pinnacle of the Hapsburg Empire, not a contemporary work of the times, but a retrospective longing for what had been, a tribute.

She opened the 1551 volume, studied pages and pages until the end. She lifted 1552 and began to turn the pages, skipping over pantry inventories and dinner parties. More pages, more volumes recorded the same. A pillow supported her head against the couch and the volume slipped to the floor as her head nodded. She sunk into the pillow and sleep took over.

A GENTLE KISS ON ONE eye and then the other woke her. Antonio's face hovered above her. "My Lady, have you spent the night here? I looked for you in your room."

"You went to my room?"

"I kissed your eyes asleep, I wanted to kiss them awake." He lifted her up in his arms using biceps honed by chopping wood and twirled her around.

"Merry Christmas."

She laughed and gasped for breath.

He kept dancing toward the door.

"What are you doing? Let me down."

She wiggled away and noticed the desktop was empty.

"Oh God. No. The painting. It's gone." She staggered and grabbed a chair. "I should have taken it to my bedroom."

"Calm, Señorita. I have it."

"You scared me. Where is it?"

Antonio had a quirky grin. "All night I thought: How can I make Christmas special for Cate? I found the perfect gift." He took her hand, opened the heavy doors, and walked toward the dining room.

She stopped at the dining room door, surprised by what was over the fireplace. "How . . . I can't believe it." She shook her head.

They stood in silence, staring at what Antonio had placed there.

A gold-leaf frame leaned against the brocade wall covering above the fireplace. The canvas was loosely taped inside the frame. Except for the part of the painting that had been trimmed, the painting fit the frame.

She walked closer and stared at the daguerreotype Antonio held out in his hand. This was the frame in the photo.

"What? But how? How did you connect the two?"

"You mentioned you'd seen the frames stored in the attic. After I said goodnight, I went to the library, measured the painting, and took the photo to the attic. After moving and sorting all the frames, I'm surprised I didn't wake everyone, this golden treasure was at the back, completely wrapped as though someone wanted it well protected. And . . ."

". . . it matched the photo." She finished the sentence.

The frame lit up *La Gloria* as was its purpose. Before electricity, gilders intended for the gold leaf to catch the candlelight and illuminate the works. She ran her finger along the leaf carved into the corner. That the frame was here combined with the discovery of Antonio's relative's photograph of the painting exceeded all her expectations. A frame like this would be worth a considerable sum, tens of thousands in New York or London.

He put his arm around her shoulder and pulled her close. "Merry Christmas, dear Cate."

"Thank you." She couldn't say more, her voice quavering because he cared so about her project. "I have no gift for you."

"Santa came to Olivares only for Americans. January 6 for Spaniards, remember?"

"I will mark January on my calendar." She sniffed, wondering where she would be, where he would be in January, so much unsettled. She took a deep breath and stared at the painting. "I think . . . do you think . . . maybe we have enough to make the experts look at the evidence that this painting was close to the Count-Duke, to Velázquez, part of the court of Felipe IV?" Out of breath, she gasped. "Look at her face."

"She's a beauty, sort of a sad beauty. Like you."

"I'm not sad." She turned her face toward his and kissed his cheek. "But yes, Gloria's face has layered complexity, beckoning and worrisome, natural and real."

She slid into a chair, exhausted from lack of sleep and the struggle. Tears would not be denied. She wiped her eyes, accepting her face was a red, snotty mess and she turned away from him. *Only movie stars look good crying.*

He put his hand on her chin and turned her face back toward his and kissed her. "And I thank you for another gift. For sitting on that train, for sharing my apartment, for coming here, for wearing my great-grandmother's dress and, most of all, for being you. I care about the *Gloria* project, but only because it matters to you."

She'd been here before—lonely and weak, unable to judge sincerity. *Go slow, be certain.* She kissed his cheek. "Best Christmas ever."

Antonio put his arm on her shoulder and they admired the painting above the mantel. "I agree."

"Looks like a masterpiece instead of a dirty, forgotten canvas," she smiled. "I'd planned to see my friend Guillermo at the Prado. He's an associate curator there. The best experts are at the Prado, the ones that matter to support a Velázquez attribution."

"Then let's go."

"Go where?"

"The Prado. Madrid. Call him. My car will be faster and cheaper than the AVE. Your break from school ends in a week."

"I'd hoped to visit him before Christmas, maybe he's left town." She dialed his number. The phone buzzed and flashed a message that the call could not be completed. No service out here in the countryside.

"Try mine." Antonio balanced his phone on his palm.

Please answer. Please be there. The phone rang and rang again.

"*Sí.*" A sleepy voice picked up. "*¿Quién es?*"

"Merry Christmas, Guillermo. It's Cate, Cate Adamson. Did I wake you?" She checked her watch. It was ten in the morning.

"Cate! You have a Seville number."

"A friend's phone." She wasn't sure what to call Antonio or what to make of the long pause and decided an apology was needed. "Sorry if I woke you."

"No, no it's fine. Are you in Madrid?"

She could hear him rustling out of bed. "Seville. Olivares actually."

"Olivares, that's interesting. I'm stuck in Madrid, officer in charge at the museum for the holidays, coverage rotated among the curators. The Prado offices are a tomb, everyone gone, but the museum is packed with tourists. I'm the guard, walking the ramparts of the fort."

She laughed. *Classic Guillermo sense of humor.* "I'm coming to Madrid tomorrow. Can we meet?"

"Want to go for tapas to Casa Gonzalez? *Un brindis.* I can leave work early."

"No, better at the museum. I have a, uh, a project to discuss with you."

"You won't rescue me from work?" He laughed. "Don't tell me you found a Velázquez in the attic? Ha."

She grimaced. "In a basement, actually." She tried to sound light-hearted. How many hidden paintings ended up at the Prado doorstep? She breathed slowly and tried to control her anxiety.

"Can you get security passes for me and my ..." She hesitated. "My Sevillaño friend?"

"What's your friend's name?"

"Antonio ... Gaspar Antonio de Olivares."

"You're joking, right? Relative of the Conde-Duque of Olivares?"

"Yes."

"*Sí. Sí.* My boring holiday just got interesting." Guillermo chuckled at his own comment.

CHAPTER 18

The Fiat chugged along in the predawn over La Mancha's sleepy plains toward Madrid. This journey propelled the two of them in the opposite direction from that train ride that brought them together toward the Prado and a moment of truth for *La Gloria*. Don Quixote's windmills waved at them as they passed the hills where Cervantes must have doubted himself, questioned whether his message to challenge the status quo would undo him. Velázquez passed this way too, traveling to become a royal painter, possibly full of doubts about whether he could impress the king.

She'd dialed Mom and Dad once Antonio drove onto the main highway and her phone had a connection. With the time difference they'd just gotten into bed on Christmas night.

"We've been waiting for your call."

"Merry Christmas! My phone connection didn't work. I'm still in Spain." It felt good to tell the truth, why not, she was working wherever she was. "I learned something in Seville. I need to finish the research in Madrid."

"Seville? We thought you were back in New York. We should know where you are." That exasperation, that desire to control and protect those they loved was something she once shared with Mom. Matty's death slapped her with the futility of it, but Mom hung on to the idea it was possible.

She shared some about the dinner at Olivares, but not much about Antonio, and promised she'd check in more often. They said goodbye with dejection in their voices. As Christmas calls went, this fell on the low end of the pathetic scale. She made a note to fix it, always trying to fix something, her failure at this, a reminder of why she fled to New York, the complicated muddle had not changed.

Time for her and the painting was running out, and rushing forward was the up-tempo music playing in her head. The stakes got bigger: the Prado, my God, the Prado, the cathedral of the Spanish Baroque. She reviewed the list of supportive documentation and it was short, missing too much. *La Gloria* was not ready.

"How about a detour to Toledo to have some lunch? There's a great parador in the same spot El Greco used to paint the city."

"Not really hungry."

"You're nervous."

"Nervous, yes nervous. I am rehearsing what I'll say. Is it enough? These art titans are about winning, about *who* is right, not *what* is true."

"Then win with what is true. You have compelling support. You brought the photo we printed of the frame, right?"

"Yes. Other puzzle parts are missing, especially provenance before the work came to Olivares. I don't have their experience. What if I'm wrong?" *A girl from a blue-collar family knocking on the door of the Prado.*

"Convince them you have enough cause for more study, right? We, both of us, must stand on top of our fears, fight those Quixote windmills."

"Ahhh what about . . . that theft thing. How do I explain it?" Even without the theft problem, she was way beyond her experience.

"In a few hours we will know something and immediately after that, you'll make it right with the university. But you know that." He smiled and squeezed her hand resting on top of the tube. Antonio turned off the freeway. "We need to stop for gas in Toledo anyway."

"Let's don't talk about the painting."

That was unfair. Antonio had been a friend and supporter in this crazy journey. He'd been so much help already.

He pulled up to the gas pump and she went inside to order food.

She found him sitting at a table, slid next to him, and handed him a wrapped ham and cheese *bocadillo.*

Antonio mumbled thanks and pulled out his wallet.

She stopped him. "You bought the gas. A sandwich—at least I can contribute that. I'm grateful for so many things—the apartment, the library, a wonderful Christmas. You've kept me going, with the photo, the frame, so much. Thank you."

He shrugged and smiled. They had not even discussed what troubled him, what weighed on his mind and distracted him from being in the moment with her.

She continued, "I've been selfish, getting you so involved in my project when you have challenges of your own. How can I help you?"

"We got through Christmas without the roof collapsing," he joked, and she tried to smile. "The distraction is welcome. All the public records institutions are closed, and nothing will happen until January."

"The estate's art may have value, money to keep things going. That little portrait might be by Velázquez, other things in your gallery look promising, and maybe we'll find a drawing or two in the library."

"Drawings by Velázquez?"

"Not likely. But by others perhaps."

Antonio slumped, his body deflating like a balloon losing air. He scrapped the crumbs from his sandwich onto the paper wrapping and folded it neatly.

She quickly added, "I know nothing is simple or quick. Your other paintings might not be by Velázquez, but his contemporaries are sought after too. Memorabilia, little notes, with or without sketches, have value. And the frame is valuable too."

He brightened up with a broad smile. She admired that about him and wished she was better at seeing the half-full part. "I will have photographs made of the portrait to make inquiries." He checked his watch. "Let's get going." He crumpled the sandwich wrappings and tossed them into the trash.

Madrid's skyscrapers appeared on the horizon and quickly the highway ended at the Atocha Train Station, near the Reina Sofia Museum of Contemporary Art where Picasso's *Guernica* had been installed. She shivered with goose bumps at the powerful art inside these buildings. The red bricks of the Prado, an art mecca of European masterworks, came into view between the trees and filled her with more anxiety. She'd risked so much and needed courage now to ask for a definitive answer, even though the response might not be the one she wanted.

Antonio U-turned into the porte cochere of the Ritz Hotel across the street from the Prado. He handed the keys to the valet. She'd protested the hotel was too expensive, but he shared his savvy student knowledge of surviving Madrid on a budget. A validation from the hotel's café would give them free parking for four hours. They could afford a three-euro coffee in the café. Antonio also arranged for them to use the apartment of a friend spending the holidays in Extremadura.

"I'll call my buddy Carlos for the keys while you meet with Guillermo."

"No. No, you need to come with me. Guillermo wants to meet you, and you talk about Olivares."

He reacted to her mini-outburst by hugging her. "If you need me, I will be there."

Those words meant what he could not know. No time for

coffee, they'd stamp the parking after the meeting. She carried the tube, he, the messenger bag with the daguerreotype, and they formed a parade, porters marching into the art jungle and its unknown dangers.

After fifteen minutes, the Spanish version of "on time," Guillermo appeared at the secure entrance door. "How are you, my beautiful friend?" He planted a kiss on each cheek and finished his greeting with a hug, and then hugged her again.

She turned toward Antonio, who looked perplexed at their reunion, and introduced them.

Antonio managed a smile as he fumbled with the tube she'd handed him to free a hand to shake Guillermo's. "Cate has told me how much she enjoyed her class with you."

Guillermo lowered his head. "Honored to meet you, Sir. Let us help you with that." An assistant handed Cate and Antonio security badges and asked to take the tube from Antonio.

Cate pinned her badge on the lapel of her black blazer, thanked the assistant, but she kept the tube.

Guillermo raised his hand. "Sorry, artwork requires a complex registration to enter the museum." He pointed to a door. "Let's go in this conference room outside the official museum, a meeting place with collectors and dealers who bring art to us. You can keep the tube." He motioned them to the open door.

Antonio looked confused. "So many people bring artwork that you need a special room?"

"They do. More with the bad economy, families selling their things for funds."

Antonio winced and looked at her.

Guillermo adjusted the lighting over the conference table. "Let's see what you've brought us."

Cate set the tube on the conference table and slid the wrapped canvas out of the tube and placed it next to the daguerreotype and the photo of the frame over the fireplace.

Guillermo picked up the photo first. "Beautiful carving. Is this frame from the Olivares' estate?"

Antonio answered, "Yes."

Guillermo's interest in the Olivares estate was not a surprise. Antonio said the press had written about his forgotten branch of the family tree because of the land dispute. Whether he wanted to keep his problems hidden or to push *La Gloria* forward she couldn't know, but he drew Guillermo's attention back to the painting. Antonio squeezed her hand as they stood against the back wall with the tube.

Guillermo walked up and down the table, leaning forward for a closer view. He was an erudite scholar, a brilliant teacher, a good friend and, most important, honest. His opinion mattered, and he would admit *La Gloria* to the next level of study—or not.

She couldn't breathe. She resisted jumping in to explain and promote what she thought about the work and instead remained silent to assure his opinions were pure and unfettered by her ramblings.

Finally, Guillermo stood erect and took a deep breath. "I was kidding, but you weren't."

"Kidding?" she asked.

"My joke about Velázquez."

"I didn't name Velázquez."

"I know *you* didn't." He winked at her and turned to Antonio. "Is this painting part of the duke's collection? Tell me the story, everything you know about the provenance."

Antonio answered, "No and nothing. Until Cate showed the painting to me, I'd never seen it."

At least Antonio didn't disclose the theft part; he made it clear she must be the one to do that. She weighed how much to share at this moment, hoping that Guillermo wouldn't pull away because of the shady way the painting arrived here. "It's complicated."

"These stories always are."

Better to wait, wait for the right moment. "We have tests from the Institute in Seville."

"I'll want to see those and see the painting under the infrared lamp."

"Infrared did show some pentimenti in certain areas."

"That rules out the work is some kind of copy."

Antonio asked, "How so?"

"Cate can explain." Guillermo, always the professor—let the student show what she knew—continued to study the brushstrokes in Gloria's dress with a loupe to his eye.

"A copyist or a forger doesn't change his mind. They replicate what is already painted."

Antonio winked at her.

Guillermo picked up the photograph of the frame.

"The canvas has been cut, hasn't it? Here at the top." Guillermo pointed to the legless body of a putto holding flowers at the canvas's top and then to the photo.

"Could be one of the missing Velázquez works? We have a list of historical references, but the matching works have not been found. It's unusual, maybe a later work like *Las Hilanderas*, an allegory perhaps." Guillermo sat down, a bit breathless, and looked at her. "Tell me your complicated story."

The words didn't come even though she'd practiced. The facts, start with the facts, her attorney coached. "I was doing an inventory for NYCU's art archives and found this canvas rolled in a sixteenth-century chest. The pigments, these quick brush strokes said it could be something, something attributable."

"What was listed on the NYCU inventory?"

"Nothing. It wasn't listed."

"Fascinating. So lost, forgotten, or . . . hidden."

Guillermo appeared to be asking rhetorical questions assuming she had no answers. And she didn't. "I wanted to know more, get it tested at the Institute in Seville."

"Good. So Jones sent you to Spain. Did Isabel give you a report? Say anything about Velázquez?"

She sidestepped the reference to Jones and talked about Isabel, a saga she had yet to tell Antonio. Her words chosen like footfalls in a minefield expecting either Antonio or Guillermo to explode at the information. "A draft report. Not the official report—holidays and all." The best she could come up with.

"I've brought it." She pulled out the draft from her bag and pointed to a specific line. "The fiber samples dated to the 1600s. The pigments are right. Some conflicts between different brushstrokes, but they might be conservation work."

"Good. I'll read it later." Guillermo again talked to himself, running through the list of things that might include or exclude the work from an attribution to the master, testing what his eyes were telling him, just as she had done.

"This is definitely exciting, but you understand all caution and also discretion must be employed. The Prado and all serious historians hold their powder until the target is clear. I'll pull the list of missing works. Some have crude or absent descriptions, but maybe something matches." Guillermo dialed the registrar's office on his cellphone and requested the list of referenced works. "We need to complete the registration." Guillermo rambled, appearing to organize in spite of the adrenaline rush they all were feeling.

Antonio spoke up. "The Prado keeps the painting?"

"We'll log it as a temporary loan and store it in a secure vault. The work is much too valuable to be carrying around Madrid in a tube. Seriously Cate!"

Antonio looked pleased that the painting convinced Guillermo enough to gain admittance to the sacred halls of the Prado. A woman came in the room and Guillermo introduced Mariana as the assistant registrar, and she handed Antonio a clipboard with forms. He pushed the forms toward Cate.

She picked up a pen, stopped at the first line, and looked at Guillermo. "The owner? The university is the owner, correct?"

It would be wrong, double wrong to lie to Guillermo and on the forms. Antonio nudged her with his foot under the table. She looked at him and saw his raised eyebrows. He mouthed the words, "Tell him." The secrets, the struggle against who she was and what she'd become, the liar, the thief, the person who'd put *La Gloria* first, needed to end, end now.

"Can we talk privately? Off the record?" She raised her eyebrows and tilted her head toward Mariana.

The assistant registrar left and Guillermo turned to Cate. "What's the mystery?"

She inhaled a big breath of the conference room's stale air and began to unravel the tale, layer by layer, highlighting the fluke find of *La Gloria* in the chest, the absence of an inventory reference, and what she referred to as the "accidental removal" of the painting from NYCU.

Antonio shifted his position in his chair and scowled.

She continued with version-lite of the Jones chapter, no reason to besmirch her mentor, and by extension, herself, but a defense of the egomaniacal professor challenged her creative explaining skills. She emphasized faculty leaving for the holidays, meeting university deadlines for dissertation topics, and making good use of her fortuitous planned trip to Spain.

Guillermo rubbed his chin and leaned back in his chair. He studied the soundproofing tiles on the ceiling and sighed. "Good you stopped the registration. Hard to undo a museum record in this place owned by the Spanish government. If NYCU doesn't know you took a work that likely belongs to them, misrepresenting the work to the Prado creates another, shall we say, deception, a criminal act."

Antonio sat up straight, his hands folded, all lawyerly. "She stipulated to the facts. No one is trying to deceive anyone."

"I don't want trouble for you, Guillermo. I believe this can be fixed."

Guillermo shook his head. "That remains to be seen. You took this work across international borders without permission, out of the university without paperwork." He scrunched up his brow, waiting for a response.

"What should we, *I* do?"

Guillermo scooped up the forms. "Let's set these aside. I'll keep the painting in the Prado, where it's safe. Yes, I'm sure Cuevas . . ." He looked at Antonio. "He is the Velázquez expert, one of the best, and will want to see this."

Guilt pangs hit her, as her mistakes drew in Antonio and now, Guillermo. "Maybe Cuevas would contact Jones and . . ." She stopped. They were rivals, famously so, a competition that made audiences nervous when they were on the same stage.

"Not likely. Cuevas and Jones don't speak. Never agree. Velázquez's 'Attributed to . . .' list. If Jones gives a nod to a painting, Cuevas will disagree. If Cuevas is convinced by another work, Jones will shoot it down."

"That's strange. With new scientific evidence, isn't it possible to have more agreement?" Antonio asked.

She knew the answer: It wasn't about getting it right; it was about who got the credit. She stayed silent.

Guillermo looked at Antonio and leaned over as though he was confiding in him. "These egos are *grande*. That's why Cate didn't show the painting to Jones. Jones didn't discover the work and wouldn't support your initial impressions. Am I right, Cate?"

She nodded, speechless to hide how her stress level was on the moon to be in the middle of this. Cuevas could be her ally, but Jones would punish her to retaliate against Cuevas.

Antonio hesitated and then asked, "What if we rebooted? What if Cate returned to NYCU, showed the painting to Jones, and retraced her steps to the Prado? We are the only ones who've seen it."

Guillermo shook his head. "Did you see the look on Mariana's face? She's probably spreading the word to her colleagues right now. Uncovering a lost masterpiece is a news-exploding event in Spain."

"Word of mouth travels faster than the Internet. Antonio is right though. Maybe we draw Jones back in and let him take credit, and then let Cuevas see it independently."

No one responded. Her contribution to this find might be lost, a price to be paid to move forward. If she had to lose recognition so *La Gloria* could shine, she'd do it.

"The director's gone, so we don't need to involve him." Guillermo paused and had the look of a man about to make a grave decision. "I can contact Jones and hopefully he is available. You decide Cate."

She took a deep breath. Either she stood up or she folded and crawled away. The only way to avoid a catastrophe of being found out, crashing to the bottom of the cliff, was to find wings and fly across the chasm.

"Guillermo tells Jones you met with an Olivares relative and learned of some significant material. All true. Ask if he can come. You want his opinion before the work is out in the art gossip circles." Was she doing it again, hiding all the facts?

"What happens when he learns you stole the painting? He'll go crazy. He's not an easy man. Of the big egos, he is the biggest," Guillermo said.

"Not stolen . . . accidentally removed," Antonio objected.

Jones had this megalomaniac personality, delusions that he knew and controlled everything. That she'd done this behind his back, for whatever good reasons, would come back to bite her. "I'll tell Jones the truth, all of it. But I want to do it in person." She took a deep breath. "I'll pick him up at the airport and tell him."

"I'll go with you." Antonio the attorney would represent her at the deposition. Nudging not nagging. And patient. Oh yes, patient.

"I need to do this alone."

Antonio smiled, maybe a sign of pride, and nodded in agreement.

Guillermo interrupted. "Cuevas? The Prado Spanish paintings expert."

Antonio slid to the front of his chair. "Don't mention Cuevas until Jones arrives and sees the work. Then call Cuevas and urge him as the Prado's expert to view the work."

Guillermo put his hands over his face and moved his fingers through his hair, a nervous tell. "It might work. We can use their competitiveness to our advantage. Cuevas is gone for the holidays. Can we get Jones here this week?"

Guillermo had just dropped into the abyss with Antonio and her. She clung to them even as they fell into the depths together.

CHAPTER 19

*A*ntonio's clunker jerked when she shifted the gears, something she had not done since driver's ed in high school. The car had to make it to Barajas airport or she'd be late to meet Jones. Sweat from her palms left marks on the steering wheel in spite of the chilly wind that came through a crack in the back window. She turned on the radio for a distraction and her heart raced to the tempo of the music, nothing soothing there. Now it was borderline panic. She turned the radio off.

Guillermo reported that Jones had planned to visit his mother in Madrid over the holidays and could come to the Prado. That was unexpected for all of them, maybe a bit of good fortune. Jones certainly wouldn't expect she'd be waiting at the airport. Surprises all around.

She and Antonio had spent the night in Carlos's apartment, huddled together more from the freezing temperature and exhaustion than romance. Antonio recognized the stress this was for her, remained respectful, maybe too much so. They both had personal mountains to climb before they could consider anything else.

Antonio had reached Carlos finally. He was not in Extremadura, but on the Costa Brava. Antonio went to spend the morning searching archives at the National Library.

Meeting Jones would be awkward—no, a stronger word, difficult, problematic, humiliating—all words that fit. When she was in trouble as a girl, she'd always bring a friend home. Mom would never scold her in front of someone else, nope she'd hold off the fireworks until the friend left. The "bring a friend" defense was only a postponement of the consequences and she needed to face up to Jones's wrath alone, here in this beat-up Fiat.

A traffic circle with cars switching lanes would swirl the Fiat into its confusion just ahead. The elegant Madrid boulevards provided a respite from city traffic, but the beautiful paseos ended in terror. She took another lap around the circle, searching for an opening to exit. A car edged between a bus and a mini-truck, which swerved and cut her off. She laid on the horn and gasped, then coughed an inhale of diesel fuel. By some miracle, the traffic cleared and she broke onto Calle Serrano heading toward the airport.

Another circle, the more complicated one, went around in her head: how to tell Jones. She searched for the opening. What would he say when she greeted him? Maybe break the ice with how she'd taken the initiative and advanced knowledge as he'd suggested. This great find could increase the prestige of NYCU, his program, his reputation. If that conversation didn't go well, she'd ask if he got the phone message she'd left with Noemi, knowing of course he wouldn't have. That would be more deception and only lead to the outcomes she feared most.

She could be extradited to the US or exiled from Spain. Lots of famous company like Goya exiled to France, the Count-Duke exiled from the royal palace.

And there was Antonio. He hadn't invited her to remain at Olivares after Christmas; they hadn't discussed what she'd do after Madrid. He'd need to go back eventually and she'd . . . well she couldn't live with Carlos. Everything was happening so fast.

She didn't fit into the art world either. Her Michigan homeland seemed as foreign as Olivares. Self-pity was not an attitude that went anywhere good. No, she'd fake being a serious professional with the hope Jones would listen like a colleague and have a civil conversation.

The airport came into view and her heart beat faster, now went to serious hyperventilation. She downshifted and rolled into the lane for parking. The roar of the planes overhead sounded like a war zone.

Five minutes until Jones's plane touched down on the tarmac. It would take him another fifteen to walk through Madrid's Richard Rogers designed airport, longest airport walk in Europe. At least, the car had made it without leaving her and Jones stranded.

She sat at a small table near the international arrivals gate and ordered a coffee. How would another doctoral candidate, her classmate Leonard, for example, tell Jones about the painting? Leonard had personal capital, had endeared himself as the sycophantic golden boy from a wealthy family. He'd have brought the work to Jones immediately. Jones would pat him on the back and they'd make a plan for serious study. The two would work happily on a paper together and Leonard would be offered an assistant professorship at one of the universities where a Jones disciple taught. That's how Leonard's story would go.

She was not Leonard and would need to do it her way, Midwest, straight up. The truth, all of it, Antonio had urged.

No, no. Terrible idea. He'd dismiss the painting because it was *her* project, *her* attribution, *her* eye. He could erupt in a rage that she was irresponsible, that he wasn't consulted. Everything throbbed, the top of her head about to explode, fueled by the fourth espresso of the day. She stood, dizzy, legs wobbling and placed her palms on her temples to hold her head together.

Drivers and tour guides, all men, dressed in dark suits, waited with signs naming various passengers. She had no sign. What would it say? "Professor Jones, I can explain."

Jones. Oh shit. He exited the elevator from the baggage area and scanned the men holding signs, looking past her even as she stood out in her camel coat.

"Professor Jones," she whispered as he walked right past her. Louder, she called after him, "Excuse me. Professor Jones."

The drivers turned their heads and so did everyone, and then finally he stopped. "Miss Adamson! What are you doing here?"

"I'm your driver."

He winced. Yeah. He did, furled his lip in a scowl.

She had to begin somewhere. "Remember I came to Madrid for research. You signed the introduction letter for the Prado archives? And well yes, there's a bigger story. . . ."

"I am sure there is." If he hadn't had luggage in his hands, he would have folded his arms over his chest in his renowned I'm-hearing-but-not-listening mode.

"I'm parked . . . not far."

They walked without speaking. He loaded the carry-on into the trunk, fastened his seat belt, and dusted off the dashboard. "Your Spanish boyfriend's car?"

"Borrowed the car, yes. The Prado wanted me to come since I would recognize you."

"Really, Miss Adamson. My photograph is on the flyleaf of a dozen books. I've given conferences, lead panels at the Prado. All museum staffers would recognize me. Get on with the *story.*"

"I had planned a few days during the holidays to come here to work on my dissertation topic." *Sort of true. Oh well.*

"Continue."

She shifted the gears with a jerk and looked straight ahead, knowing without looking he was doing that twirl thing with his finger.

"During the inventory, I found something in a storeroom." She spit out the words, increasing the pace.

"Continue." His voice was oddly calm.

"A canvas. It could be significant. I wanted to verify a few things, gather more information before I brought it to you."

He interrupted. "Is this the same canvas the Prado has, the one Guillermo called about?"

He had to know the answer; it wasn't a big leap.

She gulped.

"I hope you are not planning to tell this saga in mini-bytes, dangling me on the edge of my seat, such as it is." He brushed dust off the side of his trousers. "I've flown an exhausting three thousand miles and I don't want to beg you for installments. Out with it. What is this canvas?"

"I found the work in the basement of Hamilton, like I said." She was blithering. "A canvas rolled in a chest behind file boxes." She swallowed. "It wasn't on the inventory."

"You said that already."

"I brought it . . . to Spain. To Seville." She spit out the words now in a jumbled staccato.

"Astonishing." He shook his head. "Who does such a thing? I'm three floors above the basement and you make me fly for eight hours instead of riding the elevator and walking down the hall for eight minutes to show me this same work."

Her grip on the steering wheel tightened, her knuckles white. She'd soon hit the traffic circles of Madrid. Visibility diminished as the windshield fogged up, from either him huffing hot air against the cold window or heat from her stress or both.

"Please hold on a minute." She had to concentrate on the traffic circles just ahead. The little Fiat propelled them off the highway and jerked to stop at a red light. She turned to face him and he scrutinized her. His forehead drew together in those vertical crevices between his eyes.

She looked away. "Ah, well, I'd tried to show you, but—"

"You're running out of time, and I might add, road. If you intend to tell me something before the Prado team surrounds us, get on with it."

The light turned green and she struggled to release the clutch to move into the traffic circle, praying a Moses would part the cars so she could emerge from the Alcála Gate onto Calle Alfonso XII. A harrowing cluster of cars squeezed her out and made her think perhaps she'd die before Jones had a chance to kill her.

Jones gripped the door handle and the edge of the console, bracing for impact. "Better talk fast."

"First, I took the painting to Murphy's humidifier." Maybe she'd get credit for using proper curatorial standards. "The rolled canvas had hardened and was too stiff to unroll."

A dash between two cars took her to outside of the circle. Barely. "And then . . ."

A car blew a horn at her maneuver to change lanes.

Jones gripped the worn handle above the window and interrupted, "I changed my mind. To avoid certain death, save your story."

She nodded, grateful for Madrid's crazy traffic.

CHAPTER 20

*J*ones checked in at the reception desk. He and his luggage disappeared with the bellman into the elevator. She waited on a banquette and admired the Ritz's furnishings while the waiter got her coffee, another coffee. Her leg shook and coffee spilled into the tiny saucer when she lifted it, her hands still shaking from the prolonged agony of getting the story out. Now half-told. Waiting was worse than the telling.

The shock she'd expected from him didn't happen, and that surprised her more. He'd heard that she took a work from the basement and no big reaction, no outrage. Perhaps it was the painting the police were searching for. But that didn't seem right either.

She took in the heavenly smell of the star lilies in a large urn and checked her watch. "Excuse me, what time do you have?"

A cute waiter smiled. "It's too early for you to be late, Señorita."

She laughed, like letting air out of a balloon.

Jones surprised her from the other direction. "Miss Adamson." He pulled up a chair, faced the banquette, and set down his briefcase bulging with his latest projects, probably his new book at the ready to autograph for the Prado curators. The table served as a barrier similar to his office desk, separating him from her.

"I ordered you a coffee. But if you want something different . . ." She stammered and tried to slow down, but this was unchartered territory.

"Coffee's fine. Thank you." He flipped out his napkin with a whipping sound and smoothed it over his lap.

Civility. Maybe. She'd never sat down with him like this, socializing like they were colleagues or even friends.

"Before another interruption intrudes, finish the story. Where is this painting now?"

No turning back. She had this, the grit to do this. "The Prado. With Guillermo."

"You turned it over to . . . to the Prado? The property of NYCU." The tone-o-meter jumped past the annoyed status and reached borderline angry.

"No. Not turned over. It's in a limbo state, not registered, waiting for you."

He came off boiling to simmering. She placed her fists firmly on the cushion and pushed her spine up to its tallest. The differential in height between his chair and the banquette gave her four inches over him. He'd lost a lot of hair in the middle of his head, making him look like the friar in *The Canterbury Tales.*

"I found the painting when I did the inventory."

"You reported the inventory was complete."

"I said all items listed on the inventory were accounted for. This work was not listed. I'd hoped to share it with you, but well you, you . . ." She wanted to scream at him, to confront him about his arrogance, his rudeness, his differential treatment of her, of women. Breathe. Breathe, again. When she came off her invisible outrage, she shook her head. No defense of what she'd done. "I am aware I violated more than a few university policies."

"Well at least in that, you are correct." He leaned forward, not talking, waiting, and then leaned back to fold his arms in a resistant pose. The noise of waiters clearing tables and low whispers of other patrons filled the silence between them. Finally, he spoke in a cold voice, "Yes, you had an artwork; you said it was a poster. A lie?" He said it like a question. "Why didn't you show it to me?"

She stiffened her arms downward pushing on her hands and

took advantage of every inch of height, looking a bit down on his balding head. "I was rattled by our discussions and frustrated at your rejections of my dissertation topics. I can't undo that I took it out of the university. The reasons don't matter." She looked beyond his shoulder and pretended to study the brocade on the wall.

"The reasons matter, you can be sure." He unfolded his arms. "Go on."

"I wanted to study the painting seriously, but before I showed you, I needed support to make the case." *Say it, just say it.* "I feared you would dismiss the painting like you dismiss me."

He ignored her admission, another dismissal like the ones she'd just found the courage to accuse him of. His hand shook and the cup rattled, maybe a tell, the sign that her message got through to him. "What did you see?"

"Craquelure, hand-ground pigments, aquamarine and carmine. I wanted to know more, develop the case to establish the work could be something important." She waited for the reaction, eruption or erudite conversation.

Lava bubbled but did not flow. He gritted his teeth. "You did it for the painting?"

"Yes. For the painting. To give it a chance." The calm of her tone surprised her.

"And the image? What is the subject?"

"Not a bodegon, not religious. Maybe an allegory. Not a royal portrait, but royalty appears. Maybe Felipe IV."

"Surely not. Those royal commissions are known and documented."

"Look at the figure when you see it. The subject is different from most of his works."

"His? Whose?"

"Sorry. I'd rather not say until you evaluate it."

He laughed, a weird diabolical scoff. "Seriously Ms. Adamson, you can't be concerned I'd be influenced by your attribution."

She gulped.

"Review the details of where you found it."

"An antique chest in the storeroom, out of place, with file boxes under the stairs. Checked inside and saw a stiff canvas, couldn't be unrolled without risking damage. I wanted a good look before . . ." She paused, tried to slow the staccato sentences. ". . . I wasted your time. Could have been nothing, a minor work, a copy."

"Continue."

"When I saw the painting, spread out in proper lighting, I thought, *this is attributable*. This work deserves an identity better than school of someone."

She gained control over her blithering and proceeded with her preliminary evaluation. "With technical tests, composition and stylistic studies, we might be able to put an artist's name to this work. I brought it to your office and if you agreed, I'd write a grant proposal to fund research."

He did that thing, turning his finger in the air again, sign language for impatience.

Another breath. "If you rejected my ideas about the work, any proposal to study it would be dead. You'd rejected so much I'd brought you. That day was no different." She looked right at him, searching his blue eyes for a bit of humanity.

He plucked fuzz from his sleeve, more interested in lint than what she was saying. "I see." He lifted his tortoiseshell glasses to the top of his forehead and rubbed his eyes.

He was tired and probably not his best. If there was a best, she hadn't seen it.

"I tried to return it, but the building closed down. I found money on my own, credit cards, loans, cashed in retirement funds, and brought the canvas to Spain for tests."

The commitment, her sacrifice didn't impress him. "Do tell Miss Adamson, what was the Prado's response?"

She should have brought the Institute's report. "The Institute of Seville confirms it's a seventeenth-century work. Their draft report is at the Prado."

"Brilliant. Isabel's analysis covers several hundred artists. Who do you suggest painted it?"

The name Isabel made her cringe, and she thought it strange he didn't react to the news she'd already been to the Institute, nor ask about how they'd registered the work, how she presented the provenance, ordered and paid for tests. "The brushstrokes revealed a pattern. The Prado curators have some thoughts. Certainly it's the Golden Age, XVII century."

He took his glasses off his head and placed them on the table. "I understand and respect your reluctance to say a name." He checked his watch. "I avoid attributions, I told you that. Unless an institution requires it as the Prado will."

A deafening pause. She didn't dare roll *her* finger in the air.

"NYCU owns this painting. That reduces the problem about valuation." He inspected his glasses and pulled out a special cloth to clean them. "Has Cuevas seen it?"

"Not yet. We insisted you see it first." A small lie wouldn't hurt since that was what would occur.

"Appropriate, since it belongs to the university and you had the opportunity to show it to me last week. In my own office."

"I regret that I did not." She looked down at her lap.

He set his cup down and stared at her. "Perhaps I was too harsh with you that day, and in general."

An apology? Really? She was speechless.

"I hope there's a compelling argument for the painting. Improbable that it is important. Apparently you convinced the Prado's junior staff to set this in motion and now we shall see."

"There's more. A daguerreotype from the nineteenth century shows the work."

"Impressive." His subtle change from sarcastic to sincere suggested a glimmer of encouragement.

"Also a frame, the frame that held the canvas in the photo. The frame and the daguerreotype were discovered at the duke's estate in Olivares."

He put his glasses back on. "Olivares? The Olivares Library? The old duke, well duke-pretender, refused me access, didn't trust academics."

"The current duke, or at least the relative of the other ancestral line, is at the Prado waiting to meet you."

"You are full of surprises. Let's go see this masterpiece." He drank the last sip of coffee, stood, pulled the table out for her to stand, and helped her with her coat. They waited for the light to cross Calle Felipe IV, named for Velázquez's patron and the figure she'd speculated was the king in *La Gloria*.

"Before we enter the museum, have you discussed possible artists with Prado curators?"

"Guillermo speculated and I have an idea." A confidence rose in her with the sun's warmth on this winter day and that the worst of the story was out.

"Still not saying? Perhaps you've learned something after all."

He smiled, or was it an unintended smirk?

The conference room empty, they waited in silence except for her foot that wouldn't stop tapping. Guillermo entered with the deputy registrar.

"Professor Jones, thank you for coming, especially over the holiday. We are fortunate you were planning to visit Madrid." They shook hands. No hugs, like Spanish men.

"Where is Director Navarro?"

"He sends regards from Switzerland. We thought it best to alert you when the museum became aware the painting belonged to the university."

Jones nodded.

She looked at her feet, grateful that Guillermo didn't go into the details of the caper. She'd had no time or privacy to let him or Antonio know that she'd told Jones everything. Well, not the bit about Isabel. That she would deal with later.

Guillermo continued, "Our registrar needs you to sign the paperwork for the Prado's records. It's for an assessment."

"I'll initial as a temporary authorization. I don't have the sole authority to lend university property." He gave her that look. "Miss Adamson will follow up."

That's good news. He wasn't throwing her out of the university. Still, she could only stay at NYCU with satisfactory dissertation progress.

"Has Cuevas seen it?" He repeated the question she'd already answered for him.

"He has not. He is coming from Zaragoza where he and his family celebrated Christmas."

Maybe Jones would start to trust her now, if Guillermo and she were on same page.

"Well then, let's have a look at the main show, this painting I've heard about."

They made their way through a rabbit warren of hallways to the conservation department. The large room was empty except for one technician in a white lab coat and the registrar who took a seat at a desk against the wall. The bright lights focused on a metal table covered with a cloth.

Antonio entered the room from a different door.

Guillermo greeted him, also with a handshake. "Count-Duke Gaspar Antonio de Olivares, please meet Professor Herant Jones from New York City University."

Jones bowed his head and offered his hand to Antonio. "Honored to meet you, sir."

Antonio brushed off the greeting. Whether it was because he was not considered the legitimate duke or maybe because he was a modern, humble person, she couldn't tell. Situations like these were foreign to her. But Antonio was here, as promised, and she was glad of it.

Guillermo nodded to the registrar and lab technician, and together they removed the covering. The two stepped back from the table behind Jones and Antonio stood next to her.

The painting laid out like a naked body for an autopsy. Jones stood back, walked around the table, leaned closer, and pulled a loupe from his pocket. He examined the pigment and brushstrokes with his nose nearly on the work.

No one spoke nor breathed. The clock on the wall clicked louder with each minute.

Jones's footsteps interrupted the silence, clicking on the tile floor as he circled the table. Then he asked the staff to hold the painting upright as the artist might have painted it. He took a few steps back as far as he could to study the whole of it.

Wrinkles on his brow distracted her as she tried to catch a glimpse of his eyes, guess at what he was thinking. He rocked back and forth, moved in close and out again.

Jones finally turned and faced them. "Of course, more studies will be needed; the new radiography could tell us more. At some point, I'd like to look at the documentation from the Olivares Library."

Antonio stared at Jones, maybe also trying to decipher his reaction. Guillermo shrugged and made a motion for the registrar and lab assistant to return the painting to the table and leave.

Jones took a handkerchief from his jacket, wiped his glasses, and returned the handkerchief and the loupe to his pocket. He stretched out his hand toward her.

Surprised by the gesture, she stood there for a long moment and then took it in her trembling hand.

"Congratulations. You have found a dissertation topic," Jones said.

She nodded like a bobble head shaking and shaking his hand. She looked at Antonio, who displayed a broad grin of victory.

Guillermo picked up the forms. "Owner's name?"

"NYCU, of course. List it as Unknown, Spanish, c. XVII."

Her heart dropped, but what could she expect? It wasn't realistic to declare an artist's name, not yet, especially on an official form.

"The loan will be seven days. Enough time to organize the shipping and insurance back to New York."

Guillermo had a stunned expression like he'd been hit in the stomach. She felt it too. Guillermo recovered enough to ask, "Professor Jones, are you taking the painting back to New York?"

"Of course."

She looked at Guillermo, hoping he would say something she could not.

He argued in the most tentative terms, "Please sir, consider leaving it here. We can provide space for Cate, Miss Adamson, to work. The Prado has excellent resources to study a painting like this, including our reference library. The list of lost works is here."

She trembled, waiting for a Jonesian eruption, prideful and dismissive. Antonio looked at the ceiling, probably wishing he could disappear.

Jones harrumphed and straightened his bow tie. "We have substantial resources in New York City, the University's Art Institute, the Frick, the Met. Accessible and well-catalogued, I might add." Jones denounced the disorganization of centuries of undocumented material in Spain, tantalizing in the possibilities, but frustrating for researchers.

Guillermo motioned with his eyes for her to say something. She did not have the repertoire to intervene like she might have in an argument between her parents. She played with the fringe on her pashmina scarf. Her vulnerability on the theft and more did not allow her an opinion on where the painting should be studied.

Guillermo stepped up. "With all respect, sir, I hope you will wait until Professor Cuevas arrives to view the work. He should be here soon."

Jones paused for a moment, possibly disturbed at the mention of Cuevas. He cleared his throat and said, "My return flight is in three days. I can't see the harm in waiting. I do have one condition."

"Please tell us."

Guillermo was brilliant in working Jones. She listened to his careful choice of words and learned things that could not be learned in Ypsilanti. The value of negotiating through others, while remaining silent, something Dad never taught.

Jones leaned over the painting and without looking up, said, "My requirement is this: Do not mention to Cuevas that I have seen it or that I have an opinion about this painting. I have not stated an opinion, have I?"

They all shook their heads together like terrified school children hoping to get the answer right.

"Do not mention that it belongs to NYCU."

Guillermo's grin revealed his agreement. "As you wish, professor."

"I am tired from the trip and will be at the Ritz Hotel if you need me."

When they were back in the conference room, they congratulated each other and planned to go out for celebratory drinks if the Cuevas meeting went well. Antonio and Guillermo joined her in a relief hug that there would be at least a few more days in Madrid to move the attribution forward. Antonio winked at her, making her guess at what he might have done if Guillermo was not with them.

The shock, the anger she'd expected from Jones appeared and dissipated in minutes. He was irascible, but scholarly and even collaborative. One minute trying to get her, the painting, and himself back to New York and then in a second, being reasonable letting Cuevas have an independent viewing.

With Jones, there were always layers. There'd be time for answers before Jones might return the painting to the basement. But Gloria disappearing was not possible, not now that the world knew about her. She glowed.

CHAPTER 21

*T*hey walked side-by-side in pursuit of coffee until they tumbled into a bar known only by the street corner. Antonio looked exhausted. She was too, after a night sleeping on Carlos's couch, not that a better bed would have mattered. The windows of the bar/café had steamed up and it wasn't possible to see outside, but the Prado was somewhere in the fog across the street.

Guillermo stood at the bar. "Good morning. Bloody cold today."

She gave Guillermo an extra hug, a spontaneous gesture in gratitude for the amazing distance they'd come in a few days and they congratulated each other.

Guillermo gulped his café con leche. "Cuevas arrives on the nine o'clock train."

Careful steps were needed to not undo what they had accomplished. "When Cuevas sees the painting, I can't be there. Too many questions."

"Agreed. I won't comment about how the painting came to the Prado if I can avoid it. Also no mention of NYCU, Jones's requirement." Guillermo ordered another coffee to go and continued, "Let's hope Cuevas sees what we see and proposes additional studies. I'll text you when it's time to come." He raised his to-go cup in a toast to the day.

Nerves prevented her from saying anything.

Guillermo picked up his coat and put it on. "Antonio, will you return with Cate? Cuevas wishes to meet you and ask you about the photo."

Antonio smiled in a tired kind of way. "I'll do whatever to help Cate."

That brought a broad grin to her face. Did Guillermo know they were more than friends? She tried to be professional in his presence, but he was perceptive.

Guillermo paid the bill with two coins in the dish and made his way through the crowded space to the door. Cold air blasted the room until the door closed behind him.

Antonio leaned over close to her ear. "Did he seem nervous?"

"He has a lot on the line too—he sent out the urgent call, brought Jones to the Prado without consulting the director, interrupted the holidays for Cuevas—world's best expert on Velázquez. But don't say that to Jones."

"I'll trust you to deal with them." Antonio brushed the hair from her eyes. "I need to track down documents at the National Library. The librarian of the royal collection might have time to assist me since the library is empty this week. You don't mind?"

"No. Definitely go. I'll be at the Ritz reading articles, a good distraction."

Antonio pulled her behind a tile-covered pillar. His lips touched her forehead and then he kissed her. His strong embrace lifted the stress she felt, and her shoulders seemed lighter. "Whatever happens to *La Gloria*, we found each other and in that she's created a masterpiece of us."

She laughed and kissed him again. She pulled her coat tight as he got into a taxi and zipped it up to sprint to the warmth of the hotel. The wind howled across the plaza and even the water in the Neptune fountain shuddered. The hotel provided a welcome refuge.

The table where she and Jones had sat yesterday was available and provided privacy for work. Privacy didn't matter in the end, because she couldn't concentrate and closed her computer. Even Jones's support added to her worries. Something troubled her about his reactions and what he wanted to know and what he didn't. He never asked about the Institute or their report, but maybe he wanted to, as he'd always taught, use his expert eye before he saw analyses. He changed his demeanor in front of his colleagues and Antonio, but maybe that's not unusual. People do that; she was different here too.

If Cuevas, uninfluenced by Jones or anyone else, had a different artist in mind, it was game over. Well maybe not. Another artist could still be worthy of study. *Stop speculating.* She reopened the computer to articles on conservation.

"Here we are again, Miss Adamson." Jones stood over the table.

"Good morning. You're up early for having just arrived from New York."

Jones shook his head. "The best jet lag strategy is to adopt the local time zone immediately. May I join you?"

"Sure, I don't mind. Of course." She stammered as she moved her messenger bag to the floor so he could sit next to her on the banquette.

"What are you reading?"

"An article about Raman spectroscopy."

"I have no idea what that is."

She wasn't sure if he wanted to know but answered him anyway. "Spectroscopy is measurement of wavelengths emitted from various substances to determine their exact composition. Like varnishes. Maybe connect the varnish on the NYCU work to known works by . . ." She paused, waiting for his reaction.

He ordered sherry from the waiter, an odd choice with his time zone adjustment to Spanish morning.

"Getting Cuevas on board, in spite of his flawed scholarship, is the path to the Prado's endorsement. Scientific tests can't do that."

"Endorsement? Do you think we have enough for a definitive attribution?"

"The painting is the work of Velázquez, of course. More studies, scientific and historical, will add necessary footnotes to justify and support the attribution. But connoisseurship commands attribution."

Wow. She hung on the name he'd just put into the universe. That name, the one she'd speculated about from the first, had just become official. This time she welcomed Jones's self-congratulatory arrogance.

"You look surprised."

Surprised? Relieved, grateful, hopeful. All of those.

He didn't wait for a response. "The style is his alone."

She paused to select her words with care. "I'd hoped, but did not presume." She would not have dared to predict this. "Yes, more study is needed, but I'd hoped that you and Cuevas would see the connection to his other late compositions." She had to stop blithering, find her confidence.

He didn't give her a chance to say more. "Your work—you have been impertinent and reckless. How you have handled this matter is a near scandal. I don't fault you for thoroughly researching before asking my opinion. But seriously, Miss Adamson, fleeing to Spain, the Institute, the Prado? With a stolen artwork? Most students would have gone to the libraries at the Met or the Frick."

The contradictions, a scolding, and a hallelujah left her confused: be contrite, apologize, express thanks, or change the subject? She searched her mind madly for the appropriate reply and didn't find one.

Again, he didn't wait for her reaction. "Still a work opportunity at the Prado presents you with a new start, and I am impressed with your resourcefulness. In the end, however bumbling, you've done well to see the qualities that make this painting a masterwork. I am pleased one of my students is doing research at the Prado, a proud moment for the program."

She mumbled a combination of sorry and thank you. This turnaround, so swift after those outrageous things she'd done, left her pondering his intentions.

"After decades of studying Velázquez, looking at thousands of Spanish paintings from the seventeenth century, one distinguishes, sees finite differences, nuances. Things that no lab test or computer can see. This is our talent, our art."

"What would support a definitive attribution?"

"Cuevas matters." He paused. "Beyond his agreement, reference to the painting's provenance from a contemporary, correspondence about the original commission, an old inventory of important collections, a description in a letter or a diary connecting it to Velázquez."

"I'm searching all the library collections, including the Olivares Library."

Jones had a wistful look, or maybe it was jealousy, she wasn't certain.

She needed to ask him about the university's warning letter and where she stood. "What about my dissertation? I could polish an outline by the end of the week about a study of this painting. Before the academic deadline on January 15."

"I'll review your proposal and add to it. The study of an unknown Baroque work should be publishable in an important art journal. Colleagues who serve with me on editorial boards can expedite the publication if I am the author. Would you like to work together, a co-authorship for you, of course?"

Agree? She wanted to look in the restaurant mirror to see if she'd turned into Leonard or one of his Ivy League darlings. "Co-author? Yes, yes."

Jones continued, "Not for myself, you understand. I can edit and so on. But my name will get your work published faster, jump you to the head of the queue."

"I'd be honored." She couldn't wait to tell Antonio. Her thoughts turned to Dad, who would pretend to be unimpressed, but he'd show his daughter's name in print to everyone who'd listen, even if he never read the article.

Jones continued, "We haven't spoken of your plans after you receive your doctorate, but we need to be working on a good position for you."

Everything was moving fast. Maybe too fast. She had been so focused on the dissertation problem, she hadn't had time to think about what came next. And now there was Antonio to consider, or maybe not. They were still so new and needed time together.

"I would prefer, if possible, to be at the Prado, close to the art resources and other works. Antonio, the Duke, has offered me access to the Olivares Library, which might yield undiscovered seventeenth-century references." Together in Olivares doing the work she loved with him, made her smile. Solitary accomplishments lacked joy unless another who dreamed with you took pride in those same achievements.

"Tell me more about Antonio and how you came to know him."

She told him about the train, Christmas, and the treasures she'd only begun to study at the library.

He listened with his arms folded and then turned to her. "You lead a charmed life, Ms. Adamson. Perhaps we can arrange a visit for me as well. Why not draft a grant proposal to catalogue the collection?" he asked.

"When he joins us at the Prado, we can talk about a grant, maybe the Prado has funds."

He smiled. That was twice. Two smiles. This collaborative, collegial, gracious, and completely unrecognizable person had transformed into a mentor.

"I have little influence over positions at the Prado. Cuevas's opinion is everything, the director will follow him."

Her phone buzzed and she showed him the text from Guillermo and said, "We're about to find out what Cuevas thinks." She forwarded the text to Antonio and asked him to come to the Prado.

Jones looked at his watch. "Not even an hour. That was fast, even for Cuevas."

"Maybe too fast." Easier to reject the work than support an attribution.

She power walked to the Prado and Jones tried to keep up and control his tie flapping in the breeze. They entered the staff side of the main lobby together after fetching their security badges at the guard's desk. Guillermo greeted them as they entered the conservation lab where Cuevas was chatting with the registrar staff.

Doctor Pablo Cuevas was a rotund fellow with a mustache that looked like Salvador Dali's. His countenance did not contradict his reputation as a character. "Jones! Why am I not surprised? You sniffed out this recent discovery." Cuevas didn't bother with the traditional Spanish greeting, didn't even offer a hand. "Why are you here? How are you here?"

"How kind of you to welcome me, Pablo. I came to visit my mother for the holidays. Guillermo phoned and asked me to look at something. I suppose this canvas." He shook Pablo's hand and gestured at the table.

"And who is this?" Cuevas looked at her.

Guillermo presented her as Jones's student. Cuevas greeted her but otherwise ignored the introduction.

"Well what do you think, Pablo?"

"Why should I tell you? I might influence you."

Jones let out that sardonic laugh that made her shudder. "Influence me? Seriously. I'll learn anyway Pablo." Her professor wasn't a bad actor.

Cuevas cleared his throat and kept them all waiting. "Velázquez. Indisputable. No one painted like this at that time. The brushstrokes tell the story and there are other stylistic fingerprints." He cleared his throat. "Tests will be done for those who need them."

She suppressed her glee, but it took a mighty effort to resist the impulse to dance around the room. In her most professional voice, she asked Cuevas to elaborate. "Tell us more about your analysis, please."

"It appears to be from his late period, post-second Italian trip. Possibly 1658–59. Guillermo tells me the painting does not match any of the missing works, including those taken by Napoleon's troops."

Jones scowled and interrupted Cuevas. "Just like that? Based on eyes only you pin down the date, before the hour is over. You are good, Cuevas. Or a fool."

She and Guillermo exchanged a glance that said, "Here we go."

"How did you know I've been here an hour?" Cuevas looked at a twitching Guillermo.

"The museum opens at ten. I doubt you've been here all night."

Impressive. Jones could be in the non-liars club.

Jones stepped forward. "The Prado wanted my opinion too. Now it seems up to me to disagree with you."

What? What was Jones doing? Guillermo raised his eyebrows and looked toward her. She started to say something, but Guillermo placed his hand discreetly on her arm to hold her back.

"Nothing new about that," Cuevas grumbled.

She stared at Jones, a plea for civility. He waved her off with his finger like he was a conductor in complete control.

"I might need more than an hour to render my opinion. Have time studies been done, Guillermo?"

"At the Institute in Seville. Here's a preliminary report."

Jones scanned the papers that he hadn't asked for yesterday. He put a loupe to his eye and studied the same details of brushstrokes on the canvas he'd already examined. After ten minutes of repeating yesterday's inspection, he lifted his head. "It's clear that certain brushstrokes were not made by Velázquez's hand."

She knew it. Jones had been too easy, out of character. Jones, the shape-shifter and saboteur, what game was he playing?

Jones leaned down again over the painting. "Might be the studio, the work of an assistant."

Cuevas turned red and sputtered to respond, "Damn Americans. You know nothing. Upstairs in the galleries you will see identical strokes on *Las Meninas* and other confirmed works by Velázquez." Cuevas marched out the door without waiting for an answer.

Their only choice was to follow him upstairs. She and Guillermo followed in their wake and listened to a lively discussion in one of the most famous rooms in all of European art, the rotunda of the Prado. Tourists speaking a babel of languages from Japanese to Icelandic eavesdropped on the academic debate between the two titans.

She and Guillermo stood to the side, careful to stay silent.

Antonio arrived and interrupted them, stepping onto the battlefield without realizing shots were being fired. Cuevas responded with a deferential bow and a finger pointed to the painting of Antonio's famous relative on horseback.

Antonio greeted Cuevas. "I understand there has been an important painting uncovered that might be connected to the Olivares family."

"Yes, Don Antonio. A painting by Velázquez. Professor Jones disagrees with the obvious attribution," Cuevas said.

"Professor Jones, is that correct?" Antonio, a practiced litigator, asked in an impartial voice and hid the shock he had to feel.

"One must proceed carefully in this matter of attribution. My colleague, Dr. Cuevas, has made some important points about the brushstrokes. While there are brushstrokes that differ, they do match later paintings like *Las Meninas*."

Antonio argued the case. "There is additional evidence. Did Guillermo tell you about the old photograph from 1840?"

"A photo exists?" Cuevas looked at Guillermo who said nothing. "Did you know about this, Professor Jones?

Guillermo intervened, "Let's return to the lab where the painting is. A daguerreotype of what seems to be the original frame from the Olivares attic is in the conservation lab. Shall we return there?" Guillermo was making his best effort to remove their raised voices from the public galleries. Most art aficionados accept the hegemony of the museum and have no idea how tenuous what they read on the walls might be.

Antonio charmed the experts with stories of his relatives as they walked back through the galleries. When they arrived at the lab, she found the envelope with the photographs and placed it on the lab table next to the painting, wondering what Jones would do next.

Cuevas picked up the daguerreotype and lifted his glasses to his forehead as he angled the plate in the light. "Extraordinary. Look at this, Jones. This painting in the possession of the Olivares family."

"This photo proves that the canvas was close to Olivares at some point when daguerreotype photography was used. It proves nothing about who painted it."

Cuevas sighed. "But the connections build a case, can you agree? What would it take to convince you?"

"Then there is the matter of how it landed at NYCU."

Cuevas gasped. "NYCU? Guillermo, you failed to mention ..."

Their plan was unraveling, the tension intensified.

"Dr. Cuevas, we were asked not to identify NYCU as the owner in order to have the most objective assessment," Guillermo replied, close to a whisper.

Jones spoke next. "We'd hope to attribute it, slowly, carefully. Ask for opinions without influencing the answers. We've searched for a reference to the painting, documentation of the commission, a collections inventory naming it." Jones shook his head. "Such records remain elusive, but my doctoral student, Miss Adamson, will search the resources we have in New York."

Antonio jumped into the disagreement. "With all respect, wouldn't Miss Adamson be more likely to find such documentation in Spain? Perhaps in the Olivares Library."

Neither Jones nor Cuevas spoke, unwilling to sacrifice a connection to the duke.

Cate's head spun like that girl in the *Exorcist*. She didn't understand what the heck Jones was doing, flipping around and having more opinions than ascot scarves, Cuevas fighting for Spanish sovereignty, Antonio was in a tug-of-war about her. She wanted *La Gloria* to rise above the fray.

Cuevas looked aggravated. "This Olivares Library has been off-limits. How can we trust what comes from there?"

"My family has cared for the archives for centuries without help from the government. We have kept it private for that very reason—to assure it remained intact." Antonio gave him a look of ancestral gravitas. "Our family estate cannot receive researchers at this time. The property is fragile and in the process of restoration. But I will grant access to Miss Adamson."

Cuevas looked embarrassed and cleared his throat. "Apologies, my Lord, most kind of you to allow a researcher to use it. Perhaps Professor Jones will permit her to work from the Prado. If so, we will support a Spanish patrimony grant to catalogue and protect your library collection."

Antonio shook Cuevas's hand. "I look forward to discussing such a grant."

Cate smiled at Antonio, a silent message between them: Maybe there's money to repair the decrepit roof on the estate, especially over the library. If this project succeeded, this win became theirs together.

Jones's face turned dark. He had been beaten in his effort to get the painting back to New York and he knew it. He paced back and forth and then asked, "Miss Adamson, are you willing to take the next semester in Madrid?"

"Wherever I can best study the painting's attribution." She paused. Less was better, she did not need to overplay her hand except for one card. "I'll need some help to relocate . . . and travel."

Jones responded, "I can arrange an independent study fellowship for you."

Guillermo and Antonio were glowing like two fellas who'd had too much sangria. Guillermo said, "The Prado has a department for visiting scholars. I'll ask the director to approve support for this project. Will you also ask him, Dr. Cuevas?"

"Absolutely, the painting should stay in Madrid." He puffed out his chest like a dominant gorilla. "Are we agreed, Professor Jones?"

"It seems I have no choice." Jones offered his hand, and this time Cuevas shook it. Jones turned toward the door without seeing her sigh, relieved that the possibility of being accused of theft or having the painting returned to Isabel's clutches had ended.

CHAPTER 22

*T*he landscape below the plane displayed green patches, making a checkerboard with the flaxen tones of the fallow fields. Madrid had awakened from its winter grey to February's promise of spring. The jet landed and Cate exited into the terminal, at once exhausted from the challenge of moving here from New York and exhilarated by the *La Gloria* project that waited at the Prado. The university paperwork had been approved and the worry of being dismissed or arrested removed, freeing her to move forward.

There'd been no time to visit Ypsilanti. Her belongings, what she didn't throw out, like her beloved art library, were shipped to Michigan. The library at her new employer was world-class for her topic and far exceeded what she owned or even what could be found in New York. But the image of Mom answering the door to the UPS guy with boxes instead of her daughter haunted her as a cruel act from an ungrateful child. And for that she was sorry.

She might have made a trip home, squeezed in a weekend. Only an hour by plane and cheap too. Matty's birthday, a reminder of the life he had not lived, fell in January, she knew what that meant and wanted to avoid the painful guilt . . . again. *Was that wrong?* Things were going well for her, the life she pursued blossomed with Spring's signs of renewal, too. The good daughter, the one that kept them functioning, sacrificed all to soothe them, she had died when she left for New York. Someday she could, she would return, secure enough to lift them from that hole, and offer them a stronger hand-up to convince them happy days awaited their family.

The Prado's director set deadlines to finish the research and the restoration in order to present the work at a press conference and highlight the museum's role. She had a couple of months maximum to pull it together with a bit of flexibility for the unexpected. The deadline was driven by the museum's experience that controlling the secret of an unknown Velázquez would be difficult to impossible. A big reveal without gossip and speculation would mean the museum could maximize their visibility on the international stage and give her the ability to work unencumbered by opinions from all directions.

Antonio waited with flowers he couldn't afford. He was there, right at the customs exit. "Oh, how I've missed you." He squeezed his arms around her and held her there. She took in the smell of him, his hair, his neck, which eclipsed the scent of the roses being crushed between them. His arms, a safe place that felt right, like where she belonged, like home.

She settled into the shotgun seat of his sad little car, their transportation on the big adventure from Olivares to Madrid and now forward to the next phase.

HER SLEEPY HEAD STARTLED from the headrest when Antonio parked in front of the apartment Guillermo had arranged for her. The place was rented to Guillermo's old schoolmate, Manuel, who needed a rent-splitting roommate.

The place was functional, nothing more, probably the servant's room of an old house. She unpacked a bag onto a chair in the empty bedroom. There was no note or welcome, but Manuel emailed he'd be in class. She yawned.

Antonio sat down on the couch with a stack of papers he needed to review. She placed her head on his lap. "Just need rest for a moment."

She stirred awake. Darkness had fallen and street noise of bar patrons drinking wine and eating tapas came from below. She was hungry.

"I'm starved and I don't think there's any food here. Do you want to go out?" It didn't take much to convince him and they walked out to the street hand-in-hand.

"Madrid is always so alive. No one is sad."

Antonio held the door open to the nearest tapas bar. "New York is lively. Were you sad there?"

She didn't answer but reached for his hand across the rough wood of the table.

"Your mom and dad? You miss them, don't you?"

She nodded. "I didn't have time to get home. And also . . ." She stopped.

"Your brother. Matty, right? I always wanted a brother. I can't imagine having one and then losing him."

"I see these young people and I see him. He'd be about their age. Where would life have taken him—to study, to travel, to be like that guy?" A kid about eighteen was standing on a table leading his pals in a vulgar song with a pitcher of sangria in his hand.

Antonio shook his head and smiled. "Be glad that is not your brother."

She tried to smile but couldn't. Antonio knew too little about Matty's death.

"He was a good kid. Funny, lots of friends, a party boy." She studied her hands, looking away from his eyes. She had never said a word to anyone about her part in his death.

"There's more, isn't there? How did it happen?"

Antonio could read her, see her in ways her folks and other

friends did not. "It was a senior party, at the beach, at night. Drunken chaos like those kids."

The noise had grown to a crescendo. Their sangria pitcher was empty and so were their glasses. Antonio ordered more and added *calamares fritos.* The sweet alcohol of the sangria gave her a rush and courage.

"I always felt guilty."

"Why? How could you stop the crazy things kids do?"

She'd needed to share this for so long, to lift it from her heart, to lean on someone. He waited without speaking and finally she said, "My pills, the ones the doctor gave me to stay awake, all night for finals, disappeared. Matty had to have taken the bottle from our shared bathroom."

Antonio squeezed her hand and reached out to brush her hair off her face. "You said he'd drowned. Was it a drug overdose? Wouldn't the police have told you?" Antonio, the lawyer, was back.

She shrugged and looked away. "They found him in the water and probably didn't research much more." She pulled a tissue from her purse and patted her eyes around the edges.

"Do you want to talk about something else?"

She nodded and they did talk, talk about everything, but Matty. About how Teresa and Luis raised him after his parents died in a car accident. About Antonio's research, the history of the property, the postponement of the property legal proceedings, so typical of the Spanish courts.

Then he paused and turned to her project. "What about Jones? Did he ever explain why he changed his viewpoint on *La Gloria?*"

"He played the contrarian, said the opposite of what he wanted Cuevas to say to get him to concur with Jones's original assessment. A typical Jones manipulation."

"Manipulative and successful."

"I sense he's waiting for the research to progress and then he'll jump on the most convincing arguments. I'm suspicious that he is not trying to control it, the way he usually does, for a reason."

The lights flashed. The waiter picked up their empty *jarra* and collected the bill. Closing time put them into the street where the last of the revelers headed home singing drunken songs. Sleep came easily, both of them too tired for sex but happy to be in each other's arms.

ANTONIO KISSED HER FOREHEAD to awaken her. "I need to leave Madrid to handle a plumbing problem. Yes, a different one from last week."

She smiled to hide her disappointment and relief. A mountain of research would fill her days until they could be together. Their kiss felt different, familiar, like saying goodbye to a husband for the day, even though three hundred fifty miles would separate their offices.

The semi-empty cupboards contained no coffee, the elixir she required to face the day. The door to the other bedroom was closed and the elusive Manuel, still a stranger, must be asleep behind it. She took a shower and changed clothes and felt like a different person, unable to remember a time when she'd slept so deeply. She found the essential coffee at the bar downstairs and enjoyed the buzz of being back.

The Prado's architecture loomed over the trees on the Paseo del Prado, and she admired it from the bench where she drank her coffee. "The Temple" she called it, a place to worship art. Legions of art devotees paid homage to works by Bosch, El Greco, Titian, Rubens, Goya, and of course, Velázquez. She'd been given an office in this cathedral, sharing her workaday world with priceless art. *La Gloria* had been ensconced in her own chapel with conservators who worked with reverence to revive her beauty and complete tests to confirm her identity.

Guillermo knocked on the office door. "*Bienvenida*. You will be swept into things more quickly than we expected. The pregnant curatorial assistant went into labor and I am desperate. Will you take a group of donors on a tour in fifteen minutes? The focus is Velázquez."

She wanted to spend every minute on *La Gloria*. Guillermo had been her champion, his negotiation with Jones and Cuevas had been pivotal and she owed him. "Of course I'll help you."

Each gallery was as familiar as her folks' Michigan house. The Circle of Donors had the privilege to enter the museum before regular hours. By their profile, there was nothing she might add to what they knew. They chirped like excited children on an outing until they entered Room 12 where the works silenced them to whispers. It happened to everyone— from tourists—who'd been lured by Trip Advisor's Ten Best List for Spain—to art cognoscenti. To see one masterpiece featured in a museum had that effect but here was a room with ten of them. Canvases like *Las Meninas* measured ten by nine feet and to the left, the almost as large canvas of the Count-Duke of Olivares, Antonio's famous relative, looked down on them as he held the reins of his horse with the front legs in a levade. The viewer felt the weight of the steed and the importance of the man, smelled the dust, and heard the hooves land on the turf. The Duke had been frozen in that grand and imposing position since around 1636.

Cate waited with a dramatic pause. She described that era when the Spanish court strolled these galleries constructed as a science museum, and moved their paintings here when the Prado opened as an art museum in 1819.

Finally, she shared some lesser-known stories about the works, many enigmas in the compositions and speculation about what they meant. The group asked sophisticated questions that challenged her. She connected them to the humanity of the artist and his personal struggles. Her enthusiasm, even stumbling a bit on the art vocabulary in Spanish, combined with biographical details from her research, produced a rousing applause at the end. Their unexpected reaction made her blush as they shook her hand and left.

The banquette at the room's center allowed her to relieve her feet after walking on the unforgiving floors, the perfect place to steal a moment alone with these works.

An elderly lady sitting silently behind her surprised her. "You gave a fine presentation. Do you have time to chat?"

"A little time."

The smallish woman with gray hair wore thick glasses with large black frames, like that New York fashion maven whose name escaped her. The lady smoothed the folds of her tasteful dress appropriate for a church tea.

"The guards call me Miss Lillian."

"You must come often if they know your name. You're American?"

"New Yorker. I've lived in Madrid for a couple of decades. I miss these friends . . ." she waved her hand at the paintings, "when I travel to the US to help my son."

"Can I answer something for you?" Cate peeked at her watch, a cheap replacement for the Swatch the taxi driver took in Seville.

"These changes in Velázquez's style. From the early Seville days until these masterpieces were painted. The style, the brushstrokes changed dramatically from the controlled manner taught by Pacheco to the young painter. Do you think Velázquez adopted that style on his Italian trip?"

Lillian's knowledge humbled her. The lovely lady with the quirky glasses wasn't a socialite playing at art. She knew her stuff and perhaps even had some advice about where she might find some lesser-known research materials. "I'm impressed with your knowledge."

The woman fiddled with her hands, pressing down on her dress.

"Are you alright?" Cate asked.

"Thank you dear. You're sweet to stay with me." Miss Lillian patted her hand. "I write about Velázquez. Two books are finished, but no publisher. Especially difficult for a woman, but at my age, impossible."

"Women struggle to get recognized. It's getting better, don't you think?"

Lillian grimaced, her thin lips strained taut.

"Tell me about your writing." Suddenly time didn't matter.

She motioned to the wall around them. "Resources I spotted in the National Library made me study the changes that came after he went to Italy, especially the second trip. Do you think it's more than a maturity of artistic style, or influence of the Italians, like Titian?"

"I'm researching him too and plan to scour the archives. Perhaps we can meet and discuss in more detail what you've learned."

"I know, hard, a biography many writ—a bumble of books. I mean a jumble." Miss Lillian shook her head and tried to straighten her words, sentences Cate could not decipher. Then Lillian tried to stand and fell back onto the banquette, silent.

Cate looked across the room. A guard was just taking up his station.

"Please help, over here. Hurry."

The guard arrived and she sent him for water. He objected, saying that water was not allowed in the galleries, but she pushed back.

Lillian stuttered, trying without success to speak, and then slumped against her shoulder. Her skin had turned cold and slightly blue.

She'd know what to do in New York, but here she knew nothing about emergency services. She pulled out her cell phone and hit the speed dial for her office, a number that she had just entered into her contacts an hour ago.

"It's Cate. Medical emergency in Room 12. Get an ambulance. An elderly lady fainted . . . needs help."

The guard returned with water. Lillian was responsive, but her hand trembled and the water dribbled from her mouth. The guard blocked visitors and said the room was closed. Sounds of sirens became louder and closer. Cate tried to soothe Lillian with words of encouragement.

Paramedics arrived and placed Lillian onto the floor. Cate stepped away but watched the medics put an oxygen mask on Lillian's face, trying to make eye contact with the sweet lady. After a few seconds, Miss Lillian's eyes popped open above the oxygen mask and she raised her frail hand to pull the mask away. A good sign.

She squeezed Lillian's hand and said, "You're going to be okay." Mostly she was consoling herself. She took a couple of deep breaths and walked back down to the administrative offices.

Dalila, the receptionist, didn't look up from her computer. "Is the lady okay?"

"Don't know. Thanks for calling the emergency people."

"I didn't call. Security handles these incidents." Dalila looked up. "Happens about once a week. Older people, exhausted tourists, boring guides making people stand too long. Just wait till summer when it's hot and the hoards raise the room temperature even more."

Cate had never seen someone faint in a gallery. Dalila's indifference sent her back to a memory of Matty's drowning. Was that how it was? A precious life didn't even merit a moment of pause, stop business as usual to consider how tenuous life was. "Maybe we can send her flowers, or at least inquire how she is?"

"Sure, why not." Dalila, experienced beyond her twenty-something years, hardened by something, went back to pounding her keyboard.

Cate's office had a door, her first ever. A marvel to be able to close a door, purposefully shelter herself from whatever was on the other side. She searched the museum website to look up the Circle of Donors to find Lillian's last name. The Circle required an annual donation of €1000, not a small amount for a retired lady, but perhaps she was a wealthy expat. Ms. Lillian Smythe, very English.

She made a note of the address for Dalila to order flowers, using the museum florist. She wrote "attend next Circle meeting" on the yellow pad and headed to the staff lounge to find something to eat. Spaniards love their cuisine, something else they worshipped, evidenced by the numerous names for eating times: *desayuno, almuerzo, comida, merienda, aperitivo, cena*. A foreigner needed to check the time to understand which meal they were meant to eat.

She called Antonio while she snacked on grapes, an orange, and bread with cheese.

"You made it to Olivares? Already?"

"House problems. At least it's not raining."

"The rain in Spain . . ."

They laughed together at the corny reference. The stress of the crazy morning slipped away. "A lady on a museum tour, writes books about Velázquez. Never published anything."

"Why not?'

"She said publishers won't take on a woman. She spends a good part of her time helping her son."

He was quiet. "Does spending time with me, worrying about my financial problems, does it take away from your work?"

"Not at all. I wouldn't have this job without you."

"And don't you forget it! *En serio*, I get distracted, deep in my problems. Help me keep my perspective and appreciate you."

"Thanks, that's thoughtful. But there's more. Just when she was going to tell me about her research, she fainted or had a stroke. The ambulance came."

"Wow. What a crazy first day."

CHAPTER 23

The apartment was empty when she returned from work as per usual the last few weeks. Manuel worked as a medical intern, sometimes taking night shifts and studying for his medical license exams. Mom would object to a male roommate, something inappropriate. Manuel did satisfy mother's criteria: A doctor made a good husband because he could pay the bills and also revive her daughter if she collapsed.

Manuel was never in the apartment long enough to be a good medical responder. These weeks of "living together" revealed that Manuel, scatterbrained, overaged adolescent, had a modus operandi that included rounds at tapas bars, not patient beds. She shoved a text on histology aside to make space for her bread and coffee on the table/desk.

She'd been in Madrid for ten weeks and it was a blur to find places to do laundry, open a bank account, get a haircut, and write papers to meet independent course requirements. Daily life challenges combined with slogging through vast materials on Velázquez, resulted in bone-deep fatigue. Libraries had been her singular joy, as if learning was all that mattered. However, red stars circled the date on the calendar taped to the refrigerator door: Ten days left until the date the director had scheduled to present the painting to the press, to the world.

Scouring seventeenth-century artists' letters and journals for mentions of Velázquez's studio, writings by someone who might have seen the painting, a journal of someone who knew him exhausted her. Her thoughts wandered to Miss Lillian. She hadn't followed up after the museum received a genteel note for the flowers and now it seemed too self-serving to troll her for resources.

Reading and more reading blurred her vision. Her brain shut down. Velázquez had a studio in the royal palace where he and his family lived, a privilege of the king's royal painter. The king's accountants recorded withdrawals from the dwindling treasury from pheasants for royal banquets to pigments and canvases. Inventoried paintings became property of the Prado when it opened as a museum in 1819. *La Gloria* was not among them. Guillermo asked the staff to keep a lookout for references to Velázquez's works that might be *La Gloria*. More eyes looking might turn up something in an unrelated document or reference, but the staff appeared unenthused to help.

Eating alone with no colleagues except Guillermo wasn't the friendly atmosphere she remembered as a student. The staff resented an American in what they felt should be a Spaniard's job. She got it and might have felt the same in their shoes; still, it hurt. The way to win them was to ignore the slights and continue with friendly interactions: sharing her challenges, financial and emotional, and how she missed her family.

And that's why she went to the museum, every day, instead of directly to the library. First morning stop was to the conservation lab, to say good morning to *La Gloria*, greet the conservators, and check on the restoration. A private room for the restoration protected the painting from the hubbub of the main lab. The director had evicted other staff, adding to resentment, to protect secrecy. The staff had wanted to stay with their current projects, which she understood. Time, hours and hours, with an artwork cements a bond between art and conservator, whose close viewing results in knowing a canvas like a lover's face, every crater, blemish, and mark. The cleaning of *La Gloria* awakened the richness, the color, and those allusive brushstrokes, suggestions of reality rather than detailed representation. *Look at my child. Isn't she magnificent?*

Cleaning revealed small details like a clay pot that historians claimed nobles consumed to whiten their skin, but ended up poisoning themselves. The Infanta in *Las Meninas* held a similar pot in her hand, a shared iconography with *La Gloria*. Cleaning uncovered an unsigned sheet of paper in the corner, a device used by Velázquez to mock those who signed their works with pompous Roman script. *La Gloria* blossomed, matured toward her rightful place in the pantheon.

The little putti glowed with the cleaning, flushed cherubic faces that resembled Matty when he was that age. Time passed and impressions faded, but the echo sounded with as little as a word or an image, and that torment swooped in to take over her thoughts. The disassembling, the reassembling, and the fleeing that anguish repeated in a pattern that would not end. The agony of her part in his death, the pills she'd left out, carelessly making them accessible to him, haunted her. She turned away from the staff, placed her hands over her face, and summoned the strength to push the nightmare back into that hidden place.

Composed and relieved no one had looked up from their work, she acknowledged the restorers' talent with delight that came from the gratitude that they cared as she did. The senior staff mumbled, "Gracias." Guillermo warned her about their chilly demeanor and the conflict between budget cutbacks and the allocation of ample funds for *La Gloria*. No one could mention to them the provisional attribution, but they suspected as they had worked on other masterworks. Someday, hopefully soon, these workers would brag they had assisted with an important Velázquez in the collection.

Antonio rarely came to Madrid, the estate's problems required he be in Olivares. Guillermo lived in constant meetings. The isolation got to her and made her yearn for Michigan, something she did not see coming.

The second stop in her morning routine: Rotunda, Room 12. "Hello, old friends," she said to the silent paintings. The Infanta in *Las Meninas* greeted her and Velázquez did too, staring from behind his easel. He painted himself in this work and peered out as though he wanted to say something. *Speak, tell me about* La Gloria. *Was she your idea, a work your soul needed to create? Or a commission of a wealthy patron or perhaps the king's idea?*

In another work, little prince Balthazar sat on his pony, made giant by the size of the work as though his short life of sixteen years could be made longer with a bigger painting. The queen never recovered from the loss of her only son and the king's hope for a successor fell to his daughter, the Infanta. A story she understood.

Maybe like her, Velázquez fled to Italy to escape the depressed state of the palace. Sent on a mission to buy art for the king's collections, he found his tribe; contact with Ribera in Naples and seeing the Titians in Rome changed him. Velázquez must have felt the loss of his patron Olivares, who was fired by nobles who wanted him out for excessive expenditures on war campaigns. Velázquez ignored the king's requests to return to Spain; historians speculate about the reasons he dared to defy the king. Was it the synergy with Italian artists, the required work to purchase art for the Retiro Palace, or as some say, a mistress?

"Hola, Jose." The security guard who'd helped with Miss Lillian had taken up his post.

"*Buenos días*, Señorita Caterina. You are visiting your friends?"

"They remind me of why I do this work."

"What happened to the lady who fainted that day?"

"I need to find out." Lillian's name went on her mental to-do list.

The long walk back to the administrative quarters became the gym workout she had no time to do. Her heavy breathing wasn't only about the multiple flights of stairs but the worries she carried about presenting the painting to the world. Cuevas supported it, Jones was on board, at least she believed he was, and the case for a Velázquez attribution was as strong as it could be with the information they had. But detractors were to be expected.

Finally, she arrived to her own office that must have been servants' quarters of the museum. No windows, lots of book-cases, but enough wall space to hang a self-portrait by Anton Raphael Mengs who once guided collections at the Prado. Art staff were entitled to the perk to select an artwork from museum inventory and hang it in their office. The staff was surprised she chose a Mengs, a German who became a Spanish court painter and married an Italian. She didn't clarify how the young Mengs resembled Antonio.

A thin envelope from the International Library Foundation waited in her inbox. Thin envelopes meant bad news, a lesson from college admission days. The grant request she'd prepared to catalog the Olivares' Library had been rejected. The Foundation's emphasis had shifted to digitizing existing catalogs. Antonio's library did not have an analog catalog. What an unfortunate loss to scholars, and her summer with Antonio was not happening.

Fire had destroyed most of the duke's library and experts didn't believe anything remained. They were wrong. The duke sequestered a portion of the collection with Antonio's relatives before he died, and the duke's daughter-in-law Juana gave them the rest. An unexplored room behind one bookcase that she hadn't seen was intriguing and funds would have given her a job after the Prado project ended in two weeks. More treasures could be hidden in Antonio's library, and she would find them.

She stared at the rejection letter, another disappointment. Best to get the bad news over with. Antonio's phone rang and rang. Nine o'clock. Already somewhere away from the phone, a courtroom, a distant field on the estate, or he left the phone in the house. That she did not know his daily routine showed how the relationship suffered from absence, no matter how understanding each of them had been. It would be great to visit but there wasn't time to travel, nor money for train tickets.

Dalila came into the office with the draft agenda for the meeting about the press conference. Cate had dodged daily calls from El Pais and the ABC newspapers who'd had leaks about the painting. Pilar from the Prado's public relations department was eager to reveal what they knew at the formal press conference before it leaked everywhere. Jones, Cuevas, and she would be on the stage. She wasn't ready; she needed that final documentation connecting the work to the master. She glanced at her watch; only a couple of minutes before the meeting began and she rushed toward the conference room.

The room filled with the announcement committee, including staffers from public relations, curatorial, installation, framing, and central administration assigned to help. Someone had brought a box of sweets from Moulin Chocolat, a nice touch to celebrate Dalila's birthday with good wishes from all around.

The seat at the head of the table had been left empty for her to lead the meeting. "Let's begin. I know you all want to get back to work." Did that sound too American, or maybe they were happy taking a break with coffee and treats. She shifted gears. "You've been doing an outstanding job with the conservation. Thank you again and again." They reacted with self-congratulatory but well-earned nods. "The date is coming soon."

"If we don't hold the conference before *Semana Santa*, we'll lose the key press people to the holidays." Pilar passed out a draft of the press release and said, "Review the content and verify its accuracy. We don't want to give away our conclusions, but we need enough to attract their attention." The conservator at the meeting agreed to review the pigment reports and other chemical studies to see if they could pin down an exact date.

The draft wasn't only missing a date. A blank space filled with X's glared from the page that referred to the name of the artist. More time would likely not yield that answer. She along with the librarians had scoured everything from 1630 until his death in 1660 in the National Library and the Prado's extensive holdings. Once a Velázquez attribution was declared, research by others would strive to contradict it. But these contrarians would require documentation proving *La Gloria* had been painted by someone else, and she was reasonably sure they would not find that either.

Pilar waited for an answer, tapping her pen on the table.

Cate sighed. "Let's announce the name at the event. Say 'Golden Age master' in the press release." Let the naysayers assemble their arguments after the announcement.

"Will you write a description of *La Gloria*, some interpretation of what it's about, for whom it was painted?"

Marta from the curatorial team jumped in and volunteered, "We can draft something for the director's approval."

That would cut her out. Cate blurted a breathless impromptu analysis. "Based on the imagery, *La Gloria* was Velázquez's tribute to the Conde-Duque de Olivares and the fading grandeur of Spain under Felipe IV. The woman in the center . . ." Cate pointed to the image projected on the wall, "is the personification of Spain. She looks out at the viewer in the manner of the Infanta in *Las Meninas* as angels call her toward heaven. Perhaps she is an allegory of hope, a celestial Spain, one so grand it would continue in eternity. It's aspirational, not historical."

They scribbled with their pens, capturing her words as though she were Jones or Cuevas. Her spirits lifted and then fell as doubts made her question her own remarks. Speculation combined with self-doubt, the curse and the talent of an art historian.

"Maybe Spain died and angels are burying her," said Juan, the photographer. The group chuckled. Ana from installation added, "Say more about the Count-Duke of Olivares. Unemployed Spaniards might relate to a story about him getting fired."

Laughter rocked the room. Staff worried about money; most of them were a paycheck away from being on the minimum income system, something she'd look into if she didn't get a job offer after the press conference and wanted to stay in Spain, stay with Antonio.

She'd lost control of the meeting and Pilar looked at her with raised eyebrows that said, "Move on with the agenda."

Stephen got the meeting back on track with the next item, installation. "We received the frame from Olivares but there's a problem. The painting was trimmed, and the original frame doesn't fit. A modern copy will not equal the quality of the original, and we can't fabricate a custom carved one in ten days. This original frame is the answer if the duke will permit us to cut it. Cate can you get his permission? Also, we'll need NYCU to pay so it can remain with the painting when it goes back to New York."

"Are you able to cut it without damaging the carvings?"

"We only need to cut the sides and the main carving will remain. We can match and repair the gold leaf, but it will be impossible to reassemble. Please, can you convince the duke?"

She pretended to ponder her calendar, but she was thrilled to see Antonio, and also have another opportunity to search his library. "I'll meet with the duke to ask him."

A muffled but audible snicker passed among the staff. She and Antonio weren't a secret after all.

"Could you go immediately? We need time to redo the frame."

Pilar didn't wait for an answer and went to the next item on the agenda. "Final item: presentation. Cate, we need your draft for the director's approval, and then for the printer to make the press packets."

Go to Olivares, write that presentation, whatever else, and ten days to do it all. The academic writing had to be top quality and able to pass challenges by international experts. Everything carefully referenced to reliable sources, exact details of technical reports, and analyses of the composition, his magnificent use of color. "I'll do the draft on the train. But I'll need an AVE ticket for tomorrow."

Cate floated out of the conference room, knowing an Antonio fix was what she needed now to face her fears and gain confidence to finish the work.

Five rings. A second unanswered call.

Finally, her phone rang and she smiled at the name on the screen.

"Can you come to Olivares?" Antonio sounded excited. "As soon as you can?"

"I'm coming tomorrow. To talk about the frame and one last library . . ."

He interrupted. "Forget tomorrow. Come today. Tio Luis found something. In the library."

"Don't tease. Tell me now."

"Remember that little room? The one with no lights. Luis took a flashlight and saw a folio with parchment pages in it. Very old, we think seventeenth century. We inspected what we could but left the portfolio on the shelf as you advised in case surrounding documents relate to it."

"Good work. I'll call you from the station with the arrival time." She grabbed her coat and called back over her shoulder, "Dalila, book me a ticket for today on the 2:00 AVE. Email it to me." She flew out the door with her coat one arm on, one arm off.

Taxis were always waiting outside the Prado. The driver swung around, changing directions to her apartment as she'd asked. He waited while she packed a duffle and scurried back downstairs. They made it to Atocha in fifteen minutes, a record, and she sprinted to the track.

Her assigned seat was in first class, the only seat left according to Dalila, but she deserved the quiet to write. Her mind whirled with questions and she found it impossible to concentrate. What could be in the portfolio? Could this be the repository of Velázquez's writings and drawings, or maybe an inventory that had gone missing over hundreds of years ago? Or a journal? Or maybe it was nothing. Knowing Luis, he'd probably peeked and he and Antonio knew, knew at least it was centuries old. A journal would be amazing, *clave* as the Spanish say. An artist of his caliber had to have written a journal, musings about ideas, letters home from his Italian trips. She put her head down with renewed energy and wrote paragraphs about the history of the Baroque and the decade in which *La Gloria* had been painted.

The train huffed into the Seville station after the four-hour ride. He was there. On the platform. His whole face brightened with that dimpled grin.

"I'm so excited to see what you've found."

"No kiss first?" He welcomed her into his arms and then drew back and kissed her, long and soft, the smell of him and the touch brought back the affection she had missed. "Couldn't wait another minute to see you." He kissed her again and twirled her in a bear hug before he set her down. They linked arms, headed for the exit and the parking lot.

"I was crazy thinking of the possibilities, including that it's nothing related. Did you look into it? Tell me if you did, I won't be upset."

He laughed and put one hand on each of her cheeks. "You were thinking of old books and not me?"

"I haven't stopped thinking of you. All my unanswered calls."

"Sorry. Good news from the law library, they found related cases from over a hundred years ago, titles approved based on the owner's length of residence on the property, a squatters' rule. Brought me some hope."

"Sounds positive." She rubbed her hands together. "I can't wait. Does this car have wings?"

Antonio patted the dashboard. "This car can barely drive on roads." He squeezed her hand. "Why did you call?"

"The frame. The top portion of *La Gloria* was cut off and the museum wants to resize, cut down, your frame to fit the canvas. We need your permission."

"Should I agree? What if they find the missing piece?"

"Probably won't find the piece, very unlikely. NYCU should purchase the frame, since it will go back to New York with their painting. The frame is worth some money, thousands or more, money for roof leaks and repairs to the plumbing and fountain."

"Then yes. Sell it. How are you?"

"Stressed to the max. They've set the press conference for next Friday. The director wants my presentation on Monday. I need another source to tie the painting to Velázquez." She paused. "It's odd, even for hundreds of years ago, that there wasn't anyone who saw it or wrote about it, especially since it was painted while he was in the royal court. Those nobles at court, ruthless gossipers, wrote down everything, trust me I've read it all. But no mention of *La Gloria*."

"Sounds like we could use some wine."

"No, let's go straight to Olivares. I want to see those parchments and I will probably need the rest of the weekend to get through what's there."

"It doesn't add up, does it, why the parchments, everything in that room, was hidden for hundreds of years." He reached over the center console for her hand. "There's time to answer those questions."

Darkness covered the hills around the estate and the roads disappeared into blackness. He navigated the familiar curves like a wild race car driver, making her nervous. But she'd been here before; she'd learned to trust him.

A small lantern lit the house. The wooden door creaked and echoed up the silent staircase.

"Are you hungry? I am." Antonio motioned with his arm toward the dining room. "Once we get into the library, you won't stop to eat. Someone will find our starved skeletons in another hundred years."

She answered with a nod even though she preferred to eat and work, but he looked tired and she cared for him. She needed him, the way his wit boosted her energy, and the basics, he was tall enough to reach the top shelves.

Maria had left grapes and apples, a loaf of fresh bread, and cold cuts on the table with an open bottle of Rioja wine. "I'm too curious to eat. Can we see this little room?"

Antonio loaded a tray and gave her two wine glasses to carry. He carried a wine bottle under his arm. When they got to the library, he motioned for her to switch on the lights. She tripped on a pile of books stacked on the floor but caught herself before falling.

Books toppled as Antonio opened a bookshelf that swiveled outward to reveal a dark space, a sort of large closet. He flipped on a lamp plugged into a long extension cord. The room was about eight by eight feet, with a high ceiling, smaller than she'd remembered from Christmas. They'd left in a rush to get the painting to Guillermo in Madrid and there'd been no time to explore it. The plan was to inventory everything with the grant, the grant that was turned down. She'd tell Antonio later, bad news could always wait. Or not.

Shelves packed with books, documents, leather-bound records rose twenty feet to the ceiling. Markings on the spines indicated what the tomes contained, but the embossing on the leather was worn and often too faint to read.

"See the portfolio up there?"

She stretched her neck to survey shelves fifteen feet up to see the edge of a leather portfolio a foot or two from the ceiling. The shelves were as deep as the length of her arm and could have a second row of books behind or were made for very large books like atlases. Antonio stood behind her and the two of them barely fit into the room.

"Did Luis get up there?" She stepped back into the main room, coughing from the dust and searching the large library. "Where's the ladder?"

Antonio patted her back and offered his handkerchief. "Juan must have taken it to the stables."

"We need it." Her insistent tone sounded a bit demanding and she dug deeper to quell her impatience.

"Juan is with Maria visiting their grandchildren. I could try to get it. Usually takes two to carry it. The ladder, old school wood, is really heavy."

Fatigue was taking over when thorough careful work was required. "We'll wait until morning. Leave a note for Juan to put the ladder back early tomorrow. Please."

She scanned the lower shelves and a volume caught her attention. The title on the spine had been covered with a piece of leather. She strained to read the title page with the one light: *Dialogue Concerning the Two Chief World Systems.*

She stopped and recognized other titles. "I know why these books are hidden here."

Antonio laughed and said, "One volume and she has all the answers. What about careful work?"

"Let's have a glass of wine and I'll explain." She pulled a few more volumes and sat down. The other three books supported what she had concluded.

Antonio poured the wine. The glug-glug sound echoed in the silent house accompanied by the crackling fire. He walked behind her chair and rubbed her neck.

The fire and the wine took the chill off the cold house and her shoulders released the tension that gripped her.

"That feels great. I'm happy to be here, feels like my Spanish home."

"It is and I hope always will be." He kissed the top of her head.

She smiled. "So this book . . ." She put her hand on one of the hidden volumes without turning to look at him and risk giving into their mutual affection. "Galileo wrote a treatise about the sun being the center of the universe. Church inquisitors banned his heliocentric ideas and put him in prison for heresy."

"Why would the Count-Duke hide the book?"

"The Inquisition would have imprisoned him for having it in his possession. Especially after the nobles made the king send him from court and he had no influence. That room is filled with banned books, hidden from servants and other potential spies who might be bribed by the Church."

"No art writing or drawings? Or even land surveys?"

"Possibly. Someone, perhaps Olivares himself or his daughter-in-law Juana de Velazco, wanted to hide things from their enemies. We'll make a full inventory of the room when we get the ladder. It will probably take the three of us all weekend or longer to do it."

"I'll leave a note for Juan to bring the ladder first thing in the morning. Luis will come help."

She yawned.

"Do you want to see our redecorated bedroom?"

"Our?" She folded her napkin onto the tray and offered her hand to him.

"No relatives here now. Just us." Antonio switched off the lights of each room as they walked to the grand staircase and then to the second-floor bedroom.

A blue and white silk bedcover with a matching canopy brightened the room and was a contrast to the tattered one she remembered. "It's beautiful. But, how . . . where did you get the money?"

"Juan and I painted the walls and Tia Teresa found the bed coverings in the attic and asked a local cleaner to restore the fabric as a gift to me." He pulled back the sheets and took off his clothes while she searched her duffle for the T-shirt she slept in, wishing she had a silk négligée.

Antonio pulled her close and held her. "Give me your troubles."

"I'm putting those officially on hold until tomorrow."

"Let's make a wish you find what you want." He kissed her forehead and then his lips kissed hers, long and sweet.

She pulled away just enough to find his eyes staring back at her. "You too. Wish you find what you need."

"I already have what I need."

Another kiss, longer and deeper. The entire universe existed only in this moment, only in his arms. His hand caressed her breasts. Her body tingled when he kissed them and her head swirled as her body melded with his, his strong arms drawing her closer and tighter, thrusting, lost in pleasure. Mutual ecstasy fused them into one and his satisfaction and hers too made them collapse with joy. Antonio fell back onto the pillow, his face shining and his heart pounding in unison with hers.

Their heads shared one pillow. He put his arm around her, moving her head onto his chest, placing his hand on her cheek. He slept deep with that innocent little boy look.

She turned on her side, restless. Antonio followed, putting his other arm around her and holding her hand in his. The moonlight and shadows fell onto the walls that had stood for centuries encircling couples, cries of pleasure, and the tenderness of love. Long ago someone stared at that moon coming through the mullioned windows, perhaps with a lover that created this family's legacy.

Her eyes stayed opened, frustrating her desperation for sleep. The next week would determine *La Gloria*'s acceptance by the academy, her future career success, and a chance to build a life with Antonio, any one of which would result in a sleepless night.

CHAPTER 24

*S*unlight spread from the horizon onto the fields and drank the dew covering the wheat stalks. The sweet night enveloped in Antonio's arms relaxed and refreshed her body to return the morning kisses on her neck, arousing the desire to be close to him. She rolled toward him, and he kissed her eyes and brought her as close as two people can be. And he fell back asleep.

She stared at the bed canopy above her head. With only two days here there was no time to waste. She slipped out of bed. Separated from the warmth, she shivered, leapt into jeans and a T-shirt, and pulled on a fuzzy sweater. She searched for her shoes under the four-poster and remembered when she'd hid *La Gloria* there. The bedroom door creaked as she opened it and caught a glimpse of Antonio who slept with a peaceful face.

Maria worked in the kitchen preparing coffee, warm bread, and that marmalade made from the estate's oranges. The kind woman, a de facto mom, assembled breakfast onto a tray.

Maria nodded to her greeting with her back to her, not stopping her routine to turn around. "Do you desire café?"

She did, did always desire café. "*Si, si, bueno*. It's a beautiful morning."

Maria prepared the espresso that sent energizing smells huffing in her direction. "Juan put the ladder in the closet room."

The library's door remained open throughout the night and no magic elf had shelved the explosion of books on the floor. She wandered through the maze, entered the hidden room, and stared up at the books with anticipation and anxiety. Even a cursory evaluation of the material in the room would be impossible before she had to board the train to Madrid. The dusty mildew air made her cough and she leaned on the bookshelf to steady herself.

Maria arrived with the tray and placed it on the library table. Breaths of better but imperfect air stopped the coughing. Cate steadied herself with the hot coffee that also warmed her hands and made a plan for the task ahead.

First step, get more light, more than what was put in there. She repositioned one floor lamp closer to the room's opening, but it wouldn't reach. "Extension cord?" She raised her arms with her hands pantomiming an extension cord, if that was possible. These words never appeared in Spanish 101, but Maria seemed to understand and left the room.

The ladder was six feet short of the top shelf. So many frustrations, but no time to be a whiner. She shined the cellphone flashlight upward toward the volumes of complete collections of Galileo's writings, volumes by Kepler of his astronomy studies. She pulled the Kepler book from the shelf and balanced her rear on the lower rung of the ladder. She flipped through a few pages and stopped to read a folded page. Kepler, who faced challenges from naysayers, defended his theories and wrote, "Truth is the daughter of time, and I feel no shame in being her midwife."

Dad would like that. Time would eventually bring out the facts, including proof that planets did move around the sun. The value of art history depends on uncovering the truth. The history part owned her heart and pushed her onward to learn what this room's secrets could add to that record.

"Señorita Cate."

She jumped and the ladder rattled.

Maria held out a cord like a dangerous snake. Cate descended the ladder and took the cord, but it wasn't long enough to bring the lamp into the room.

She lifted the floor lamp higher toward the upper shelves. Books were shelved in orderly rows, but the exact system wasn't clear. The ability to locate a book was as important as having it in the first place. She spotted the worn leather portfolio Antonio found squeezed between two volumes, probably atlases, of a similar height.

She set the lamp down and climbed the ladder, but the portfolio was still beyond her reach. Dad had scolded her when she put a foot on the top rung, repeating the warning every year when they cleaned the rain gutters. Lately she'd cleaned, he directed, too weak with his heart problems to do the job.

If she stepped on the top step, she might reach the portfolio, but could fall. She needed Antonio, a foot taller than she was, and with a longer reach too. But he needed restorative sleep and she wouldn't wake him.

"Maria, can you hand me the walking stick from the corner?"

She reached the last few inches with the walking stick and nudged at the leather binding. The folder tumbled beyond her waiting fingers and parchment papers with elaborate calligraphy floated down with a snow of dust particles. She grimaced at the floor covered in pages, because of her impatience. This was exactly what she wanted Luis and Antonio to avoid: Losing the order of the documents, an order someone chose almost four hundred years ago.

She rushed down the ladder with the portfolio cover and stopped on the bottom step. She placed one foot in an empty spot on the floor and the other remained on the ladder, balancing like a ballerina, leg on the barre. With surprising flexibility, she gathered the dozen or so documents to create a place for her feet and then a path out of the room. The individual edges did not appear to have been bound and she slid them back into the portfolio, her hands shaking for fear she might crease or crimp something important. She sneezed.

Maria, standing behind her, ready like a surgical assistant, handed her a linen cloth.

Cate wasn't certain if she was to wipe her nose or dust off the pages. She pulled on her cotton gloves to avoid getting oil from her hands on the pages. The elaborate calligraphy required a magnifying glass and a reference book on seventeenth-century spelling. The language was Castilian, not Latin, and she was grateful for that. She sat at the large library table and pulled the lamp closer to illuminate the faded ink. She read aloud, drawing out the phonetics, and extracting meanings from the odd spellings. Her heart pounded in an escalating rhythm. The list contained ten or so well-known paintings that were in the royal collection of the Prado. Nothing was listed that sounded similar to *La Gloria*. The list was from Velázquez's era, a good sign that perhaps other documents were too.

She paged through, trying to keep from missing something important. One parchment appeared to be written in Italy making references to visits and the kindnesses of hosts on Velázquez's second journey to Italy. Extraordinary. Not a journal by him, but stories about him. Next in the jumble was a lengthy document, paragraphs of text written in difficult, shaky script like that of her grandmother after her stroke. She held it directly under the light.

On this day the second of the month of July in the year one thousand six hundred sixty of our santísimo Jesúscristo, I, Diego Rodríquez de Silva y Velázquez declare my final testament . . .

Extraordinary! The page shook in her trembling hands. Velázquez wrote this.

The year 1660, July, a month before he died in August. She struggled to read on, dizzy with joy, forcing herself to continue, but she could not.

"Señorita, Señorita. You okay?" Maria touched her shoulder and like a concerned mama, tried to lift her head to look at her.

"More than okay." Moving away from the precious parchment, Cate took the napkin, wetted it with water from the tray and wiped tears from her eyes. She laughed and took Maria's hands in hers to twirl her around until the dizziness made her stop.

"Crazy. She is crazy." Maria shook her head and walked away, saying something about old dusty papers.

Antonio came through the door, "Dancing before coffee? Or with coffee? Good morning." Then he noticed her face. "Crying? What's wrong?" Antonio planted a kiss where the tears had been.

"The portfolio. Velázquez." She pointed her shaking finger near the first sentence of the document.

Antonio moved closer and lowered his head to read the words. He stopped abruptly. "Velázquez himself?"

"Velázquez's own hand." The words shattered the air.

Antonio's sleepy eyes popped alive, and he appeared too stunned to speak.

Swirls and tails did not stop with each word but connected letters between words and above and below the lines of writing. She read the first word, *Declaro*, and stopped.

"Let me try." Antonio read, slowly deciphering each word.

Declare this final testament for the disposition of my worldly possessions, the inventory of my artworks and other artists' works in my possession . . .

He paused. "It is a will. See this word *testamento*—testament, a legal will."

She blurted words in staccato, keeping pace with her heart rate. "Lists of paintings? Are there?"

He ran his finger down the document. "No list. Did he know he was dying?"

"No. He fell ill after he'd traveled to France to coordinate the marriage celebration of the Spanish Infanta Margherita to Louis XIV. All that way and the French king sent a stand-in."

He winked. "Outrageous. I'll attend my own wedding."

"Am I invited?"

He placed his hand on her cheek and gently turned her head toward his. "Yes, definitely yes." His lips touched hers, teasing her to kiss him, which she could not resist. They stayed there until she separated from him with a gentle nudge.

"Let's keep reading—this is important."

He pouted like a small boy and then turned to the parchment to read faster, skimming the formal declarations to the details of his bequeathal.

I declare that an Italian woman, Flaminia Triva, recorded as my slave has been my faithful companion while I stayed in Italy and since arriving from Rome with my child Antonio whom I recognize as my legal son and heir, to join me in Madrid. My lady Flaminia needs no grant for her freedom.

"Why didn't he free this slave? He freed Juan de Pareja, his longtime studio assistant." She'd never heard of Flaminia, not in any biography or in the details of the Italian trips.

"I'll transcribe while you read." Antonio pointed, stopping short of touching the document, to the spot he'd left off.

. . . because she is a free woman, daughter of the Italian nobleman Francisco Triva and sister to artist Antonio Triva. Flaminia Triva with loyalty and dedication sacrificed her homeland, her family, and her talent as my companion.

Cate gulped in disbelief. "He had a mistress, a muse, and a child with her." Her heart pounded and the paper shook in her gloved hands.

I have suffered since the second voyage to Italy from severe tremors brought neither by my sins nor disaffection from the sacred catholic faith, but by some defect in my worldly body. At first, I could and did continue to paint with this wretched palsy. Long brushes and quick strokes made it possible to complete the compositions. The tremors increased and dominated my hands so that even this was no longer possible.

"He was afflicted with some neuromuscular problem?" Antonio asked.

"Not recorded in any biography. Many experts commented on changes in his brushwork after the Italian trips, thought to be the influence of Italian painters like Titian."

She could not continue, and Antonio took over reading.

It is with humble gratitude that I confess before God and all mankind my sin of deception. The paintings after the second Italian trip have been a collaboration of my thoughts and the gifted hand of Flaminia Triva. Because of her generous spirit these works were presented to his Majesty King Felipe IV as the work of this, his humble servant. I herewith declare Flaminia Triva is the sole genius, with some poor guidance from this, his Majesty's Court painter, of these works. I declare this to be true and correct for all of history to recognize the work of Flaminia Triva and beg forgiveness from his Majesty and God Almighty for my deception.

She stopped him from continuing, running a list in her mind of which paintings might be included with this reference. She nodded for Antonio to continue reading.

I give my worldly goods including the paintings I possess, my own and works by others, to my wife Juana Pacheco de Velázquez. The works painted by Flaminia including unfinished works belong to her and our son, my rightful heir, Antonio.

He had a son, also named Antonio. Flaminia was no ordinary mistress. A son born in Italy had been mentioned in some biographies but nothing about the mother. Juana Pacheco, his legal wife, died only two weeks after him. Both of their daughters were already dead. Cate turned the parchment over, hoping to see another list of artworks, but nothing was written there. She flipped through the other parchment pages, nothing there either. Her voice barely audible and wavering, she read to the end.

The brittle parchment rattled in her hands as she placed it on the table. She slumped back in her chair, removed her gloves, and stared at the ceiling. No words came with her long sigh, only feelings of being overwhelmed by the exhilaration of the extraordinary find and stunned by the shock of what it revealed.

Antonio set the pen down. "This changes everything, doesn't it?"

CHAPTER 25

"*Y*es." She could barely speak, whispering, breathless. "Velázquez did not paint *La Gloria*."

She said it but could not believe it. The dates she'd worked so hard to verify, the ones the master himself identified meant Velázquez could not have painted *La Gloria* if he stopped painting in 1652. A cloud of confusion hovered over her, the papers on the table, the library and her research all the way back to Madrid.

Antonio questioned her mumblings, but she didn't hear him. The document had crushed what the world had known or thought it knew about this artist. Antonio nodded, mumbled a few words, and then stopped, leaving the room silent except the sound of the clock echoing its tick tock against the library walls.

Finally he spoke and she heard, "Explain it to me."

"Velázquez's most important later works, or the works assumed to be by him, were not painted by him. That's what it means. *La Gloria* was not painted by him." She almost shouted it. A list of masterpieces raced through her mind. "Perhaps he composed the work but the canvases were painted by this Flaminia . . . maybe a collaboration." Studio assistants often painted works assigned to the master of the studio and historians speculated about who did how much of the work. But Velázquez's own words . . . he could not hold a brush. Hope slipped away.

Maybe the document was a fake, outrageous information not corroborated by history, other documents, or known fact, a forgery by a zealous noble or rival. Unlikely, given where they had found it and all the associated circumstances. Adding false expectations would only result in more aspirations to be shattered. The revelation represented a scorched-earth version of the Spanish Golden Age. International experts had been convinced to agree with *her* about the Velázquez attribution. She had convinced them. Her work was wrong. *She* was wrong. Her face fell into her hands, eyes hidden from what she did not want to accept, battered, catatonic unable to move.

He placed his arm around her, pulled her onto his chest, and she remained there listening to his heart pound in counterpoint to her breathing.

He wrinkled his forehead and held her hands still. "Could this revelation be good news? Flaminia Triva, new Golden Age genius. Establish your reputation as scholar."

She shuddered. "You're being sarcastic, right?"

He bristled. "Not sarcasm. I'm a lawyer. Seriously, explain the facts of the case."

"What do you think those academics will say when I tell them half the paintings in the Prado attributed to Velázquez aren't by him? Maybe the works are not even Spanish, but Italian? An unknown art history student brings an old parchment that declares another painter, a woman no less, someone not even mentioned in Jones's famous biography, painted those works in Room 12."

He frowned and pulled back.

"You know what they're like. You saw Cuevas and Jones together. They'll both look like fools for not spotting the difference in Velázquez's brushwork. Never considered someone else right in the royal court had painted them." She added the devastating coupe de grace: "Flaminia won't be a genius in their eyes."

He moved away from her and asked a reasonable question, "Why not?"

She tried to keep her voice from betraying her emotions and respond to his lawyerly inquiries. "If you owned, say, a Rembrandt, and then found proof it was painted by an unknown someone, an apprentice maybe, the value would plummet."

"But a painting admired for centuries as a masterwork is still a masterpiece. True?"

"Names matter. A revised attribution creates doubt in the experts and their opinions that extend beyond a single painting. Maybe the odd reattribution for good reason happens. But a dozen, maybe two dozen? A treasure trove of masterworks!" She gulped the words, searching her memory for such a massive shift in the chronicles of art history. She turned her eyes downward, away from his stare.

"But that's the work, to understand the art, declare who painted what. Jones himself flipped back and forth about *La Gloria*; he claimed he manipulated Cuevas. None of this is cemented in stone."

"You've no idea. Would you challenge the authority of hundreds of years of history around the Magna Carta or some legal treatise? The provenance of those paintings in the Prado showed a direct line to the royal collection; documents and inventories showed Velázquez painted them." She lifted up the parchment. "And they *were* from the royal studio, but Flaminia was right there too, doing the work. The provenance is correct, except for the artist." She paused to control the uncontrollable trembling in her voice, in her head and her soul. "Powerful people in the Academy will fight me. The Spanish government owns those works that bring in hundreds of millions in tourist dollars."

Antonio moved his head up and down as though he was grasping the implications. The clock ticked seconds, then minutes, and finally chimed the quarter hour before either of them spoke.

Antonio straightened his back as if his posture could correct the shock of this find. He broke the silence and asked what worried him most. "The Velázquez portrait, the little one in the gallery? His painting or not?"

"Painted in the later years. We can't be sure of the date, but later years means . . . Flaminia." She lifted her hand to his cheek and looked into his eyes. "I'm sorry."

"I'd hoped to sell the painting to get the funds for the estate repairs, for us, for our . . ." He pushed her hand away.

In less than an hour she'd moved from tears of joy to desolation, all because she'd found what she'd been seeking.

He put his handkerchief in her hand and lifted it to dry her cheeks. He stood, giving her a minute, and paced and moved toward the windows, away from her. "It's worthless?"

Emotions spent, she found her voice. "Not worthless. Thousands of dollars, maybe. Very few women from that time like Anguissola, with a few sales at auction."

"If something is rare, it's more valuable, right?"

"Not always. Anguissola was painting tutor to Felipe II's wife and she painted court portraits. Not many survive. In spite of their scarcity or maybe because of it, they fetch very little in the marketplace."

He sat on the window seat and looked away. His head was framed in profile against the bright sun coming through the glass, a silhouette that gave him a quiet strength, even in his confused state.

She sat next to him and rubbed her hand along his arm. "We'll find another way to get money. There are other things of value here on the estate. Even here in the library."

He ignored her words and continued talking to himself as though she wasn't there. "How much of the family legacy must I sell? The library was one of the last things still intact. The money from that painting could have been enough for me, and

I had hoped for us . . . to survive while the estate developed the agribusiness."

"Us?"

"Of course." Antonio returned his gaze out the window. "You had to know, ever since Christmas. I was planning . . . well it doesn't matter now."

She placed her hands around his and brought them to her lips.

"I struggled with selling that little painting. Like the tiara in great grandmother's portrait. The estate shrinks each year and becomes only the bones of a shoddy house. Now not even that painting can save me." He pounded his fist on the window seat cushion, sending a plume of dust into the air.

"That painting and the others, irreplaceable. His name, her brushstrokes. Her sacrifice to protect him, to protect them. Their love story." She released his hands and stared down at her own. "Maybe a Flaminia will be worth more because of the history, a tangible link to their love." She didn't even believe the words herself, too exhausted with his dilemma to absorb the consequences for her, her goals, her career.

Just outside the window, a bed of neglected plants surrounded the cracked fountain, empty of water and silent above the carved basin. Antonio rubbed his finger on the window frame sending paint crumbles onto the faded cushion. "Do I destroy the place to save the place? As soon as there's hope, it evaporates. Like a curse." He turned to face her, gripping her shoulders.

"Let's put the parchments back and hide them. No one will know."

She gasped. "No." Not him, not at all. Lover of history, his family, and his country. "Ignore the truth? You can't be serious."

He paced and ranted, like an attorney trying to convince the jury. "Hidden for centuries. Imagine how much we don't know about who painted what. Why not put them back where they were? Leave them hidden."

This. From Antonio. He'd criticized her for taking the canvas from NYCU. He had the moral compass to know this would be wrong. She couldn't think straight. Living with another lie after she'd just been freed of a serious one, returning to that person on the precipice of dishonoring her family, shaming them and herself. As much as she wanted the will to go away, she pulled back and moved away from him. She would not, could not go there.

Antonio pulled her closer and whispered, "No one would know."

She raised her head. Her voice wavered, searching for the strength to speak. "We would know." She paused. "Antonio, you were the one who scolded me; taking the painting was wrong. But destroying the will would be no accident. A secret lie would become part of us, always be between us."

He ignored her words and jumped up. "Throw the damn will in the fire, like it had burned up with the rest of the duke's library. No one will miss what they didn't know existed."

The fire roared in the large fireplace on the other side of the library. She stood in front of him and held his arms, shaking her head in disbelief.

"Someone wanted that truth hidden. They did a good job of it too. Until you . . ."

She glared at him, dark and fierce, a fire blazed inside her.

"We . . . I meant to say, we, found them. You're unhappy too. This ruins all your work."

"I can't ignore this." She shook her head and tightened her lips. "Spain's treasure, *Las Meninas*, painted in 1656, Flaminia Triva's work? No one will believe it."

"For you, it's a career. But for me, it's my family, the legacy, funds to save it." Antonio talked into the air to someone, somewhere else. "I am so fucking tired of having no money, being broke. ¡*Qué asco de vida!*" His voice cracked and then he was silent, his face puffed red to the point of exploding.

He picked up the documents and marched five paces toward the fireplace.

"My God, no." She ran and stood between him and the flames. "You can't. There's no getting them back if we . . . you destroy the documents." She grabbed his arm and held tight.

Then he pushed the parchments toward her hands. "You do it. If you love me, you'll burn them."

She gasped and took a step backward. She put her hands behind her back and refused the documents he was pushing at her. The room darkened, her knees weakened. "How dare you test my love like that? I'd never destroy them, no matter what was at stake: my career, the reputation of others, even you."

"You? Tell me right from wrong. You on the high ground? You sacrifice morality when it works for you—like stealing the painting."

"I owned what I did to make it right." She lifted her chin and planted her eyes on his. "What a hypocrite you are to tell me to do something we could never put right!"

Blood rushed from her head. She stepped away from his rage, trying not to make it worse. "More than a career, I wanted respect for my work. From Jones, my family—I wanted them to be proud. You too, I wanted you to be proud." An unfamiliar shrill sound accompanied her words.

He shouted, forcing her backwards. "And you think you're better than me because I need money. What is your career? That's about money. Money to survive. Am I not entitled to that?"

She lowered her voice to a calming tone. "You're frustrated, I get that. I am too." She placed her palm on one of his burning cheeks. She eased the parchments from his hands.

He didn't resist.

She stowed them in the portfolio and pressed it to her chest. She stepped slowly backwards putting the desk between her and the flames.

He sat on the window seat, as far from her as he could be without getting up. He stared out at the Olivares estate. Anger's friend, silence, sat between them in the old library whose walls could tell stories of survival from the Inquisition to wars and fires, and now bankruptcy.

The clock chimed. She moved closer, touched his arm. "I don't know what we do with this. I care about the estate and the financial problems." She turned toward him. "Mostly I care about you."

He sat with his arms folded like a petulant child and didn't answer.

She continued anyway. "I've got to validate a document that I wished we'd never found."

"Validate?" Antonio looked up, unfolded his arms, and stood. "Is it possible the documents are fakes?"

She looked at him and waited. Maybe offer him hope. "It's possible. They're old, I can tell that."

"People fake documents to look old. Find antique paper, old ink."

"I know. But what's the motive?" She needed to plant doubts, reduce his false hopes, or this drama would replay. "Why would someone want to undo a Velázquez attribution? A forger's goal is to make something more valuable, not less."

"Maybe it was a fake in its time. Nobles wanted to challenge the king and his court. Maybe Flaminia was scorned when Velázquez died. Juana his wife died immediately with no living children. Think about it."

Ideas bounced around her head. Leaving the documents with Antonio was out of the question. With time he would get perspective and realize how wrong he was. "Maybe you're right. Maybe they're fakes. First, let's authenticate the writing on the will. If it appears to be false, we can forget it. Problem solved."

"How do you analyze the writing without asking an expert? The document will become public instantly."

"I could do a preliminary comparison to samples of Velázquez's handwriting from the archives. If there are some characters, a loop or a swoop that are dissimilar, it'll be enough to suggest the document was not written by Velázquez."

He put his hand on the portfolio. "One condition: Don't show the will to anyone. Don't log them into the Prado records. Don't tell anyone they exist."

Sneaking around with *La Gloria* had been the worst. To do that again, after she'd solved that with the university, was not what she'd choose but might be the only option to satisfy Antonio and protect the documents.

He repeated his demand. "Agreed?"

"Agreed. No one will see them or even know about them." The Prado was a tough place to hide anything. She'd figure it out.

"The leather portfolio will raise questions. Put them in here." He picked up a canvas briefcase with torn corners marked with the logo of a law firm. He slid the old portfolio into it and handed it to her.

CHAPTER 26

*T*he parchments were secure underneath the bed where she and Antonio slept on separate sides, him kissing her with an obligatory peck across the distance that had become a chasm. She spent the day in the library trying to organize and straighten, checking volumes with limited motivation to find something that might contradict what they already found.

Antonio worked with Juan in the fields, in the barn with the horses, riding off that morning with no invitation for her to go along. Another day passed. She did not know how to fix this.

Maria entered the room and picked up the empty coffee cups. "Señorita Cate, I placed luggage in the hallway." She handed her a small canvas bag. "Lunch. My lord asked me to make lunch for you."

Cate forced a smile, a useless attempt to hide the tension from Maria, who knew everything. "Thank you, Maria." She picked up the frayed briefcase. That someone created a fake will and hid it in the library, not likely. She'd do what she promised: check the handwriting and buy time until she could figure out a plan. She walked through the house that now appeared more sadly dilapidated than ever, and arrived at the entrance.

The gravel drive crunched under her feet. Juan loaded her overnight duffle into the back seat of the car and reached for the briefcase with the documents, but she hung on to it. Juan shrugged and wandered off toward the stables.

Maria hugged her and kissed her cheeks, a different type of goodbye. Maria was the center, the heart of this house and perhaps now sensed something different—the possibility they might not meet again.

Cate got into the front seat where Antonio waited, turned back, and waved to Maria. Antonio drove down the gravel drive, crushing more than pebbles in his wake.

He said little during the hour drive to the station, driving with his shoulders leaning forward and arms rigid, folded around the steering wheel.

She guessed his head was spinning with money issues. His plans, their plans, all suspended like clouds over the plains. Passing across these lands, she reflected on his fear that the estate would crumble to rubble while he fought for it, or worse be razed by developers if he lost.

The stakes for her loomed like storm clouds too, but those didn't concern him. She, an unknown student, declares Velázquez masterpieces documented and attributed since the days they were painted in the royal palace, were instead painted by an unknown woman. She'll be laughed off the stage, recorded in every media imaginable, unemployable in the art field without a reference from anyone. If she shared what she'd found as her principles required, she'd lose him. There'd be no them.

Antonio exited the highway toward Seville's train station. The passenger drop-off line was just ahead. He stopped, brakes grinding at the curb, pulling to the side of the road to let cars pass. He leaned across the seat and took her hand and kissed it as he had done when they first met on the train, a bookended goodbye kiss to match the introductory one.

"I can't promise what will happen next." She turned her head toward the terminal to avoid his eyes. "But I will honor my word. No one will see it."

"I'm sorry."

"I understand." But she didn't. His apology softened the wounds. But the fear that he was a man who, in a moment of crisis, insisted to have his way, beyond all reason, capsized her illusions about who he was.

"Call me when you know something. I'll come to Madrid for Friday's press announcement."

Yes, Friday. Announcement, what could she announce? The presentation she dreaded for the week ahead, the drafts she'd written, worthless.

The driver behind them sounded his horn as cars lined up behind them. She jumped out, grabbed her duffle from the backseat, and clutched the documents case. "Thank you for letting me take them."

He nodded. "Call me when you arrive." His words were the same as always, but his eyes were empty and there was no message of love. His outstretched hand felt cold when she touched it to her still hot cheek. A chill ran from it to her fingers as she released it, and the rest of her body turned numb. More than attributions had changed.

THE TRAIN PUFFED A FINAL sigh of arrival into the Atocha station and echoed her deflated mood. Twilight transformed the streets where diesel-smelling buses and masses of cars turned into a kaleidoscope of lights and motion, but the colorful whirl failed to energize her. Streetlamps sparkled through the trees on the Paseo del Prado as though nothing had changed. Her apartment was fifteen minutes walking, a walk more pleasant and safer than the subway. Traversing the subway tunnels, bumping into people against the flow, presented a risk that someone would knock the case filled with papers from her arms or worse, grab it and run. The Paseo in the evening air along the old route taken by carriages gave her room to breathe, to clear her head protected under the umbrella of trees. Children playing and lovers, arms entwined, reminded her not of Antonio, but of Mom and Dad and little Matty, playing with his friends.

The crush of emotions from the argument with Antonio weighed her down and she could add the dread of disappointing her parents, failing to secure the career that might have healed them with pride in their daughter's accomplishments.

Her cellphone peeked out from a side pocket and she considered phoning him as promised, but the fear remained that they could not talk about this. Geography separated them now, time was needed to assess what happened, how differently they saw things, what it all meant.

Clutching the bulky case reminded her why she wanted to be a scholar, a careful student of the facts, pursuer of truth, a way of thinking and seeing the world, work that matched her character or maybe, like now, character defined the work.

Jones, her mentor, had nurtured these qualities in his students and in her. His words provided a guide: "Epistemology involves the ability to separate mere opinion from rational conclusions based on the available evidence." He pushed careful investigation through comparison, painterly qualities, familiarity with similar works, and the scientific approach instead of conjectures about an attribution. Consider all the possibilities, including the ones easy to reject. She made a mental list as she continued her walk in the evening breeze.

Who was Flaminia? Why had she never heard of her? Maybe Flaminia wrote the will, a revengeful mistress trying to discredit Velázquez for leaving her defamed and destitute with their child. Cate tried to make the case but couldn't. Flaminia had a family, a noble family. It was logical she'd return to Italy.

Perhaps the Triva family had rejected her, an unmarried mother not worthy of her noble heritage. Research on the internet recorded their baby born in 1652 after Velázquez had returned to Spain at the king's order. Piero's ship logs! She'd forgotten the female slave. Why did she follow him? To learn from him, to paint with him, and to love him, passionately love him hidden in the severe and strict Catholic court.

Slaves worked in the household, in the bedroom, in the studio. Flaminia, pretending to be a slave, could work in all areas of the house, including the studio where she could paint and he could guide her hand. No one faulted a gentleman for having sex with a slave in the 1600s, but loving a noblewoman was an affront to the Catholic sacrament of marriage.

Circles of bright lights shone on the corner of the Paseo and Calle de Cervantes. Sunday crowds spilled out of the bars singing soccer club songs and made the walking slow going. She entered the crosswalk to climb one short block to her apartment.

Manuel probably sat in one of these bars watching soccer. Or maybe, but improbable, he was studying for exams in the apartment. If he was there, she couldn't work. No one else could see these papers, even him. She should not go home.

A street musician, wedged between stalls selling Real Madrid scarves, strummed *Concierto de Aranjuez* on his guitar. The haunting melody from another era pushed away all that worried her and reminded her of where she was, what she'd accomplished. She retraced Felipe IV's steps when he walked these ramparts, farmlands belonging to the Conde-Duque of Olivares, Antonio's relative. Their historical presence grew a vision inside of her, a thrumming to learn more. No time to waste, she needed to know what could be known now. She turned around and walked toward the museum.

She set the portfolio on a bench to search the duffle. She'd left from the museum, it had to be here somewhere. She pulled out her security badge. Hopefully the guards would check her duffle with her clothes but ignore the briefcase.

Gabriel, a forty-year veteran of the museum guards, led the

team and worked Sundays, the museum's busiest day, to free his young staff. Fingers crossed he would be tired and ready to end the shift. He stood guard behind the glass door as Sunday's final visitors exited.

He shook his head while he greeted her. "You work too much, go have fun. A *caballero* wants his *novia los domingos.*"

His unsolicited advice was offered with fatherly protectiveness, something she would not accept from a man her own age. *Caballero* Antonio didn't want his girl this Sunday. Perhaps he was chopping wood to purge his anger. "I traveled to Seville, a nice weekend," she lied.

"Open the bag."

"Sure, sure." She pulled the zipper and held the duffle open.

Gabriel peered into the jumble, zipped it up, and hesitated, looking at the briefcase. He reached out for her to give it to him.

Her hands were sweating. "Just a quick trip to check something. Let me get that out of your way so you can process all the people leaving." *Brave, unlike her.*

He put his hand down and winked.

She acknowledged the favor with a nod and passed through the turnstile. Her key card opened the door where her office was. She turned on the lights of the empty, silent office. A pang of loneliness merged with the hurt from Antonio's outburst. Naive, believing and trusting, when she should have known him better before diving into a relationship.

Only twenty minutes remained before the museum closed and she set the alarm on her cellphone to mark the time. Tomorrow morning, there'd be no private time, staff in and out of her office working on Friday's deadline for the press conference.

She removed the will from the case and placed it between two pieces of acid-free mat board to protect the pages. Her curator key card opened the secured area where two Velázquez writing samples should still be in the flat files, awaiting return to the fireproof vault. A curatorial assistant had reviewed the specimens and completed a report for a course project that Cate had not yet read and hadn't given much importance as *La Gloria* was unsigned. Now those papers could determine *La Gloria's* attribution. She raised the archival portfolio from the drawer, placed it on top of the flat file, and held her breath. She put on her gloves, holding the parchment with the lightest pressure to avoid damaging the brittle paper, and placed it on the light box.

The will glowed with illumination from underneath and above. She aligned the first sample, a short note with a signature, but no date, next to the will. The swooping letters, deliberate and distinctive on the sample, did not match the letters on the will. She examined them with the loupe again making sure. They didn't match. Either the will was a forgery, or this sample was.

Analyzing artists' signatures, looking for basic differences, was not her expertise. She'd studied many signatures as an undergraduate and received a "superior work" faculty designation for a paper about Miró fakes. Handwriting experts could date the chemicals in the ink. Still, specialists admitted nothing substituted for comparison and examination of the letters under magnification.

The LED magnifying lamp with the adjustable arm brought the swoops and turns into high relief. The dissimilarities were clear, especially when she lingered over the q, an unusual and distinctive letter in his name. The q on the first writing sample did not match the one on the will that was less bold and the tail smaller. She sat back in the chair, breathed a deep sigh, and considered what this meant. Antonio would be happy.

The disparity between the sample and the will might be due to the author's age. The will was written at the end of Velázquez's life and if it was true, his hands shook from palsy. The sample's exact date could not be determined, but had to be earlier than the will.

A curator's note attached to the second writing sample indicated the paper had been attached to the back of a painting with the address of a patron and the title of the work, signed and dated 1653, closer to the 1660 date on the will. A comparison of the two Vs and each letter that followed including the tails on the q and the two z letters, matched. The swoops were identical. The same shaky letters as those on the will appeared on the handwriting example.

Tired to the bone, she sat back in the chair. Conflicting specimens, like a second medical opinion, eliminated a clear conclusion. The evidence tipped toward the will being genuine.

The more significant question was motivation. Objects were forged to create value, not diminish it. The will made Velázquez's works less valuable and provided limited benefit to Flaminia. She pushed the magnifying lamp aside, turned off the light box, and closed her eyes. Sitting in the dark, she wanted to moan, howl, scream at the universe for upending her work, creating uncertainty about everything, and putting insurmountable challenges in her path. *Why, why, why her?*

This self-pitying persona had become a familiar, unlikable companion, returning her to a pattern she'd left, tried to leave, back in Michigan. She took a deep breath, sucked in tears and issued a warning to herself to avoid that place she'd tried to escape.

Step up to this challenge. What historians knew about Velázquez, their assumptions about women painters of the era, and the valuations of masterworks would raise questions and deserved more study. Her mission, her resolve, to study *La Gloria*, to open the Academy's eyes to the contributions of women, endured. Antonio was right. The will changed everything, but some things in a good way.

Maybe the Prado director would cancel or delay the press conference until experts, including handwriting specialists, could study the new information. But she'd need to show them the will, break her promise to Antonio—which would require hiding or even lying about what she had found. She leaned back in the chair, folded her hands in her lap, opened her eyes, and stared up at the ceiling.

Her watch buzzed. Five minutes to closing. She was too tired to make sense of anything. The samples went back into their acid-free storage box. Security cameras would have recorded her in the room and she needed a story. She signed the log showing that she had viewed the writing samples to critique the student's paper.

Janitors swept up the crowd's residue from the galleries, preparing for the next day's onslaught of visitors. Their brooms banged against the walls and echoed between the giant salons. She stopped at Velázquez's *The Surrender of Breda*, painted before he knew Flaminia. Perhaps they'd met on his first trip to Italy in 1634 and he'd returned a second time because of her. *Surrender* was precise and strong with details and a brilliant composition of gracious Spanish victors over the clumsy-looking Dutch. No palsied hand executed this painting.

In *Las Meninas*, the focal point of Room 12 rotunda, the center of the Prado, eleven figures populated the canvas, all gathered together with a lovable dog. The composition had parallels to *The Surrender of Breda*, complex iconography, open to interpretation.

A janitor stood next to her admiring *Las Meninas*. *"¡Que maravilla! ¿Verdad?"*

She smiled and nodded. It didn't take an art history degree to recognize this as a masterpiece—whoever painted it.

Velázquez appears in the painting holding a brush in front of a canvas. A mysterious composition, pondered by the experts asking if it was a self-portrait or one of the king and queen that sit out of the frame reflected in the mirror. Flaminia as the painter made sense: This was a portrait of her lover in his glory days, brush and palette in his hand. Maybe the two contrived the composition together to quell rumors about the master's reduced production of artworks, which history blamed on his other court duties. And maybe Flaminia was the one who painted the Cross of Santiago on his tunic, a noble rank Velázquez had coveted but had not yet been granted until eight months before his death. Flaminia could have painted the cross as she finished the portrait after his death. The differences between early work and these paintings was something that developed with every artist as he or she found a voice, a rhythm.

If the master sat next to her, sharing a *copa*, how would he write the ending? Velázquez had intended for the world to know. She had the burden to decide if they *would* know.

The janitor moved on to another gallery and she sat alone on the bench. Dad was right: Looking at paintings was not work. For her, it never had been.

The gallery lights flashed, signaling the museum's closing. She quickened her steps back to the office with the parchment under her arm. She locked it and the other documents in her office cabinet with the security and fire protection of the museum.

Velázquez was long gone. Flaminia dead and unknown. Antonio very much alive and in her life. She should take the papers out of the museum, toss them in the public trash on Paseo del Prado, burn them on the kitchen stove, or return them to the hidden room as Antonio first suggested.

Maybe she was making things harder than they had to be.

CHAPTER 27

*S*he hadn't eaten since breakfast. She munched a few chips from an open bag on the kitchen table. Graphs and charts with colored lines that looked like a Mondrian painting traced histories of a disease she couldn't pronounce, Manuel's stuff, covered the table. The television displayed a soccer match paused with a midfielder's leg in mid-run, time stopped at forty-six minutes, the break between halves.

Someone opened the street door on the ground floor and throbbing hip-hop music traveled up the stairwell. Manuel appeared in the apartment door, headphones protruding like an alien. A beer in one hand and a sandwich in the other, he nodded, followed by air kisses in her direction.

And this, this . . . alien would be someone's physician in less than a year?

"Hola, *Desaparecida*. Where've you been?"

"Olivares. Kinda last minute."

"No problem. I figured nobody kidnapped you and you were with the lover." He laughed at this own remark.

Were they? Still lovers?

Manuel rolled back the brown paper and chomped the *boccadillo*. "What a face, *mujer*. What's the matter? A breakup?"

Maybe Manuel would make an insightful doctor after all.

"Did the Seville guy dump you?"

Manuel had no finesse, no social boundaries, and she had no energy for him. "Can we talk about something else?"

He nodded, or was that chewing with a head bob? "You want part of this? Some tortilla left in the fridge. Not too old, maybe a week."

Didn't they teach food safety in med school? The smells of his sandwich filled the air and stomach pangs wouldn't stop. She remembered the lunch Antonio told Maria to make. She unzipped her bag and pulled out the plastic box.

Antonio did care, at least enough to make sure she ate something. Sharing his apartment, the magical Christmas, taking the canvas to the Prado, joining this attribution journey, he had been with her. Until now.

She squeezed into a space between Manuel's papers and spread out a napkin. Manuel chomped at thin slices of salami buried inside the thick bread.

She hadn't ever eaten with him, only chats standing at the bar downstairs, but here at the table, his open-mouth chewing was unsettling. But his company distracted her from her own dilemma. "What are you working on?" She pointed her free elbow at the papers.

"A case study from medical rounds at the hospital. It's my turn to present," he said with a mouthful of sandwich.

She looked away, grateful for Antonio's impeccable manners, and waited until he was between bites to ask another question. "What's wrong with the patient? Something weird?" She braced herself for one of his gruesome descriptions of an accident victim or some unknown infectious disease. "Should I get vaccinated?"

"Can't. Not for this."

She waited and chewed, mouth closed.

"Death. A forty-year-old man, wife, two children. Presents with a cough. Advanced stage lung cancer, dying. Nothing to be done." Manuel shuffled the papers, stacking them away from her food.

His expression, usually full of energy, conveyed a solemnity that drew her in. She studied his face like she'd analyze a painting. Manuel's eyes, his inward glance, showed helplessness. A young father dying trumped her problems; her work was not life and death. Or was it? The death of her career. The death of an artist's reputation. The death of Antonio's dreams. The death of their relationship.

She dumped the self-pity and conceded a man dying trumped art stuff. "What do you write about something like that? What's the case if there is nothing to be done?"

"The topic: Do we tell the patient?"

She lifted her eyebrows. "Don't you have to tell the patient? Medical ethics require it."

"Would you want to know that you were dying?" he asked.

"Absolutely," she answered too quickly.

"I thought that too. Then I considered he'd be robbed of any joy in his final days. With his kids and his wife. Overwhelm them with sadness, hard decisions, and helplessness."

Her thoughts drifted to Matty's abrupt death, a kid, with no wife, no children, no will.

She pushed back. "What about getting things organized? Isn't that a gift too, to be able to die with the peace of knowing your wife and children," she hesitated, ". . . maybe someone else dear to you, will be taken care of?" Being taken care of was more than economics. There were hearts to care for too.

"That's good. I'm going to use that. Most people are not organized." He scribbled something in the margins of a notebook.

She added more. "But also, a chance to say goodbye, to say what needs to be said, that you're sorry, to ask forgiveness, to say how much you love the dying patient." She couldn't look at him and did not want to tell him about Matty.

Manuel stood to refill his cup, leaned against the kitchen counter, and stared out the window. "I suppose so. Want coffee?"

Manuel sipped. No, slurped.

She picked up her plate, put it in the sink, and tossed the crumpled paper napkin into the trash. "I don't have a will. Do you?"

"Wills are for people who own something. My entire estate—right here, this cup, a coffee cup and a few pairs of jeans." Manuel chuckled.

"Me too. Nothing to leave behind."

"Don't you own some art?"

"Not really. Once I had a valuable canvas with a confused ownership. Not really mine." Her smile faded.

"Confused ownership." Manuel pondered the phrase. "Sounds like a reason to get organized. Get clear about who owns what, make it so the people left behind know what your wishes are." He scribbled some notes.

Velázquez tried to get it right, make sure the world knew what he wanted them to know. Was the will ever read as was the custom, and did Flaminia receive paintings? His wife, dead two weeks after him, probably never heard the disclosures the will contained and the revelations would not have served the nobles who took over.

Her shoulders slumped, beat down with fatigue. "That's my answer. Got to tell the patient. I'm getting some sleep."

"No, stay. Once we tell the patient, we can't take it back."

She really didn't want to do this. She raised her voice from the frustration of the day, the work, her life. "There's no way to know. How can you predict the reaction? If you don't tell, you will never know if it was a good thing or a bad thing. Until you do it." She lowered her tone and whispered, "Tell him."

He appeared shocked at her outburst, resigned and confused at the same time.

She felt bad and picked up the notebook with a half page of handwritten words. "What have you written already?" She stared at the illegible script.

He shook his head and took the notebook back. "Consult with colleagues, including others who work with the patient. Might have insights to patient's state of mind. Relationships. Practitioners must consider in context of patient's situation."

"That's good." She paused surprised at his words. But there was a flaw. "Moral dilemmas aren't decided by majority vote, are they?"

He scrunched up his mouth. "You're tough, *Mujer*. Sometimes talking with people helps clarify your own thinking. That's the final point of my outline. It really comes down to how you, yourself would want to be treated. Final decision made by your own conscience, your own compass."

"You've just robbed me of a night's sleep."

"That's my world. No sleep ever." He looked like a sad boy, as lost as she was.

Manuel was a guy who could sleep on a dime, on a park bench, the back seat of a car. She couldn't picture him awake worried about anything except his beloved Real Madrid losing a match.

"Guess they don't have decisions like this in art."

"You'd be surprised." She kissed him, real kisses on both cheeks. "*Buenas noches.*"

Her dark room felt like a protective nest. Cracks in the ceiling got bigger, deeper in the blackness, something she'd never noticed until now. Maybe light blinds the eyes and hides the imperfections.

Manuel and his dying patient. How much do people want to know?

She turned over to the side where she slept best. Manuel said he'd discuss the patient's case with the medical team. Ask colleagues. Clarify his thinking.

Jones would arrive on Wednesday to chair a panel entitled "Velázquez and His Studio" the next day. And he would speak at the press conference on Friday, alongside Cuevas. Jones had become less a curmudgeon professor, more a mentor who took her phone calls, responded to her emails, and built trust between them.

She could question him about his Velázquez biography without revealing anything. Perhaps Jones knew details about the master's final days.

When New York woke up, she'd phone Jones and set up a meeting with him upon his arrival.

CHAPTER 28

*C*ate wove her way through the Monday morning crowds gathered outside the Prado, carrying espresso in a paper cup, something no Spaniard would have done before Starbucks. Sluggish, she needed a gallon of espresso to face this day. She sipped what she had while a full complement of guards rifled through purses and work papers in compliance with their mission to protect the irreplaceable art. When her turn came, she got the thorough routine, removing everything and returning the jumble. Without a word, she clutched the link necklace around her neck, relieved she'd left the Olivares documents in her office yesterday.

PR Pilar and her assistant sat in chairs outside her office, waiting. Cate forced a half-smile in their direction and said nothing. They stood at attention, awaiting their orders without any idea how the landscape had shifted.

"Another coffee?" Dalila asked. She lifted Cate's empty espresso cup and tossed it into the trash. Dalila bowed with a sarcastic curtsy and disappeared.

Not even nine o'clock, three coffees downed. She checked her work phone and the message slips on her desk. Nothing from Antonio. He probably assumed she wouldn't have compared the signatures yet.

Pilar cleared her throat and pulled out two folders, handed one over, and kept one for herself. "Let's review Friday's agenda."

Cate put her phone down. "Go ahead." Dalila arrived and set the coffee into her eager hands.

Pilar rolled her eyes. "The program begins with a reception in the lobby. We expect three hundred representatives of the press."

"Three hundred. Seriously? Are that many newspapers still in business?"

"There's a couple hundred in Spain alone. The small Spanish papers from Alicante to Vigo will attend. Representatives from the major European papers, plus US, Latin America. Now that I think about it, we should plan for four or five hundred."

"At the Metropolitan, print press would come, but if something was visually exciting, television crews and photographers might come."

"Oh, they'll be here too. We need time for stage setup—light and sound checks. It's on the schedule for 8:30 a.m." She pointed at the paper.

Espresso ate at her stomach but she ignored that pain and substituted the terror of Friday's Waterloo moment. Predictions about how Friday would evolve were impossible but withholding what she knew felt wrong. She imagined the headline on Rome's *la Repubblica*, newspaper of Flaminia's home country. If she introduced this unknown Baroque painter, the Italians might be happy. To attribute Spanish masterpieces to an Italian, especially a woman, that would be something.

Pilar tapped her fingers on the desk, a not-so-subtle message to demand attention. "A newly discovered Velázquez. Cate, it's huge. The Prado competes to be on the world stage against the Louvre, the National Gallery in London, the Uffizi, people who think Europe ends at the Pyrenees. The Spanish Golden Age will return to the consciousness of Europe. You did this for us." Pilar glowed.

She could not tell Pilar to cancel or postpone. This train, the thing she dreamed of, now about to become reality, could not be stopped. The press would be relentless and there would be dead bodies on the tracks, including hers, if the train didn't arrive.

The Prado's impressive Italian section included Titian, Tintoretto, and Caravaggio, and other works some of which Velázquez had purchased on behalf of the king on that Italian trip. It was the trip where he discovered or renewed his passion for Flaminia. She couldn't imagine the Prado renaming the rotunda an Italian gallery.

Pilar clicked her fingers near her face. "Hola—where are you?" Pilar flipped a couple of pages. "Look, page three. You need to know this. At 9:00 a.m., you will be seated on the podium with the director, Jones, and Cuevas. The director will introduce you and then you speak. How long do you need?"

"I need to write it."

"You haven't written it?" Pilar gave her a look that could set a building on fire. "The printer needed it two days ago, I gave you until today. Journalists need the facts."

Yes facts. Which facts would they choose to share with the press? "I can have it late Wednesday. I need to review some things with Jones and he doesn't arrive until tomorrow."

Pilar scowled. "*Muy bien*. We want you to get it right." She turned to the assistant who had been scribbling notes. "Let's go so Cate can write, write, write."

Pilar remained in the doorway after the assistant left. She took a step back and closed the door. "You can do this. It's daunting but you're smart, organized, know everything about this painting."

Yes, know everything and then nothing. How does anyone ever know anything with certainty when information is incomplete and upended when new facts are discovered?

Pilar continued, "Don't be nervous. Don't. Millions of people will see your face on the evening news, it's the same as talking to one person." Pilar put her arm around Cate. "You can do this. No interviews until next week. Gives you the weekend to prepare, anticipate questions and research answers. The bonus is we get a second follow-up story." Pilar smiled.

If she meant to make her feel better, she'd failed. Breakfast rose into her throat. "Excuse me. I need to go to the restroom." She scurried out of her office and down the hall.

Cate locked the staff restroom door to keep her panic attack private. Supporting herself at the sink was a dismal place, so she moved to the chaise longue provided for . . . who knows . . . swooning female employees? Like her. She gagged but did not lose her breakfast. She tried deep yoga breathing, other calming techniques without success.

Flat-out bad karma. She'd gone down a wrong path by taking the painting, challenging Jones but survived, even prevailed, to tell the tale of a Velázquez attribution. But Flaminia could not be denied and if she didn't disclose what she'd found, more bad karma, and someday she'd be called to account for the deception. Dad's words, one lie requires another, then another until it all blows up.

If she revealed the will, she—a junior art historian—would not be able to manage the turmoil that would result.

But if she did not introduce Flaminia, what kind of a scholar would she be, or the more important question, what kind of person? Not the one her parents had loved, not what they had dreamed for their only surviving child. She had to do better, fulfill even the low expectations they had for her.

She gave the mirror a determined but fake smile and staggered back to her office.

The afternoon's work resulted in a frustrated effort evidenced by the volume of crumpled paper, tossed and failing to reach the wastebasket. She turned to the computer and dashed off lots of words and then deleted them, the digital equivalent of crushed paper. The deleted paragraphs ended up parked on a second word doc in case they were better than the rewritten ones. In school, she did her best writing after she had an idea, understood what she wanted to say.

Jones must have an idea; he'd been generous with advice in the last few months. But their history of his repeated shifts between sabotage and support made him unreliable—less a leaning post and more an erratic weed bending with the wind. That wobbly weed was all she could cling to now.

She turned off the light and left to find space, breathing room, open sky, and an idea of what she would write.

CHAPTER 29

*I*n two mad days, she'd reviewed all the primary and secondary sources in the Prado archives, including letters, journals, and royal court documents, searching for any reference that might confirm or deny the existence of Flaminia, a Velázquez will, a son, any bit of the story. Pacheco described the first Italian trip and Palomino wrote about Velázquez's second visit to Italy. Palomino mentioned a Flaminia with a different last name, Triunfo. Difficult to believe there were two women named Flaminia, both with surnames beginning with T. Palomino's respected history from 1715 was a record that Velázquez knew her, speculation about her as the mother of his bastard child, and that Flaminia was even possibly the model for the nude in the *Rokeby Venus*. Palomino wrote this more than fifty years after Velázquez died, so it had to have been recounted to him.

Embarrassment flushed her cheeks with the realization she'd read Palomino before and she too had overlooked the role of women in Velázquez's life. How easy it was to fall into the comfort of accepted history and forget how much historians leave out or don't know.

Noise in the kitchen brought her out of the bedroom dressed in her ragged T-shirt and sweatpants. A tired-eyed Manuel sat catatonic at the kitchen table.

"Exams?"

He nodded but didn't look up.

She didn't have the bandwidth to sympathize with him. She faced a mega challenge in front of the world's press that would decide her entire career. Maybe his test was epic, life-changing if he fell short, and in that way, they were two souls spinning like separate planets trying to hold their orbits.

Perhaps Jones would consider the Flaminia discovery to be a gift. *La Gloria* could be a scholarly coup and she'd let him be a champion of this revised history. Hell, she'd let him own the discovery if he'd help her maneuver through the minefield ahead. She could not predict anything about how Jones would respond.

She'd offered to pick him up at the airport. In a moment of atypical graciousness, he said, "You're too busy I'm sure and, I might add, important to our upcoming events." Perhaps he wanted to avoid the traffic circles with her at the wheel.

The "busy" part was correct regarding the research, but she had not written a word for the presentation. Mostly she'd avoided Pilar whose bleating for the final presentation continued. Responses about various states of completion had escalated to something she'd called a final draft and promised to deliver after she met with Jones.

She opened her laptop, committed to write the introduction. No matter who painted *La Gloria*, words of love flowed over the keyboard and onto the digital page about the painting. Three minutes of the ten-minute talk filled the screen, describing the painting's woven linen canvas prepared with a mixture of lead white oil paint and clay in the first layer of ground to achieve the luminous effect he'd developed during the second Italian trip. The compositions fit with his later paintings, his signature white lines around the figures, or lines repositioning the image on the canvas, altered as he painted instead of using drawings and studies. Pigments were consistent with the master's practice, never using green but mixing blues, white, yellows, and ochre to achieve a precise palette for sky and vegetation. Her initial thought was the red was carmine from the cochineal beetle, used by the Aztecs in Mexico, but *La Gloria*'s red derived from crushed kermis beetle native to Europe. The props, the models' faces, the positioning of the figures, all consistent with Velázquez's studio. These facts supported a Velázquez attribution but did not rule out Flaminia as the painter.

The empty paper scroll in the corner, his device to mock those who signed their works, took on a different meaning. Was it Flaminia's way of inviting the world to consider who had painted *La Gloria?*

Just write it, damn it. She pounded the keyboard like an airline employee changing a ticket. "The attribution appeared to point to Velázquez. That hypothesis changed when we . . ." She stopped. "We," who was we? She and Antonio? She and the Prado? Certainly not. She'd told no one at the Prado. She and Jones, unlikely. There was no "we." Not yet.

She saved the file and closed the laptop. Manuel had left and either didn't say goodbye or she didn't hear him. The shower energized her like a rehydrated plant, lifting its leaves to face the sunshine. The black suit, too funereal, she chose the grey instead, neutral softer, less threatening, not that she ever intimidated Jones.

She enjoyed the brisk walk to the Ritz. The golden sconces on the porte cochere glowed in the morning light and the doorman greeted her in his archaic livery. "May I open the door for a beautiful lady?"

"*Buenos días.* I love the smell of these gardenias." The ornate pots never displayed dead or wilting flowers. The front desk clerk stood ready to receive her request. "Professor Herant Jones. For Cate Adamson. Please."

The clerk pulled a note pinned to the desk and read from it. "The professor asks that you wait at the entrance to the Garden Restaurant."

Blue umbrellas dotted the terrace like a convention of butterflies enjoying the spring sunshine. The maître d' welcomed her in English, pegging her as American. Hard to shake that look even after all these months living here. Her mind filled with distractions to avoid the crucial discussion awaiting her.

She sat on a banquette next to a grouping of thick palms. An animated conversation at the table on the other side radiated tension where she'd come to expect tranquility. She couldn't resist poking her head around the plants to see who was there. Jones, dapper in a paisley ascot, argued with a gray-haired woman facing the opposite direction. That voice, something about it, had a familiar gentleness in spite of the emotional conversation.

Their discussion got louder. "After years of helping you, now I need your help. Your objections don't make sense."

Miss Lillian! Lillian Smythe, the woman who'd fainted and required an ambulance, was meeting with Professor Jones.

"I won't explain nor defend my position. Our arrangement does not include publishing under your own name," Jones said.

"I've done the research, developed the ideas, drafted, and revised. If it weren't for me, you wouldn't have a career!"

Cate sat up straight, couldn't believe what she'd heard.

Miss Lillian, not Professor Jones, wrote the tomes she and other students revered. Jones never used graduate students for research or to draft his publications as other faculty did. Students assumed he never slept, had no life to produce the volume of writing listed on his curriculum vitae.

But this was something else. She shrunk down into the banquette.

Jones pushed back. "You were my researcher. The writing, the polished drafts were mine alone. I cannot discuss this here. Let's meet in your apartment later after the presentation on Friday."

Through the palms, Miss Lillian appeared to put her shoulders back and lift her face toward him, ignoring his request. "This new project based on the journal from the National Library revises the biography of his final years. All my work."

Eavesdropping was wrong, it was. But the words "final years" persuaded her to continue listening. She leaned the other direction and pretended to read a newspaper and not be so obvious.

Jones responded, "Not the point, Mother."

Unbelievable! Miss Lillian was his mother. Cate scooted over, farther away from the palm fronds, lowering her head and trying to absorb the shock.

Frail Lillian raised her voice. "Your lack of gratitude infuriates me. Those books that won awards, your books—my books—?"

"Calm, please. People are listening. We are meeting here at your insistence. I prefer to discuss this in your apartment, but this trip I have no extra time. At least, keep our discussion quiet and confidential if we must meet at all." Jones lowered his voice and Cate strained to hear the next bit, but couldn't.

He spoke louder again against his own admonition in response to whatever Lillian had said. "Nonsense. My ideas, theories about the Baroque period, not to mention my position at the university, my status in the Academy, that's what gets books published. Your research provided the foundational material, yes, and thank you for that. My knowledge, analysis, and reputation built those facts into something more."

"What about the facts you omitted?" Lillian's voice wavered.

He paused and moderated his tone. "Never let that journal out of your control. My god Mother, you stole it from the National Library."

"Don't threaten me."

Missing facts? Journal? Overhearing this became too awkward and it was wrong. Cate got up from the bench, walked to the lobby, browsed the gift shop, and then reentered the dining room, walking directly to their table. Their conversation ended mid-sentence when she approached.

Jones spit out a terse "hello," and then the gentleman in him jumped up to pull out her chair as his mother must have taught him. "Lillian Smythe, this is Miss Catherine Adamson, a NYCU doctoral student."

Lillian looked up at her, studied her face, and reached out a veined hand to delicately shake Cate's outstretched hand. "We've met before. How are you, dear? Son, remember the lovely woman who helped me when I had that mini-stroke?"

Cate feigned a surprised look at the word "son." "Professor Jones is your son?" She didn't wait for an answer. "Small world. How are you feeling?"

"The doctors said your quick action made all the difference. I wanted to thank you, but I didn't remember your name."

Cate looked at Jones still holding the chair. "I'm happy you are well. May I join you? I could wait. . . ."

"Mother was about to leave."

Cate ignored the comment, something he'd taught her, and sat down. "Have you published the book you were working on?"

A shocked expression returned to Jones's face. *Perhaps she'd gone too far.*

"We were just discussing publishing certain projects," Lillian replied.

An awkward pause took over. The waiter handed her a menu, large enough to hide behind.

"It's important to include all the facts. Don't you agree, Ms. Adamson?"

Cate peeked over the menu to look at Jones, who checked something on his phone. She didn't want to get in the middle of their argument, nor annoy him, not now. "Some facts are stronger than others, some might be redundant or not facts at all."

"Yes. Reliable, primary sources," Lillian said with a bit too much emphasis. Her son poked out some words on his phone.

"A fruit plate, please," Cate said, closing the menu. Church bells nearby chimed out the time. Four hours before Pilar would be tapping her foot, expecting a completed presentation.

"Ms. Adamson and I must discuss our upcoming presentation. And you have a busy day, Mother."

Saved from being drawn into the middle of their dispute, Cate was at once relieved and disappointed. She sided with Lillian and a woman's need for recognition of her work, but the facts in the journal, maybe about Flaminia, were imperative now.

Miss Lillian put a cape over her shoulders, protection from the chill. "Very nice to see you again. Perhaps we can meet for lunch."

"I would like that," she answered. She'd hoped Lillian would offer her card or write her number down, but she didn't.

Lillian squeezed her hand and wobbled off toward the lobby.

Jones spread the napkin across his lap with his classic flourish. He checked a massively expensive Patek Philippe watch for the time. "How can I help you?"

She'd rehearsed the opening lines to secure his guidance, but they seemed useless after what she'd heard. She had no other option. "The press will ask about the central figure in *La Gloria*. Who was the model? Was it a mistress? The same as the mysterious nude in the *Rokeby Venus*, perhaps?"

Jones straightened his tortoiseshell glasses and pushed them up his nose. "Ridiculous. The identity of the nude in *Rokeby* remains a long-standing mystery. The woman's nude back is to the viewer and her face a blurred image in the mirror she holds. Her identity has never been confirmed, but most experts, including me, conclude she was a paid model." Jones turned on his professorial robot.

"Your biography says little about the women in Velázquez's life. His wife died two weeks after he did. His two daughters both died before their parents. A mistress during his Italian trips is documented in Palomino's book. On the second trip, he disobeyed the king when asked to return to Madrid. Defying the king was an extraordinarily bold move. Some say it was because of the mistress."

"Mistresses, typical of the time, are of no consequence, not worth writing about." He took another sip of coffee and sloshed some into the saucer. Unusual for this fastidious professor.

She pushed ahead. "An Italian mistress could have modeled for the *Rokeby*. Or a paid model. Or a woman who was both."

He fidgeted with his Harvard signet ring.

"Perhaps there's a connection between the figure in *La Gloria* and the model in the *Rokeby Venus*. The nude Venus in *Rokeby* is holding the mirror at an odd angle, not showing her reflection, but possibly that of the painter."

Jones shook his head before she finished the sentence. "The face in the mirror can't be the painter. The image is a woman."

"Yes."

He appeared stunned at her suggestion. "The painter, a woman? Absurd. Velázquez painted it." His hand visibly shook now.

She poked at a strawberry and considered taking a bite, hoping her silence might encourage him to say more. But he did not.

"Your mother mentioned when we met in the Museum that she'd found something in the National Library, related to Velázquez." She waited, nudged him gently, not wanting the old Jones to rear his head.

He took an impatient breath. "Don't take her seriously. She's a hobbyist, an art history enthusiast, nothing more." His tone shifted to defensiveness.

Something awakened in her, an intuition. She'd come to ask his guidance on what she'd learned, but now what he knew mattered more.

She chose her words and considered her promise to Antonio. "The information might corroborate documents I uncovered." She turned to her plate and speared a melon piece with the fork. "Is it possible Velázquez had another family, in addition to Juana and their daughters?" She looked up, waiting, and the room became a swirl of images encircling the table with Jones's face in high relief.

He twirled his finger.

She'd have to speak first.

"An Italian noblewoman, a painter he met in Italy may have had a child with him. Is there any chance . . . ?"

Jones mopped his brow with a monogrammed handkerchief. She observed his poker player tell, that mopping of his forehead when he was concealing something. She looked over her shoulder to check the bench and, seeing it was empty, leaned forward. "Flaminia Triva. Do you know about her?"

He lowered his voice. "Know what?"

"A previously unknown document in Velázquez's own hand . . ." She regretted it as soon as she said it.

"What document?"

"Flaminia was his mistress, had a child with him, and . . ." She waited for a reaction that would reveal what his words might not.

His voice lowered to a whisper, tight and controlled. "A discredited hypothesis, surely you were aware of the nonsense of that Englishwoman historian."

Her pulse raced. So he'd read something about this. "This document says Flaminia painted with him, painted *for him*."

He dropped his coffee spoon. His head stiffened and he glared. "Groundless leaps. Where's the evidence?" He set his water glass down and steadied his fingers on the table's edge.

He had not denied hearing it. Time to end this dance.

"Does the journal Lillian found state that canvases painted by Flaminia have been attributed to Velázquez?"

He pretended to laugh. "Preposterous." His fingers trembled as he clutched his napkin and brought it to his forehead.

Waiters clearing tables, clanging dishes and speaking in low tones filled the air.

He clenched his jaw, suppressing the eruption of anger and mumbled, "Mother betrayed me."

"Your mother did not tell me. You did." She folded her hands, sat tall until her spine could go no higher, eyes directly on his.

His breaths were coming faster, almost hyperventilating. "Mother found a journal in the National Library, an item not in their catalog, and she brought it to me. The writings of an Italian nobleman in whose home Velázquez had stayed. The journal has not been authenticated." He stopped. "It would be reckless to publish anything from it."

"Ship logs show Flaminia came to Spain from Italy, pretended to be Velázquez's slave. Velázquez was ill with a palsy that made his hands shake. Maybe from the skin-whitening clay, or the toxic chemicals in white lead paint, mercury, or other toxic pigments he used. Doesn't matter how he became ill, but the result was he could not control his brushes to paint."

"Absurd. Nothing supports this." He spit out the words in an angry whisper. He tapped frenetic fingers on the table.

Her promise to Antonio had been breached. She couldn't help Antonio, she couldn't help herself or even Flaminia, any of them without disclosing the will's details. Enough of secrets, she needed answers. "Velázquez's will surfaced in the Olivares Library, untouched for centuries, written in his own hand. He wrote Flaminia painted for him, possibly everything after 1652."

His face looked stunned and his head shook back and forth as though his resistance could hold back the incoming tide of information.

"Does the journal corroborate this history?"

Jones put his hands over his face and rubbed his forehead with his fingers. He looked up at her and shook his head. "And you were the student I believed would bumble around and never . . ."

"Around what?" Like a bolt it came clear. "*La Gloria*! You knew! Oh my God, you hid it."

He pursed his lips and huffed.

She tossed her napkin down on top of her plate and stared at him. If she didn't push now, she would not have another opportunity. "Why?"

He moved his hands from his eyes to press his temples. She waited in silence until he finally spoke. "No one could know about the painting. No one could make the connections to this woman, this Flaminia and his illness. When I learned you'd taken the canvas . . ." He stopped.

She panted, struggling for air, shaking her head. "Isabel."

"Yes, Isabel, she tried to seize the painting and save you from your own naiveté, your ill-gotten project. You, a know-nothing, found the painting locked up in a place you weren't meant to go. And scandalously, took it to Spain." He glared at her.

The bullying, the name-calling didn't faze her, not anymore. She sat frozen, struggling to process the revelations that poured out like hot lava, too dangerous to touch and too perilous to ignore. "Why didn't you contact me when you learned I'd found *La Gloria*?"

"Why didn't you bring the canvas to me?"

She shook her head, still second-guessing what she could not undo.

"Within days, I'm summoned to the Prado. Olivares, Cuevas, and half the curatorial staff are present. Even Cuevas believed it a Velázquez." Jones mopped his head and returned the handkerchief to his pocket. "Your limited talent, your lack of competence would keep the Flaminia story buried in history. Fortunately, Cuevas didn't see the F. T. initials in the fabric folds."

Initials. What initials? She made a mental note and challenged him. "This discovery could have been your discovery. A Flaminia Triva attribution would explain so much about the change in his style, the freer brushstrokes, Italian luminosity, a new genius, a woman."

"I spent my life analyzing his career, defining and defending those works to arrogant Europeans who had no respect for Spanish art or American art historians."

He stopped to gulp air and scanned the room to make a tardy assessment of who might be listening. The few remaining guests turned inquisitive heads toward the tension rising from their table, again.

"If art history titans believed the works were painted by an amateur, a woman no less, these paintings would be returned to the attics. This work deserves a place in the pantheons of Europe, of the world."

"You did it for the art? That's your answer?" she scoffed with an unfamiliar cruelty. "You did it for yourself, not to look a fool, a discredited expert."

He paused and then added, "You too, Ms. Adamson, and everyone at the Prado."

He'd fall farther than most, and the art with him. But *La Gloria* was the big one, the one that would cause the others to tumble. Jones had tricked her into supporting the misattribution. Used her, Cuevas, and his own mother.

He straightened his ascot. "Not everything in history should be revealed. Art lovers lose by diminishing Velázquez with the tawdry story of his tart."

She bit her lip to avoid calling him an asshole. "Flaminia was no tart; she was an educated noblewoman. And an extraordinary painter—my God, she may have painted *Las Meninas*."

"Ridiculous. *Las Meninas* is a masterwork, the most important European painting of its time." He paused. "If she had a role, it was as a studio assistant. Like Juan de Pareja."

"Don't you see a different painter explains its mysteries? Velázquez is in the painting, looking out, someone painted him and then the royal couple reflected in the mirror, and the Cross of Santiago on his tunic. Who painted the cross, when he received the Santiago appointment a few months before he died and after the work was completed? Pigment tests show the cross was not overpainted at a later date."

For a minute he appeared intrigued by her command of the historical details, but then folded his arms across his chest and shook his head.

She persevered, "What about facts over opinions? Follow the evidence. That's what you teach."

He laughed that scornful laugh. "Truth. Splendid."

She suppressed the rage bubbling inside and kept from screaming. "The stakes are high for me too. Many days I wish I didn't find the painting, but with what you know and what I have . . . the attribution of *La Gloria* is clear."

He lowered his voice and said, "Show me the document. Where is the evidence?" He leaned back in his chair and then forward, reaching for his briefcase like he was he going to walk out.

She pushed her chair back from the table. "I can't. I gave my word."

"Your word? The word of a thief? One phone call from me and the university will dismiss you. Consider carefully the implications of what you do next." He tossed his napkin on the table, stood, turned on his heel, and left the terrace.

CHAPTER 30

Cate rushed past the doorman who opened the door with an urgent swoosh before she ran into it. The stoplight to cross the street to the Prado took forever and she considered crossing against the traffic, the chaos of which could not be predicted. All was turmoil now, lies and deception. The foundation she'd trusted crumbled, and she was falling with no way to save herself.

She studied the Prado with its imposing entrance from across the street and saw no salvation there. Pilar would be waiting outside her office for a presentation that if she revealed the truth, loomed as an international art scandal.

She needed to sort what she'd just learned and turned to walk in the opposite direction, a detour physically and mentally to the green of Retiro Park. A curved path led deep into the trees where a vacant bench offered refuge. Except for a nanny pushing a stroller, the park was empty. She could break down in private, but no tears came.

She took deep breaths and stared at the sky, cloudless and vast. She checked her phone. Three calls from Antonio, after days of no calls, but no voice messages. A panic set in that he'd been in an accident or gotten sick and that had been why he hadn't called. Ghosting him would not end that worry. She hit the return call button.

"Three calls. Are you ok?"

He answered, "Yes. I was worried about you."

"I'm fine—well not fine, struggling, confused . . . ." The conflict of last weekend piled onto today's battles. "I was in a meeting with Jones."

He was silent and then said, "Jones is back?"

She did not want to go there. "Are you calling to ask about the will?" He didn't deserve her anger, anger that belonged to Jones.

"I do want to know and I waited for you to call."

The silence was long and she wanted to say something, but what? Antonio wanted an answer she didn't have.

"A lot has happened."

"The writing matched the samples, didn't it?"

"Everything points in that direction. Analysis by an expert is needed to be conclusive but you asked me not to show it to anyone. I refused to show it to Jones."

He was silent. His disappointment about what it meant to the value of his Velázquez portrait, his finances, needed no words. "I'm sorry it's not what you wanted." She caught her breath to find the strength to say it. "There's more. Jones knew. He knew!"

"Knew what? About Flaminia?"

"He hid the painting in the cellar. *La Gloria* proves Flaminia's role in Velázquez's world, or better said, it was proof of her existence, her presence in his life, and her talent."

He took a deep breath. "We didn't suspect Jones was deceiving you, us, all of us."

"We probably wouldn't have found out if I hadn't overheard him."

"This is crazy. I'm driving to Madrid now to be there on Friday as I promised you. Can we talk? Meet for dinner tomorrow?"

Badly. She wanted to meet him for dinner, spend her life with him, forget about art, make all this go away. "Yes, maybe. I don't know. The pressure. Friday is speeding at me."

"You have to eat. There's a quiet place behind the Ritz called Goya. I'll be there at nine tomorrow evening. You'll come, no?"

"I'll try." They hung up with strained voices, her pressures, his too, and without the usual sweet words shared between them.

She was grateful he didn't make her explain more about Jones's cover-up. His liar's excuses had rattled her in a way she could not shake. Even as arrogant and rude as he could be, this behavior was a new level of reprehensible.

The phone's message light flashed again. Mom had called while she was talking to Antonio. Four in the morning in Michigan had to be an emergency. "Mom. Is everything okay?"

"Yes. Well yes, mostly okay."

Midwestern understatement. "What's not okay?"

"We can't come to Spain for your big day. Dad and me, we aren't coming." Mom was shouting in the phone as though by raising her voice's volume she could cover the distance between Ypsilanti and Madrid.

This was non-news news as she didn't really expect them to come. "Don't worry. Expensive travel for a single presentation."

Cate had added them to the press release list so they'd have a memento from her career, something to brag to the neighbors, the canasta group, and yes, distract them from their chronic sadness. But now, she wanted them here, a bedrock to support her.

She slumped on the park bench, stretched out her legs, and stared up at the treetops. Flecks of sunlight struggled to shine through the trees and reach the dead leaves on the pathway.

"It's not just that." Mom choked back words she couldn't get out.

She sat up straight, alarmed by the tone of Mom's voice.

"Just a second. I need to go to the hallway."

"Hallway? Where are you?"

"Your Dad had a heart attack," Mom's voice wavered.

She jumped up from the bench. "NO. Is he okay?"

"The ambulance took him to the medical center. He's in the cardiac unit sleeping and the doctors said he'll be . . ." Sobbing took over Mom's words.

"I'll come, right away." She grounded herself back on the bench, gripping the edge of the seat to keep from tumbling into the chasm. "If anything happens to Dad . . ."

"The doctors say he's stable."

"I'll get a ticket today." She got up and started walking back to her apartment to pack a bag.

"Dad's grumpy as ever, proof positive."

Cate heard mom shuffling, moving back inside Dad's room. Dad's voice came through the telephone, loud as though he was speaking into it.

Cate stopped walking and sat down on another bench, warm from the sun's glow.

"That our girl? Damn it woman, why did you call her? Give me that phone."

"Dad? I'm so worried about you." Stabbing memories of those minutes before she knew for certain Matty had drowned rushed back, shadows that blocked the light. That treasured moment before she knew, when he still lived for her, and then that smack in the face that destroyed her innocence forever. Dad walked away at the mention of Matty, like her brother never existed, or that he existed still if they never mentioned he was gone.

There was a pause and then a rustle. "Get this damn bed upright. Okay there. How is my budding artist?"

"Art historian. Forget about me—what happened to you?"

"My ticker needs a tune-up." He laughed, a real laugh.

She joined the laugh, a relief laugh. "Will you need surgery?"

"Nah. Some pills and got to eat different. Mom's meat loaf with gravy, can't give that up. Go home tomorrow."

Tomorrow. How would mom handle it without her? She was all they had. "I'm coming home."

"Will not. You got your thing." His voice quavered but he continued, almost in a whisper, "I really wanted to see that museum of yours."

"That's not important now," she lied, the burden of the press conference disappeared to some distant corner of her thoughts. Then she blurted in a halting voice, "I don't want to lose you, like we lost . . . Matty."

She regretted them as soon as the words were spoken.

This time Dad cleared his throat as though he was suppressing his emotions. He faltered and began to sob.

She'd never heard him cry, not even at the funeral. Together, emotions united leaping distance and stopping time, they wept, not from pity, not solace, nor nostalgia, but burdens released. A flood of tears flowed unabated, sending waves crashing against the walls that had kept secrets hidden.

"I miss your brother every day."

"Me too Dad. I'd hoped, I mean I wanted to tell you, to be honest."

"About how you felt, hard to talk about it."

"No, other things." The words would not come, the part she had hidden so long, she could not. "It was me, my fault. The pills, those amphetamines."

Hospital noises, banging, pumping, and wheezing in the background. His tears stopped and he whispered, "Knew about Matty, his stupid-ass friends, his drinking and the marijuana."

Her eyes lifted and she managed to speak. "I should have told you. Maybe we could have . . . He took them Dad, they were gone from our bathroom. My fault." She cried quietly.

"No, no he didn't take them. I did."

She swallowed her sobs. "You took them?"

"I took the bottle from your bathroom. Threw the pills in the toilet. Whatever Matty took that day, if he took anything, it wasn't from you."

The tortured hours, days since Matty died, years of blame and shame she had placed on herself now were not what she had assumed. Disbelief took over. "You did, you're sure, that bottle, the one I had?"

"Yes Catie. I didn't want you or your brother to use drugs. I should have been watching Matty, paying attention, looking out for him. I failed him."

"No Dad, you tried. I tried. A horrible accident like the coroner said."

She could hear him sniffling. "I wish I could be there. I don't want . . . I can't lose you."

"I will be fine, don't you worry."

"I wanted to be more for you, more than one child, be *enough* to fill that empty place Matty left. Achieve something that would make a daughter be enough."

There was silence and then he squawked at Mom. "Make this bed go up higher. Now you listen to me, Miss Catherine Adamson. Don't you say, don't you even think that. *Enough?* Hogwash. You give me more pride than ten kids. More than any kid in this town, more than a simple man like me could dream."

She did know, hoped it was true. To hear him say it put a salve on her shattered heart. "Thank you, Dad."

"Could I give you a hug? Like I used to when I came home from work. Scoop you and Matty up and twirl you around."

"I would love that."

"Here you go. Arms around you." He chortled.

She could hear the echoes of two innocent children laughing, filled with joy.

"Are you ready for Friday?"

"It's complicated."

"Those hoity-toity types being mean to my girl? They'll answer to me." His voice went up a few octaves and sounded like his normal crotchety self. She welcomed it now.

Mom hollered from somewhere, "Calm down. The doctor said no stress . . . ."

"Quiet woman. I'm fine."

She could picture him switching the phone to the other ear away from Mom so she wouldn't take it from him.

"What is it? You won't upset me."

She bit her lip and weighed her need for guidance against worrying him. "Last weekend, I found some documents in Antonio's library. A will that disproves, ah changes, the announcement. I was wrong about the painter."

"Hmmm. That's a problem alright. What do your work friends, those museum people, say?"

"I haven't told them. When I told Professor Jones, he already knew about *La Gloria*. He hid it, deceived everyone, including me."

"Well damn him. Bullshitters, keep away from 'em."

She was fourteen again, him yelling at her instead of advising, counseling, and yeah, parenting. "I'll try Dad. Lots of consequences to many people. Complicated."

"It's not complicated. You make it so. You are raised right. Show that professor, those museum people." He paused and lowered his voice. "Believe in yourself. You know what to do."

She heard voices in the room.

"Doctor's here."

"Tell me what he says. I love you, Dad."

"Love you, Catie girl."

CHAPTER 31

$\mathcal{A}$ll the traffic lights were green in perfect synchronization, and she appreciated their cooperation on her power walk toward Armageddon. The energy in her step came from an important bit of peace, a moment of absolution thousands of miles away. The revelation that it could not have been her pills that ended in Matty's drowning lifted a weight that had burdened her from moving beyond the grief.

When she entered the office, Cate raised her hand to stop Pilar, who snarled like a guard dog ready to attack. "Before you even ask . . . I'm finishing the last paragraph now. I have what I need from Jones and must check the painting for one thing." She didn't mention the new information about the initials Jones let slip. If she could find Flaminia's initials, another valuable piece of evidence would support what she already had.

"Can't. The painting's offsite for framing, Antonio's frame, remember? The installers will place both in the auditorium Friday morning."

"Oh, not good." Cate thought for a minute and realized she might find the initials on the transparency of the painting they'd used for the PR packet.

"We are out of time, *mujer*." She checked her watch. "In forty-three minutes, I'm back for those pages." Pilar bustled away to be somewhere else.

This deadline drama was her own doing, well hers, Jones, history, whatever.

She reviewed the half-written presentation and leaned back in the chair against the drawer where she had hidden the parchment documents. She laid them out on the desk with the will on top to run her fingers over the sheepskin, feel the texture and a physical connection to Velázquez. The parchment's rough composition, the tactile sense of connection formed an aura over the documents, the spirit of a dying man struggling to write them.

She reread what she'd written and considered the dilemma Velázquez faced. Patrimony ruled the world and his only male heir was Flaminia's bastard child. There was no future in the 1600s for Flaminia as an unwed mother. Her life and that of their son could only be secured if patrons knew of her talent. He risked his legacy to introduce the world to Flaminia. So he wrote the will, but when his wife died, his intentions to protect Flaminia were likely interfered with by nobles who did not want the truth to be known, especially that there was an heir. Perhaps that's why the will was hidden with his old friend's family, the Olivares, knowing it would be found one day. *Time is the midwife of truth.*

Dad was right; it wasn't complicated. She knew what to do.

Twenty minutes left. She centered the cursor, pounded out the final paragraph: "All of the compositional factors, along with laboratory and radiographic testing led me, in consultation with Dr. Jones and Dr. Cuevas …" She stopped, deleted that phrase and typed, "…in consultation with Dr. Cuevas and Dr. Jones." A small victory. She continued, "to conclude that the painting *La Gloria* was painted by Diego Rodriquez de Silva y Velázquez, the Master of the Golden Age of Spain, and of the European Baroque."

She had a plan and she'd follow through. Courage. She hit print, stood, and opened the door to retrieve the document from the shared printer outside her office. Pilar almost fell into the room, hand raised, about to knock.

"Presentation in the printer tray," Cate said before Pilar could speak.

Pilar placed her hands together and looked toward heaven. "Thank God." The public relations director turned and leapt the ten steps to the printer, grabbed the pages, and held them aloft.

Cate reached for them. "I need to proof them."

"We'll do the proofing. Can't risk any more delays. Go take a break. See you in the morning for Jones's panel."

Oh jeez. In the same room with that hypocrite, plagiarist, liar. Ay. She had to face him at some point, resign to being with the scoundrel and then . . . she'd become a . . . travel guide, tour American seniors through Spanish museums, or open a Spanish restaurant, whatever.

Better to encounter Jones at the panel than when she took the stage with him on Friday. He could charge her as a thief, but a public investigation would force her to reveal what she knew. Dad would say truth *and* consequences, not truth *or* consequences.

In her life, it was truth not the consequences. She'd kept secrets, the stress of that was worse than any consequences they might cause. She'd come to know this about Matty's death, about stealing a painting, and now about Flaminia.

A HALF-DRESSED MANUEL SAT on the couch staring at the television in his underwear. Real Madrid slugged it out against Barcelona.

"Exams over?"

He waved her away and mumbled, "Penalty kicks."

Even the television held its breath as the Real Madrid player ran toward the ball. The crowd moaned. She didn't need to look to know.

"Ouwf," Manuel said to no one. "Still tied."

She closed her bedroom door and collapsed onto the rumpled sheets, wondering how long it had been since she'd had time to do laundry. She had nothing to wear for her big moment in front of the cameras. She rolled over to avoid the almost empty wardrobe and tried to nap. Maybe she should leave Spain, go home to her ailing Dad. The museum would understand, but Jones would take over. The press might track her down wherever. She'd have to leave the art world, give up this field.

She could marry a rich doctor, some Michigander or Manuel. *Ah, no to that.*

Antonio. She'd be a countess or a duchess. The wife of a duke-pretender with debts and drama. She'd forgotten about dinner at Goya tomorrow. The pressure, explaining and trying to satisfy Antonio, she couldn't do it. The lawyer in him would read her thoughts, pull the plan out of her or she'd feel the need to share it. Or worse, he'd try to change her mind.

Her reflection in the wardrobe mirror stared back and she cringed at what she saw. Dark depressions under her eyes, freakish hair, and sallow skin would be replayed again and again in the television broadcast. Her fifteen minutes of fame or infamy on the world stage would not be what she'd imagined.

WWMS. What Would Mom Say? "Get your hair done up, honey." That was it. New haircut = new life. She hadn't slept a whole night since they'd found the will. She threw on a sweater and headed for the late evening salon. A butterfly was about to emerge.

SHE AWOKE AT SUNRISE AND couldn't believe nine hours had passed since she put her head on the pillow. The girl in the mirror, unrecognizable, stretched herself to meet the day, sleep, new hair, and yes, clarity where chaos had ruled.

The flowers now blooming along her daily walk and even the traffic noise of the Paseo del Prado sang the music of Madrid. The entrance to the museum, unchanged physically, smiled to welcome her.

She found a seat in the back row of the panel discussion on the Baroque. Tomorrow the chairs in this same auditorium would be filled with reporters. She clung to her plan like a life preserver to keep from drowning in doubts.

Jones appeared from behind the crimson curtain and walked into the seats toward her. She'd ignored three messages from him after the breakfast debacle and looked the other way to study the technical guy with the video camera. When she turned back, he was sitting next to her.

"Your presentation. Congratulations. Succinct, careful with the ah . . ." he paused, "proven facts, and to the point. Your wisdom in this surprised me. No reason to upset the academy over one painting."

She looked away, toward the video guy who seemed to be struggling to make the camera work. This praise, after so much effort to win his approval, gave her no joy. The opposite.

"An assistant professor position will open in the department next fall. Julia Monahan is going on sabbatical and we need, of course you understand, someone to teach her class."

"Contemporary art is not my field. You need a woman and I'm the only one you've got. Keeps the Office of Diversity from questioning you, doesn't it?"

"Don't get a chip on your shoulder. Of course, you'll need to study up on Picasso, Miró, Calder, and other contemporary artists from the Catalan group. The temporary appointment will lead to a tenured position after you publish your work on the painting."

It wasn't exactly extortion. He'd jumped ahead based on the printed presentation. Only a fool would trust him about the position or anything else. Now was not the time to call him on his character failures.

Pilar waved for him to come onto the stage. Most seats in the auditorium had filled with art aficionado types and artists who attend these sorts of things. Jones turned to her as he waited for a stocky man to exit so that he could pass. "Lovely hairstyle."

She couldn't thank him, not for the gratuitous compliment nor the job offer. Not for anything.

The lights lowered just enough so the speakers on the stage couldn't see the audience. The panel flooded the room with words not to communicate but impress, self-important and pompous in two languages. How bizarre, embarrassing almost, that she had once aspired to this. She squeezed around the legs of two older women and past the man, and from force of habit as a student, bending down so her early departure would not be recorded on the video camera.

She went to her office and retrieved her personal items. The Mengs portrait that looked like Antonio seemed to bid her goodbye before she turned out the light. The breeze in the museum foyer drew her outside into the fresh air.

She checked the time, middle of the night in Ypsilanti. Mom texted her that Dad was asleep in his own bed and left her to guess at what wasn't said. She'd get a ticket to go home to see for herself, no matter tomorrow's outcome.

The travel agency in the lobby of the Palace Hotel remained open all hours and she could get a ticket there. Booking tickets online was not easy in Spain, especially with a credit card from an American bank. She waited in one of the two chairs. The agent projected an annoyance that he had been asked to *work* and punched angry strokes on his computer without the customary Spanish cordiality. Bad day, all around.

Finally, ticket in hand, she left and then circled back to the hotel lobby and took a white card, like a florist would use from the front desk. She placed it with the envelope in her purse and headed across the Paseo del Prado toward Goya restaurant.

Goya, the eighteenth-century artist, never ate here, she was certain. The restaurant was empty at the five o'clock hour, not *merienda*, not *cena*, maybe early *aperitivo*. Waiters organized table settings and ignored her. The smells from the kitchen made her wish she could stay in Spain forever. She took a stool at the bar and ordered a Campari and soda to toast herself. The bartender placed a terra-cotta dish with some exquisite olives in front of her. She popped one in her mouth and flavors exploded when she crushed it with her tongue. The hotel note card would serve the purpose of what she needed to write. But she paused, uncertainty plagued her.

Finally, she wrote a single word and put the card into the envelope. She scribbled Antonio's name on the outside.

The bartender placed a glass in front of her filled with the glorious Campari, in carmine red with a lemon twist bobbing on top.

With the first sip, her shoulders lowered. "Do you have a reservation at nine o'clock for Antonio?"

The bartender pulled out a rumpled notebook and opened it to a dog-eared page. "Antonio de Olivares, for two."

"Could you give this note to him?"

The bartender nodded and held up the envelope before placing it in the clip that held the book open to today's date. "That's why a pretty one like you drinks alone?"

She never thought of herself as pretty, maybe she should have gotten this haircut sooner. "Not what you're thinking."

But maybe the bartender guessed right. This relationship was no more, not happening like their dinner. No need to explain what she barely understood.

"Whatever you say, *Guapa*. He's a donkey's ass if he loses you."

She smiled, took another olive, and tossed enough coins to cover the bill and a tip onto the bar.

$\mathcal{T}$he journey wasn't supposed to end like this. The game clock ticked down the minutes, but the game plan kept changing, all night tossing and turning, doubts eroded her well-thought plan. Not complicated, Dad had said, and yet, it was.

She got out of bed, opened the draperies, and stepped onto the tiny balcony with just enough room for her feet. She lifted her arms and released her fate into the heavens. That blue sky promised a day without rain. Flakes of paint fell from the rotten doors and the cracked platform wobbled with her full weight. A bit of concrete tumbled from the decorative trim and bounced to the curb below. Her hands tightened on the railing, even though it wouldn't save her if the thing detached from the building.

Some wrinkled items remained to pack into the rolling suitcase that had been her loyal companion from Michigan to New York, Seville, and Madrid. Now back to Michigan. Better to be prepared, for whatever the outcome. Return to Dad, stay at the museum, work with Jones, or love Antonio. She'd call an audible about the next step.

It wouldn't be fair to disappear without letting Manuel know she hadn't been kidnapped, but what if she didn't leave? Hard to predict what would happen. She pulled out a yellow tablet and wrote: "Leaving Madrid. Use my security deposit to pay rent until you find a new roommate. *Abrazos*, Cate." She placed the note on top of her winter coat and hid them both in the closet, in case the plan changed.

She could leave for Olivares and a life different from what she'd planned, if he asked her, but he wouldn't, she was sure of that. He hadn't called last night when she no-showed at Goya, and that was okay. What she needed was alone time. *Stand on top of your fears*, Dad's mantra repeated in her head.

God, keep Dad safe. She could be at his side by tomorrow and tell them both how much she loved them. She could explain in person how the art career went all wrong and then ... then what?

She put the presentation with the margin notes into a museum envelope and slung the worn strap of her purse over her shoulder. That new Loewe bag, the one she admired in the hotel boutique, the hip one Dalila would approve of, and the one she had planned to buy to celebrate, would have to wait.

THE MUSEUM AUDITORIUM WAS empty except for Gabriel who stood guard by the easel. The registrar's staff had placed *La Gloria* there with a red velvet drape covering it. "Your day, Señorita Caterina," Gabriel said.

"Not my day, her day."

She pointed at *La Gloria*, and acknowledged to herself the double entendre that there was another woman. "I need to check something. Can you secure the doors so no one enters?"

He opened a detailed schedule. "Video technicians will set up in thirty minutes." He left to lock the door.

She lifted the cover that dressed Flaminia's work like a woman in an elegant gown awaiting a curtsey in front of the king. The cloth caught on Antonio's refitted frame as she lifted it. She unhooked the velvet and gazed at *La Gloria*. A stunner, restored colors, missing paint replaced, new varnish, and luminous like a proper masterpiece. The artist's virtuosity could not be denied. *La Gloria* was glorious like her name, prepared for a splendid debut. She resisted the urge to linger; there was work to do.

She held the loupe to her eye and moved it over the entire surface including the folds of the central figure's skirt. Jones had said initials. She stood up and moved back. If the initials weren't there, why would he say anything? He couldn't be trusted, and perhaps this was a set up to erode her credibility.

The sound of people gathering in the lobby, greeting each other, outside the locked door distracted her. She doubled down with urgency and examined the canvas inch by inch, reviewed each brushstroke, gestures that created the fabric of the dress and the draperies. No "F. T." initials anywhere.

More might be seen from a distance like the expressive brushstrokes. She moved to a middle seat in the empty auditorium and stared at the exposed masterpiece. The luminous tones of *La Gloria's* face stared back, her eyes yearning. *La Gloria*, paint and canvas, transformed like magic to reality.

"I'm trying, Flaminia, I'm trying." She whispered, "Help me." What was fabric and folds became paint and strokes. Not shadows, but lines and, yes, letters. Initials.

There they were.

Subtle still from a distance, near the face in the folds of the collar. Five strokes of paint. Velázquez rarely signed his work, and it would have been unfitting for Flaminia to sign, even on the blank scroll begging for the artist's words. Of course, she would have hidden her initials.

She rushed back to the stage, examined the marks, and made certain they were not a hopeful illusion. The downward and crosswise strokes of F and T buried in the folds were intentional and seamlessly hidden in the composition.

Gabriel opened the door. "The video crew is here." A journalist entered the room and began snapping photos.

She scrambled for the velvet cloth and covered the painting. "What are you doing in here?"

"Gabriel is my cousin. Can't blame me for wanting the scoop on a new Velázquez."

"Don't send out anything until the presentation is over. Please."

The technical crew with rolls of cable and camera cases began filing in. She left to collect her thoughts and review the presentation.

The barista in the café near the gift shop started to prepare her usual double espresso, but she asked for water instead. The barista raised her eyebrows as though she was about to ask a question but didn't. Cate sipped the water from a seat at the back and stared at her notes. She scratched out words on the copy of the original she'd given Pilar and scribbled bullet points in the margins.

Pilar entered the turnstile of the café and flitted around the room like a fashion director preparing to send out models. "Oh good, you're here. Someone said they'd seen you."

Cate placed her hand to cover the margin notes. "A moment of solitude."

"No espresso I see. Let's review the set up." Pilar spoke in a staccato tone, betraying her nervousness. She ticked off the times and what was supposed to happen, monotone recitation that fuzzed into words Cate did not hear.

She finished her water, got up, and walked with Pilar, still chattering, toward the check-in table. Inside, journalists greeted each other, banged chair seats, shifting from one seat to a different one, moving closer for a better photo angle on the easel. Nametags identified important journalists, their publications or media stations and matched labels stuck on the front row seats. Every field had its pecking order.

Director Navarro and Dr. Pablo Cuevas appeared from backstage, deep in a dispute over symbols in Bosch's *Garden of Earthly Delights* triptych. Scholars have been debating the meaning of the erotic religious work since it was created in the early 1500s. She imagined how what she was about to say would carry over centuries and poured herself another glass of water from a pitcher. Instead of drinking it, she offered it to Cuevas, who took it, smiled, and extended some encouraging words.

A journalist approached the stage and greeted Cuevas, who replied, "Stanley Harding, thank you for traveling to Madrid for our little presentation."

"Not a small thing, Professor Cuevas: A newly attributed Baroque masterpiece."

"Ah you've heard. Have you met Catherine Adamson, our young protégé? Mr. Stanley Harding, Arts Editor of the *London Times*."

She shook his hand and barely heard him say congratulations as her mind drifted.

"Will you give us an interview?"

She didn't even know what continent she'd be on by tomorrow and referred him to public relations.

A *Times* interview would place her in art historical archives. The "V" attribution would provide an opportunity to make a mark, a false mark that later she could reverse, write a paper revealing the truth. Notoriety was a big step down from respect. Maybe this was Jones's plan—to hide the work and eventually reveal it.

Dalila arrived with a headset perched around her ponytail and grabbed the pages of Cate's presentation from her lap. With her other hand, Dalila took the manila envelope with the parchments.

"Wait. I need those." If someone saw her margin notes, they might not let her speak at all.

"Notes go on the speakers' podium. No chance you'll misplace them."

Cate sat silent, open-mouthed, not wanting to disagree in front of the assembly.

Dalila continued, "Give that to me." She took her old bag.

"Coach bag? Really Cate. I'll put it with the security officers." Dalila huffed out, mumbling the Spanish equivalent of "whatever" about the American designer and disappeared.

Jones arrived and kissed her on each cheek.

She kept her arms pinned to her sides.

"A momentous day for you, for us, NYCU. We're counting on you to shine."

He was riding high on his victory over her, a successful bribe of a faculty position. His Puig cologne penetrated the air, a smell that she'd once found pleasing. But now, the fumes made her nauseous, adding to a rebellious stomach.

Antonio entered the auditorium and made his way to an empty seat in the back row. He looked up at the stage, his face absent of emotion. He wore a navy sweater under his camel jacket, the cashmere one she loved.

She waited for him to smile, something, encouragement, but he offered only a nod in her direction. She yearned to go to him, grab his arm and leave the room, and live out a different life's journey. But what did he want?

Guillermo spotted Antonio, invited him to move to sit in the front row where there was a seat with his name taped to it. Antonio moved right in front of her, so close, three steps off the stage and she'd be in his lap.

A nervous sound engineer sweating gobs attached her to a portable microphone, adding his jitters to hers. She closed her eyes and visualized a walk in fields near home with the cold spring air refreshing her face.

Dalila appeared from behind the curtain and handed her a package. "A lady in the lobby insisted I give this to you now, before you begin."

Cate mumbled a confused thank you and took the package. The paper crumpled when her anxious hands struggled with the envelope flap. Inside was a worn leather-covered book with

Italian words embossed on its spine. She opened the fragile cover to the title page. Handwritten, in Italian. A business card "Lillian Smythe—Art Historian" marked another page in what appeared to be the journal Lillian spoke about. Cate scanned a marked page in the journal and found the words Flaminia Triva. A few sentences later she saw the name Diego de Velázquez. In between were sentences in both Latin and Italian. No time to translate the curlicue script.

She searched the audience for Lillian and instead her eyes found Antonio. So close, she could almost feel him breathing. Stage lights came up, turning the audience to a midnight without a moon and blinding her to everything.

Director Navarro stood at the podium, tapped the microphone to quiet the audience. "Welcome to the Museo Nacional del Prado. We're pleased you have joined us for an extraordinary, rare-in-our-lifetimes announcement."

She exhaled slowly, several times, to stabilize her voice.

"Rising star" and other superlatives came from Navarro's introduction of her but blurred as her head was stuck repeating "extraordinary" over and over. The audience applauded and like a robot, she rose. Navarro shook her hand. In a fuzzy unreality, she found herself transported behind the podium, looking into the blackness, her body pulsating with anticipation.

She opened the folder, pulled out the presentation. "Thank you, Director Navarro. Ladies and gentlemen, I'd like to introduce *La Gloria*, the name we've given this untitled Baroque painting." She nodded to two curatorial assistants.

With a grand gesture raising their arms high in the air, the assistants lifted the velvet cover. An audible gasp rose from the darkness. Cameras flashed every direction, sending more blinding lights toward the stage. The lights illuminated another face in the back: Isabel. The sight of this devious woman lifted Cate with renewed resolve.

Flashes blurred her vision and she squinted, willing her eyes to focus.

Pilar's voice interrupted from an offstage microphone. "Please refrain from flash photos. An image suitable for publication will be provided by public relations."

Cate continued, "It's clear from your reaction that you too see the work is exceptional." A few flashes continued as uncooperative photographers wanted an image they could own the rights to. Then the room was quiet.

Her eyes adjusted, but her heart rate did not. She cleared her throat, looked up, and proceeded. The story of the discovery, the documentation, the dating, historical background, chemical tests, the royal studio, the similarities between the face of *La Gloria* and the one in the *Rokeby Venus*'s mirror, she read from the pages even though she'd committed the words to memory, the message, like describing a love, had been engraved on her heart.

Margin scribbles, her handwriting messy and illegible up the side of the page, she set them aside and in spite of the stage lights found Antonio's face staring back with intense concentration.

"The brilliance of the work, even more evident after cleaning and restoration, caught my attention in that dusty NYCU storeroom. The research supported an attribution of this painting to the Golden Age Master Diego de Silva y Velázquez."

Stanley Harding nodded as though he agreed. The ABC art reporter sitting next to him scribbled on his notepad.

The description of the piece, the brushstrokes, the Golden Age were in the press release. No doubt the pundits would compare it with what she was about to say. She lifted her head and presented the most earnest face she had. "All the facts and laboratory tests supported an attribution to Velázquez, until . . ."

The word "until" hung in the air and the reporters lifted their pens from their notebooks, looked up, and waited.

Antonio too. She didn't need to turn toward Jones to feel his burning stare.

Now or never.

She shuffled the pages, aligned them into a stack, and set them on the podium. A big exhale. "We concluded Velázquez painted *La Gloria* until the artist's will was discovered in the library of Antonio de Olivares, the estate of descendants of the Count-Duke of Olivares."

A whoosh sound rushed past her ears, the sound of the air leaving the room in total silence. Her courage waning, she needed to liberate the truth. Now. "The will, likely written in Velázquez's own hand, lost for almost four hundred years, reveals *La Gloria* was painted by Flaminia Triva, an Italian noblewoman, a painter, and Velázquez's mistress."

She fumbled with the string on the envelope, removed the will, and held the parchment up. Cameras exploded, photographers moved closer to capture Velázquez's words with their long lenses. Reporters scribbled and punched texts into their phones.

Antonio's restlessness caught her attention. He leaned back and put his hand on his forehead. Promise broken. She lowered the parchment onto the podium.

"This document supports a Triva attribution. Professor Herant Jones had access to an Italian journal found in the National Library, which connects this young woman, a painter Velázquez met on his Italian trips, to the master." She held the little leather book high in the air, this time allowing the cameras to flash away and a moment for her to turn to the panel. Director Navarro held his middle section like he'd taken a punch to the stomach. Next to him, Cuevas, well . . . confused, lost, mumbling to the director. Jones looked at his shoes.

Buzzing among the reporters reached a crescendo and she waited for it to dissipate. "Ship's records document Velázquez brought Flamina to Spain as his slave with their child. This newly discovered work has Flaminia's initials 'F. T.' in the folds of the collar." She approached the painting and pointed out the initials. "We discovered this new information in the last week."

Arms flew up, journalists with burning questions, called from the darkness, "Professora Adamson." Another shouted, "Doctora Adamson."

For a brief second, she basked in those unearned titles, lamented what she was about to lose.

Miss Lillian appeared at the back of the room, near an exit light, with an anticipatory look, the older woman's courage hit her like a slap about the face, the risks she'd taken, her life's purpose, the possible loss of her son from her life. The risks Flaminia took, her courage, her talent. That too. *For Flaminia, for Lillian, and for every woman struggling to be recognized for her accomplishments.*

She held up her hand to silence the audience. "Another revelation came from the Olivares' papers." She lifted the parchment again without looking at Antonio. "In his will, Velázquez confesses he suffered from a palsy, unable to control his brushes, and he stopped painting when he returned from Italy around 1652."

There was a stunned gasp from the audience, familiar with Spain's most famous artist's life story.

"The ailing master devised a plan with his . . ." She would not call her an assistant nor a mistress. "Flaminia Triva, to paint the works dated to these years that we have wrongly attributed to him."

The press at first stunned to silence, erupted, calling out questions. A reporter near the front blurted out a question with the words "*Las Meninas?*"

She looked down and then up. "This new information requires serious study. The will declares that Flaminia cared for Velázquez, helped him when he was afflicted, and painted canvases for him to hide his condition. The exact role she played deserves careful research."

Photographers came forward, crowded into the small space in front of the stage, blocking her view of Antonio. Cameras flashed from the center. She put her hand over her eyes, pulled the microphone closer to her mouth, and turned toward the men seated on the stage. Jones folded his arms tight across his chest, turning his hands white and his face red, his lips firm and pinched together. Cuevas shook his head and stared.

She added, "Other mysteries, like the identity of the nude *Rokeby Venus*, why Velázquez's own figure is painted in *Las Meninas*, the changes in painterly style, the different brushstrokes in these later works, might connect to this new information."

Questions flew: Is the will a fake, is *Las Meninas* painted by a woman, is *La Gloria* a fake? Derisive comments about American scholars of Spanish art erupted. A reporter in a Televisa España logo shirt called out with his hand up, "Professor Jones?"

She lifted her arm to invite Jones to the podium, picked up the documents, including the journal, and stepped away, edging toward an opening in the curtain.

Jones rose, steadying himself on his chair, and wobbled to the podium. He adjusted the microphone to his height and cleared his throat.

"It's always exciting to discover an unknown artist."

She stopped, paralyzed and shocked. He had plan B ready in case she told the truth. Or was this another reverse psychology moment?

The reporters scribbled wildly. They paused and waited, looking at Jones, pens poised to write.

"Perhaps a Golden Age mistress." He smirked at his own sarcasm, continuing to pretend he endorsed this attribution.

A nervous chuckle arose from the audience. Cuevas and Navarro sat rigid, without laughing.

"Your Velázquez biography, Professor Jones?" the *ABC* reporter called out. "You say nothing about this Flaminia person, but you saw the journal where apparently she is mentioned. What did you know about her?"

The video crew moved forward, focusing a big camera in a close-up of Jones. She peeked around the curtain to watch him squirm. She resisted the temptation to stay and moved completely behind the curtain where she could hear, but not see or be seen.

Jones stuttered, "Ah, ah, the journal has not been authenticated. We only recently learned of the will." Then he mumbled inaudible words, only heard by her. "Histories may need to be rewritten."

A reporter called Jones's attention back to the audience. "Were there differences in the technique of this *La Gloria*? Surely you noticed this painting was different."

She waited with the rest of the press corps for the answer, straining to avoid missing a word.

Cuevas coughed during the silence that followed the question.

Jones gained some composure. "I want to recognize the generosity of Antonio de Olivares for sharing the resources of his library with scholars."

She couldn't see Antonio from where she stood, but she felt his disappointment in her at her broken promise.

"Did you examine the documents, Professor Jones? Could they be fake?"

Jones's flustered words trailed backstage. "Ms. Adamson will . . . ah, ah Ms.?" The cacophony of three hundred reporters buzzing drowned out Jones's stammering.

His awkward response faded away as she tiptoed into the back hall. Truth never evolves, it just is.

CHAPTER 33

*T*he guard, one she didn't know, stared at her from the security desk. She lifted the museum badge hanging from her neck and declared, "I'm staff." She choked on the words, knowing in a moment she'd be *former* staff.

Gabriel rushed over from his auditorium post and inspected her messenger bag himself. "He's new, Ms. Cate. Are you okay? You disappeared."

She wanted to hug him goodbye but could not telegraph what she knew and he did not. "It's been a hard week, a hard couple of years."

"*Si, si.*" Gabriel pushed the button to open the exit gate.

A vacant seat tucked behind the café counter, a spot not visible from the lobby, provided the hiding place she needed now. She lifted her phone and texted Antonio.

"In the lobby, behind the column of the café. Meet me."

The depressions surrounding her eyes had deepened from yesterday. She snapped the mirror shut, exhausted and regretful that she'd looked at herself.

Antonio touched her shoulder. "Are you alright?"

She forced a smile and motioned to the bench for him to sit next to her.

He squeezed her hand. "It's a fire storm. Reporters shouting questions, without waiting for answers. Cameras pressing forward. Jones like a bull cornered in the arena by the picadors, weak explanations about the diary, the will. Cuevas took over, but he was no better. He couldn't resist attacking Jones. Lots of bickering."

She placed a hand on her forehead, a futile attempt to stop the throbbing. "Not what I wanted. Jones expected me to protect him by lying. I can't say he doesn't deserve the spot he's in, but it's not what I wanted."

"Where did you get the diary?"

"From someone close to Jones. Long story." She wanted to protect Miss Lillian, who could face consequences for taking it from the National Library. "Counselor, would you keep it until we know what to do with it?" She handed him the fragile volume.

Antonio nodded and didn't ask her to explain. "Jones's own doing. He knew and hid the truth. That's different than the will, which he didn't know about."

Now beyond the indecisiveness, an unwavering calm took over like a handhold on a rock in a receding sea. "I did it for her, for Flaminia. She deserved a voice, a place in history."

"I know that. I was a wrongheaded fool. Can you forgive me?"

"I was surprised and disappointed at your reaction to the will. I'm sorry too. Sorry that the pressures of your family made you forget the good person you are. The person I still believe you are."

Antonio looked down and didn't speak.

After an uncomfortable silence, he pulled the card she'd left at the restaurant from his pocket and pushed it toward her. The word *Veritas* was written in her handwriting.

She took the card and read aloud, "Truth."

Antonio touched her arm with his hand. "I wrote you a response. Turn it over."

The back of the card read, "Courage."

"Most people think courage means bravery, facing your fears. It does mean that." He paused. "There's another meaning. The

Latin root *Cor* . . . heart, the center, the source of your strength. You showed us heart, Cate."

She pulled a hankie from her bag and dapped the tears running down his face.

A journalist and a cameraman rushed out of the auditorium, past the guards and the visitors milling in the entrance, on deadline to file a story.

"There's not a lot of time. I need to leave soon." She nodded toward more journalists. "This is for you." She put the oversized envelope into his hands and lingered there touching his fingers. "I kept part of my promise. No one has read them but you and me."

"Didn't you just show them to the world's press corps?" He squeezed her hand, without any anger in his voice.

"Yes, I'm sorry and . . ." She couldn't finish. "Open the envelope."

Antonio pulled the documents onto the table.

"We never had time to study the others."

He examined one of them comparing the writing to the will. "This one seems to be a letter in Latin."

"It is. I could only decipher a few words. A love letter perhaps. The signature. Look."

Antonio held the parchment up to catch more light. "Flaminia. Incredible."

"This correspondence, the initials on *La Gloria*, and the diary support what the will says."

He pulled her closer. "We can get this letter translated."

"The debate in that auditorium . . ." she motioned toward the door where more people exited. "Showing the will increased the document's value. The Spanish government, the Prado, and Cuevas's Institute will ask you to donate the parchments. Don't. Sell them to the highest bidder. This rare documents dealer in Berkeley Square in London will bid." She put a small paper in his hand with the contact information.

He stared at the documents, his hands shaking, and then at her. "Thank you. I'm so sorry I let you down."

She rested her head on his shoulder. He brushed her hair from her face and kissed her forehead.

She lifted her head and turned toward him. "I'm leaving Madrid, going home to Michigan. Now."

"Don't. Please don't."

She placed her hand on his. "Dad had a heart attack."

"Is he okay?"

"Mom says yes. I need to see for myself. Been crazy with worry that I might not get back in time. I need them to know they're important to me."

"Of course, you must go." Antonio drew her close and whispered, "You're important to me. I want you to know that." He shifted his face to look at her and more tears came. He held up the limp handkerchief and laughed. "A lot of good this will do."

She laughed with him.

"Will you come back? What does all that in there . . ." he motioned with his head toward the auditorium, ". . . mean for you?"

Many questions, including the one he didn't ask. She didn't have an answer for that one either. "I don't know. Not yet."

Antonio looked away into the distance. He lifted the documents and turned to her. "Will there be enough money left for a trip to Michigan?"

"If you get a good bid on the roof repairs or it doesn't rain again." She smiled.

Doors banged. A stream of video technicians left the auditorium. Cuevas and Jones would exit soon. She jumped up. "I need to go."

"Let me drive you. We've hardly talked."

"I'm rushing to my flight."

He helped her with her coat and carried her messenger bag along with his briefcase containing the precious parchments.

They wove between the tourists toward the exit. The fresh air blew away the indecisiveness that had plagued her, and in their place, clarity and strength sprouted except for . . . yes that.

She reached for her bag, let her hand remain on his, and looked up to kiss him, time waited, their lips together in a transient farewell. For now.

He handed over the bag and they embraced until she freed him to walk away, knowing his gaze followed her.

Green buds appeared on the barren sticks of the nettle trees along the Paseo del Prado; soon the promenade would transform into a protective tunnel for lovers and seekers. Menacing clouds had formed over the Guadarrama mountains dropping a surprise shower. Rain always a certainty when she forgot her umbrella, but storms no longer concerned her as clouds in their time would drift away.

She stretched upward, turned her face toward the refreshing raindrops before she covered her head with her coat, and ran toward the taxis.

AUTHOR'S NOTE

*Y*ears of research provided the foundation for this novel, but *Attribution* emerged and remains a work of fiction. Over a decade ago, the first spark of the story came from a lecture at the San Diego Museum of Art about the challenges of attributing a painting dated to the Golden Age of Spain. The attribution of artworks with incomplete centuries-old histories can be upended with the discovery of documents or previously unknown records. These accounts and several others, combined with my memories of studying art history at the Prado inspired this art history puzzle.

In early drafts, I invented a fictional mistress who was a painter. As I discovered more obscure sources, I was stunned to learn Velázquez did have a mistress, an Italian noblewoman who was a painter, bore his only son, and possibly modeled for or perhaps helped paint the *Rokeby Venus*. And yet, Flaminia Triva does not appear beyond a footnote in any important English-language biography of the artist. Perhaps his relationship with her explains why he did not return to Spain when the king summoned him. No record has been found that she traveled to Spain, but one source suggests there is a police record of her resisting when Velázquez ordered their son sent to Spain. Antonio Palomino mentions her in his 1724 biography, and there are thin references elsewhere. Hopefully, future biographers will search for more documents and expand the historical record of this important relationship.

Unresolved mysteries about Velázquez's life and his later works continue to plague art historians, but the neurological disease is a fictional explanation for changes in the artist's style and the lack of production in his later years.

Gaspar de Guzmán, the Count-Duke of Olivares, had one son, a bastard whom he recognized toward the end of his life in order to continue the line of the House of Olivares. Unfortunately this son, Enrique Felipez de Guzmán, died a year after his father, leaving a baby son who died at age two. That Enrique could have had a bastard son who survived is a fictional leap that creates the ancestral line from which the character Antonio de Olivares is descended.

The voices of many female painters like Flaminia that have been lost to history, call out to have their stories and their works researched and their contributions added to the historical record.

For more about Spain's Golden Age, the Baroque, and the story behind *Attribution* visit www.lindamooreauthor.com.

ACKNOWLEDGMENTS

Writing a novel is a solitary pilgrimage to invented places accompanied by imaginary people. And it's not. Real people, brilliant practitioners of this challenging craft and extraordinary friends, writers and readers jumped on this train to an uncertain destination. They have earned my gratitude by their boundless generosity. I am grateful to many, but especially:

Writers and seekers who struggled together with me in a sturdy alliance, including Karen O'Connell, John Maly, Natalie Hirt, Maryam Soltani, Judy Bernstein, James Burnham, Dave Putnam, Michele Morris, Mark Radoff, James Albert, Cat Darby, Van Thaxton, Cynthia Dillon, Carl Vonderau, the writers of the Stanford Writers Program, the Community of Writers, the Asilomar, and DeLuz Writers groups. Friends and beta readers, especially Beth Rowley, Iraina Hofsteede, Jane Piccard, Lynn Krominga, Maureen Brown and Stephanie Buckley.

Mentors who patiently molded the clay of my flawed writing into something better, especially Caroline Leavitt, Stacey Swann, Josh Mohr, and Angela Pneuman. Art experts who provided scholarly opinions through their writings and helpful conversations: Edward J. Sullivan, John Marciari, Ariel Plotek, and Sarah Murray. Publishing team members lead by the extraordinary Brooke Warner who makes dreams happen, copyeditor Annie Tucker, cover designer Julie Metz, project manager Lauren Wise, and Crystal Patriarche and

Tabitha Bailey of the Booksparks team. Boundless gratitude to the supportive authors at She Writes Press, especially Leslie Johansen Nack, Sally Cole-Misch, Margaret Rodenberg, Rebecca D'Harlingue, and Suzanne Parry.

Anything good about this book belongs to these generous friends, collaborators and experts. What falls short is all mine.

This would not have happened without family, including daughter Adrienne who gifted me a pen purchased with her first lawyer paycheck and encouraged me to write, son Craig, insightful old soul who convinced me when I'd almost given up that I could do this, Gina who gave honest advice about covers and photos, and Terry who deserves huge gratitude as proofreader, word genius, lover of books, and patient husband who has supported my crazy adventures since Madrid college days. And to my grandchildren who inspire me every day with their energy and fresh view of the universe, there is no not.

AUTHOR BIO

L inda Moore is an author, traveler, and a recovering gallery owner. She studied art history at the Prado while a student at Complutense University of Madrid and received degrees from the University of California and Stanford University. Her gallery featured contemporary Hispanic artists, she has published award-winning exhibition catalogs, and her writing has appeared in art journals and anthologies. Born in the Midwest, she resides with her husband in California when not spending time at their cottage on Kauai or traveling the world.

Author photo © Daren Scott

SELECTED TITLES FROM SHE WRITES PRESS

She Writes Press is an independent publishing company founded to serve women writers everywhere. Visit us at www.shewritespress.com.

Estelle by Linda Stewart Henley. $16.95, 978-1-63152-791-3. From 1872 to '73, renowned artist Edgar Degas called New Orleans home. Here, the narratives of two women—Estelle, his Creole cousin and sister-in-law, and Anne Gautier, who in 1970 finds a journal written by a relative who knew Degas—intersect . . . and a painting Degas made of Estelle spells trouble.

Beautiful Garbage by Jill DiDonato. $16.95, 978-1-938314-01-8. Talented but troubled young artist Jodi Plum leaves suburbia for the excitement of the city—and is soon swept up in the sexual politics and downtown art scene of 1980s New York.

Peregrine Island by Diane B. Saxton. $16.95, 978-1-63152-151-5. The Peregrine family's lives are turned upside-down one summer when so-called "art experts" appear on the doorstep of their Connecticut island home to appraise a favorite heirloom painting—and incriminating papers are discovered behind the painting in question.

Beautiful Illusion by Christie Nelson. $16.95, 978-1-63152-334-2. When brash and beautiful American newspaper reporter Lily Nordby falls into a forbidden love affair with Tokido Okamura, a sophisticated Japanese diplomat whom she suspects is a spy, at the Golden Gate International Exposition, a brilliant Mayan art scholar, Woodrow Packard, tries to save her.

Portrait of a Woman in White by Susan Winkler. $16.95, 978-1-93831-483-4. When the Nazis steal a Matisse portrait from the eccentric, art-loving Rosenswigs, the Parisian family is thrust into the tumult of war and separation, their fates intertwined with that of their beloved portrait.

The Black Velvet Coat by Jill G. Hall. $16.95, 978-1-63152-009-9. When the current owner of a black velvet coat—a San Francisco artist in search of inspiration—and the original owner, a 1960s heiress who fled her affluent life fifty years earlier, cross paths, their lives are forever changed . . . for the better.